Skip·Beat!

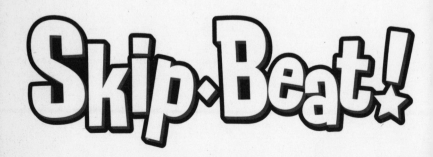

Shojo Beat

Skip·Beat!

3

Story & Art by Yoshiki Nakamura

Skip·Beat!
Volume 3

CONTENTS

Skip•Beat!

Volume 3

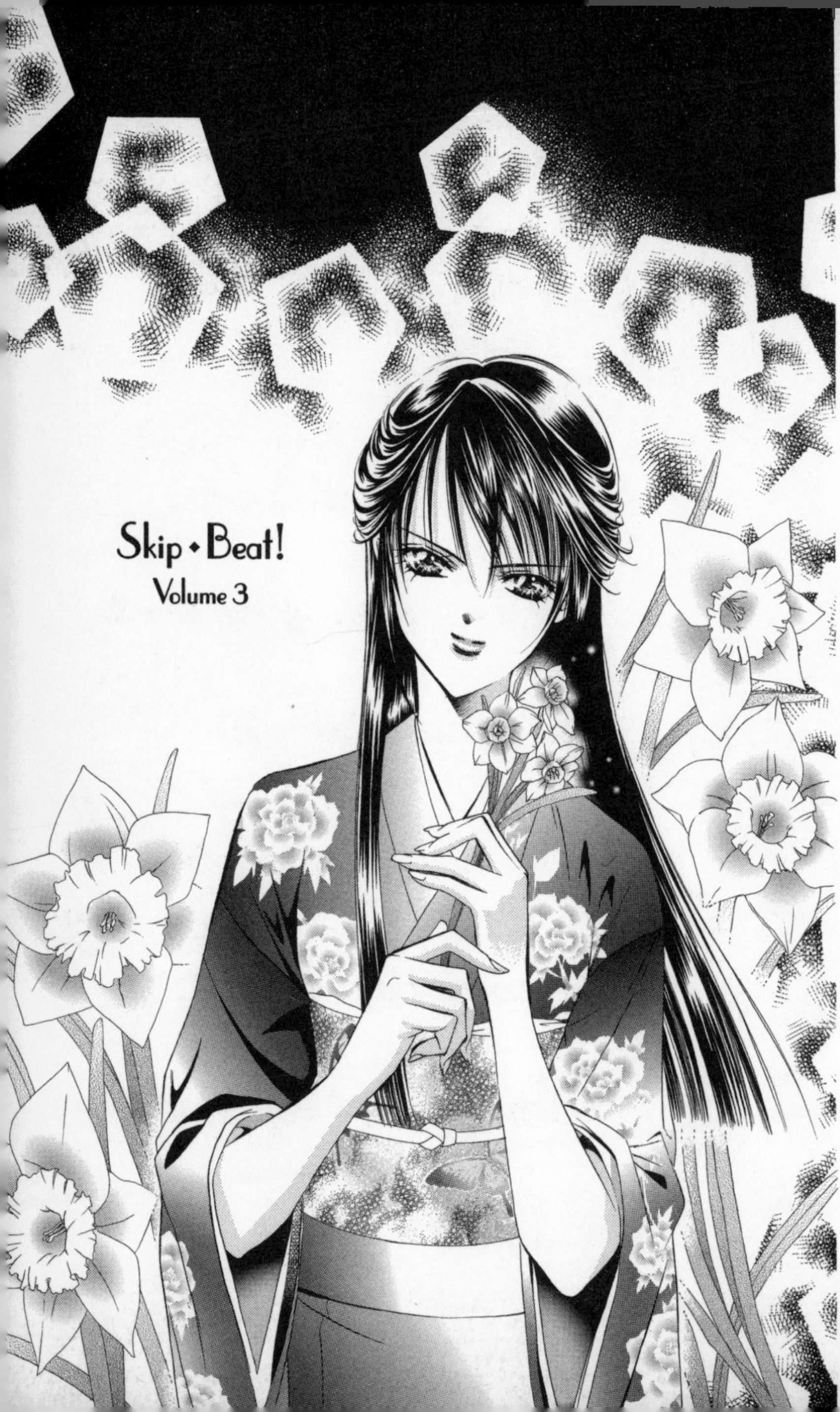

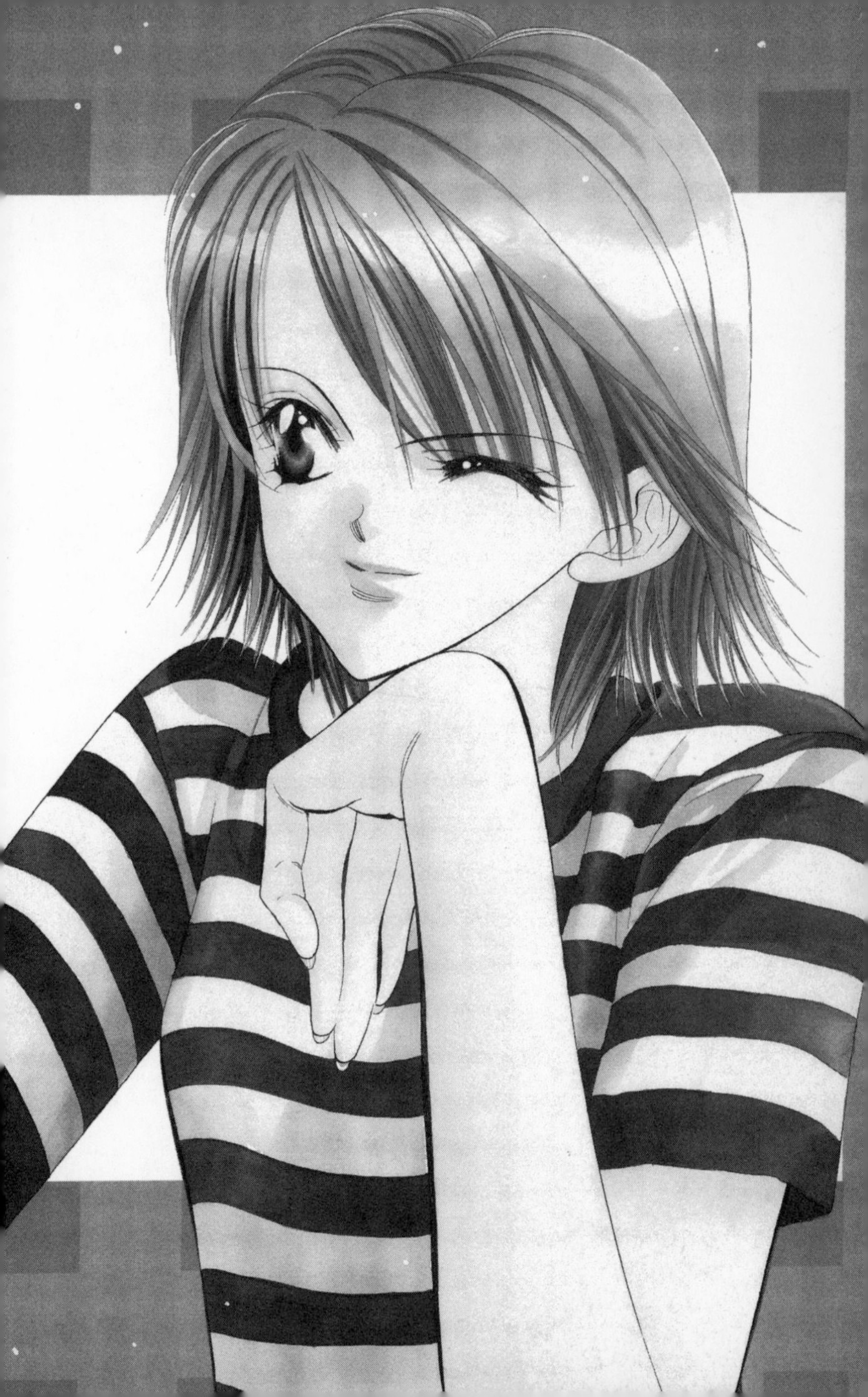

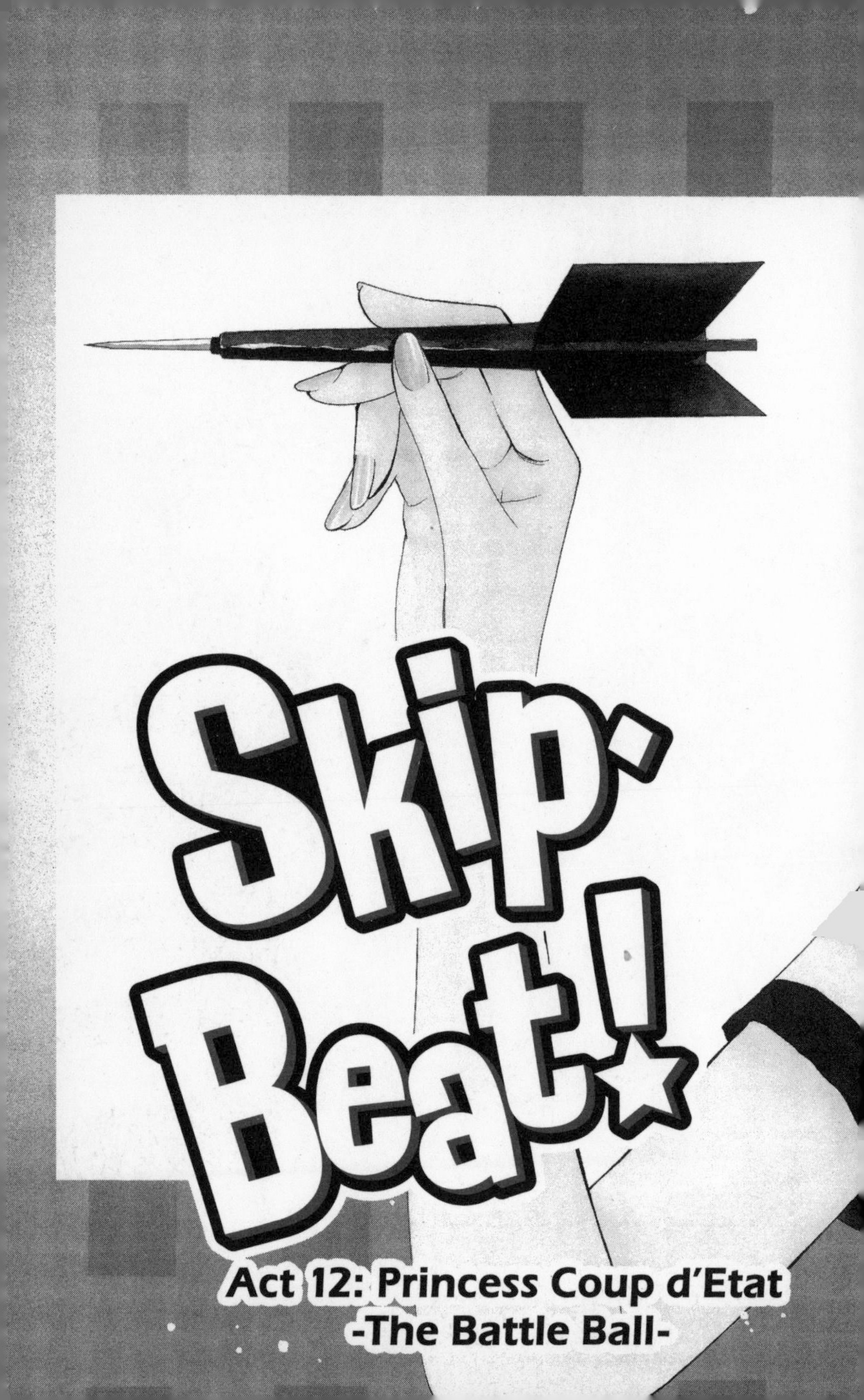
Skip·Beat!
Act 12: Princess Coup d'Etat
-The Battle Ball-

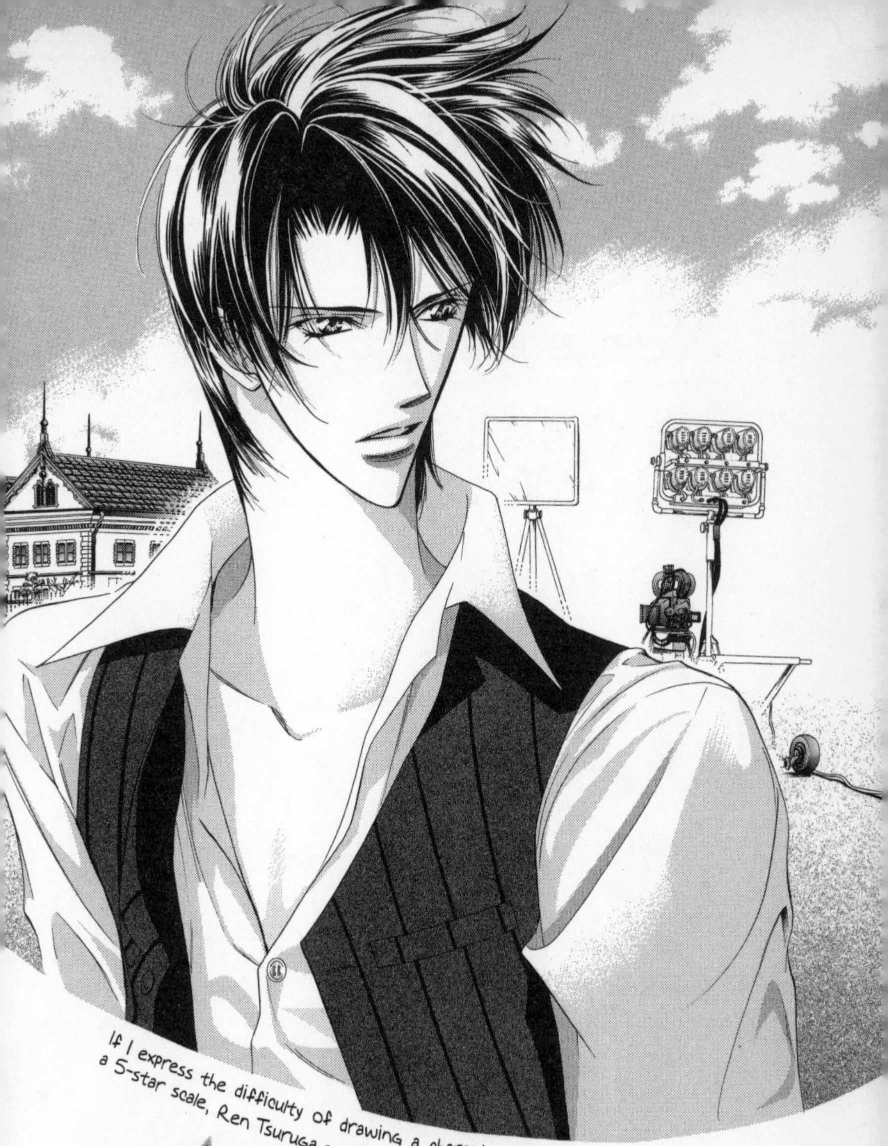

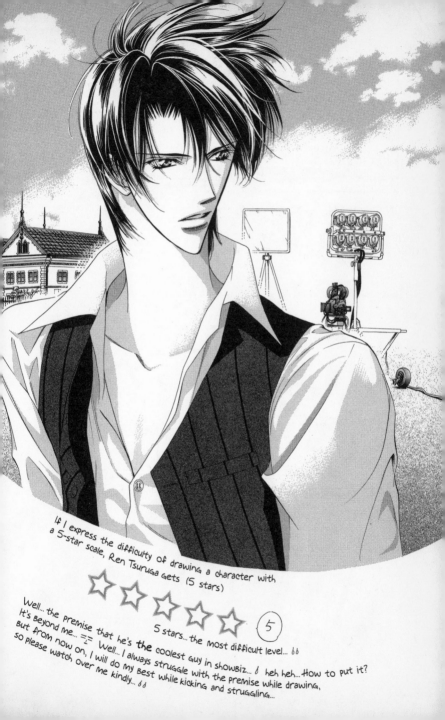

If I express the difficulty of drawing a character with a 5-star scale, Ren Tsuruga gets (5 stars)

☆☆☆☆☆ (5)

5 stars... the most difficult level...

Well... the premise that he's **the** coolest guy in showbiz... heh heh... How to put it? It's beyond me... Well... I always struggle with the premise while drawing, but from now on, I will do my best while kicking and struggling... so please watch over me kindly...

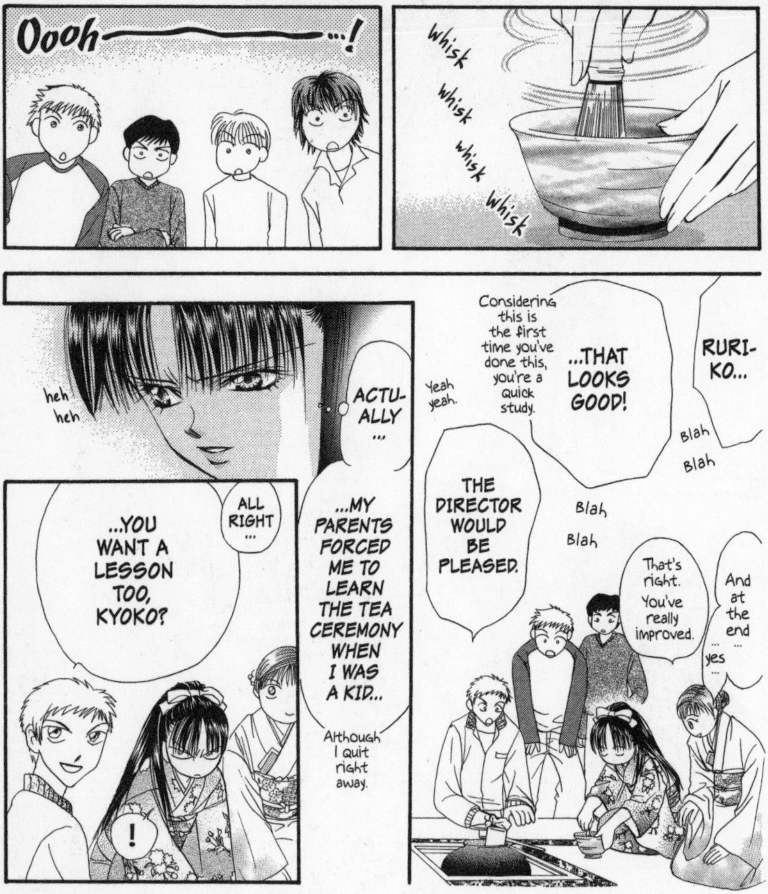
whisk
whisk
whisk
whisk
Oooh———...!
RURI-KO...
Blah
Blah
...THAT LOOKS GOOD!
Considering this is the first time you've done this, you're a quick study.
Yeah yeah.
Blah
Blah
THE DIRECTOR WOULD BE PLEASED.
And at the end ... yes ...
That's right. You've really improved.
heh heh
ACTU-ALLY ...
...MY PARENTS FORCED ME TO LEARN THE TEA CEREMONY WHEN I WAS A KID...
Although I quit right away.
ALL RIGHT ...
...YOU WANT A LESSON TOO, KYOKO?
!

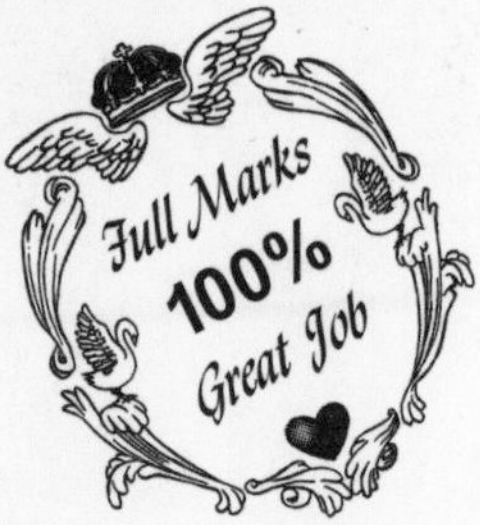
Full Marks
100%
Great Job

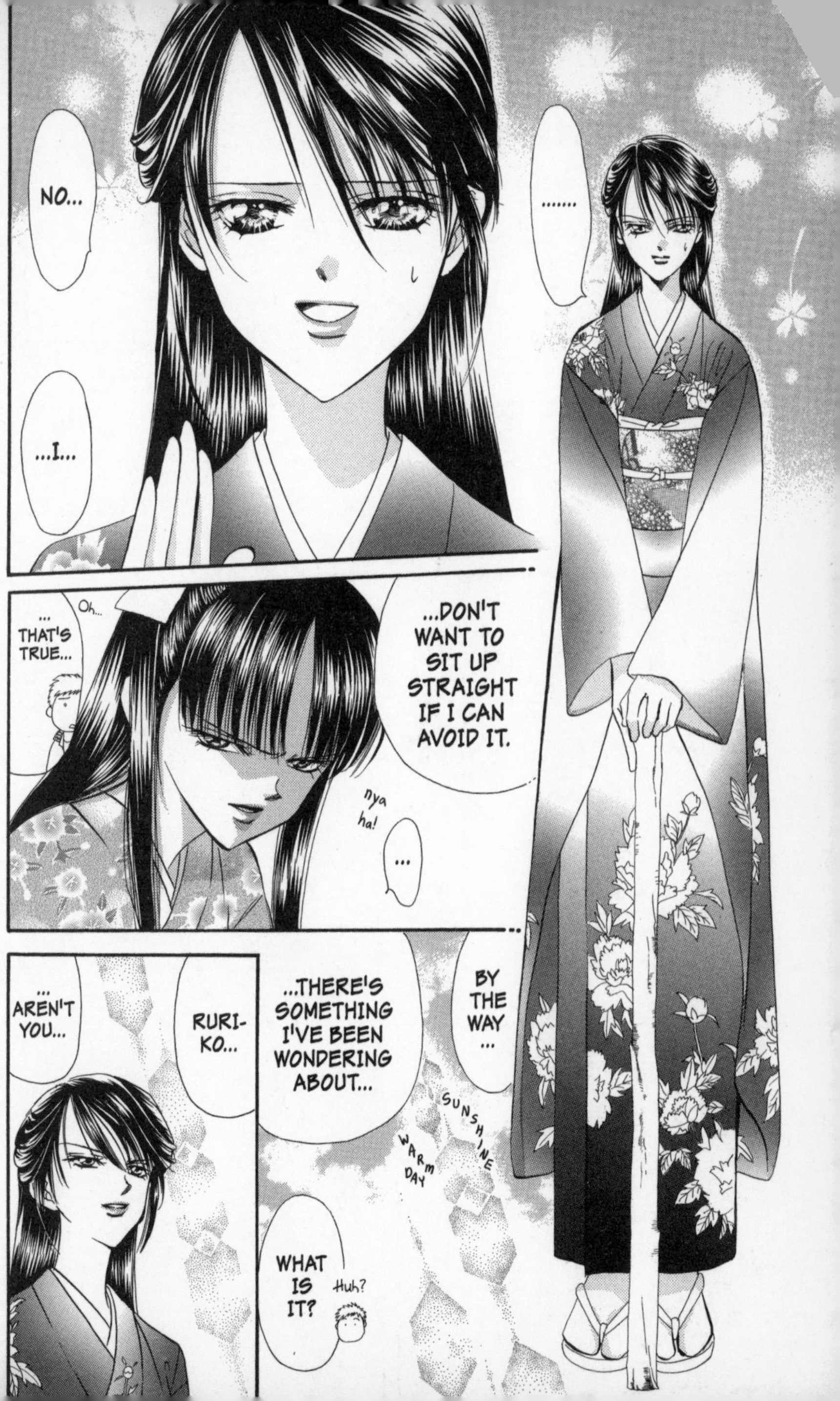
....
NO...
...I...
...DON'T WANT TO SIT UP STRAIGHT IF I CAN AVOID IT.
nya ha!
...
Oh...
... THAT'S TRUE...
BY THE WAY ...
...THERE'S SOMETHING I'VE BEEN WONDERING ABOUT...
RURI-KO...
... AREN'T YOU...
SUNSHINE
WARM DAY
WHAT IS IT?
Huh?

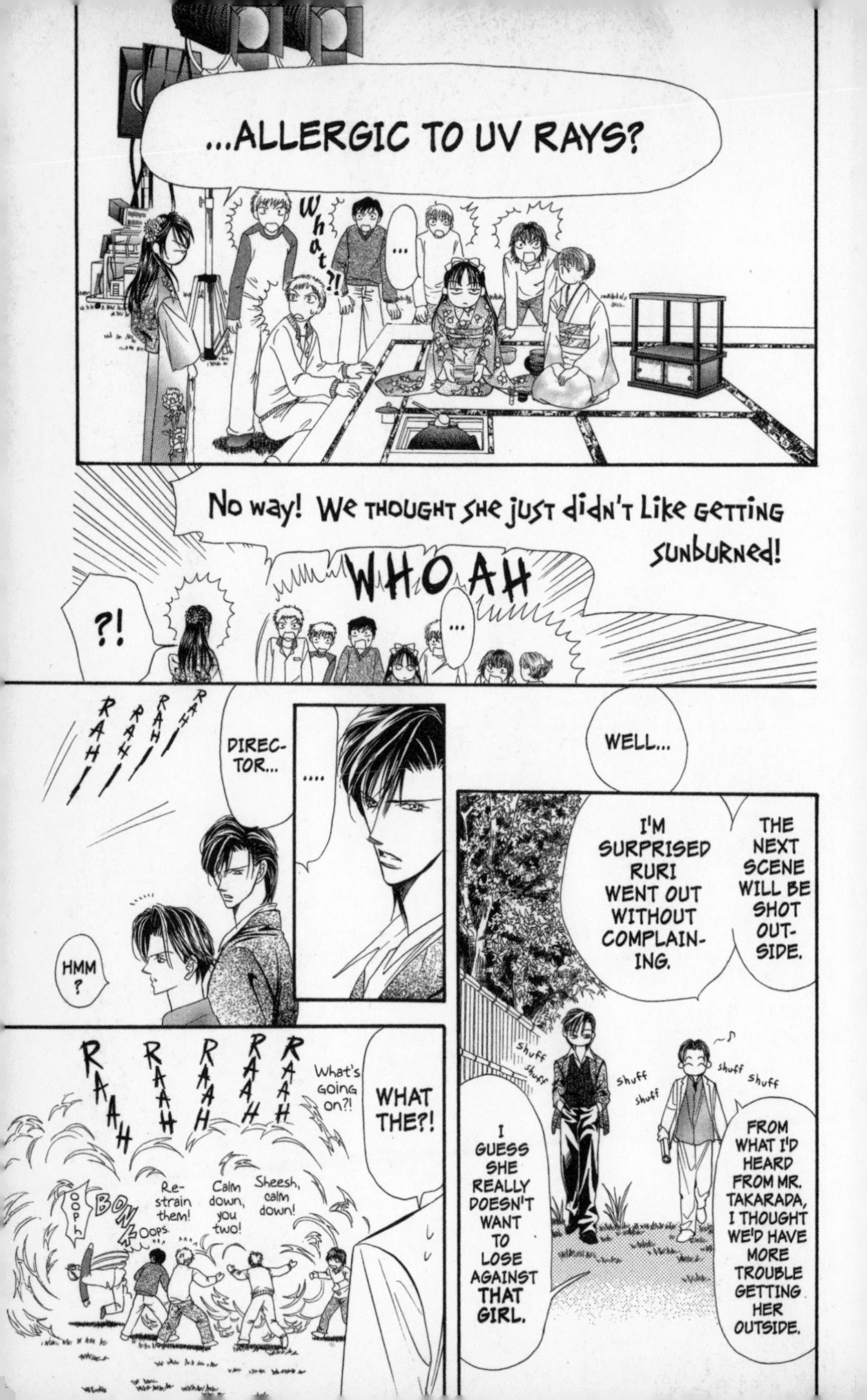
...ALLERGIC TO UV RAYS?
What?!
...
No way! We thought she just didn't like getting sunburned!
WHOAH
...
?!
WELL...
THE NEXT SCENE WILL BE SHOT OUTSIDE.
I'M SURPRISED RURI WENT OUT WITHOUT COMPLAINING.
shuff shuff
shuff shuff
FROM WHAT I'D HEARD FROM MR. TAKARADA, I THOUGHT WE'D HAVE MORE TROUBLE GETTING HER OUTSIDE.
shuff shuff
I GUESS SHE REALLY DOESN'T WANT TO LOSE AGAINST THAT GIRL.
....
DIRECTOR...
RAH! RAH! RAH! RAH!
HMM?
WHAT THE?!
What's going on?!
RAAAH RAAAH RAAAH RAAAH RAAAH
Sheesh, calm down!
Calm down, you two!
Re-strain them!
BONK
OOPS.
OOPh

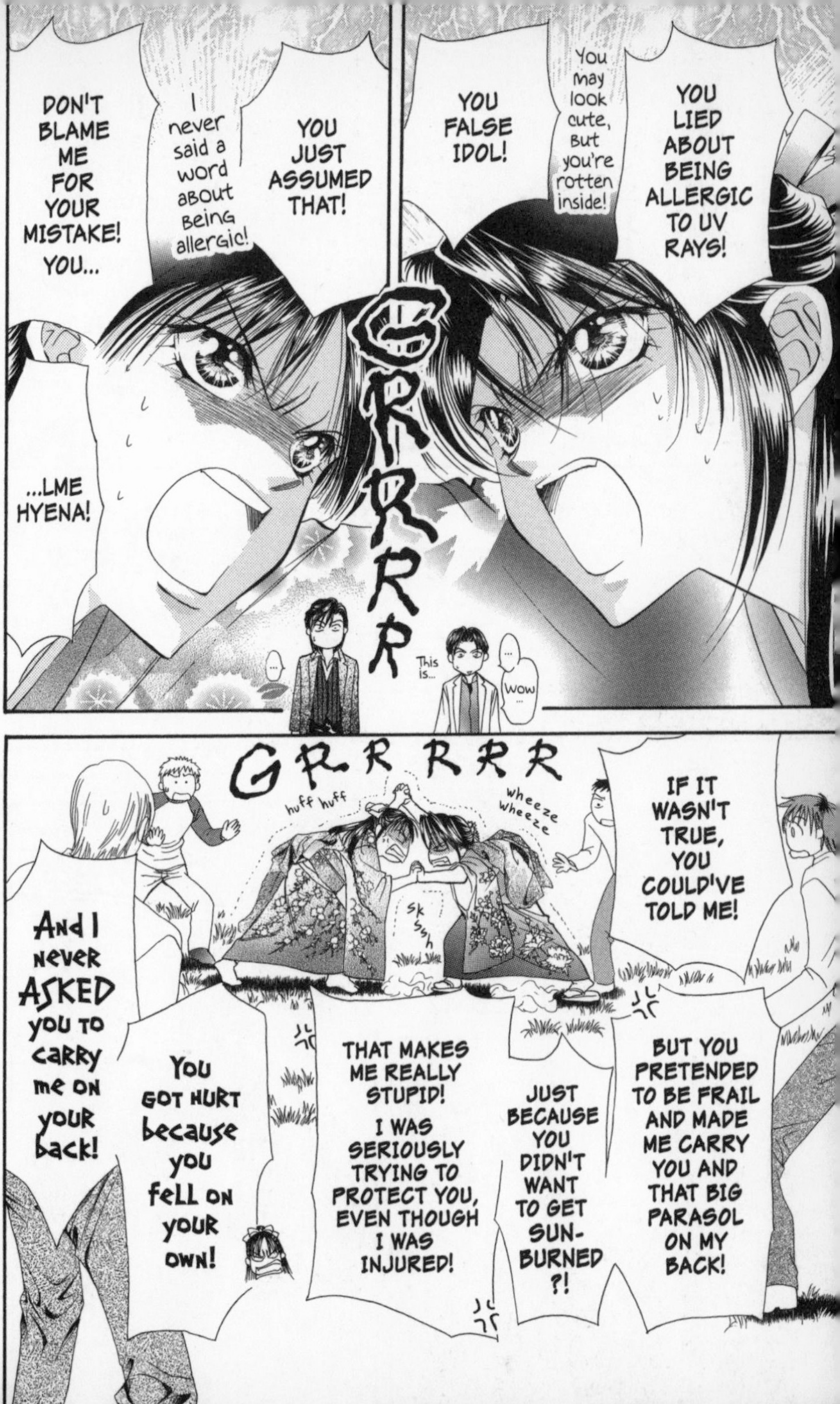
YOU LIED ABOUT BEING ALLERGIC TO UV RAYS!
You may look cute, but you're rotten inside!
YOU FALSE IDOL!
YOU JUST ASSUMED THAT!
I never said a word about being allergic!
DON'T BLAME ME FOR YOUR MISTAKE! YOU...
GRRRR
...LME HYENA!
...
This is...
...
WOW...
GRRRRRR
wheeze wheeze
huff huff
IF IT WASN'T TRUE, YOU COULD'VE TOLD ME!
And I never ASKED you to carry me on your back!
BUT YOU PRETENDED TO BE FRAIL AND MADE ME CARRY YOU AND THAT BIG PARASOL ON MY BACK!
JUST BECAUSE YOU DIDN'T WANT TO GET SUN-BURNED?!
THAT MAKES ME REALLY STUPID! I WAS SERIOUSLY TRYING TO PROTECT YOU, EVEN THOUGH I WAS INJURED!
You got hurt because you fell on your own!

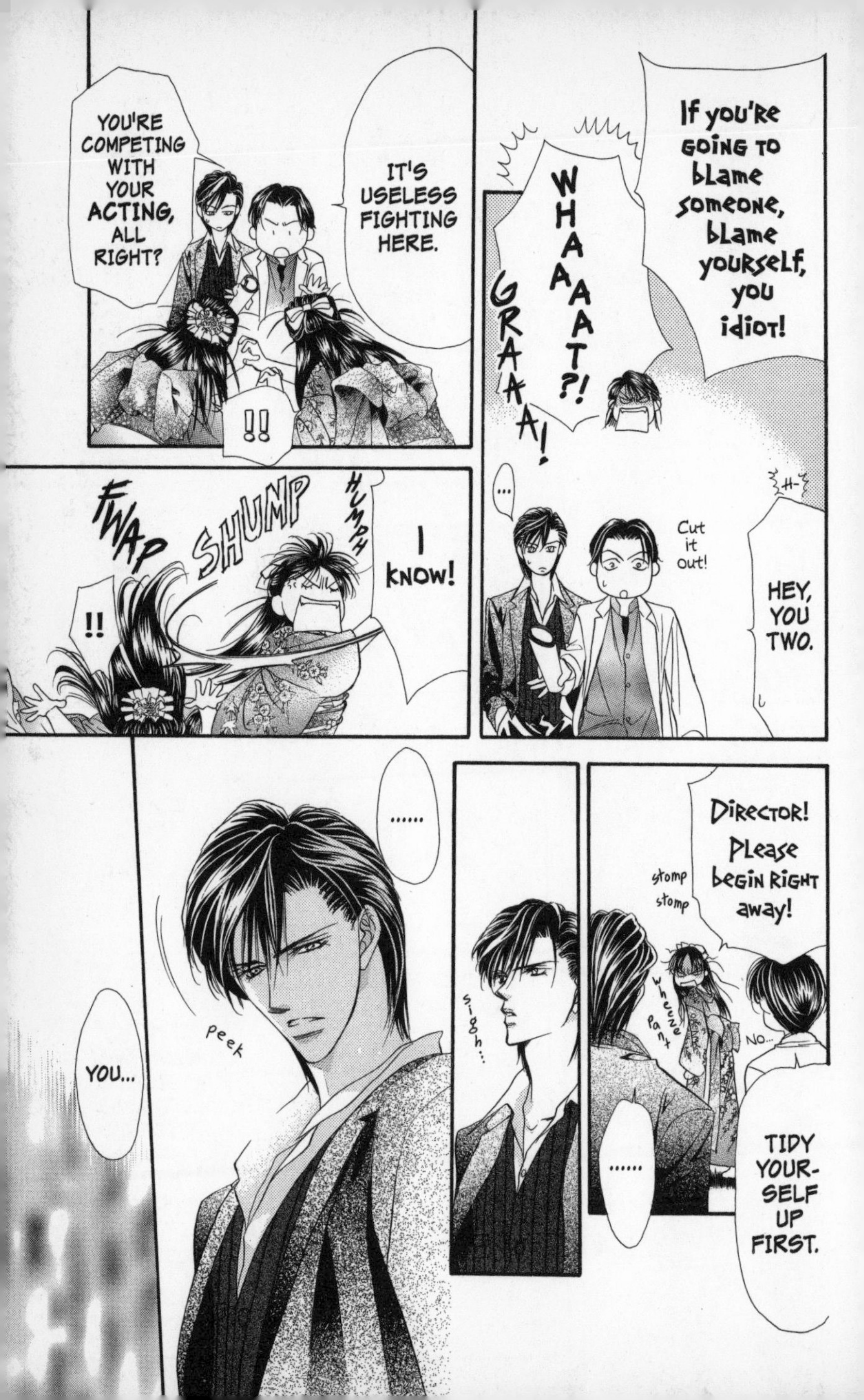
If you're going to blame someone, blame yourself, you idiot!
WHAAAAT?!
GRAAAA!
HEY, YOU TWO.
Cut it out!
...
IT'S USELESS FIGHTING HERE.
YOU'RE COMPETING WITH YOUR ACTING, ALL RIGHT?
!!
I KNOW!
HUMPH
SHUMP
FWAP
!!
Director! Please begin right away!
stomp stomp
wheeze pant
NO...
TIDY YOUR-SELF UP FIRST.
......
sigh...
......
peek
YOU...

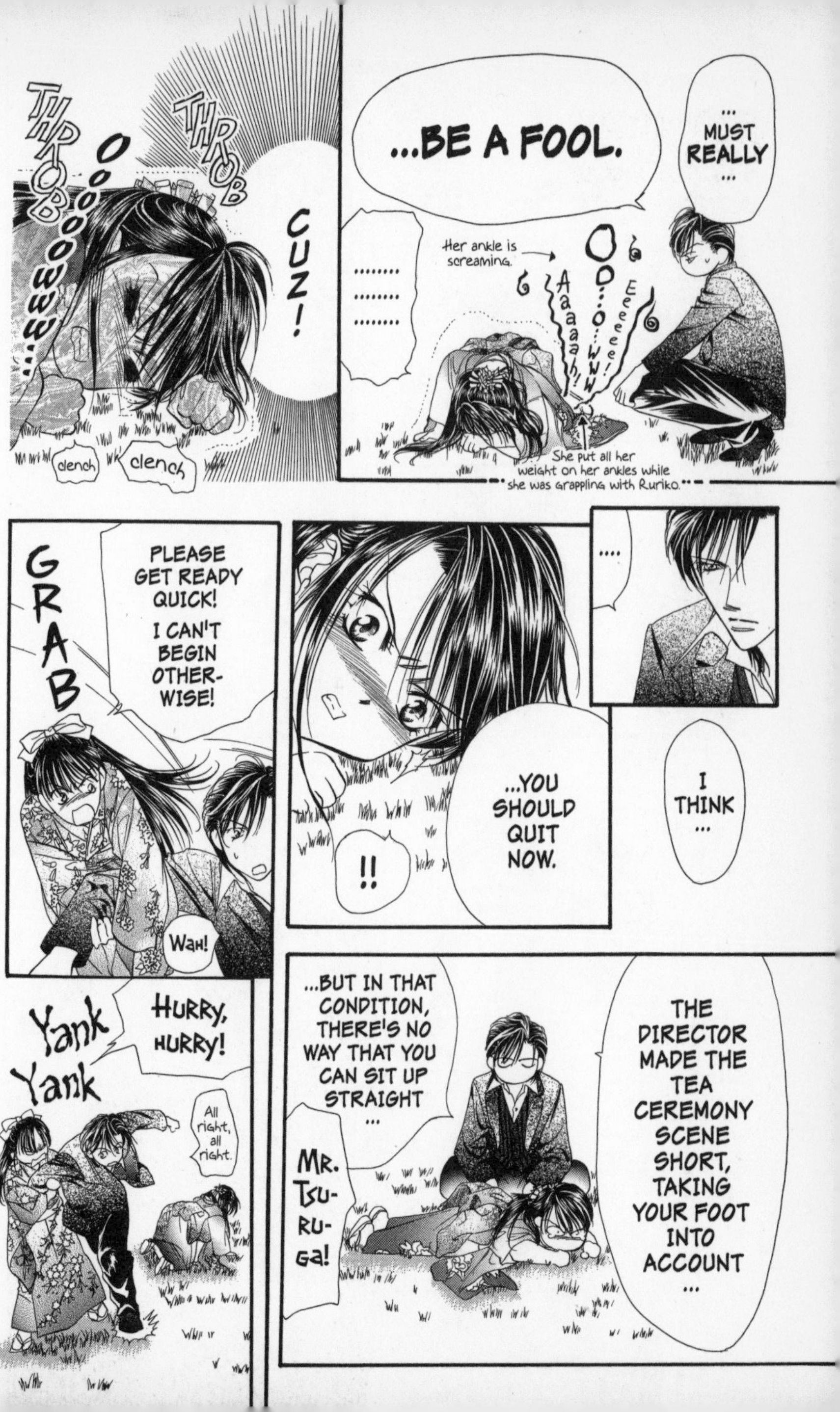

...MUST REALLY...
...BE A FOOL.
....
....
....
Her ankle is screaming.
Aaaaah!
Oo...oWWW
Eeeeee!
She put all her weight on her ankles while she was grappling with Ruriko.
THROB
THROB
OoooooWWW...
CUZ!
clench
clench
....
I THINK...
...YOU SHOULD QUIT NOW.
!!
GRAB
PLEASE GET READY QUICK!
I CAN'T BEGIN OTHER-WISE!
Wah!
THE DIRECTOR MADE THE TEA CEREMONY SCENE SHORT, TAKING YOUR FOOT INTO ACCOUNT...
...BUT IN THAT CONDITION, THERE'S NO WAY THAT YOU CAN SIT UP STRAIGHT...
Mr. Tsu-ru-ga!
Hurry, hurry!
Yank Yank
All right, all right.

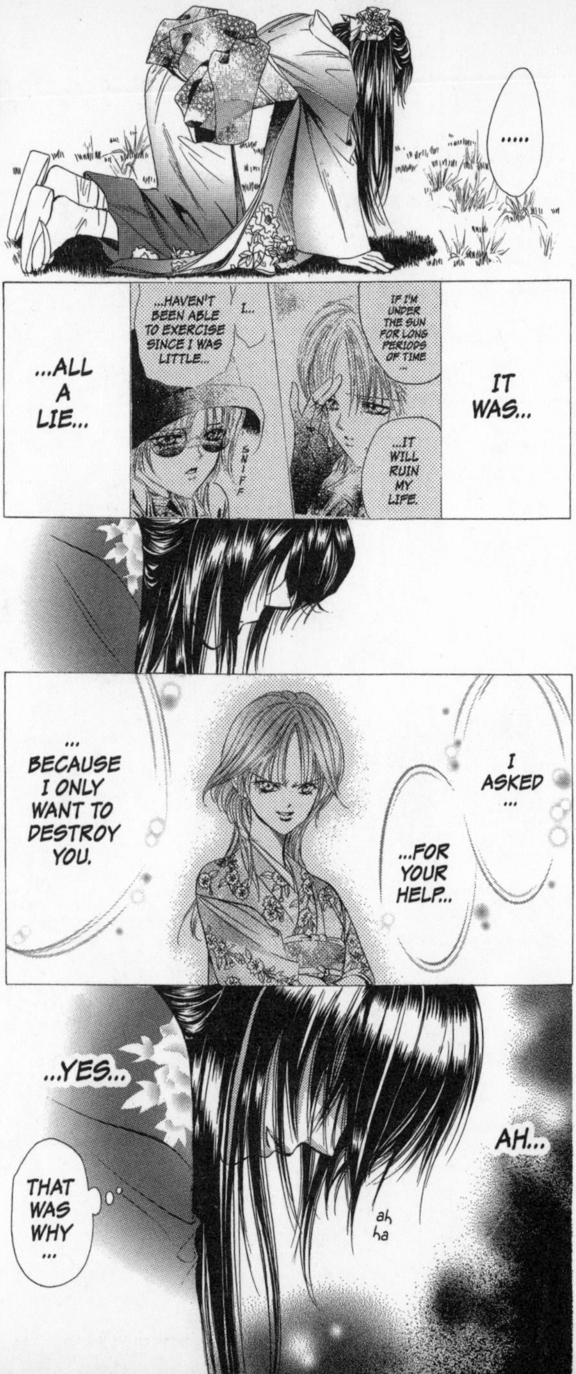
.....
IT WAS...
IF I'M UNDER THE SUN FOR LONG PERIODS OF TIME
...IT WILL RUIN MY LIFE.
I...
...HAVEN'T BEEN ABLE TO EXERCISE SINCE I WAS LITTLE...
SNIFF
...ALL A LIE...
I ASKED...
...FOR YOUR HELP...
... BECAUSE I ONLY WANT TO DESTROY YOU.
AH...
ah ha
...YES...
THAT WAS WHY...

Greetings

Hello. I'm Nakamura. Thank you for reading *Skip•Beat!* this time around, too. It happens with me often, but I redrew some of the panels that I wasn't satisfied with for the manga volume (sometimes I redraw the same panel about five times...)

My drawing ability isn't enough to satisfy my ideals. I've been a mangaka for at least ten years. It's pitiful...

...so...it took more time to fix things for the manga volume than I thought it would... Especially with Ren and Lory... If other people looked at it, I don't believe they'd think there's been much of a change...the change is veeeery subtle... probably...heh...

But...(and this happens every time) Ren always makes me cry...why? Somehow the Ren that I draw doesn't look like he's good-looking... It's because the type of male characters that I like are well-built, have single eyelids, look super evil, kind of like a savage (?!)...(The assistants who know what I like sometimes say "Nakamura-san...please don't go after dangerous-looking guys"...)

I won't go... yeah... I think... so...for sure...

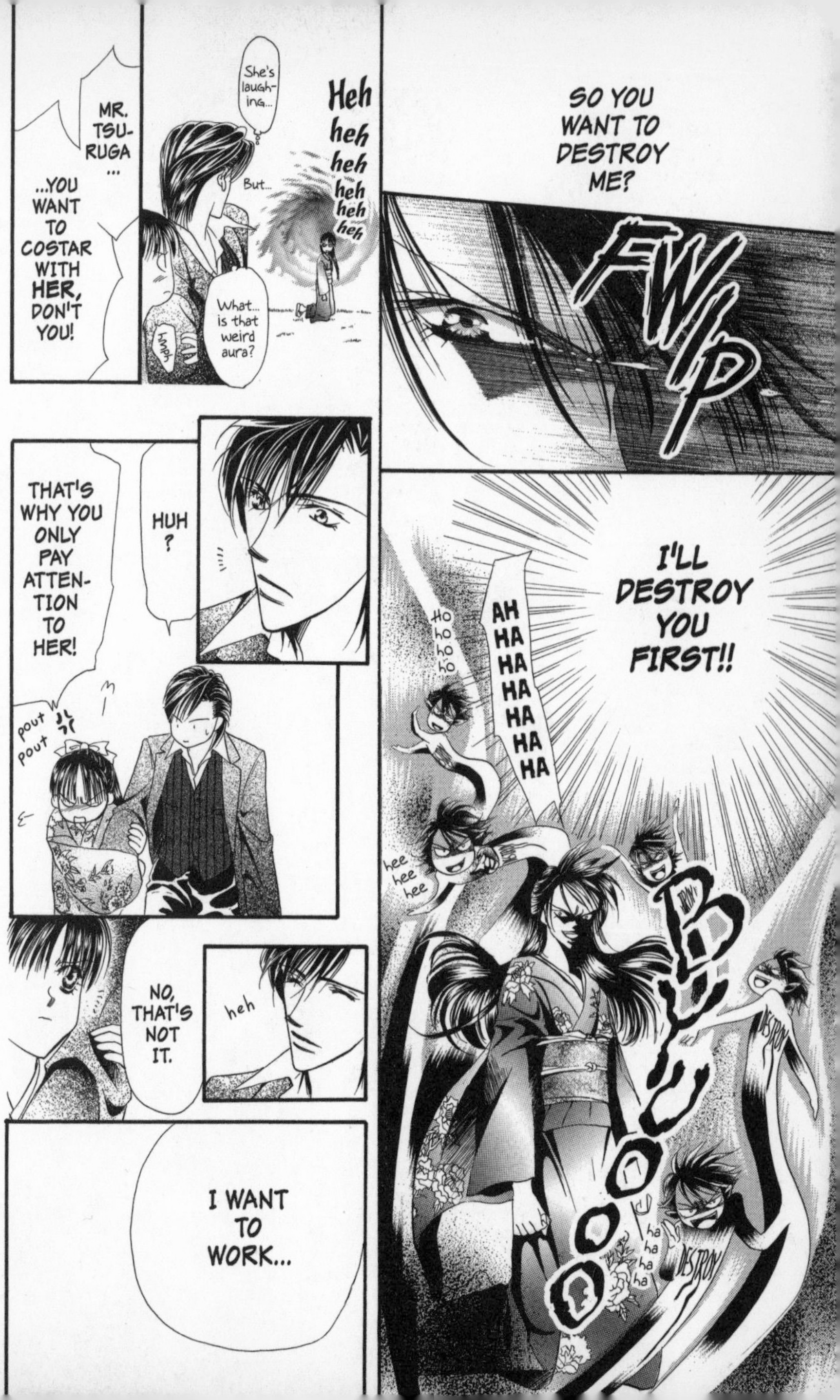

SO YOU WANT TO DESTROY ME?
FWIP
I'LL DESTROY YOU FIRST!!
AH HA HA HA HA HA HA HA
Ho ho ho ho
hee hee hee
DESTROY
ha ha ha ha
DESTROY
Heh heh heh heh heh heh
She's laughing...
But...
What... is that weird aura?
Hmph
MR. TSURUGA...
...YOU WANT TO COSTAR WITH HER, DON'T YOU!
HUH?
THAT'S WHY YOU ONLY PAY ATTENTION TO HER!
pout pout
heh
NO, THAT'S NOT IT.
I WANT TO WORK...

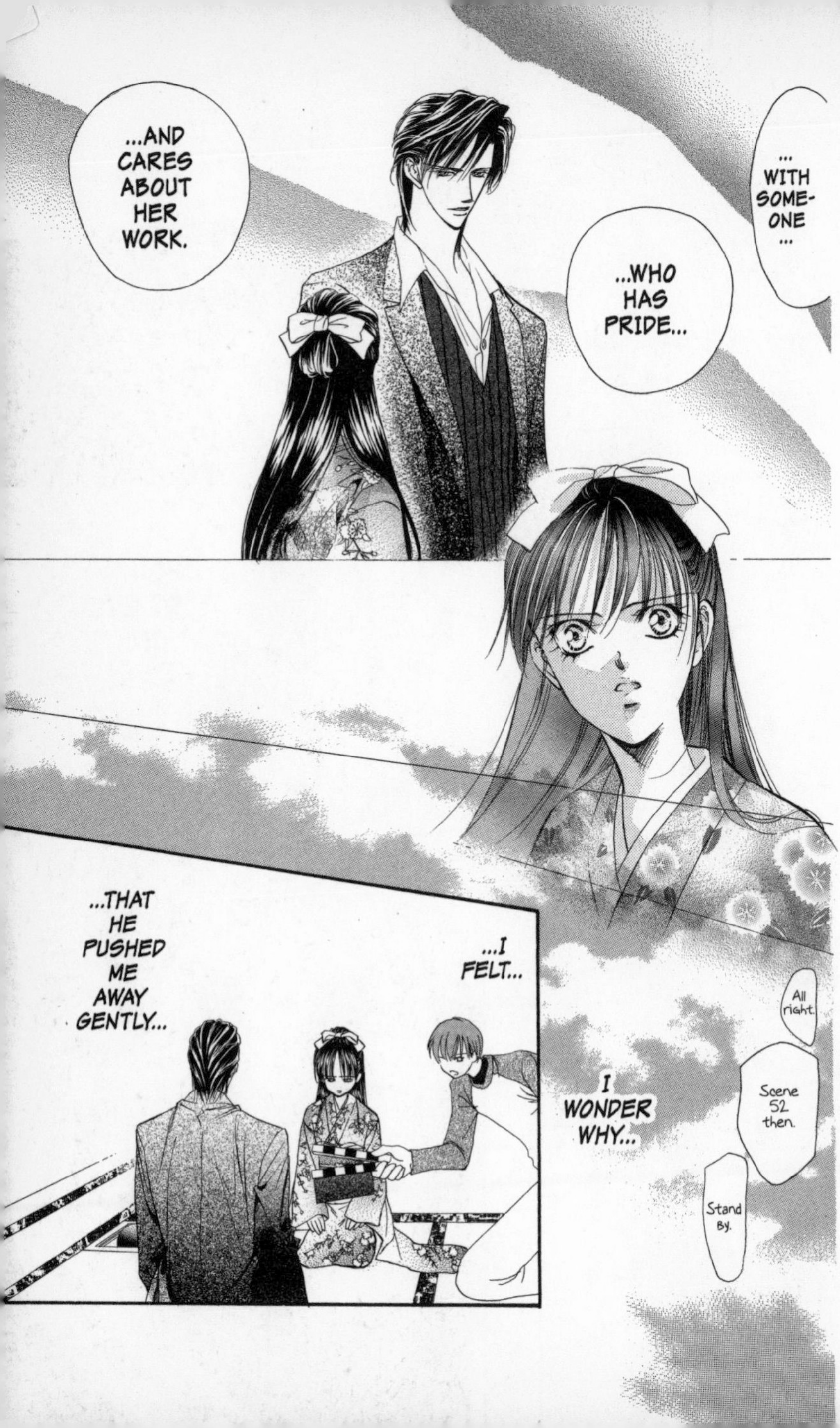
...WITH SOME-ONE...
...WHO HAS PRIDE...
...AND CARES ABOUT HER WORK.
All right.
Scene 52 then.
I WONDER WHY...
Stand By.
...I FELT...
...THAT HE PUSHED ME AWAY GENTLY...

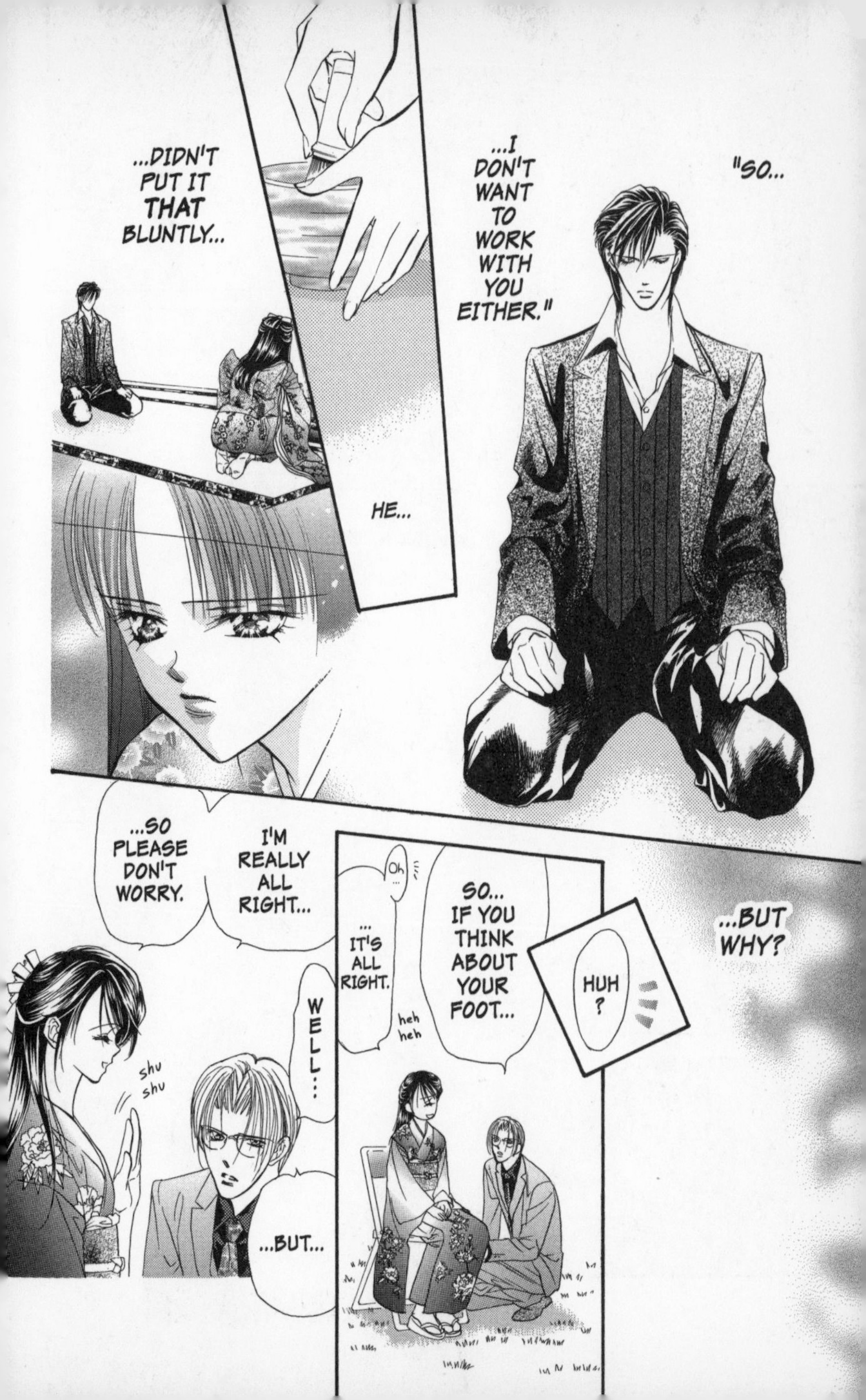
"SO...
...I DON'T WANT TO WORK WITH YOU EITHER."
HE...
...DIDN'T PUT IT THAT BLUNTLY...
...BUT WHY?
HUH?
SO... IF YOU THINK ABOUT YOUR FOOT...
Oh...
...IT'S ALL RIGHT.
heh heh
I'M REALLY ALL RIGHT...
...SO PLEASE DON'T WORRY.
WELL...
shu shu
...BUT...

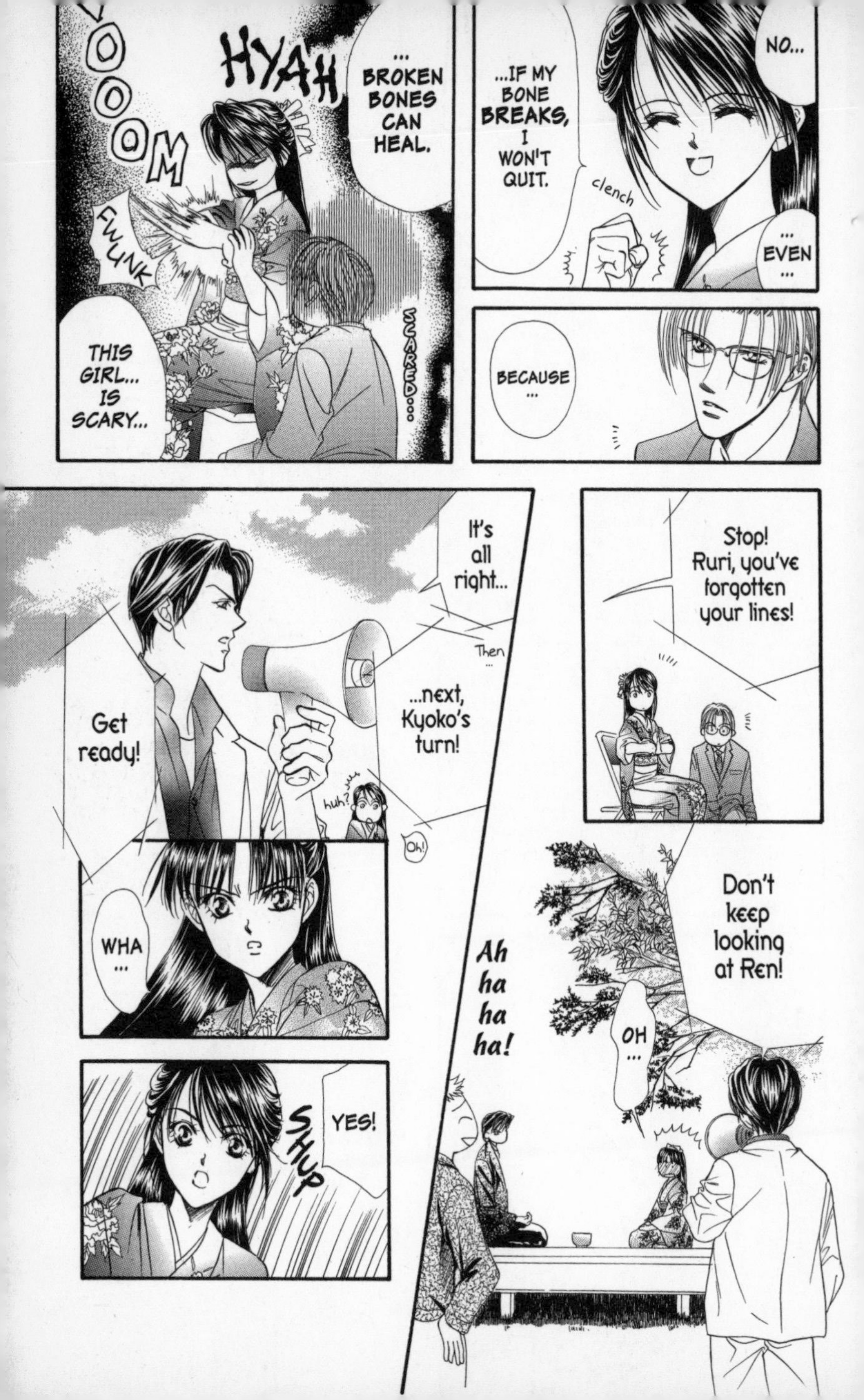
NO...
...EVEN...
...IF MY BONE BREAKS, I WON'T QUIT.
clench
BECAUSE...
...BROKEN BONES CAN HEAL.
HYAH
VOOOM
FWUNK
THIS GIRL... IS SCARY...
SCARED...
Stop! Ruri, you've forgotten your lines!
Don't keep looking at Ren!
OH...
Ah ha ha ha!
It's all right...
Then...
...next, Kyoko's turn!
Get ready!
huh?
Oh!
WHA...
YES!
SHUP

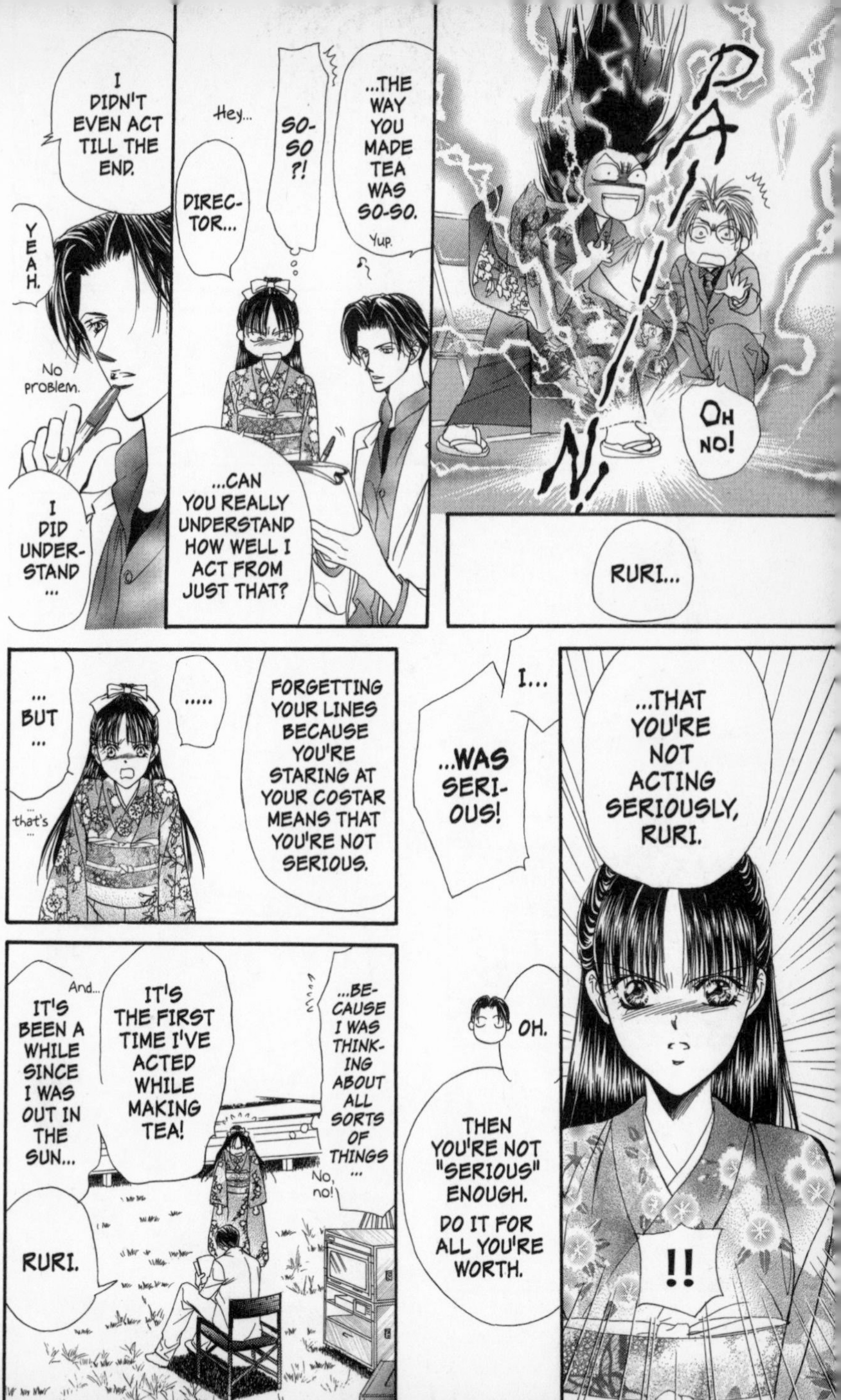
PA-I-I-I-N!
OH NO!
RURI...
...THE WAY YOU MADE TEA WAS SO-SO.
Yup.
SO-SO?!
Hey...
DIREC-TOR...
...CAN YOU REALLY UNDERSTAND HOW WELL I ACT FROM JUST THAT?
I DIDN'T EVEN ACT TILL THE END.
YEAH.
No problem.
I DID UNDER-STAND...
...THAT YOU'RE NOT ACTING SERIOUSLY, RURI.
I...
...WAS SERI-OUS!
OH.
THEN YOU'RE NOT "SERIOUS" ENOUGH.
DO IT FOR ALL YOU'RE WORTH.
!!
FORGETTING YOUR LINES BECAUSE YOU'RE STARING AT YOUR COSTAR MEANS THAT YOU'RE NOT SERIOUS.
.....
...BUT...
...that's...
...BE-CAUSE I WAS THINK-ING ABOUT ALL SORTS OF THINGS...
No, no!
IT'S THE FIRST TIME I'VE ACTED WHILE MAKING TEA!
And...
IT'S BEEN A WHILE SINCE I WAS OUT IN THE SUN...
RURI.

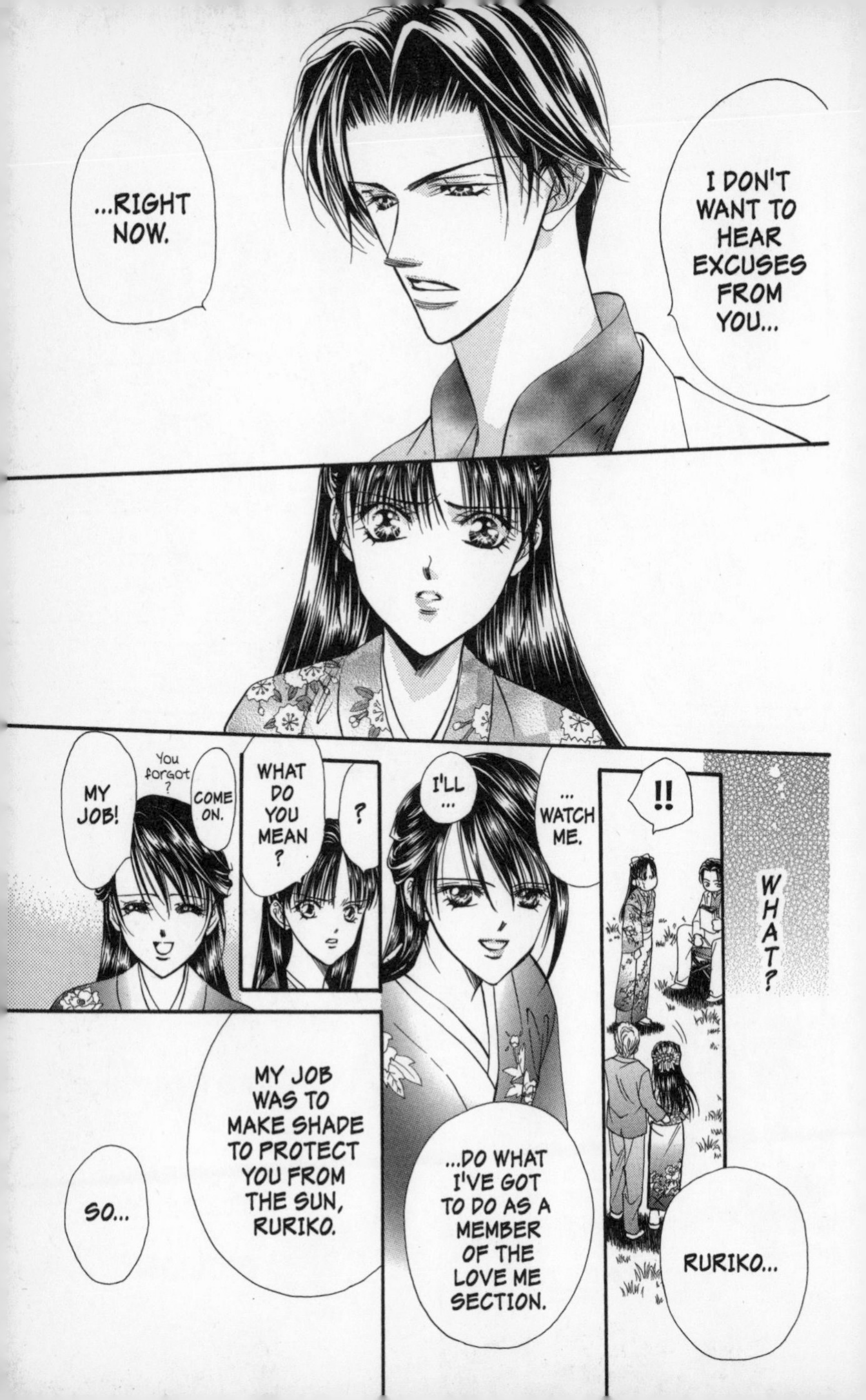

I DON'T WANT TO HEAR EXCUSES FROM YOU...
...RIGHT NOW.
!!
WHAT?
RURIKO...
... WATCH ME.
I'LL ...
...DO WHAT I'VE GOT TO DO AS A MEMBER OF THE LOVE ME SECTION.
?
WHAT DO YOU MEAN?
COME ON.
You forgot?
MY JOB!
MY JOB WAS TO MAKE SHADE TO PROTECT YOU FROM THE SUN, RURIKO.
SO...

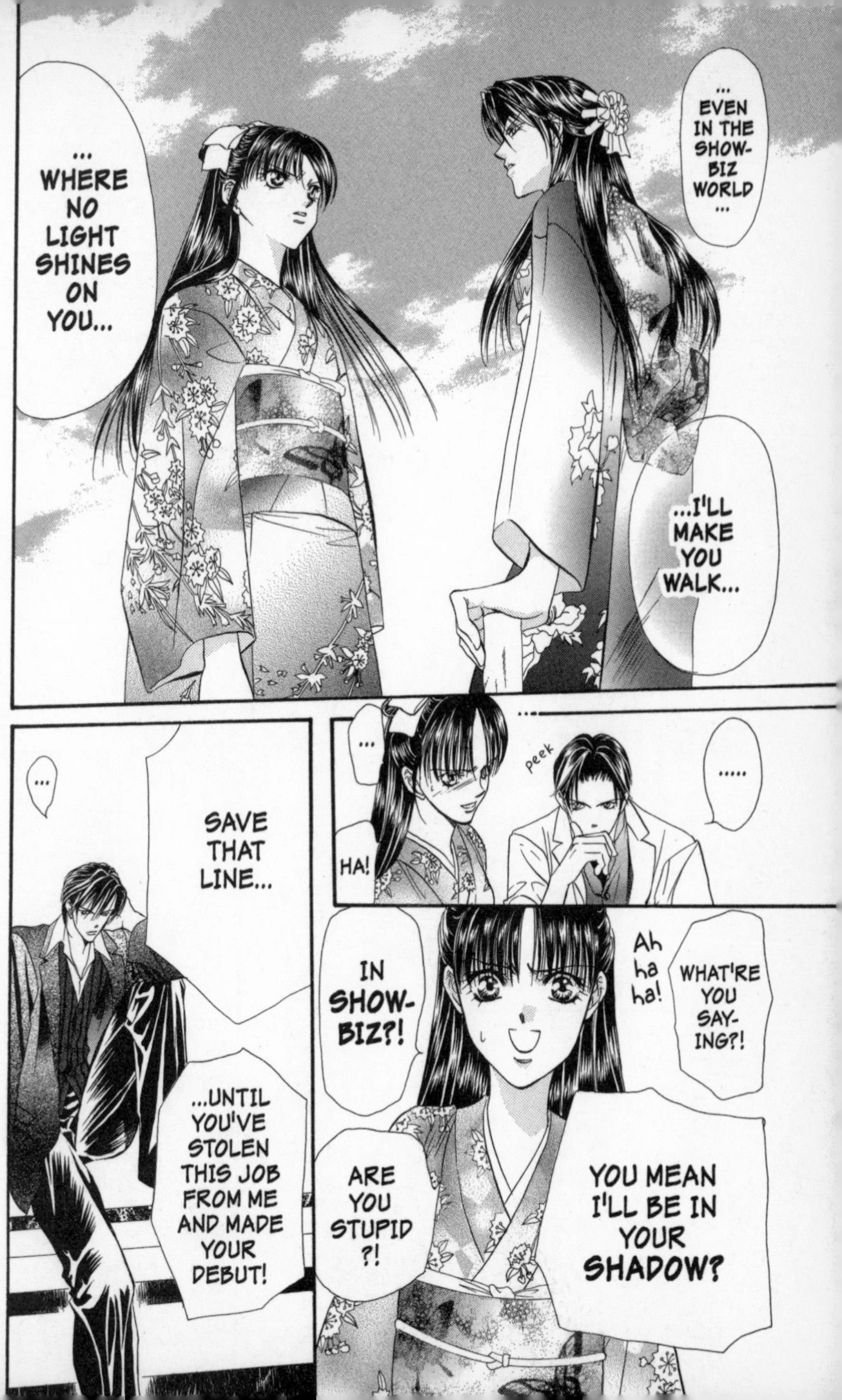
...EVEN IN THE SHOW-BIZ WORLD...
...I'LL MAKE YOU WALK...
...WHERE NO LIGHT SHINES ON YOU...
.....
peek
...
HA!
WHAT'RE YOU SAY-ING?!
Ah ha ha!
IN SHOW-BIZ?!
YOU MEAN I'LL BE IN YOUR SHADOW?
ARE YOU STUPID?!
...
SAVE THAT LINE...
...UNTIL YOU'VE STOLEN THIS JOB FROM ME AND MADE YOUR DEBUT!

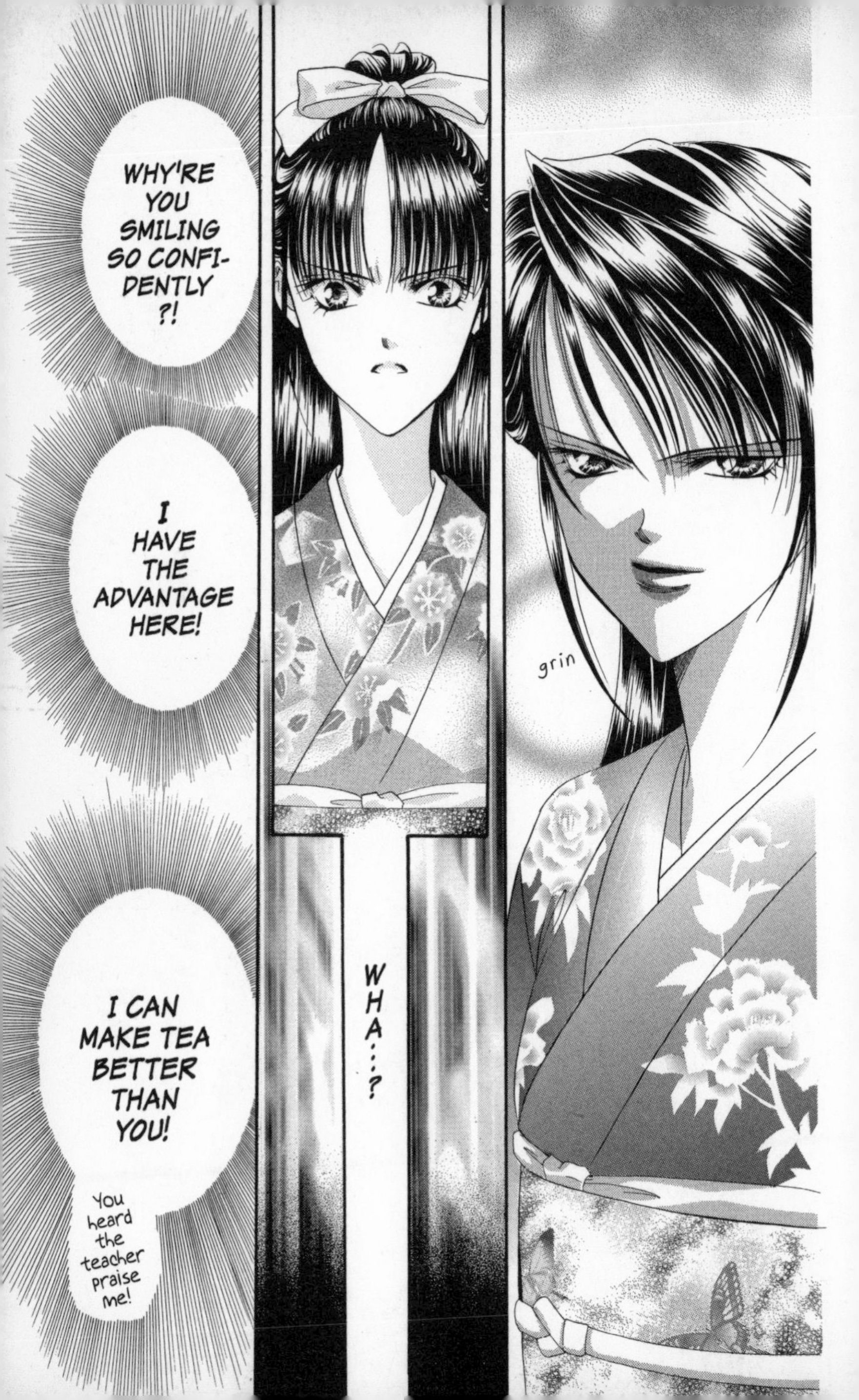
grin
WHA...?
WHY'RE YOU SMILING SO CONFI-DENTLY ?!
I HAVE THE ADVANTAGE HERE!
I CAN MAKE TEA BETTER THAN YOU!
You heard the teacher praise me!

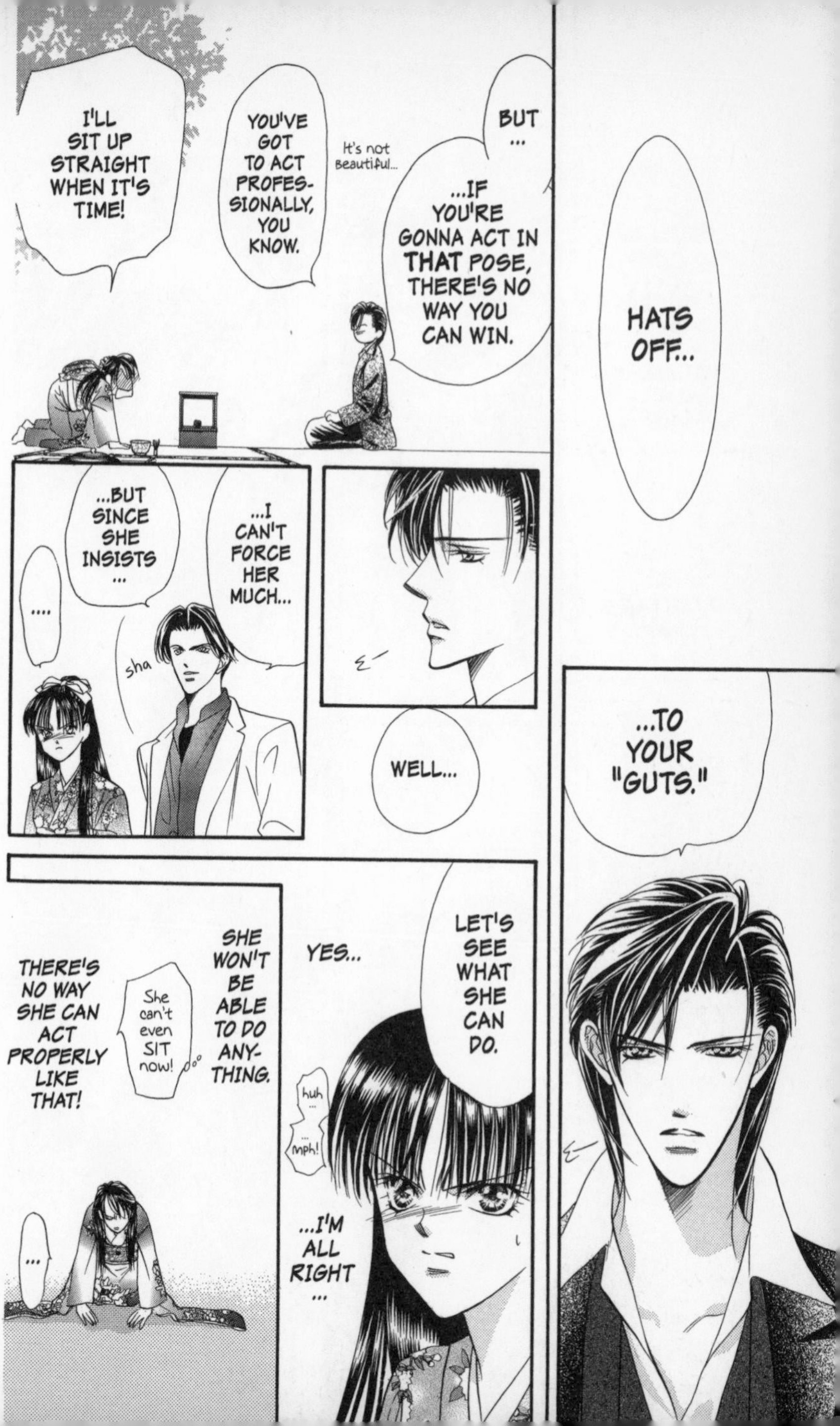
BUT ...
...IF YOU'RE GONNA ACT IN THAT POSE, THERE'S NO WAY YOU CAN WIN.
It's not Beautiful...
YOU'VE GOT TO ACT PROFESSIONALLY, YOU KNOW.
I'LL SIT UP STRAIGHT WHEN IT'S TIME!
...I CAN'T FORCE HER MUCH...
...BUT SINCE SHE INSISTS ...
sha
....
WELL...
HATS OFF...
...TO YOUR "GUTS."
LET'S SEE WHAT SHE CAN DO.
YES...
huh ...
... mph!
...I'M ALL RIGHT ...
SHE WON'T BE ABLE TO DO ANYTHING.
THERE'S NO WAY SHE CAN ACT PROPERLY LIKE THAT!
She can't even SIT now!
...

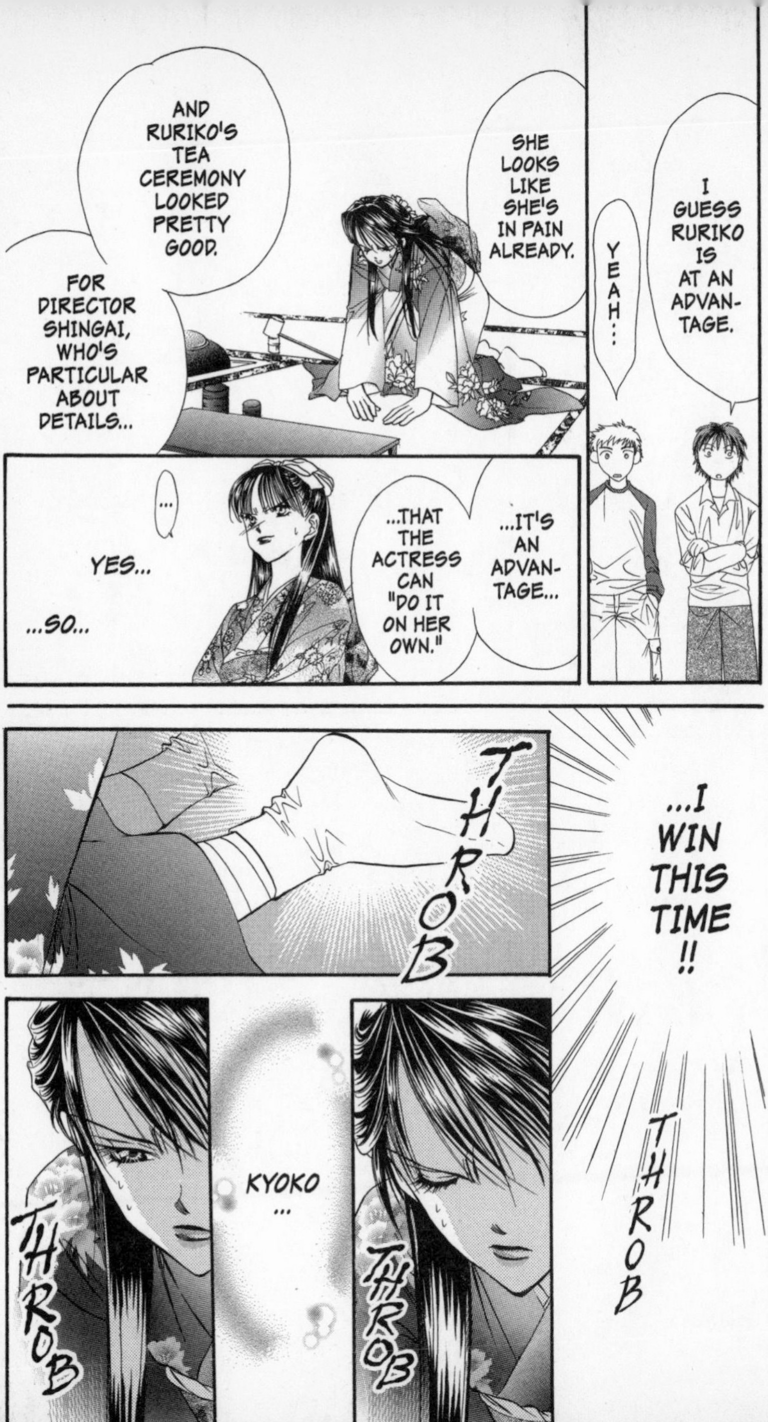
I GUESS RURIKO IS AT AN ADVANTAGE.
YEAH...
SHE LOOKS LIKE SHE'S IN PAIN ALREADY.
AND RURIKO'S TEA CEREMONY LOOKED PRETTY GOOD.
FOR DIRECTOR SHINGAI, WHO'S PARTICULAR ABOUT DETAILS...
...IT'S AN ADVANTAGE...
...THAT THE ACTRESS CAN "DO IT ON HER OWN."
...
YES...
...SO...
...I WIN THIS TIME!!
THROB
THROB
THROB
KYOKO ...
THROB

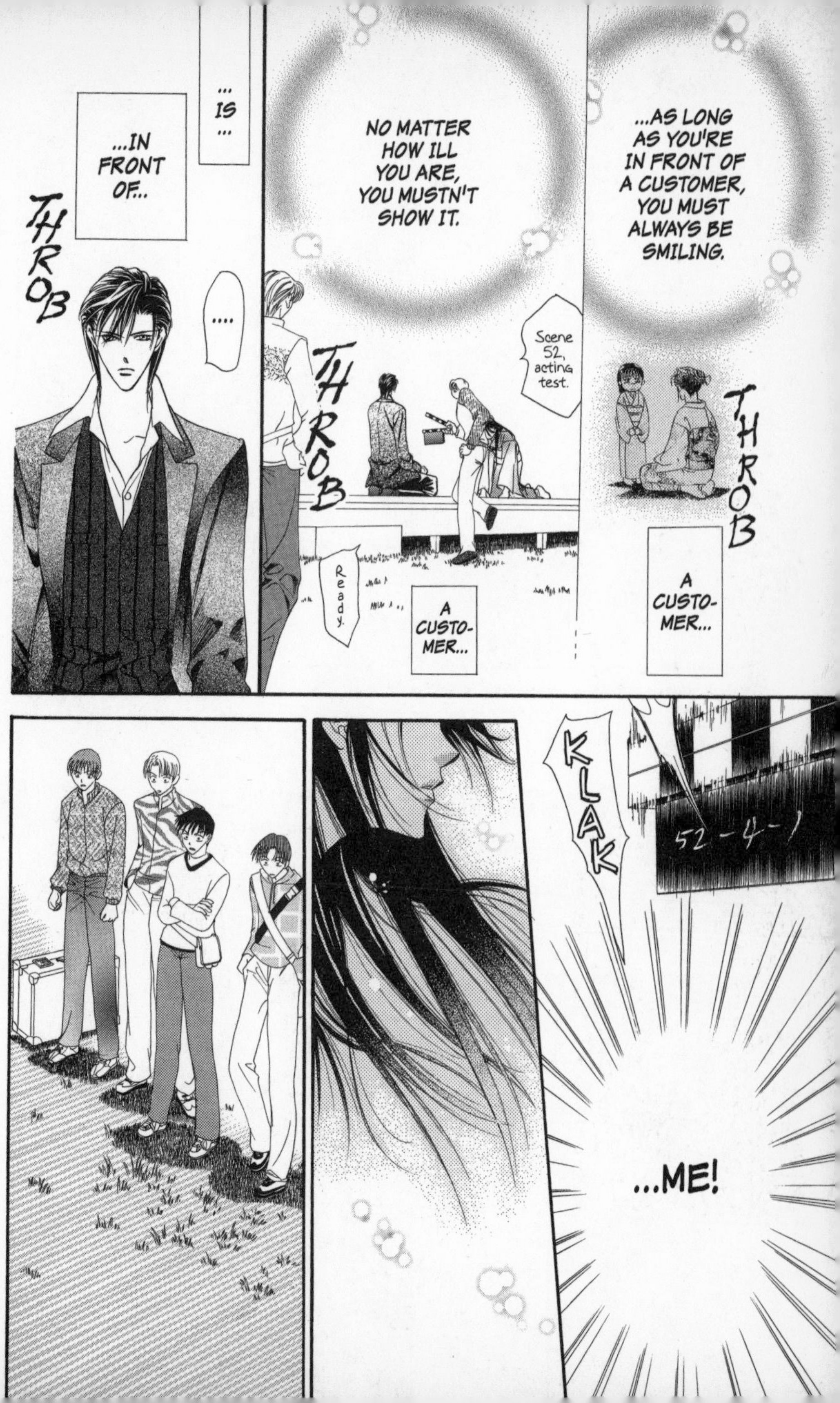
...AS LONG AS YOU'RE IN FRONT OF A CUSTOMER, YOU MUST ALWAYS BE SMILING.
THROB
A CUSTOMER...
NO MATTER HOW ILL YOU ARE, YOU MUSTN'T SHOW IT.
Scene 52, acting test.
THROB
Ready.
A CUSTOMER...
... IS ...
...IN FRONT OF...
THROB
....
52-4-1
KLAK
...ME!

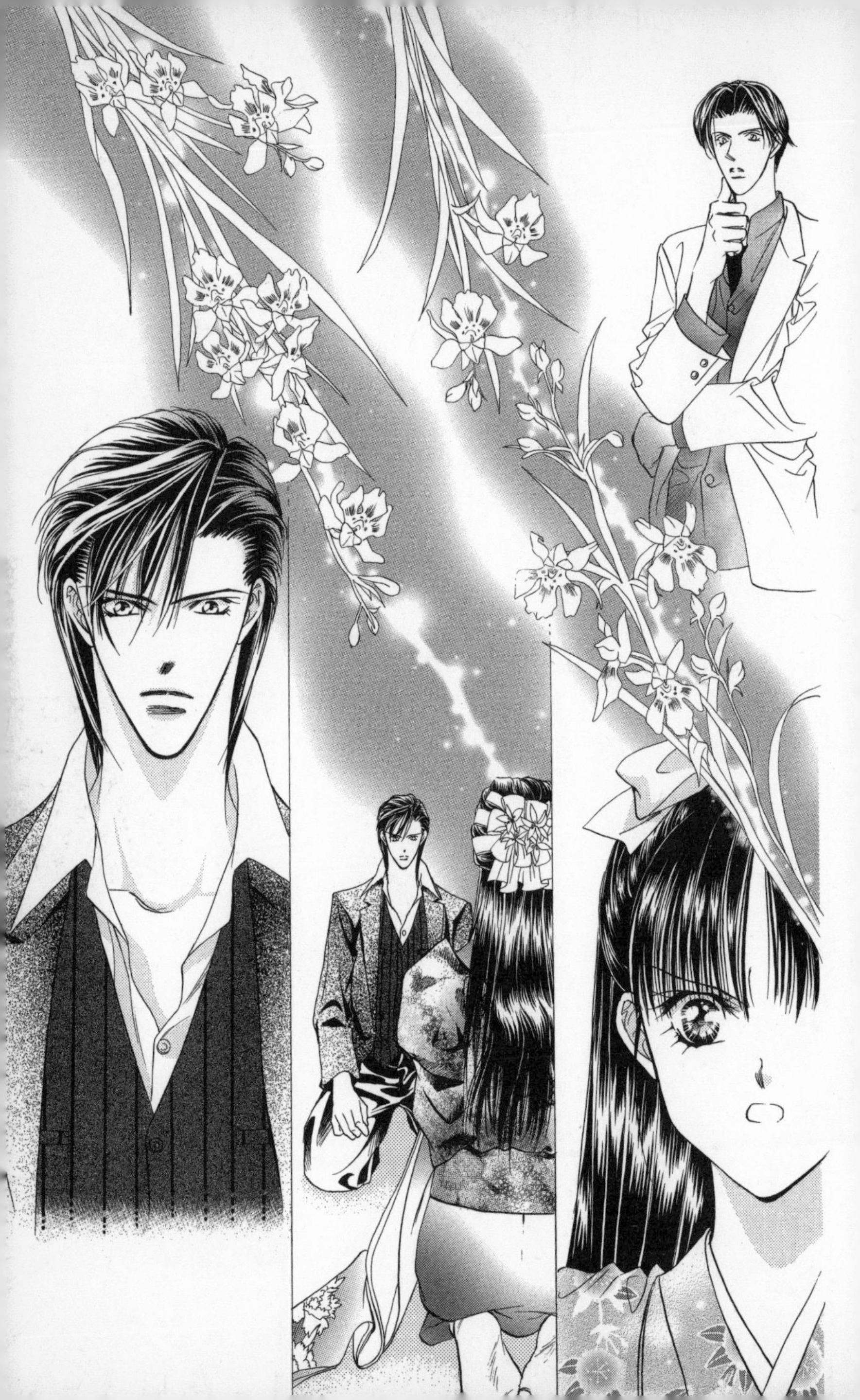

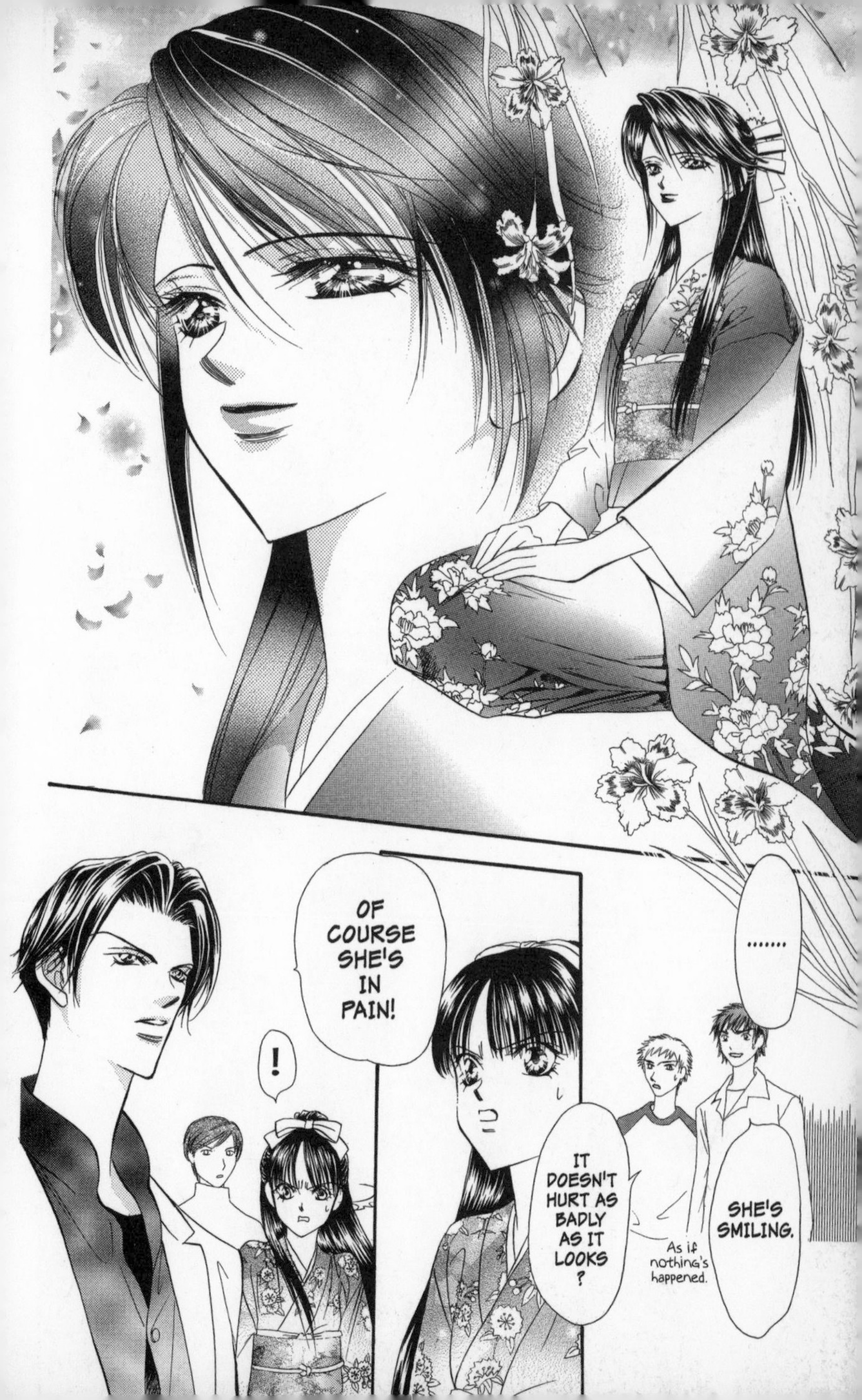

......
IT DOESN'T HURT AS BADLY AS IT LOOKS?
SHE'S SMILING.
As if nothing's happened.
OF COURSE SHE'S IN PAIN!
!

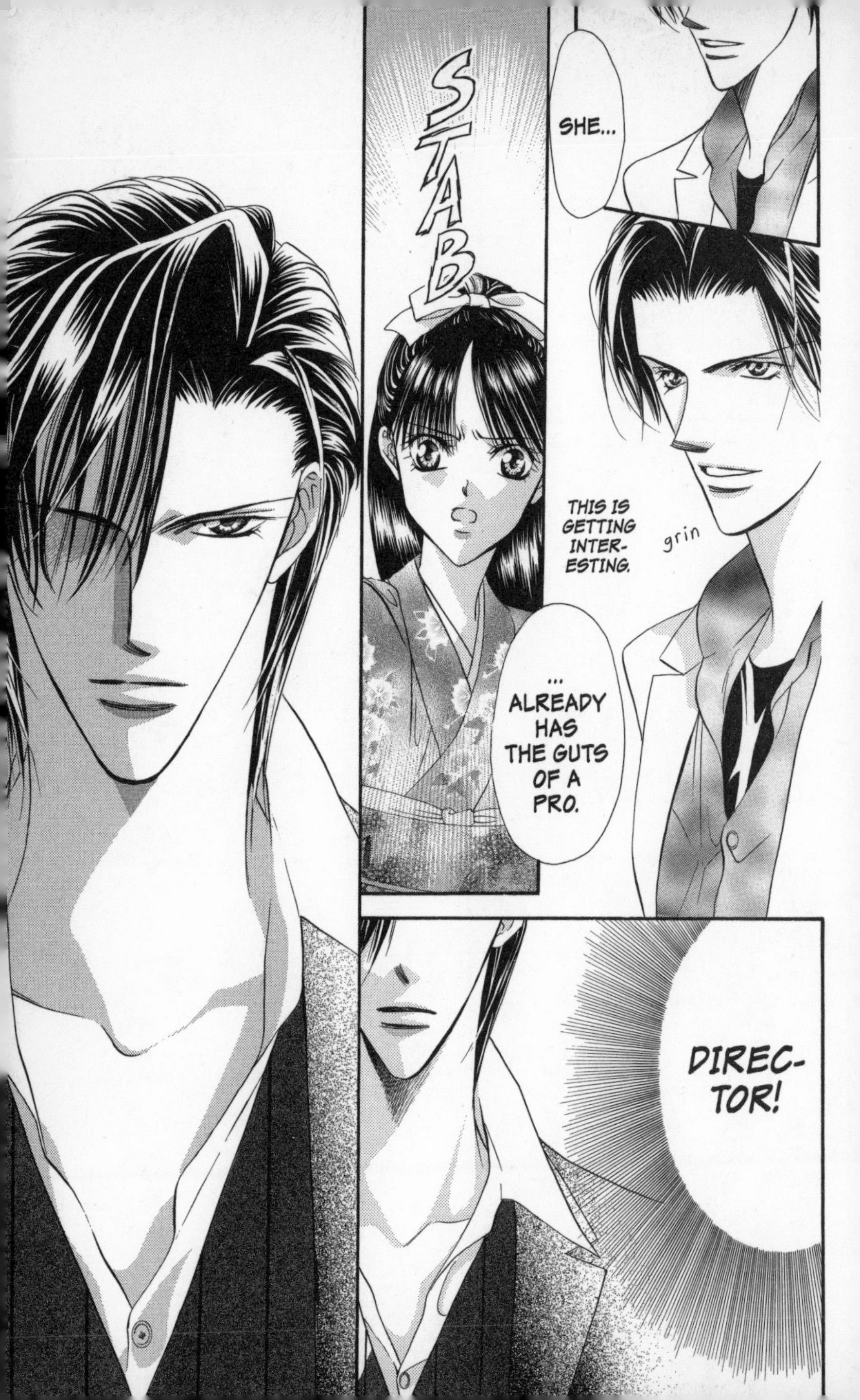
SHE...
... ALREADY HAS THE GUTS OF A PRO.
THIS IS GETTING INTER-ESTING.
grin
STAB
DIREC-TOR!

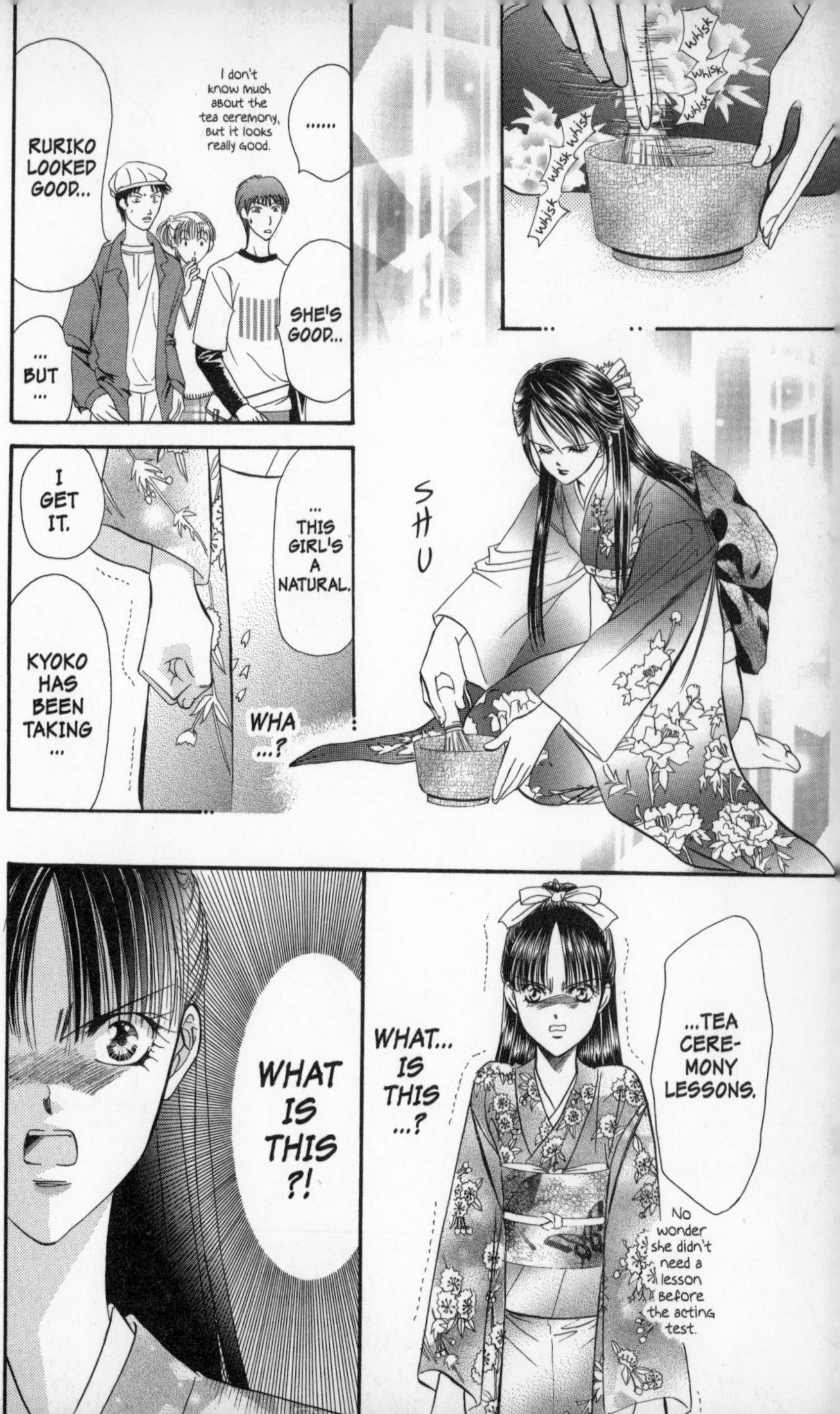
whisk whisk whisk
whisk whisk whisk
......
I don't know much about the tea ceremony, but it looks really good.
RURIKO LOOKED GOOD...
SHE'S GOOD...
... BUT ...
SHU
... THIS GIRL'S A NATURAL.
I GET IT.
WHA ...?
KYOKO HAS BEEN TAKING ...
...TEA CERE-MONY LESSONS.
No wonder she didn't need a lesson before the acting test.
WHAT... IS THIS ...?
WHAT IS THIS ?!

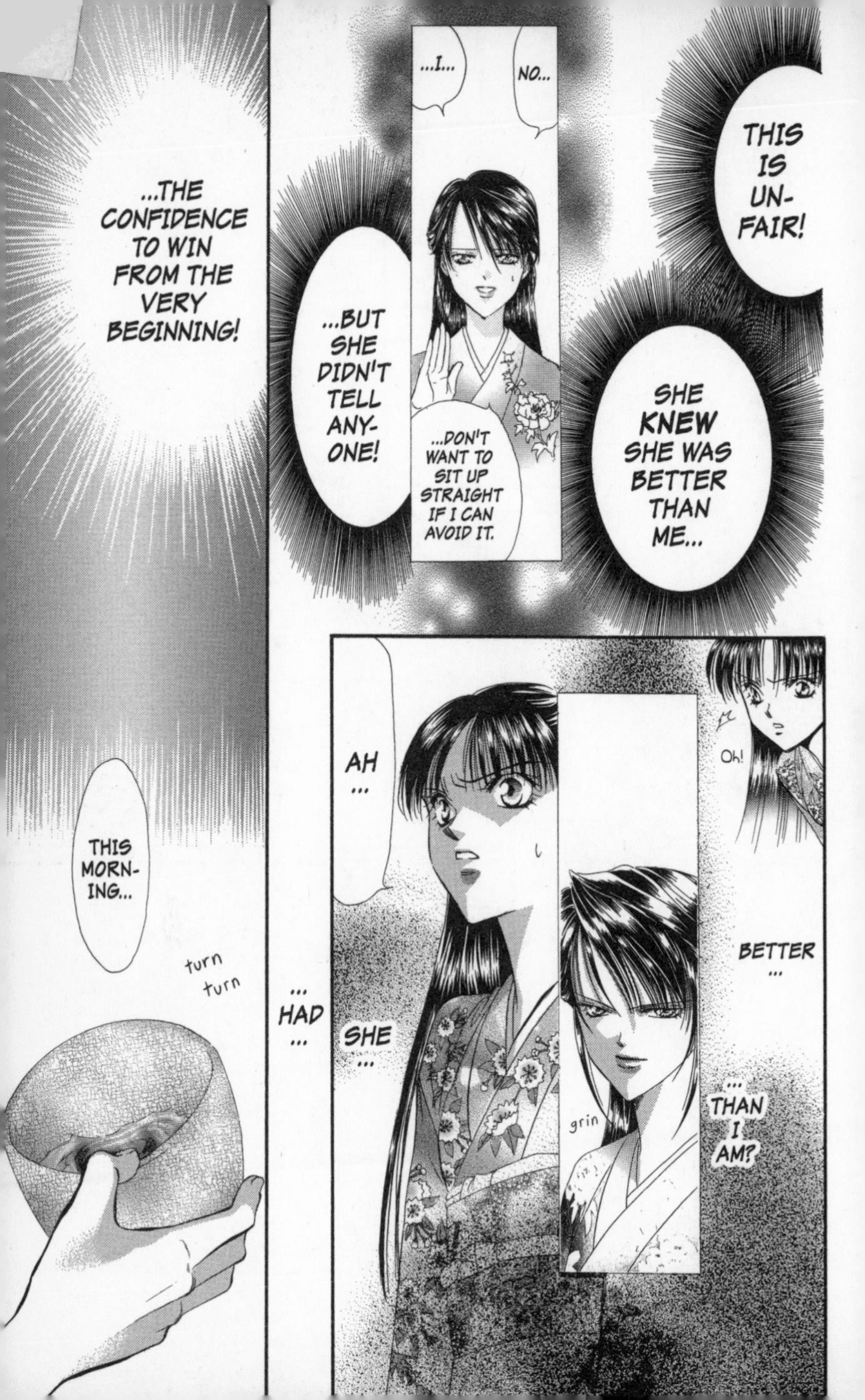
THIS IS UN-FAIR!
SHE KNEW SHE WAS BETTER THAN ME...
NO...
...I...
...DON'T WANT TO SIT UP STRAIGHT IF I CAN AVOID IT.
...BUT SHE DIDN'T TELL ANY-ONE!
Oh!
BETTER...
...THAN I AM?
grin
AH...
SHE...
...HAD...
...THE CONFIDENCE TO WIN FROM THE VERY BEGINNING!
THIS MORN-ING...
turn turn

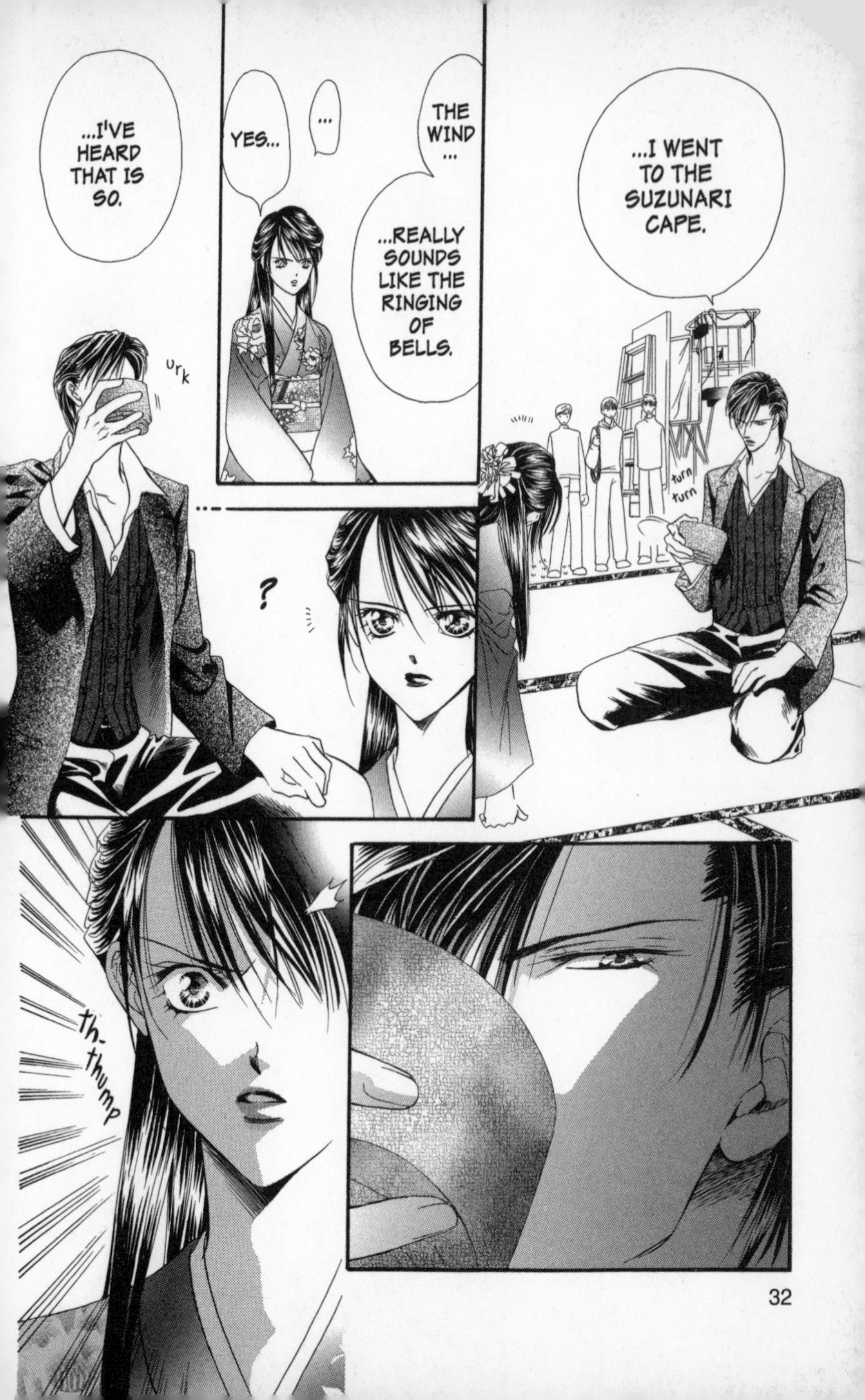
...I WENT TO THE SUZUNARI CAPE.
turn turn
THE WIND ...
...REALLY SOUNDS LIKE THE RINGING OF BELLS.
...
YES...
...I'VE HEARD THAT IS SO.
urk
?
th-thump

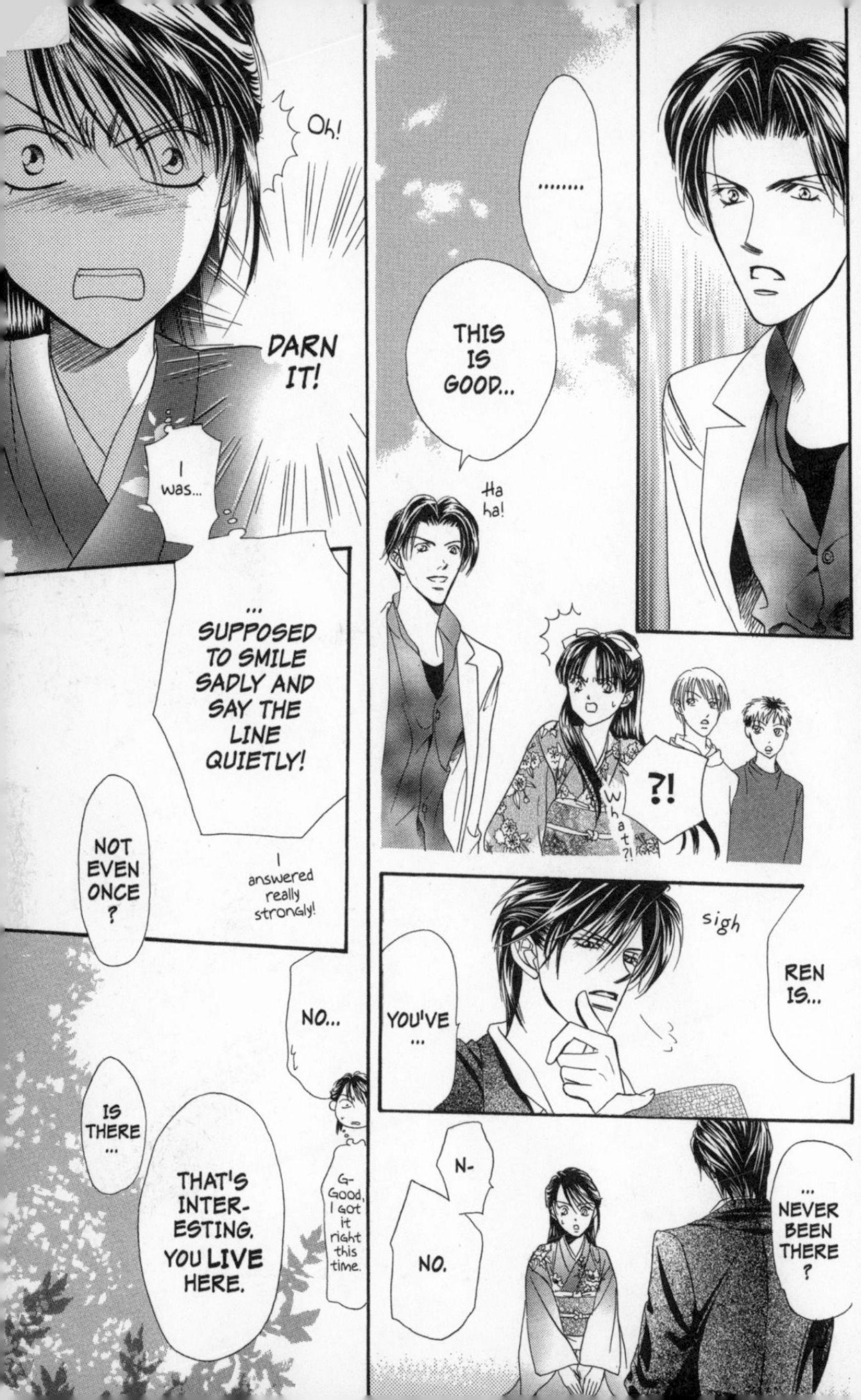

....
THIS IS GOOD...
Ha ha!
?!
What?!
sigh
REN IS...
YOU'VE ...
... NEVER BEEN THERE ?
N-
NO.
Oh!
DARN IT!
I was...
... SUPPOSED TO SMILE SADLY AND SAY THE LINE QUIETLY!
I answered really strongly!
NOT EVEN ONCE ?
NO...
IS THERE ...
THAT'S INTER-ESTING. YOU LIVE HERE.
G-Good, I got it right this time.

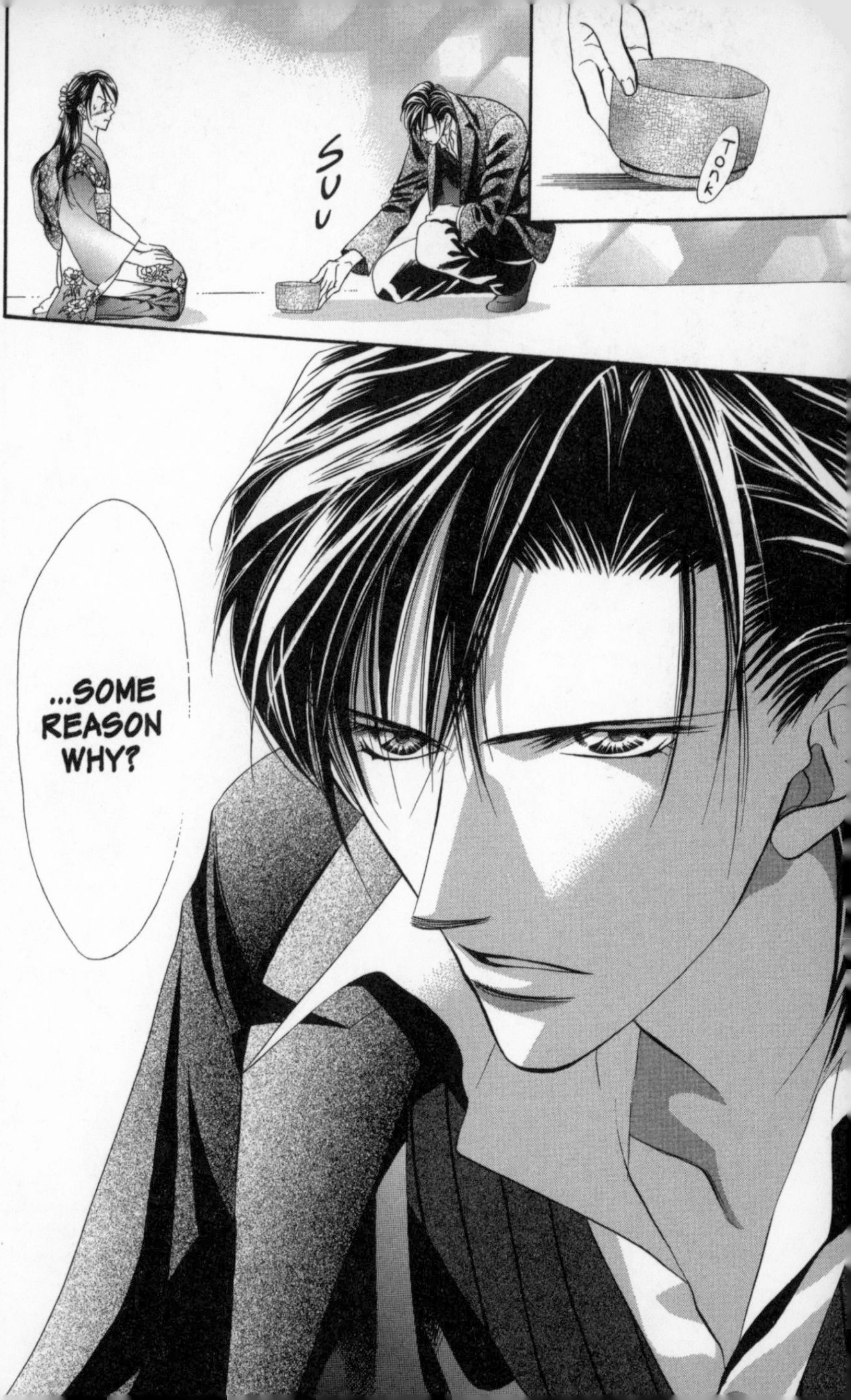
Tonk
SUU
...SOME REASON WHY?

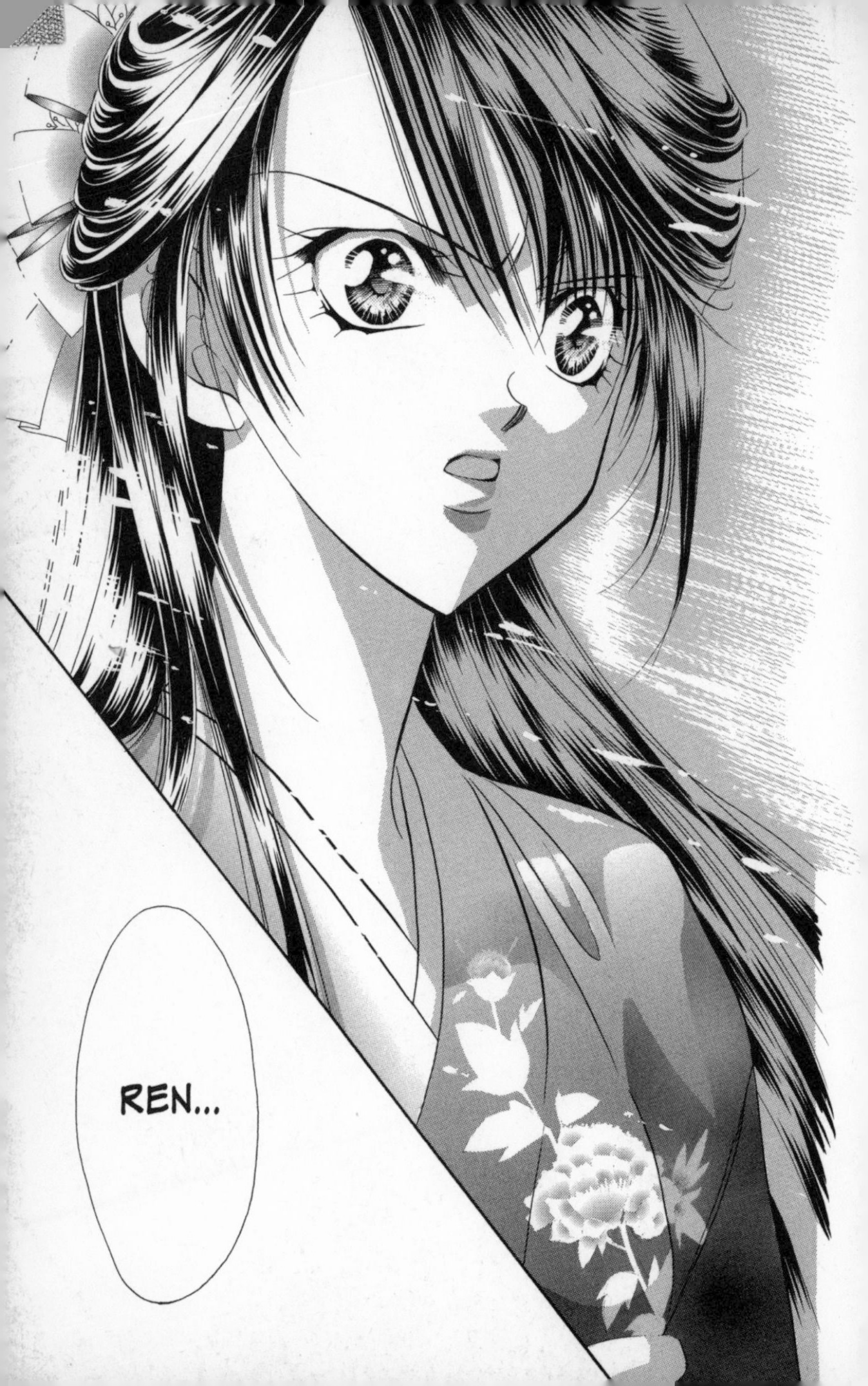
REN...

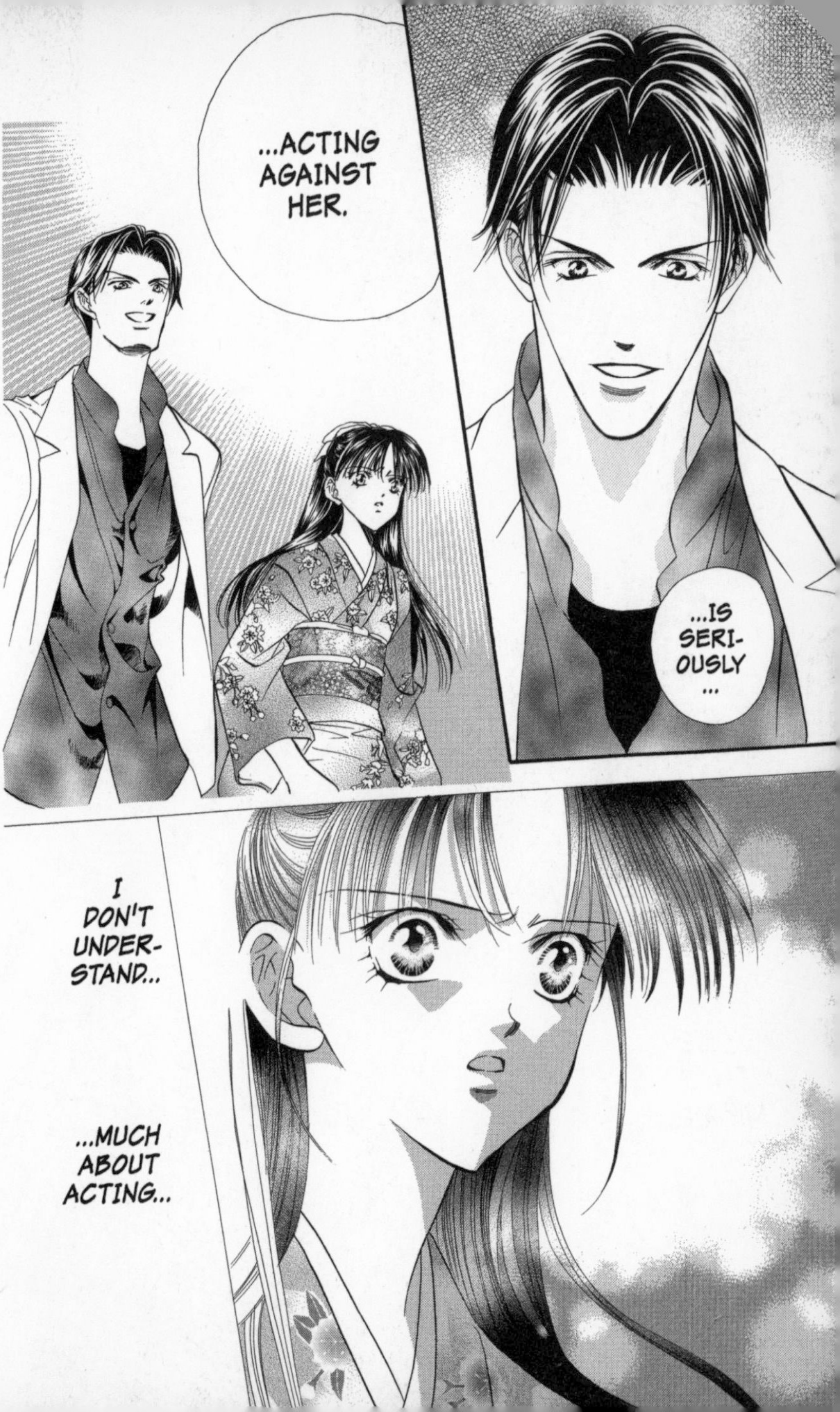
...IS SERI- OUSLY ...
...ACTING AGAINST HER.
I DON'T UNDER- STAND...
...MUCH ABOUT ACTING...

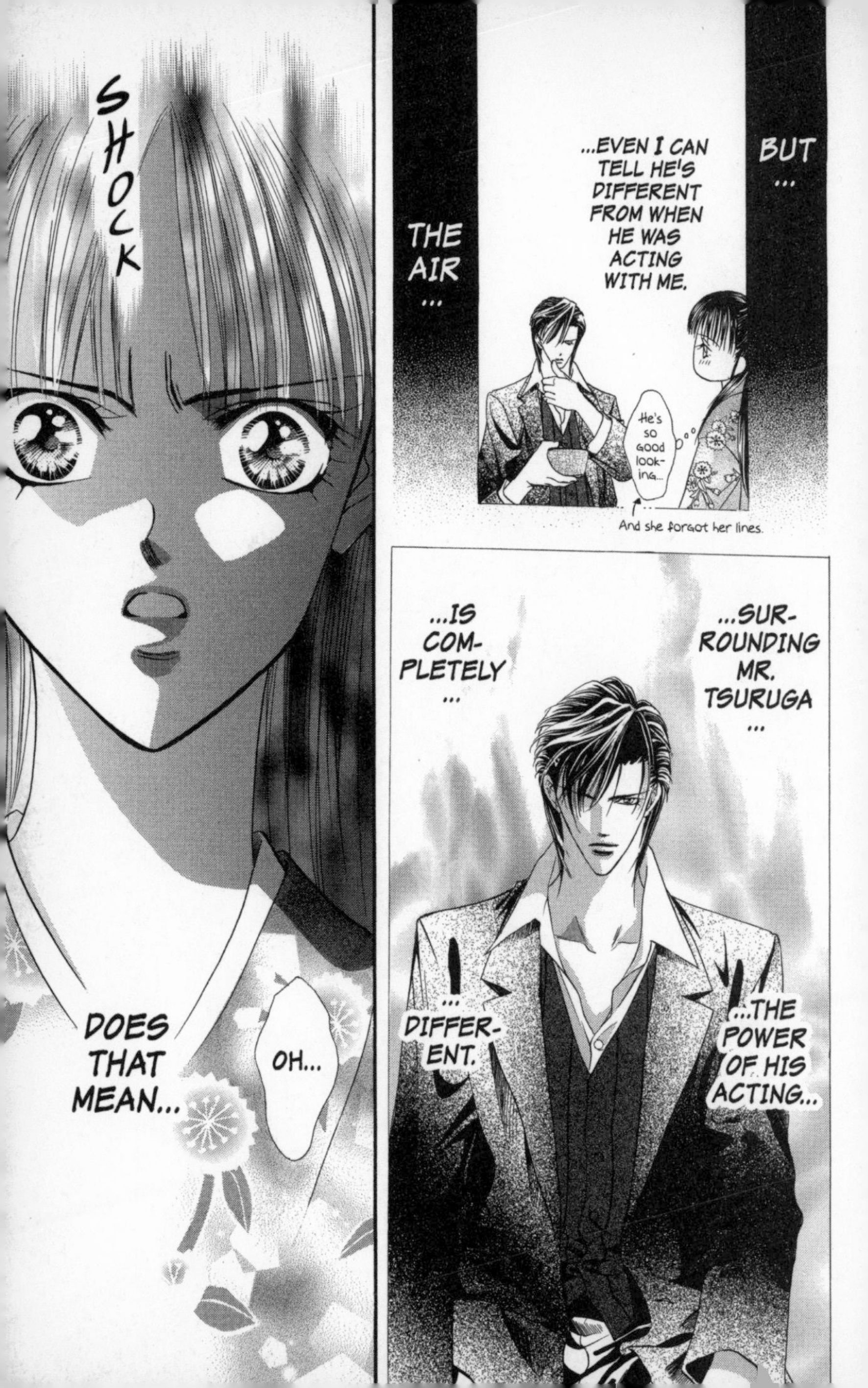
BUT...
...EVEN I CAN TELL HE'S DIFFERENT FROM WHEN HE WAS ACTING WITH ME.
THE AIR...
He's so good looking...
And she forgot her lines.
...SUR-ROUNDING MR. TSURUGA...
...IS COM-PLETELY...
...THE POWER OF HIS ACTING...
...DIFFER-ENT.
SHOCK
OH...
DOES THAT MEAN...

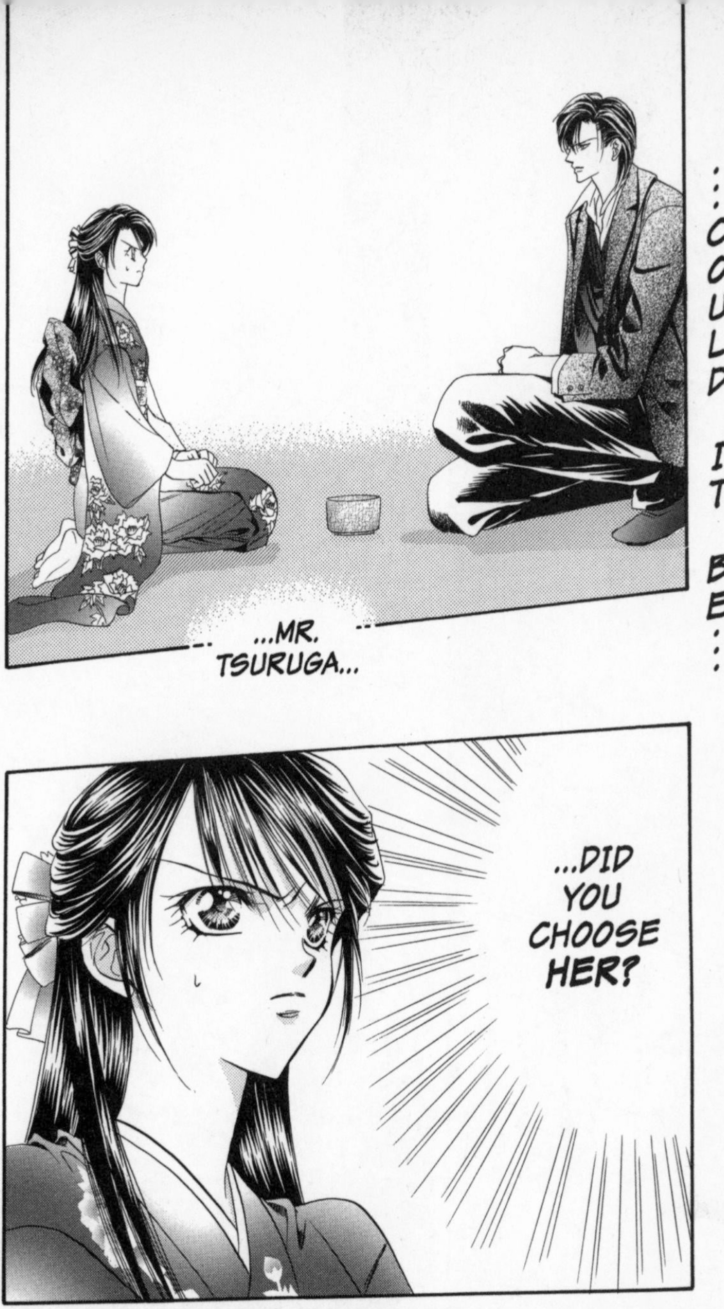
...COULD IT BE...
...MR. TSURUGA...
...DID YOU CHOOSE HER?

End of Act 12

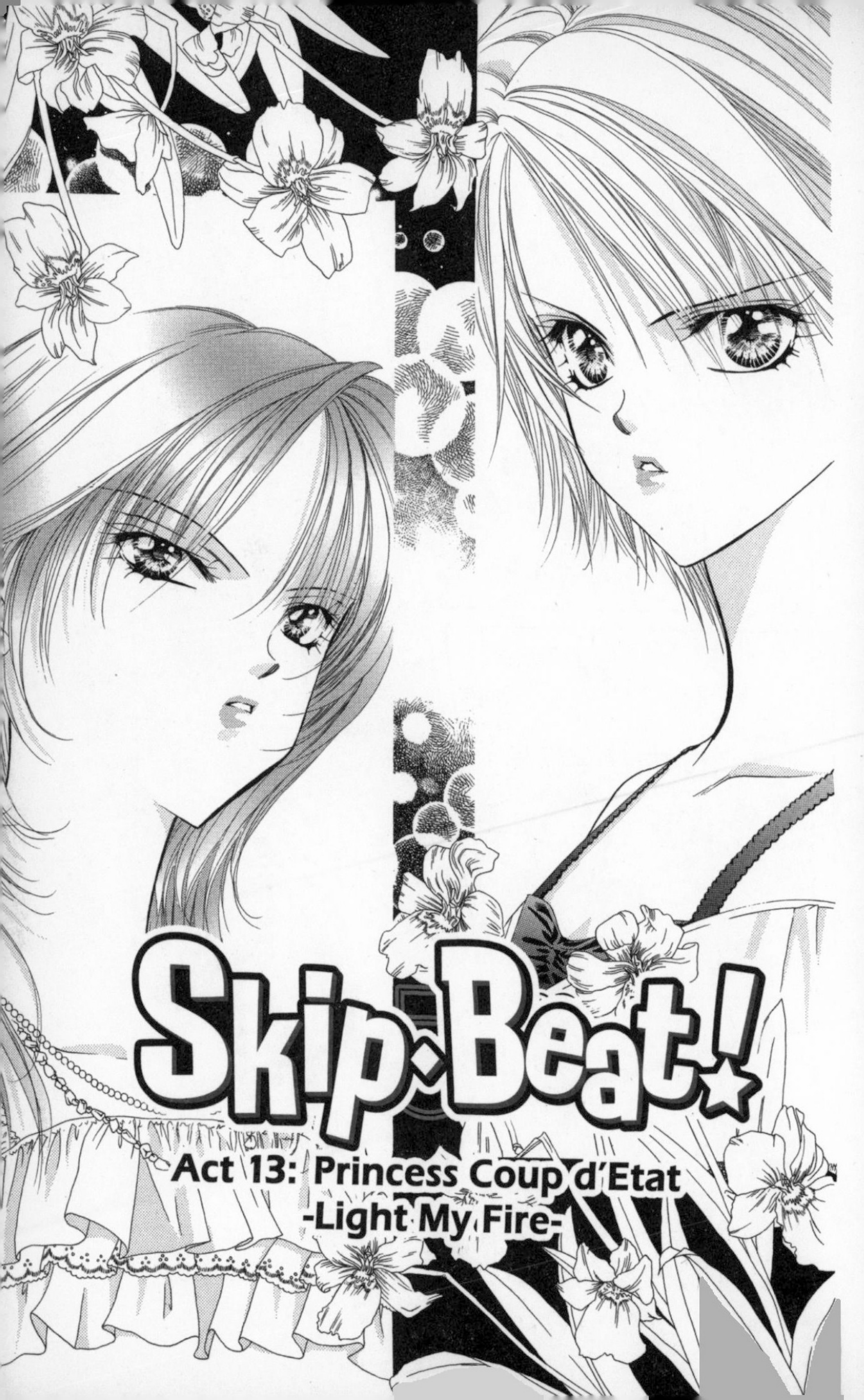
Skip·Beat!
Act 13: Princess Coup d'Etat
-Light My Fire-

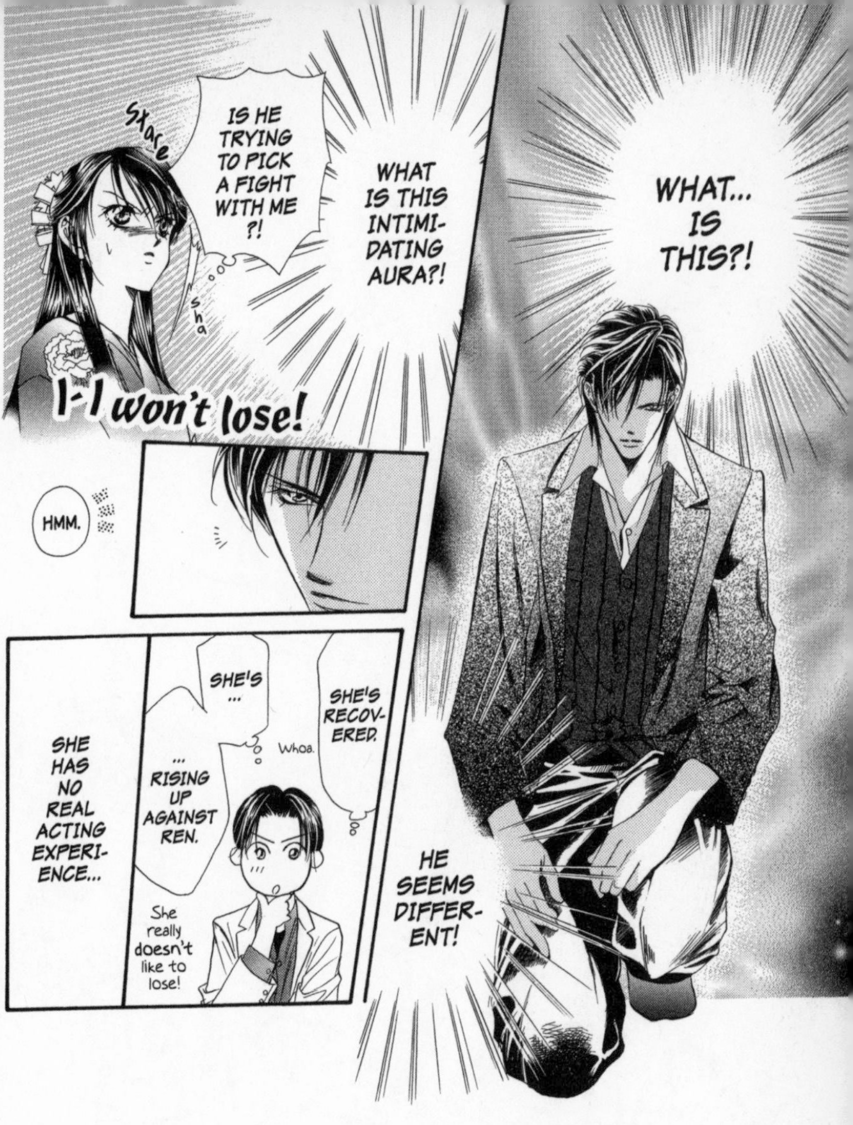
WHAT... IS THIS?!
HE SEEMS DIFFERENT!
WHAT IS THIS INTIMIDATING AURA?!
IS HE TRYING TO PICK A FIGHT WITH ME?!
Stare
sha
I-I won't lose!
HMM.
SHE'S RECOVERED.
SHE'S...
... RISING UP AGAINST REN.
Whoa.
She really doesn't like to lose!
SHE HAS NO REAL ACTING EXPERIENCE...

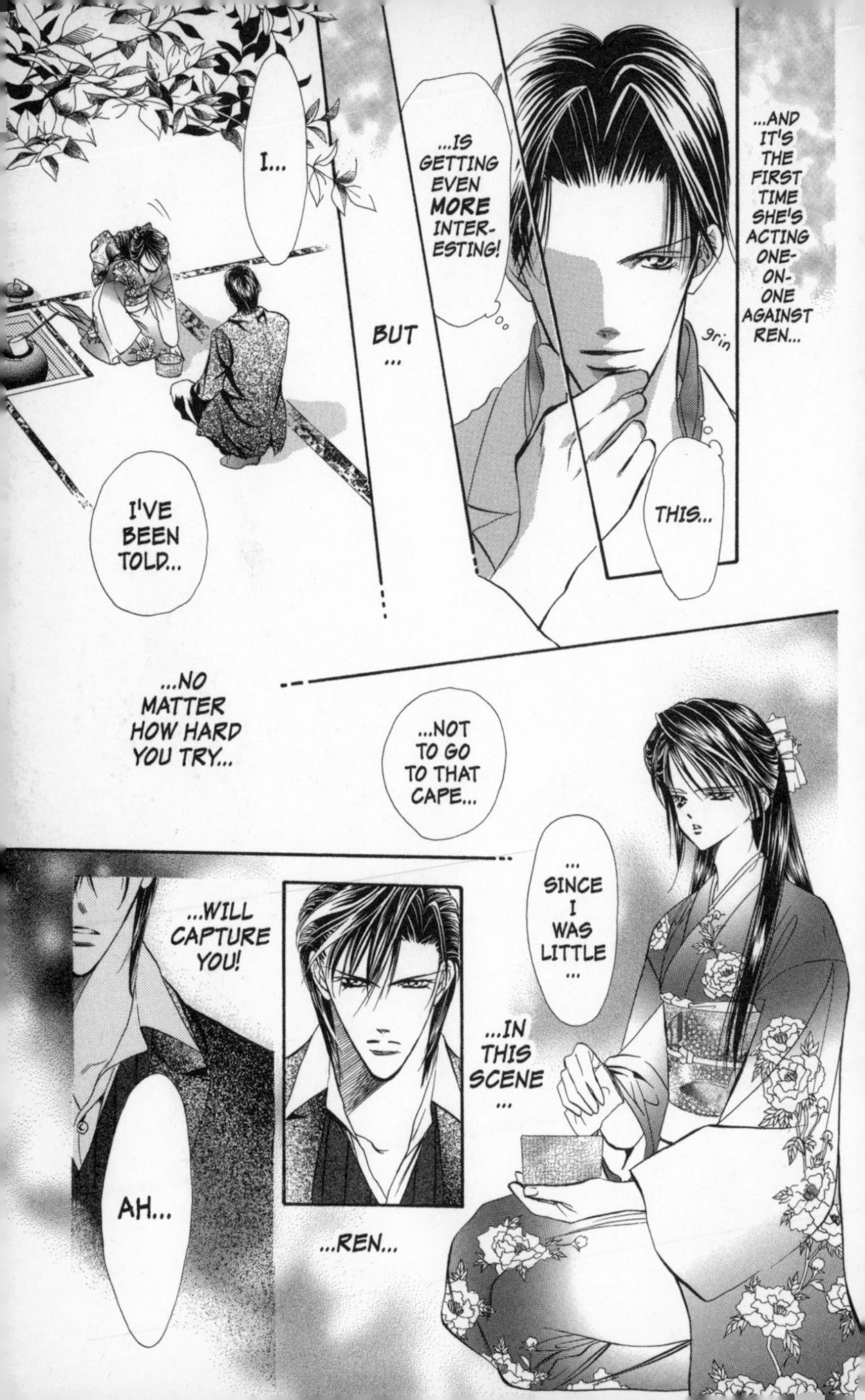
...AND IT'S THE FIRST TIME SHE'S ACTING ONE-ON-ONE AGAINST REN...
grin
THIS...
...IS GETTING EVEN MORE INTERESTING!
BUT ...
I...
I'VE BEEN TOLD...
...NOT TO GO TO THAT CAPE...
... SINCE I WAS LITTLE ...
...NO MATTER HOW HARD YOU TRY...
...IN THIS SCENE ...
...WILL CAPTURE YOU!
...REN...
AH...

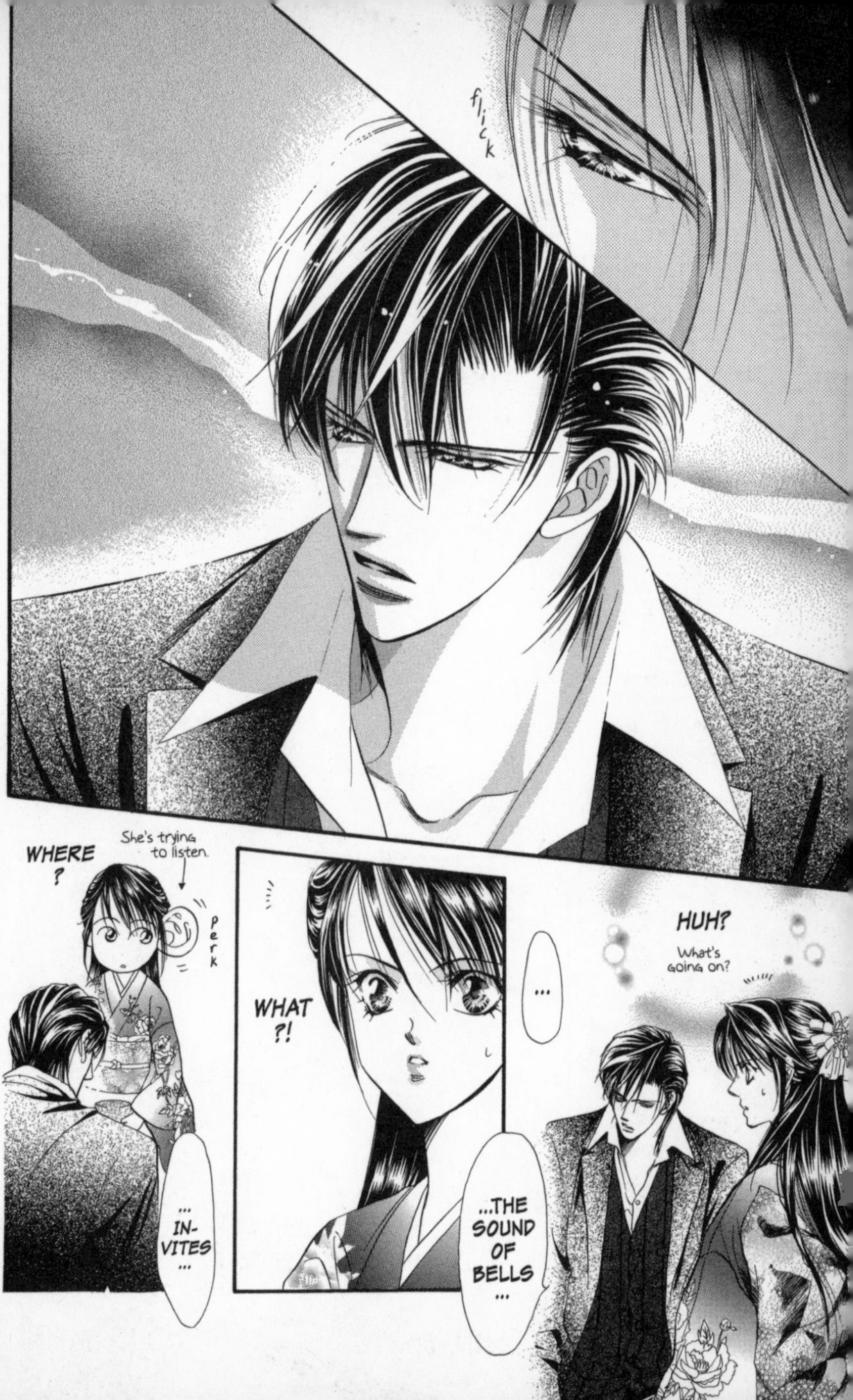
flick
HUH?
What's going on?
...
WHAT ?!
...THE SOUND OF BELLS...
WHERE ?
She's trying to listen.
perk
... IN-VITES ...

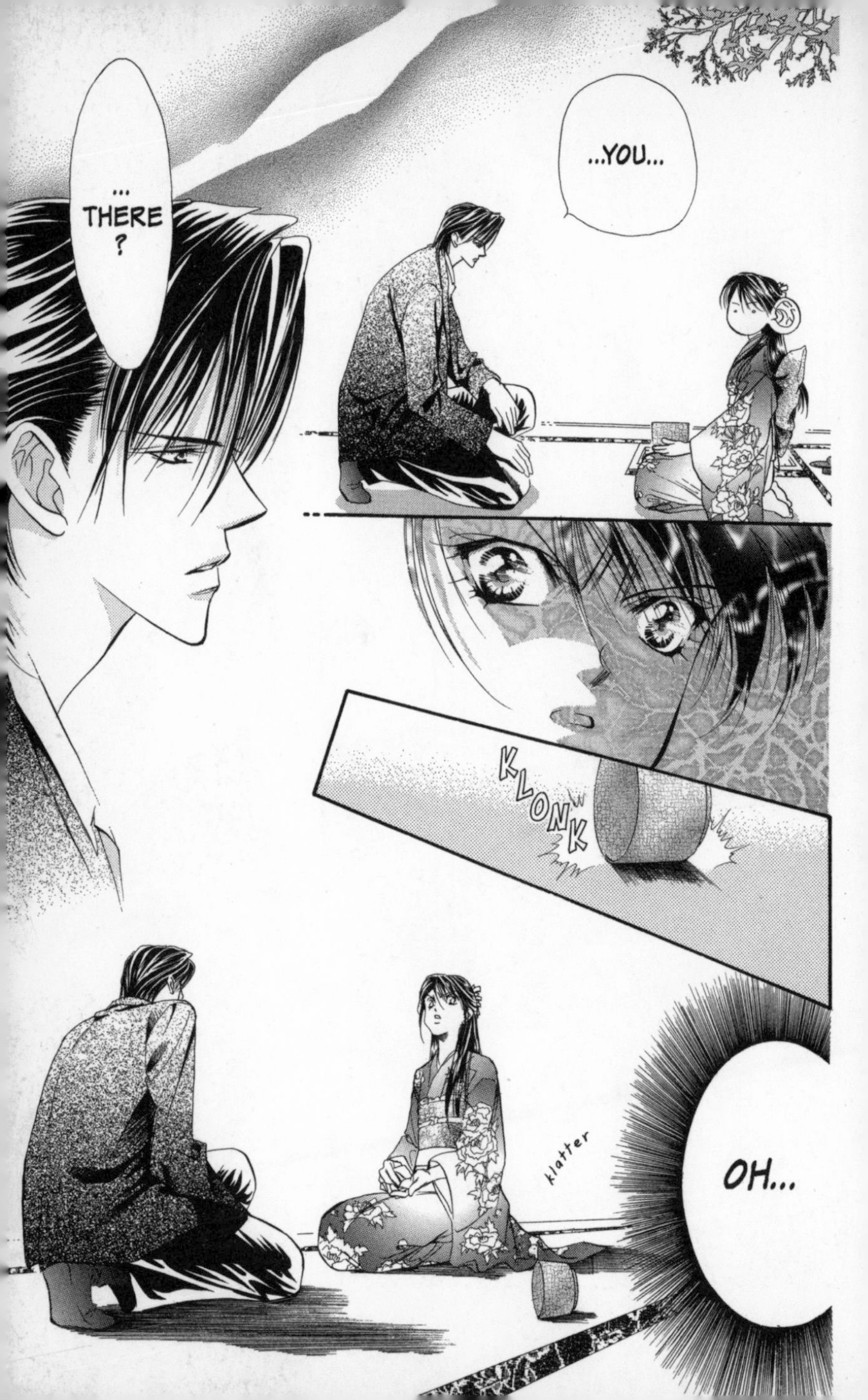
...YOU...
KLONK
... THERE ?
OH...
klatter

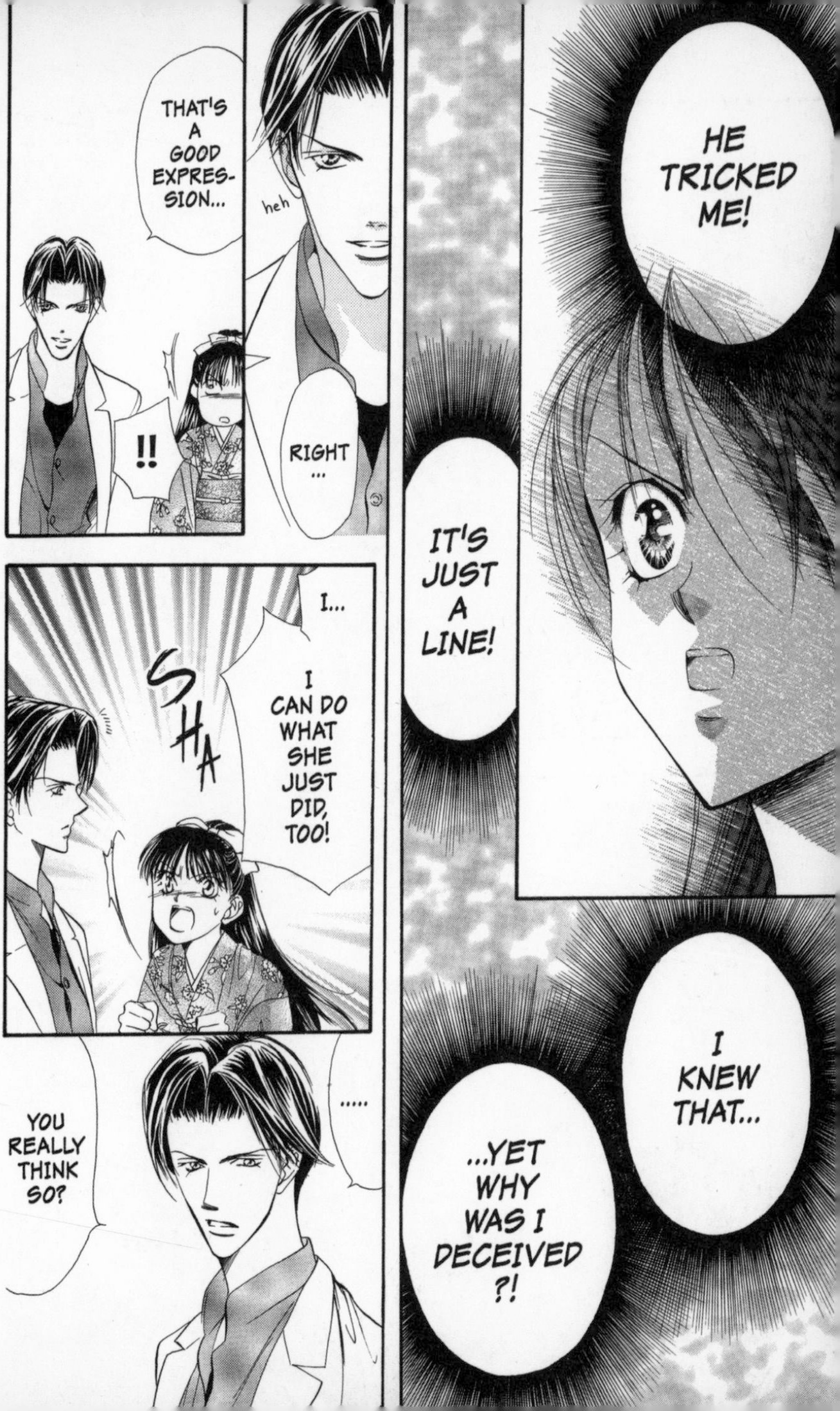
HE TRICKED ME!
IT'S JUST A LINE!
I KNEW THAT...
...YET WHY WAS I DECEIVED?!
THAT'S A GOOD EXPRESSION...
heh
RIGHT...
!!
I...
I CAN DO WHAT SHE JUST DID, TOO!
SHA
.....
YOU REALLY THINK SO?

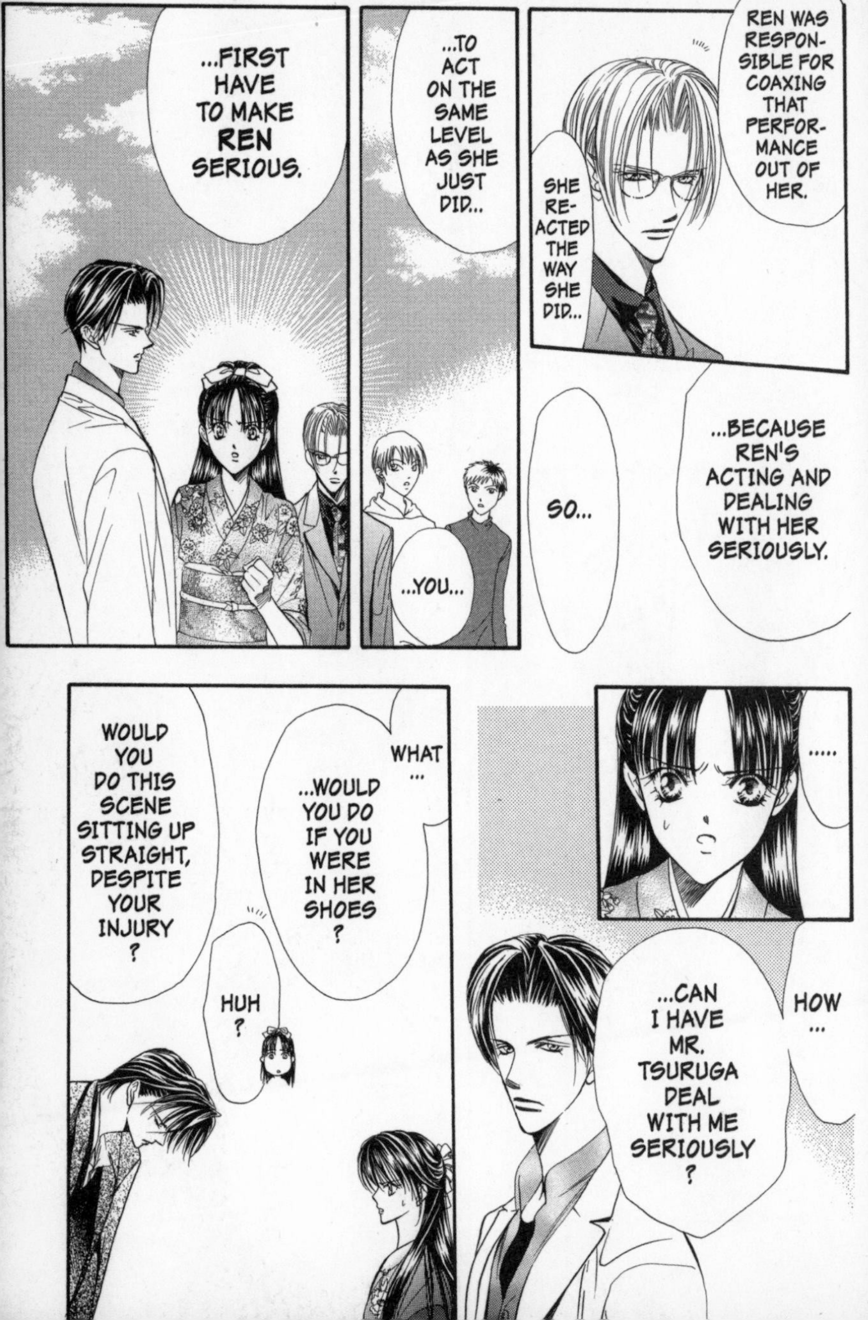
REN WAS RESPONSIBLE FOR COAXING THAT PERFORMANCE OUT OF HER.
SHE REACTED THE WAY SHE DID...
...BECAUSE REN'S ACTING AND DEALING WITH HER SERIOUSLY.
SO...
...YOU...
...TO ACT ON THE SAME LEVEL AS SHE JUST DID...
...FIRST HAVE TO MAKE REN SERIOUS.
.....
HOW...
...CAN I HAVE MR. TSURUGA DEAL WITH ME SERIOUSLY?
WHAT...
...WOULD YOU DO IF YOU WERE IN HER SHOES?
HUH?
WOULD YOU DO THIS SCENE SITTING UP STRAIGHT, DESPITE YOUR INJURY?

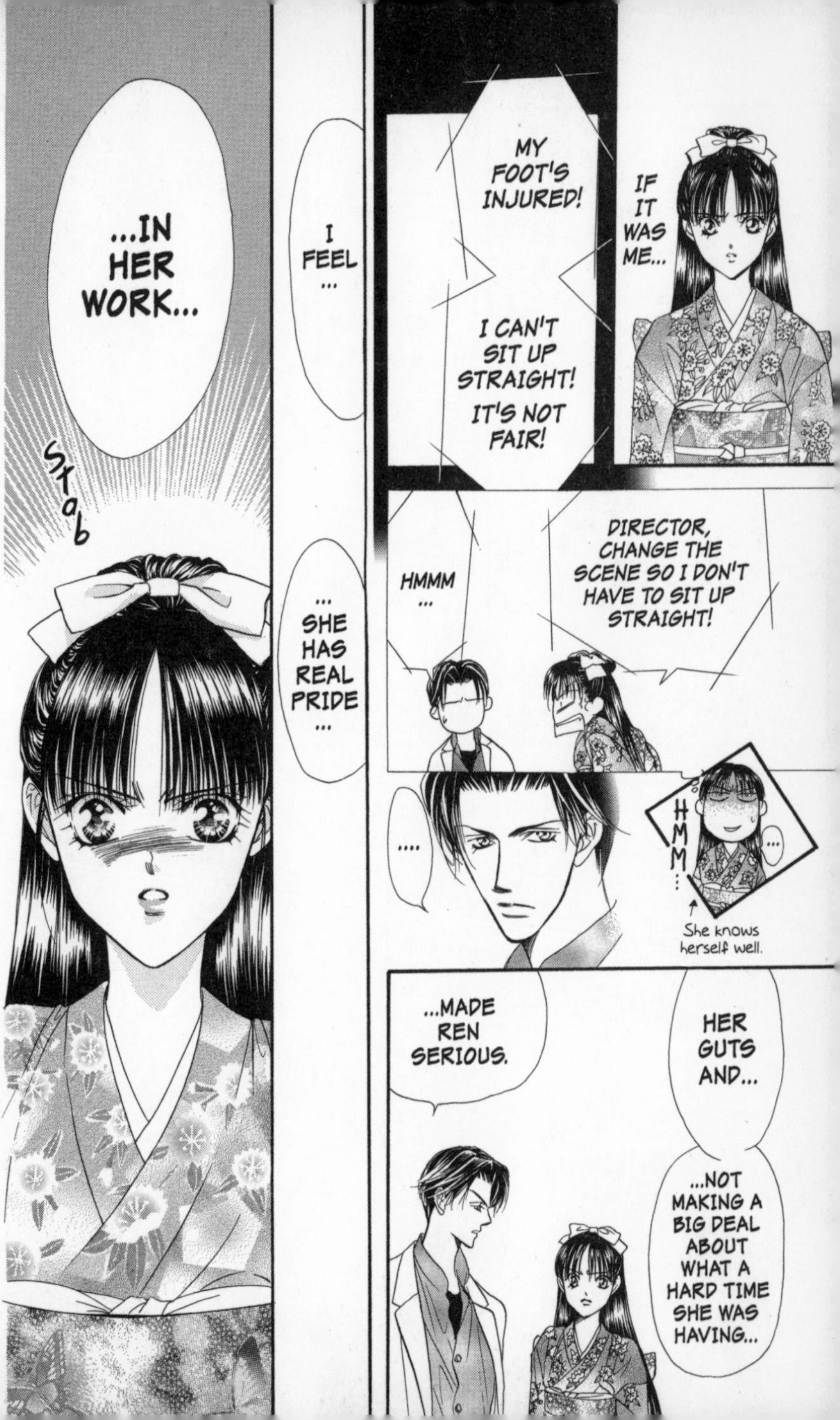
IF IT WAS ME...
MY FOOT'S INJURED!
I CAN'T SIT UP STRAIGHT!
IT'S NOT FAIR!
DIRECTOR, CHANGE THE SCENE SO I DON'T HAVE TO SIT UP STRAIGHT!
HMMM...
HMMM...
...
She knows herself well.
....
HER GUTS AND...
...NOT MAKING A BIG DEAL ABOUT WHAT A HARD TIME SHE WAS HAVING...
...MADE REN SERIOUS.
I FEEL...
...SHE HAS REAL PRIDE...
...IN HER WORK...
Stab

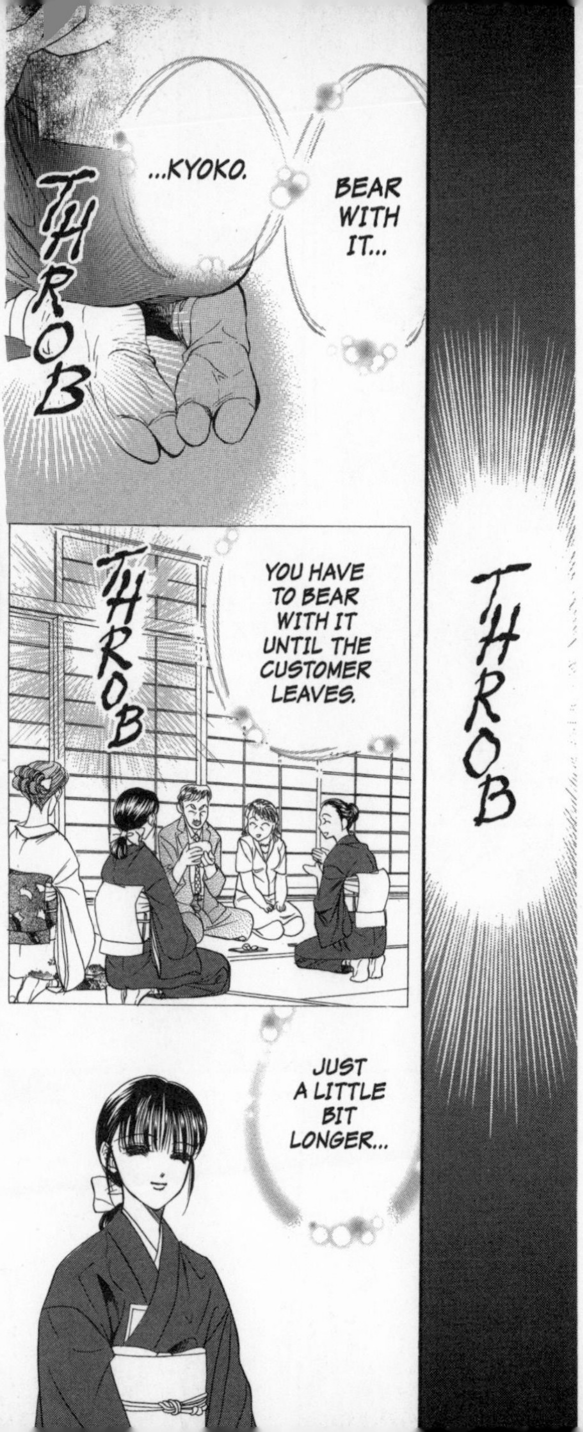
THROB
BEAR WITH IT...
...KYOKO.
THROB
YOU HAVE TO BEAR WITH IT UNTIL THE CUSTOMER LEAVES.
THROB
JUST A LITTLE BIT LONGER...

Ruriko Matsunai

Difficulty level

☆ ☆ ②

The thing that was difficult with Ruri was expressing how her fair skin is beautiful and white like snow...

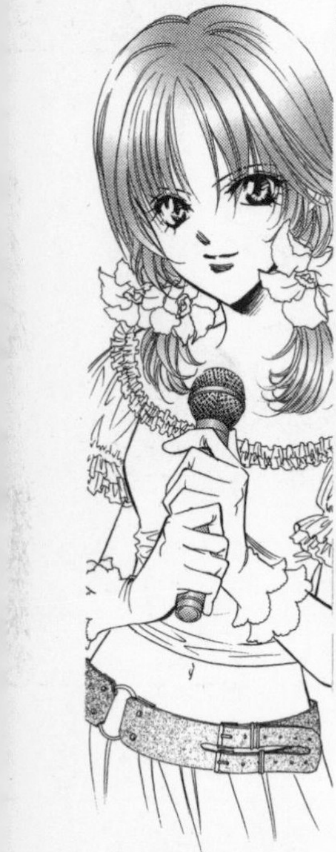

That's impossible to do in black-and-white... I have to have the dear readers imagine this... 6

Anyway, she has fair skin that all women would be envious of... 66

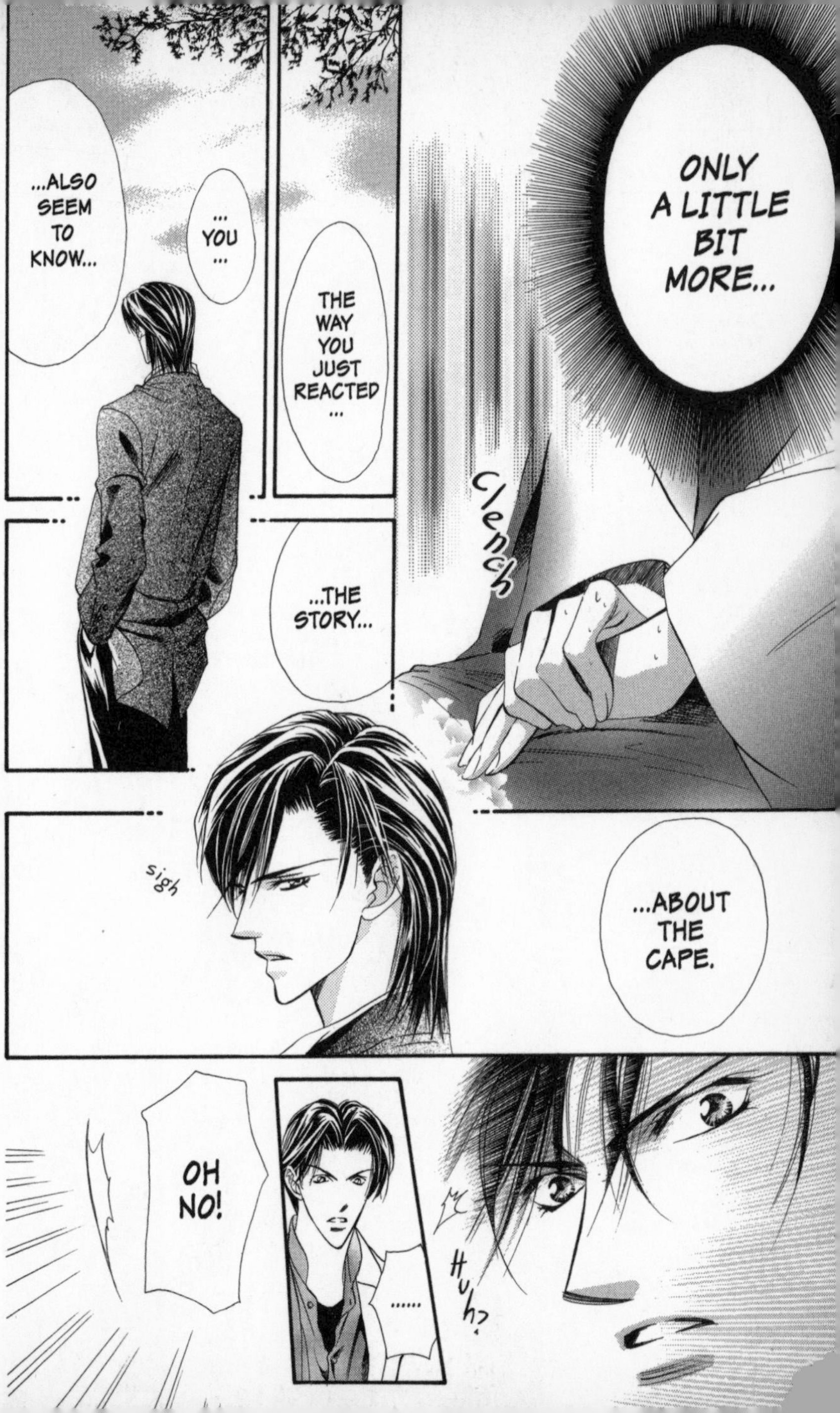
ONLY A LITTLE BIT MORE...
Clench
THE WAY YOU JUST REACTED...
...YOU...
...ALSO SEEM TO KNOW...
...THE STORY...
...ABOUT THE CAPE.
sigh
Huh?
......
OH NO!

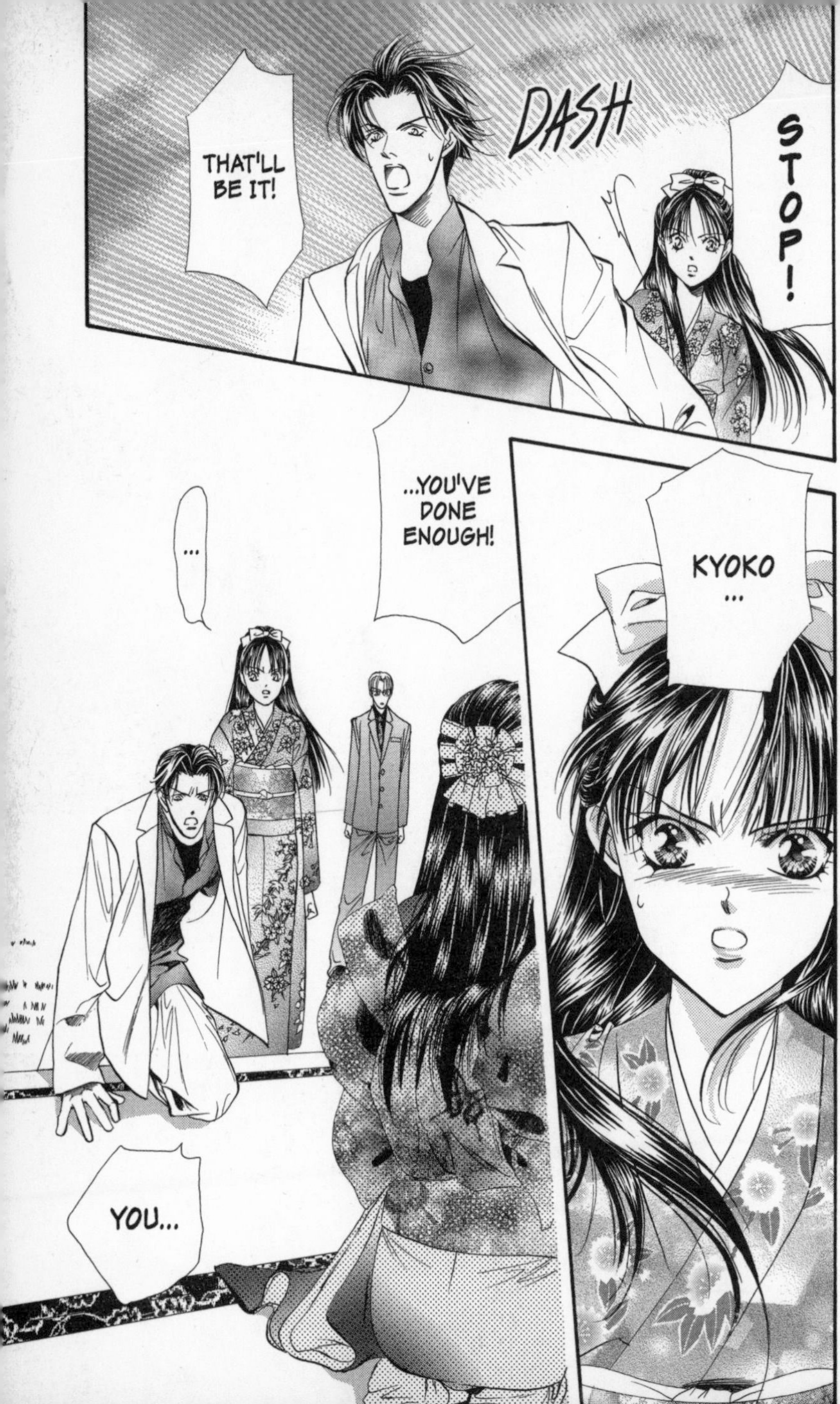
STOP!
DASH
THAT'LL BE IT!
KYOKO ...
...YOU'VE DONE ENOUGH!
...
YOU...

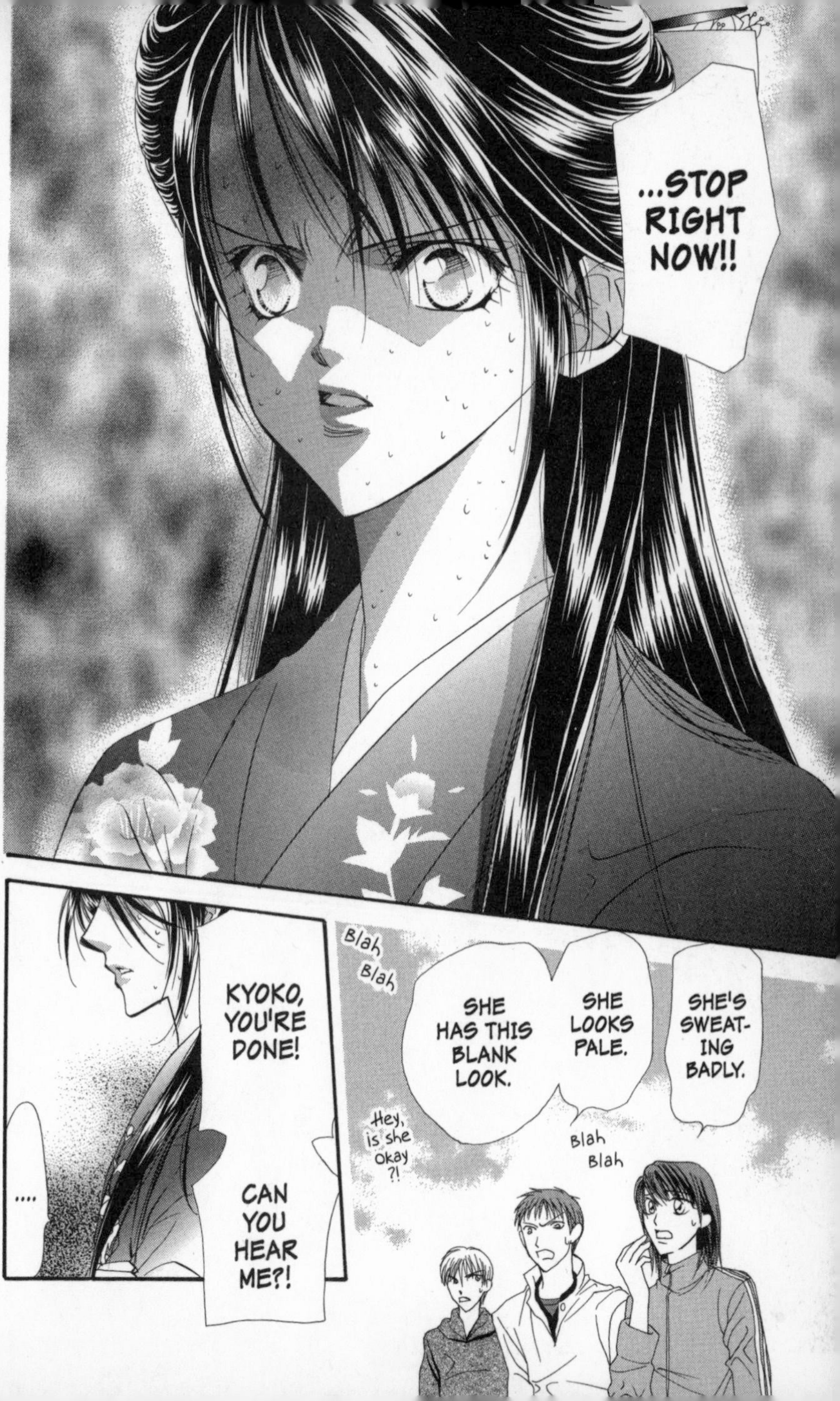
...STOP RIGHT NOW!!
SHE'S SWEAT-ING BADLY.
SHE LOOKS PALE.
SHE HAS THIS BLANK LOOK.
Blah Blah
Blah Blah
Hey, is she okay ?!
KYOKO, YOU'RE DONE!
CAN YOU HEAR ME?!
....

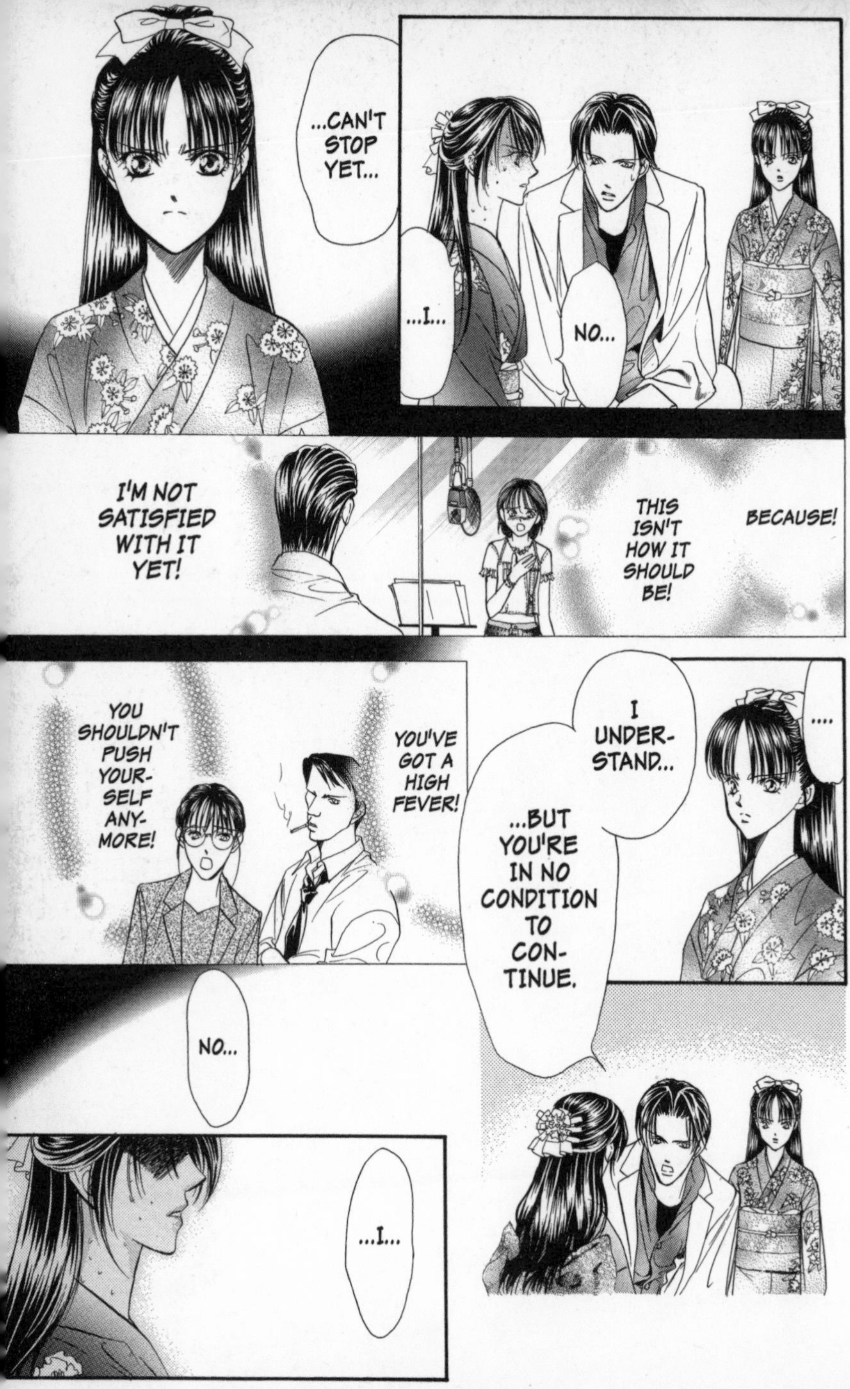
NO...
...I...
...CAN'T STOP YET...
BECAUSE!
THIS ISN'T HOW IT SHOULD BE!
I'M NOT SATISFIED WITH IT YET!
....
I UNDER-STAND...
...BUT YOU'RE IN NO CONDITION TO CON-TINUE.
YOU'VE GOT A HIGH FEVER!
YOU SHOULDN'T PUSH YOUR-SELF ANY-MORE!
NO...
...I...

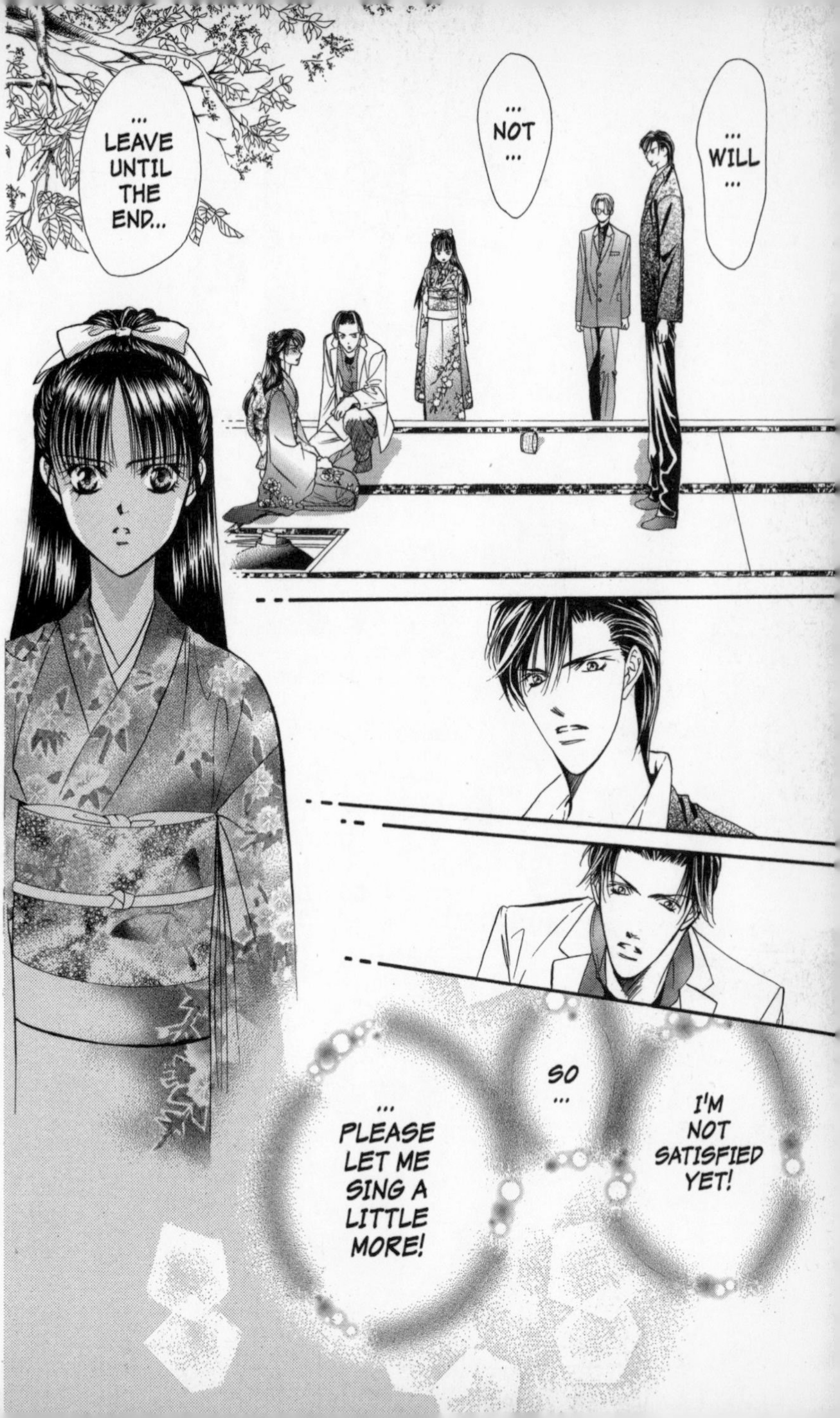
... WILL ...
... NOT ...
... LEAVE UNTIL THE END...
I'M NOT SATISFIED YET!
SO ...
... PLEASE LET ME SING A LITTLE MORE!

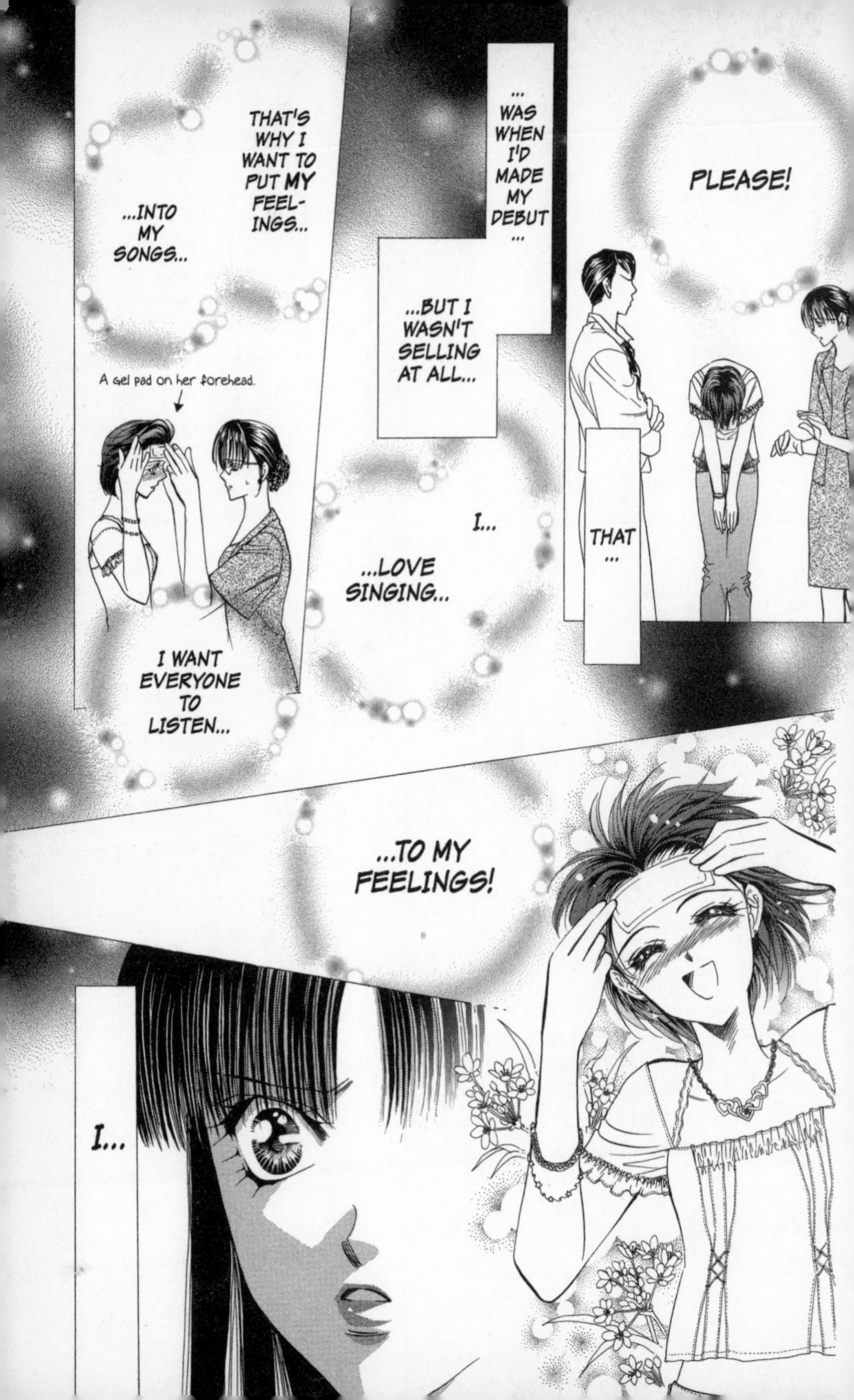
PLEASE!
THAT...
...WAS WHEN I'D MADE MY DEBUT...
...BUT I WASN'T SELLING AT ALL...
I...
...LOVE SINGING...
THAT'S WHY I WANT TO PUT MY FEEL-INGS...
...INTO MY SONGS...
A gel pad on her forehead.
I WANT EVERYONE TO LISTEN...
...TO MY FEELINGS!
I...

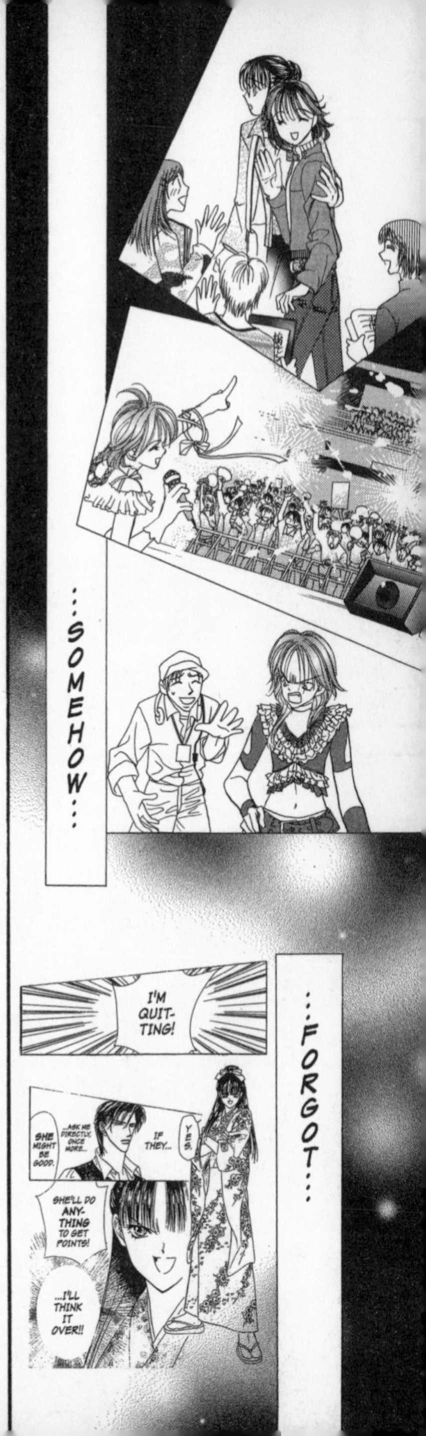
...SOMEHOW...
I'M QUITTING!
...FORGOT...
YES.
IF THEY...
...ASK ME DIRECTLY, ONCE MORE...
SHE MIGHT BE GOOD.
SHE'LL DO ANYTHING TO GET POINTS!
...I'LL THINK IT OVER!!
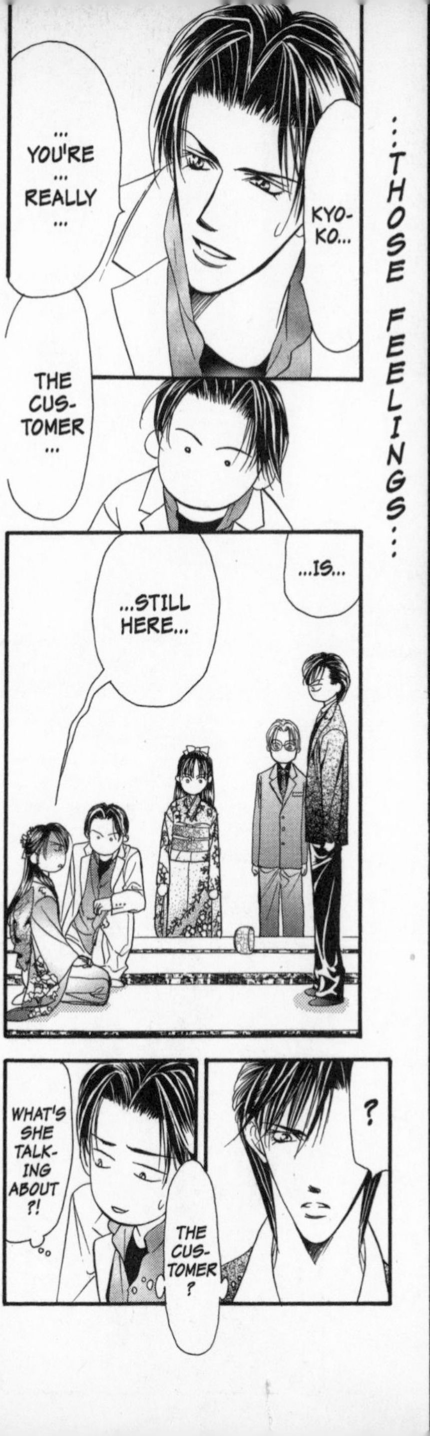
...THOSE FEELINGS...
KYO-KO...
...YOU'RE ...REALLY ...
THE CUS-TOMER ...
...IS...
...STILL HERE...
?
THE CUS-TOMER ?
WHAT'S SHE TALK-ING ABOUT ?!

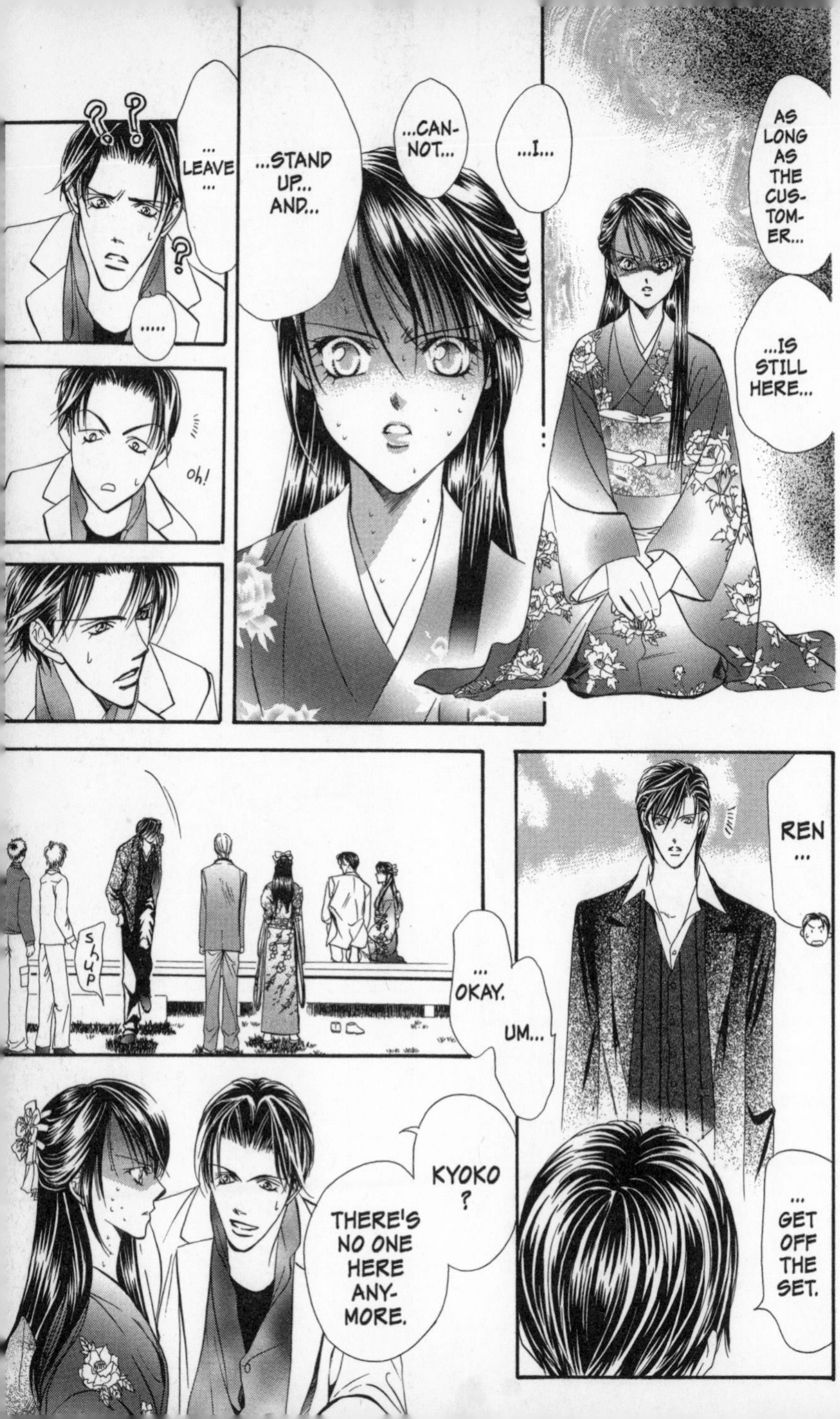
AS LONG AS THE CUS-TOM-ER...
...IS STILL HERE...
...I...
...CAN-NOT...
...STAND UP... AND...
... LEAVE ...
??
?
......
oh!
REN ...
... GET OFF THE SET.
... OKAY.
UM...
SHUP
KYOKO ?
THERE'S NO ONE HERE ANY-MORE.

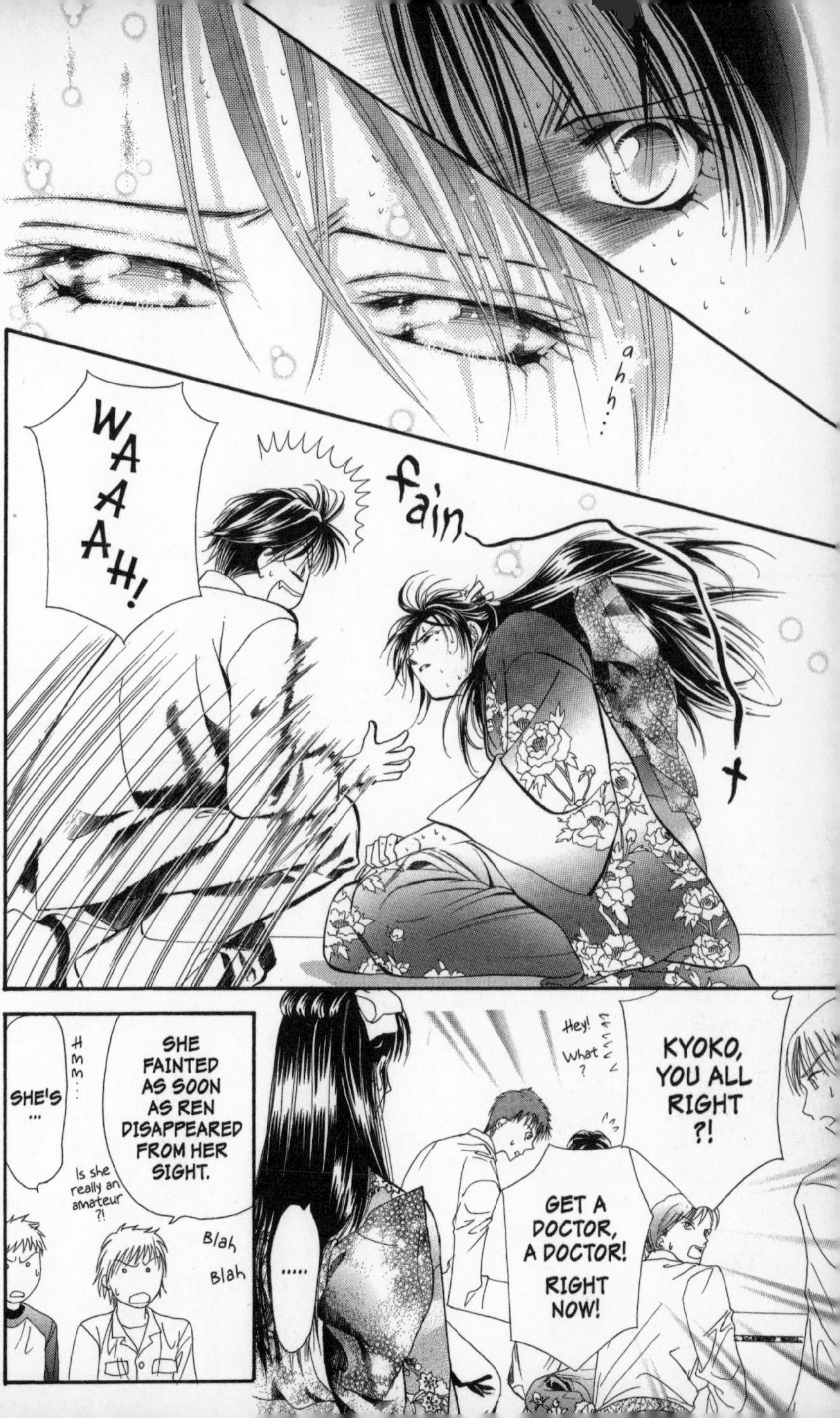
ahh...
faint
WAAAAH!
KYOKO, YOU ALL RIGHT?!
Hey! What?
GET A DOCTOR, A DOCTOR!
RIGHT NOW!
......
SHE FAINTED AS SOON AS REN DISAPPEARED FROM HER SIGHT.
Hmm...
SHE'S ...
Is she really an amateur?!
Blah
Blah

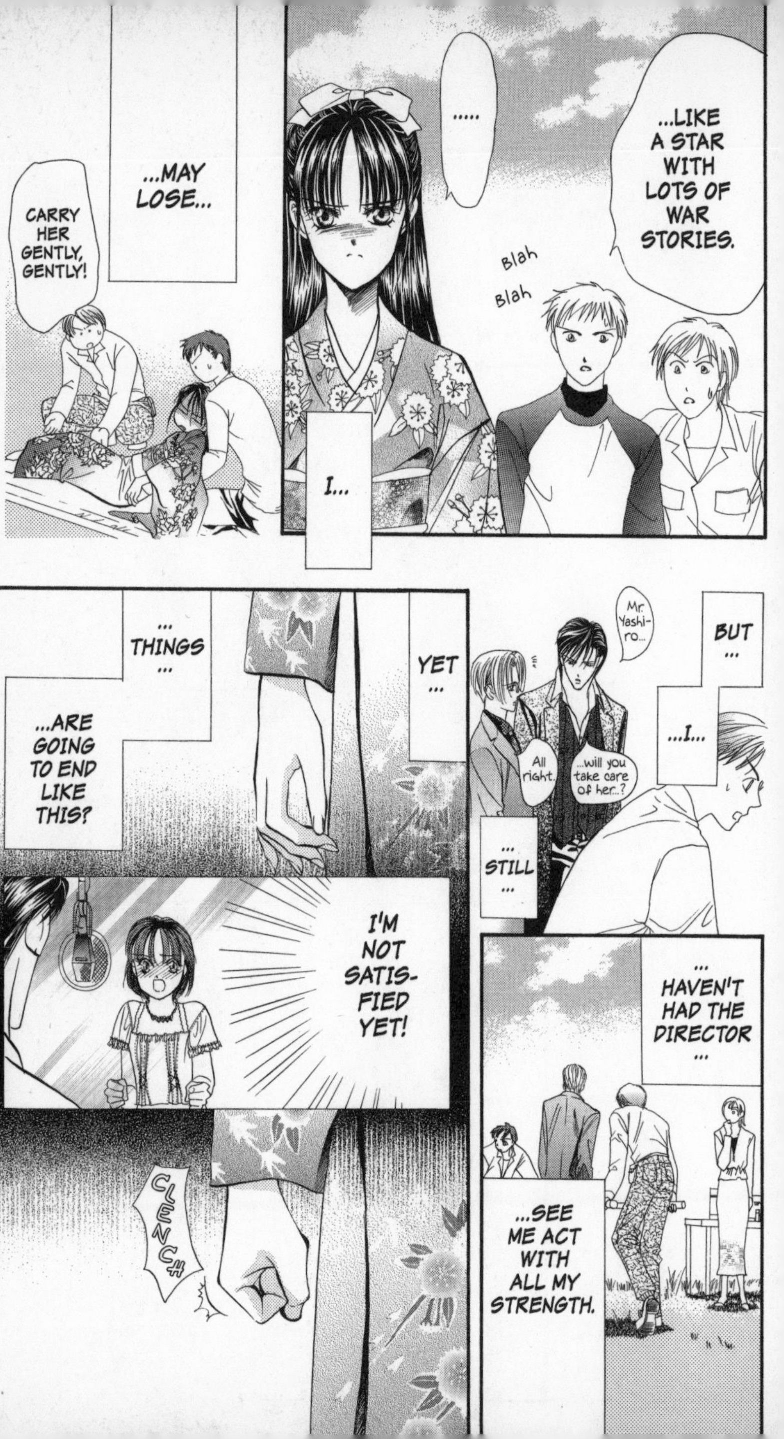

...LIKE A STAR WITH LOTS OF WAR STORIES.
.....
Blah
Blah
I...
...MAY LOSE...
CARRY HER GENTLY, GENTLY!
BUT ...
...I...
Mr. Yashiro...
...will you take care of her..?
All right.
... STILL ...
... HAVEN'T HAD THE DIRECTOR ...
...SEE ME ACT WITH ALL MY STRENGTH.
YET ...
... THINGS ...
...ARE GOING TO END LIKE THIS?
I'M NOT SATIS-FIED YET!
CLENCH

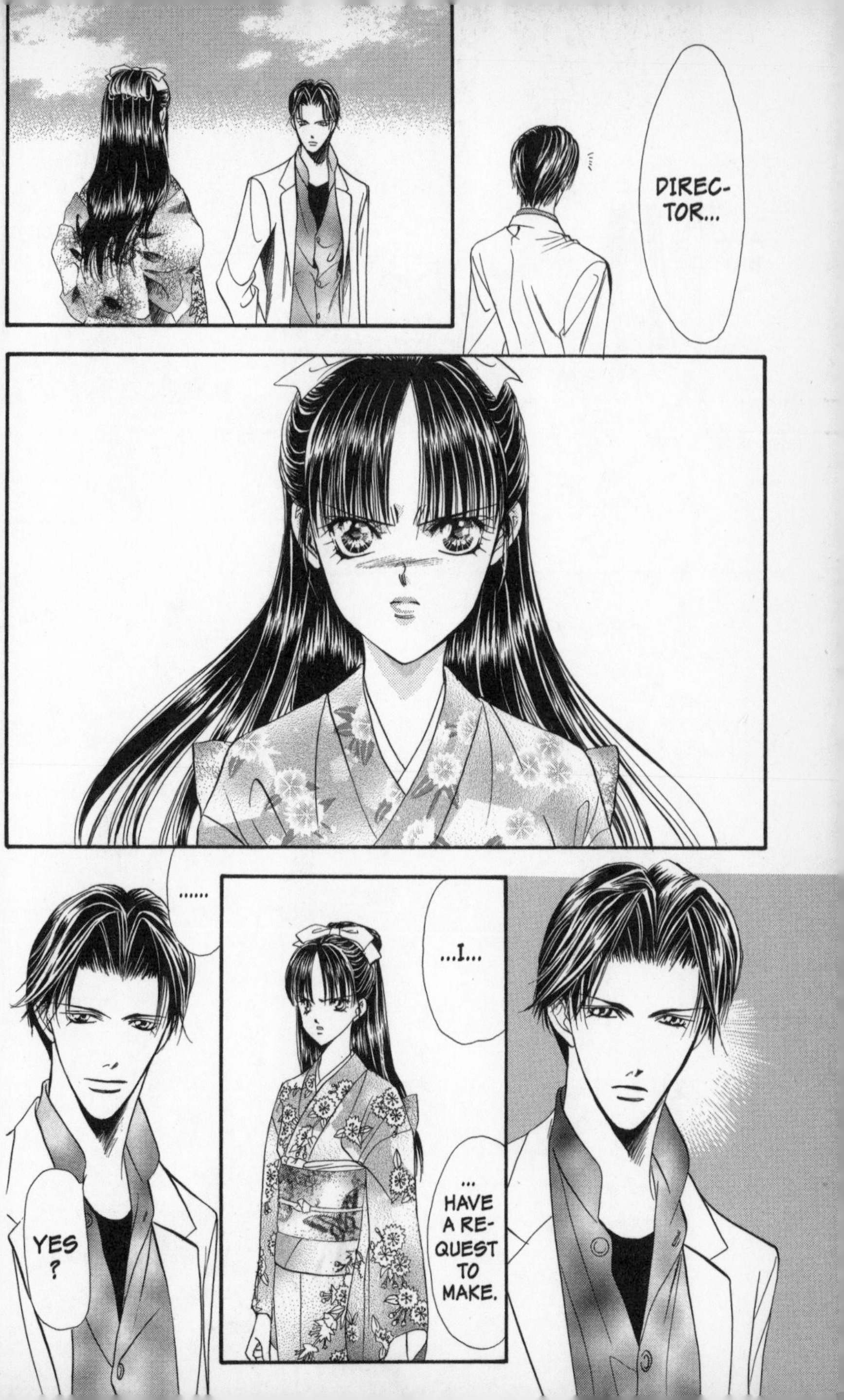

DIREC-TOR...
...I...
...HAVE A RE-QUEST TO MAKE.
......
YES?

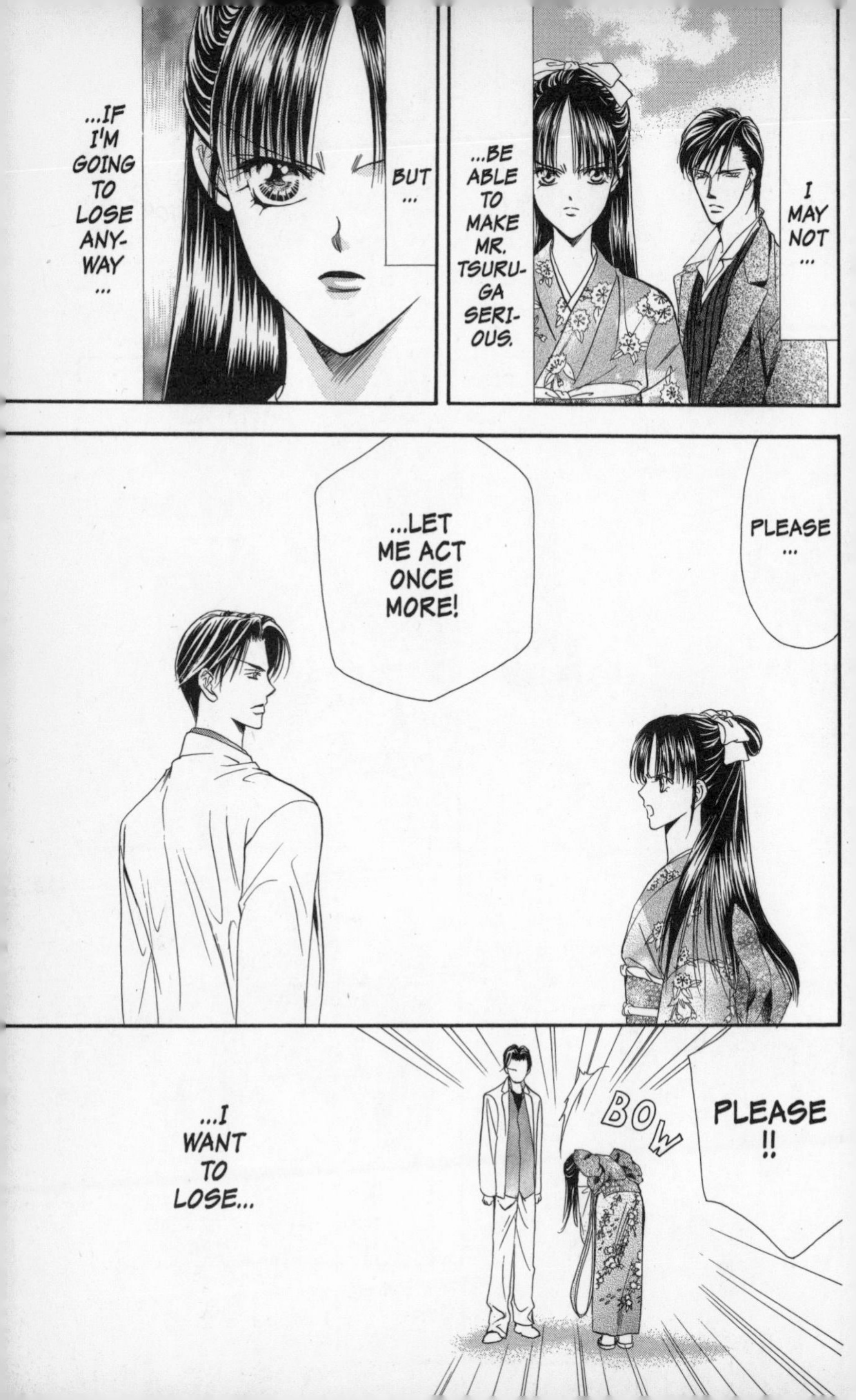
I MAY NOT...
...BE ABLE TO MAKE MR. TSURUGA SERIOUS.
BUT...
...IF I'M GOING TO LOSE ANYWAY...
PLEASE...
...LET ME ACT ONCE MORE!
PLEASE!!
BOW
...I WANT TO LOSE...

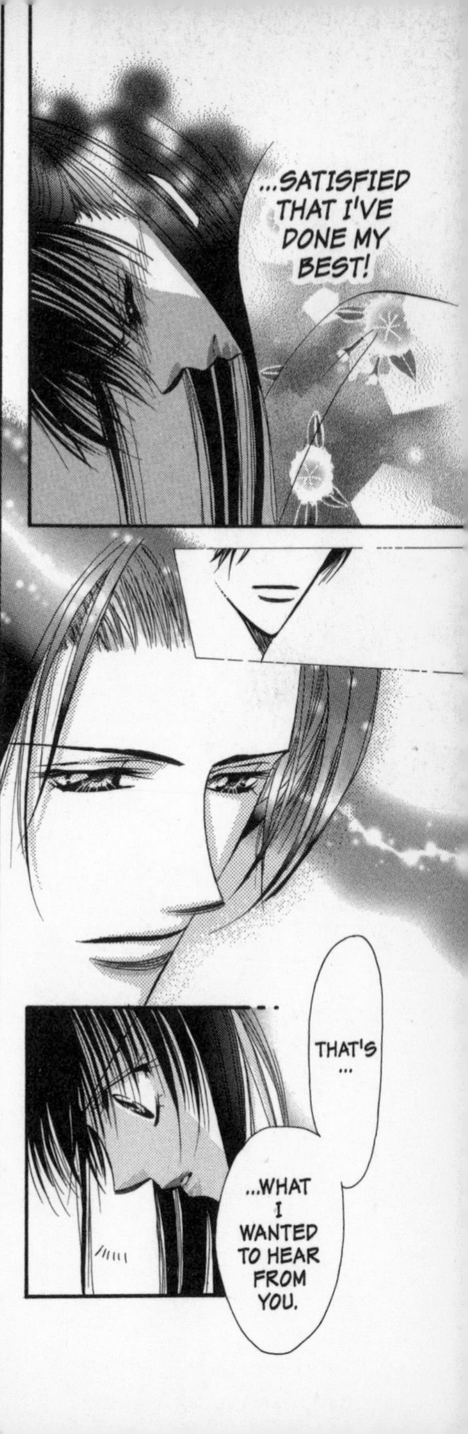
...SATISFIED THAT I'VE DONE MY BEST!
THAT'S ...
...WHAT I WANTED TO HEAR FROM YOU.

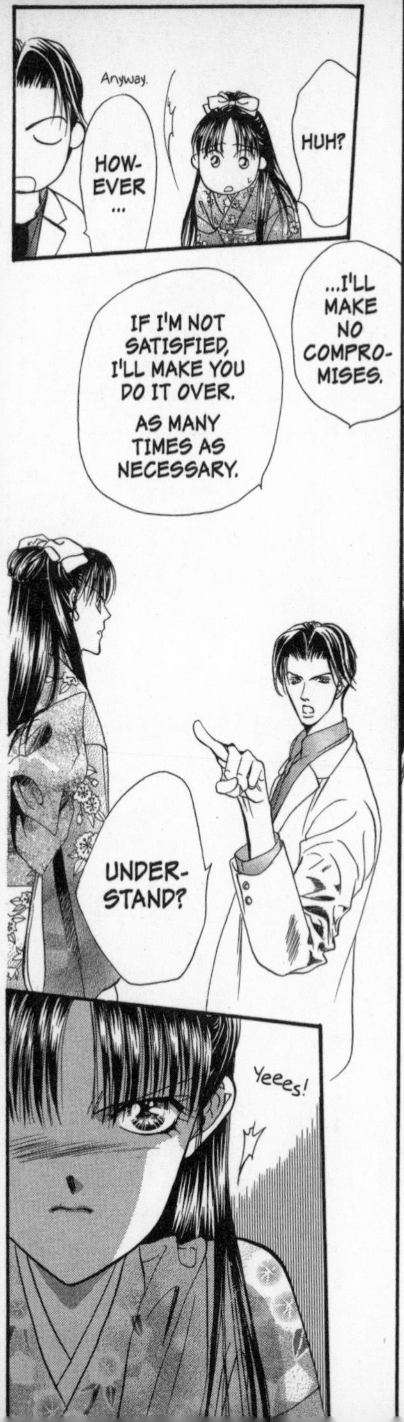
HUH?
HOW-EVER ...
Anyway.
...I'LL MAKE NO COMPROMISES.
IF I'M NOT SATISFIED, I'LL MAKE YOU DO IT OVER.
AS MANY TIMES AS NECESSARY.
UNDER-STAND?
Yeees!

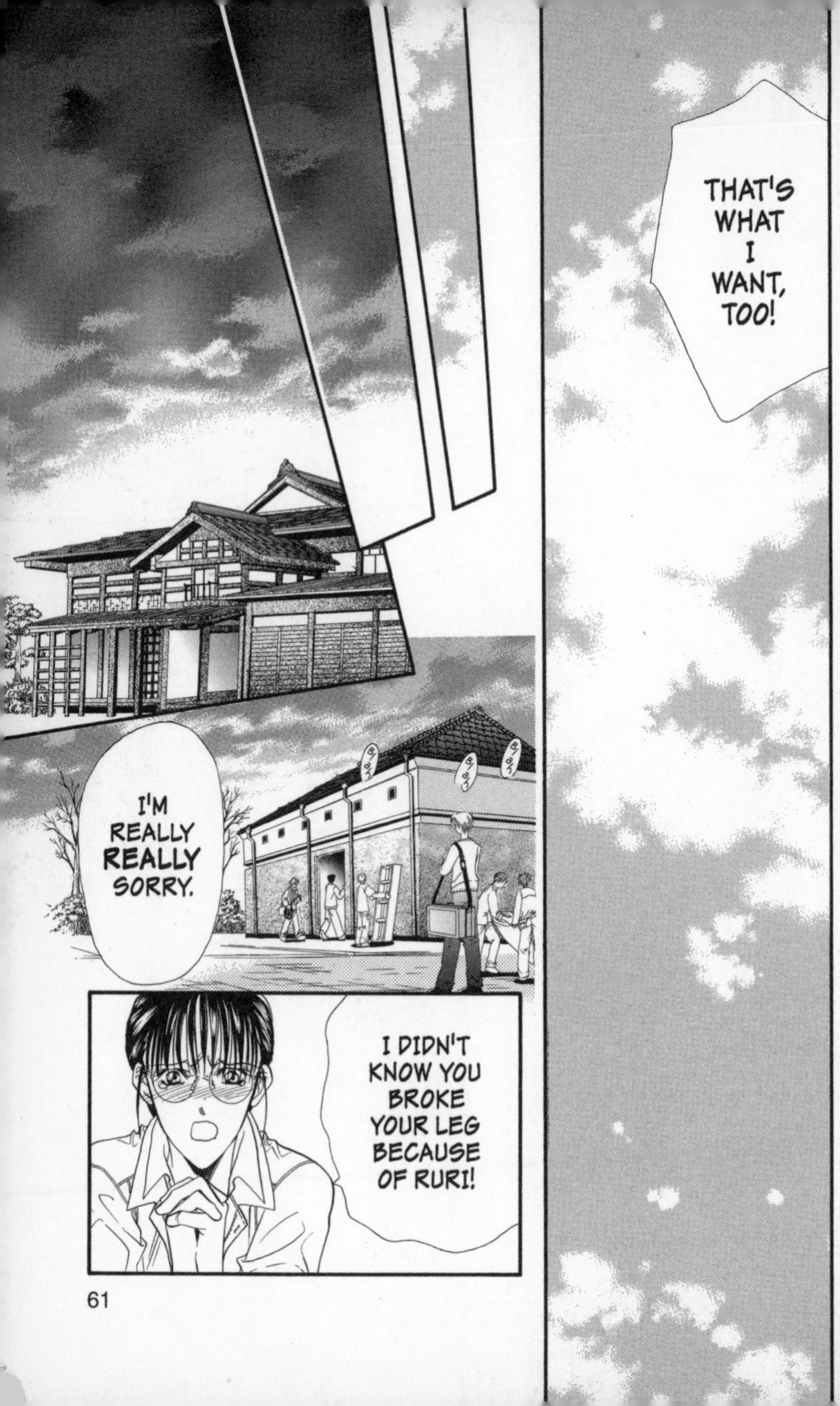
THAT'S WHAT I WANT, TOO!
I'M REALLY REALLY SORRY.
I DIDN'T KNOW YOU BROKE YOUR LEG BECAUSE OF RURI!

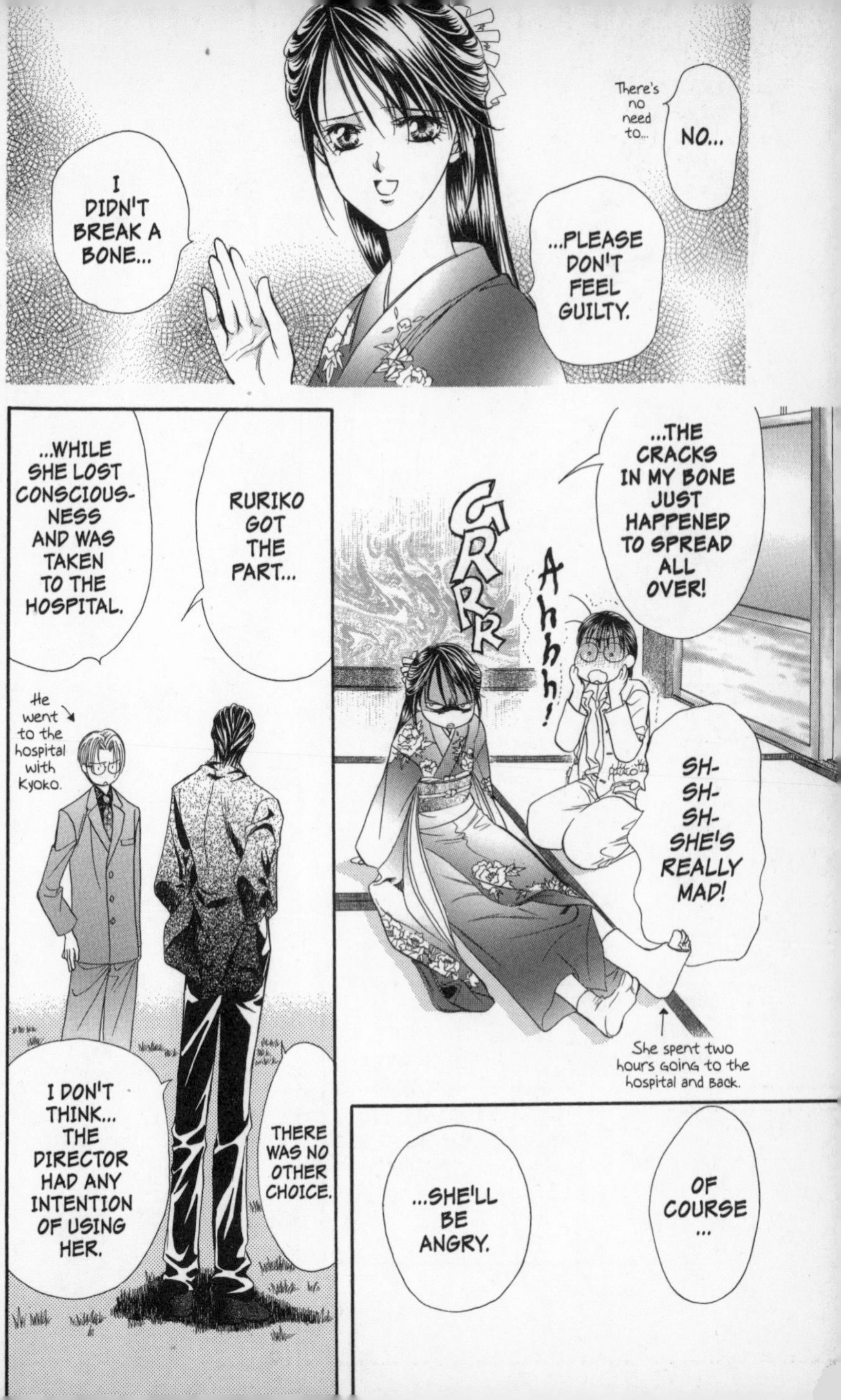
There's no need to...
NO...
...PLEASE DON'T FEEL GUILTY.
I DIDN'T BREAK A BONE...
...THE CRACKS IN MY BONE JUST HAPPENED TO SPREAD ALL OVER!
GRRR
Ahhh!
SH-SH-SH-SHE'S REALLY MAD!
She spent two hours going to the hospital and back.
OF COURSE...
...SHE'LL BE ANGRY.
RURIKO GOT THE PART...
...WHILE SHE LOST CONSCIOUSNESS AND WAS TAKEN TO THE HOSPITAL.
He went to the hospital with Kyoko.
THERE WAS NO OTHER CHOICE.
I DON'T THINK... THE DIRECTOR HAD ANY INTENTION OF USING HER.

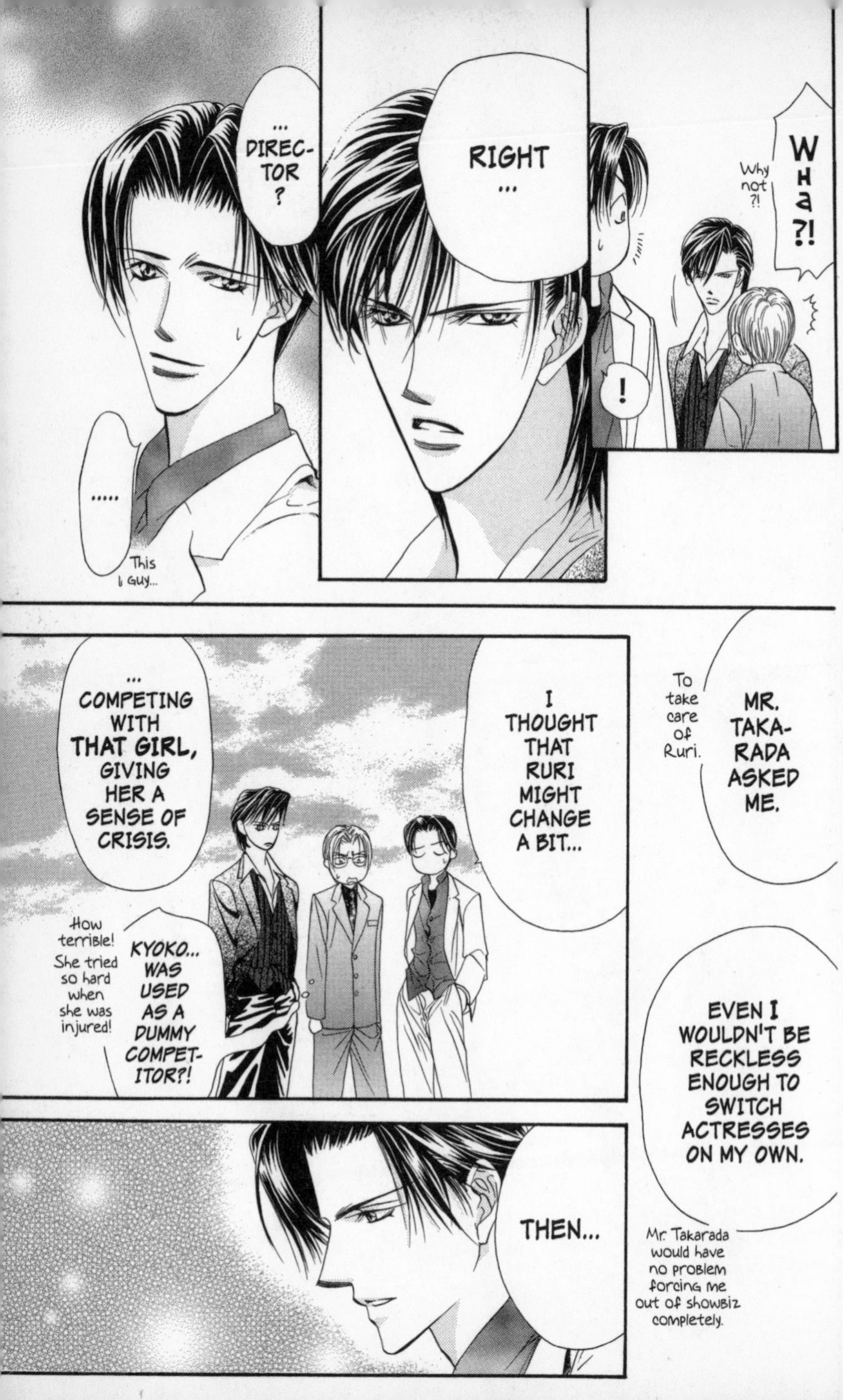
WHA?!
Why not?!
!
RIGHT...
...DIRECTOR?
.....
This guy...
MR. TAKARADA ASKED ME.
To take care of Ruri.
I THOUGHT THAT RURI MIGHT CHANGE A BIT...
...COMPETING WITH THAT GIRL, GIVING HER A SENSE OF CRISIS.
KYOKO... WAS USED AS A DUMMY COMPETITOR?!
How terrible! She tried so hard when she was injured!
EVEN I WOULDN'T BE RECKLESS ENOUGH TO SWITCH ACTRESSES ON MY OWN.
Mr. Takarada would have no problem forcing me out of showbiz completely.
THEN...

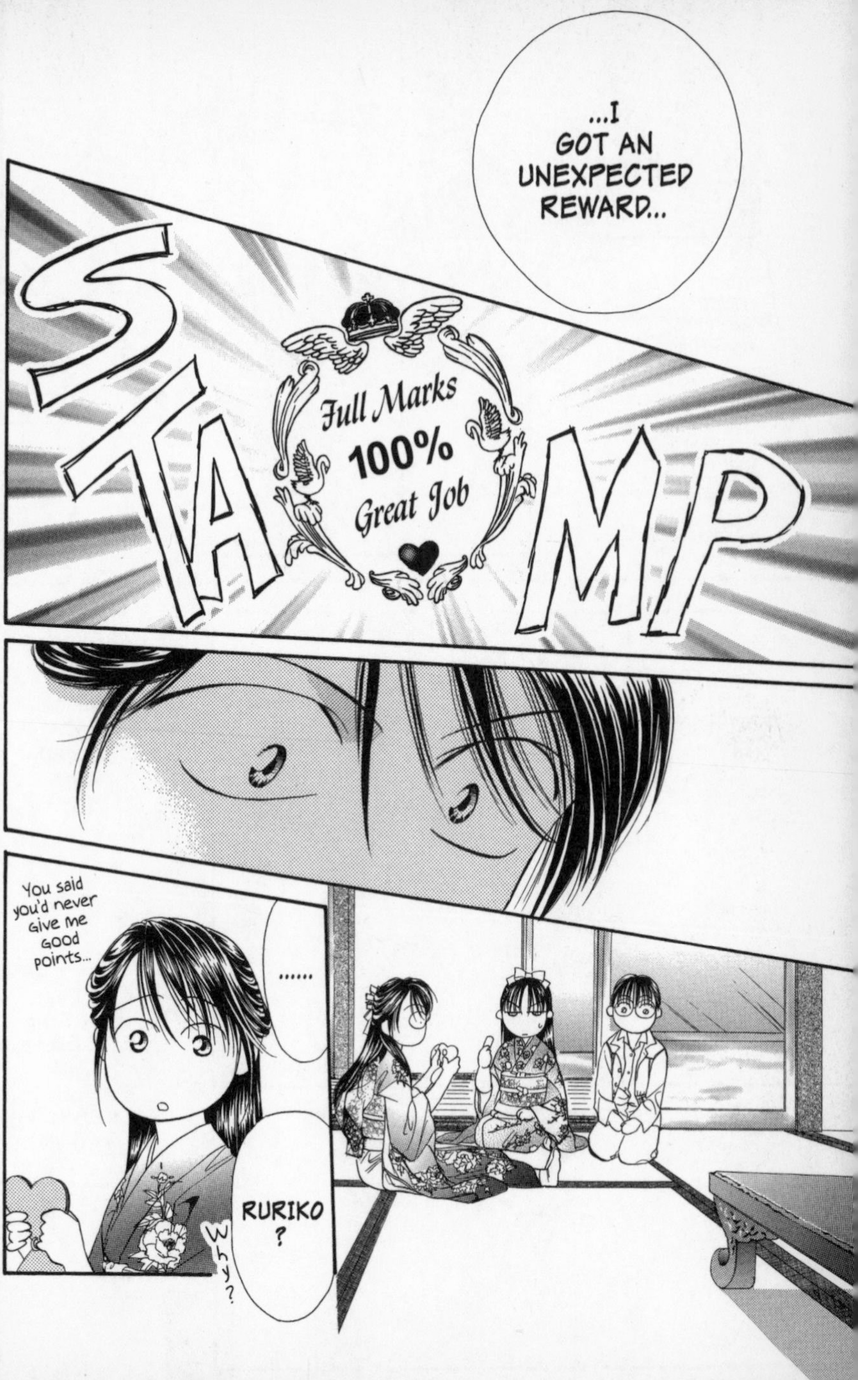

...I GOT AN UNEXPECTED REWARD...
STAMP
Full Marks
100%
Great Job
......
RURIKO ?
Why?
You said you'd never give me good points...

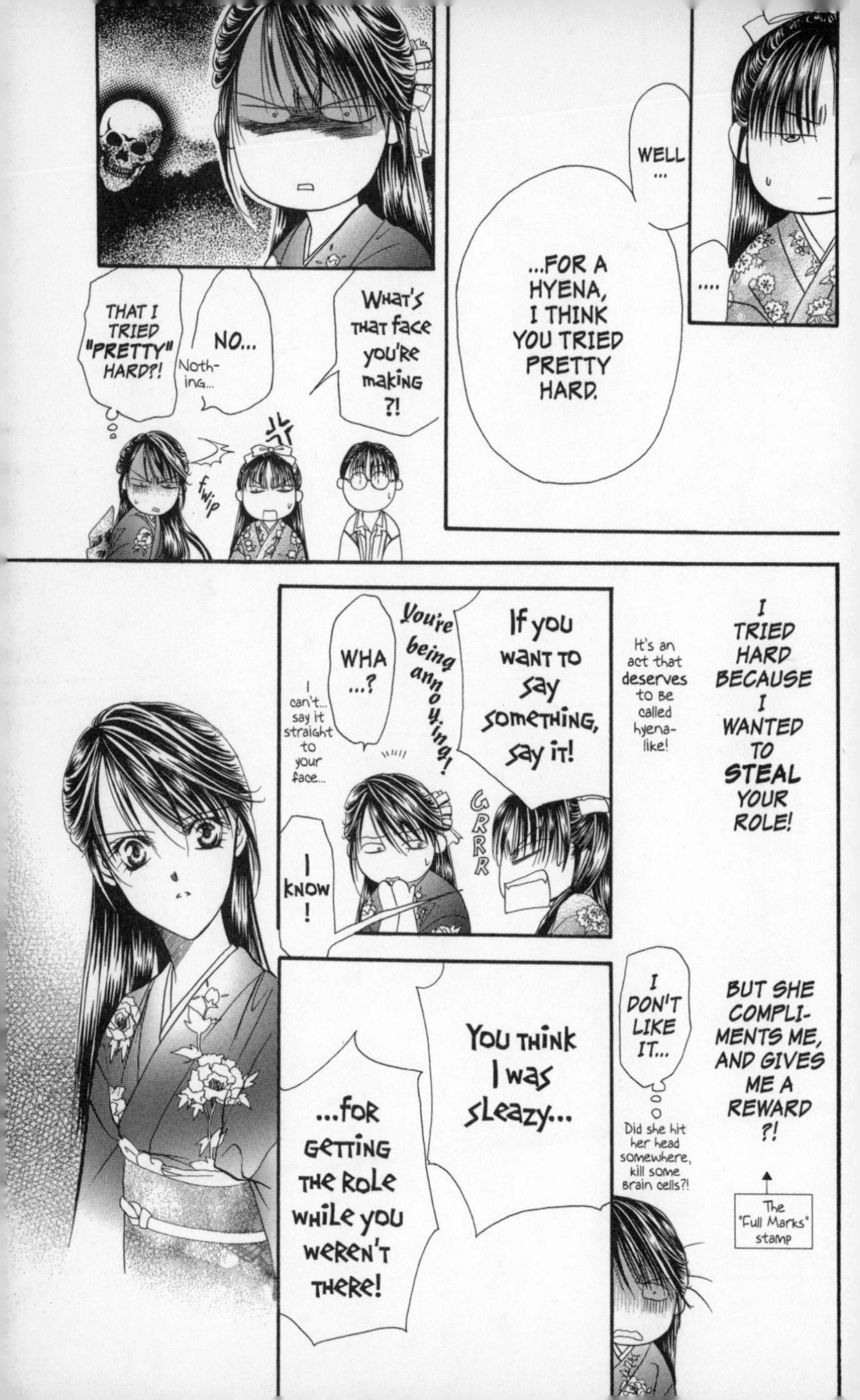
....
WELL...
...FOR A HYENA, I THINK YOU TRIED PRETTY HARD.
WHAT'S THAT FACE YOU'RE MAKING?!
NO...
Nothing...
THAT I TRIED "PRETTY" HARD?!
fwip
I TRIED HARD BECAUSE I WANTED TO STEAL YOUR ROLE!
It's an act that deserves to be called hyena-like!
If you want to say something, say it!
You're being annoying!
GRRR
WHA...?
I can't... say it straight to your face...
I KNOW!
BUT SHE COMPLIMENTS ME, AND GIVES ME A REWARD?!
The "Full Marks" stamp
I DON'T LIKE IT...
Did she hit her head somewhere, kill some brain cells?!
YOU THINK I WAS SLEAZY...
...FOR GETTING THE ROLE WHILE YOU WEREN'T THERE!

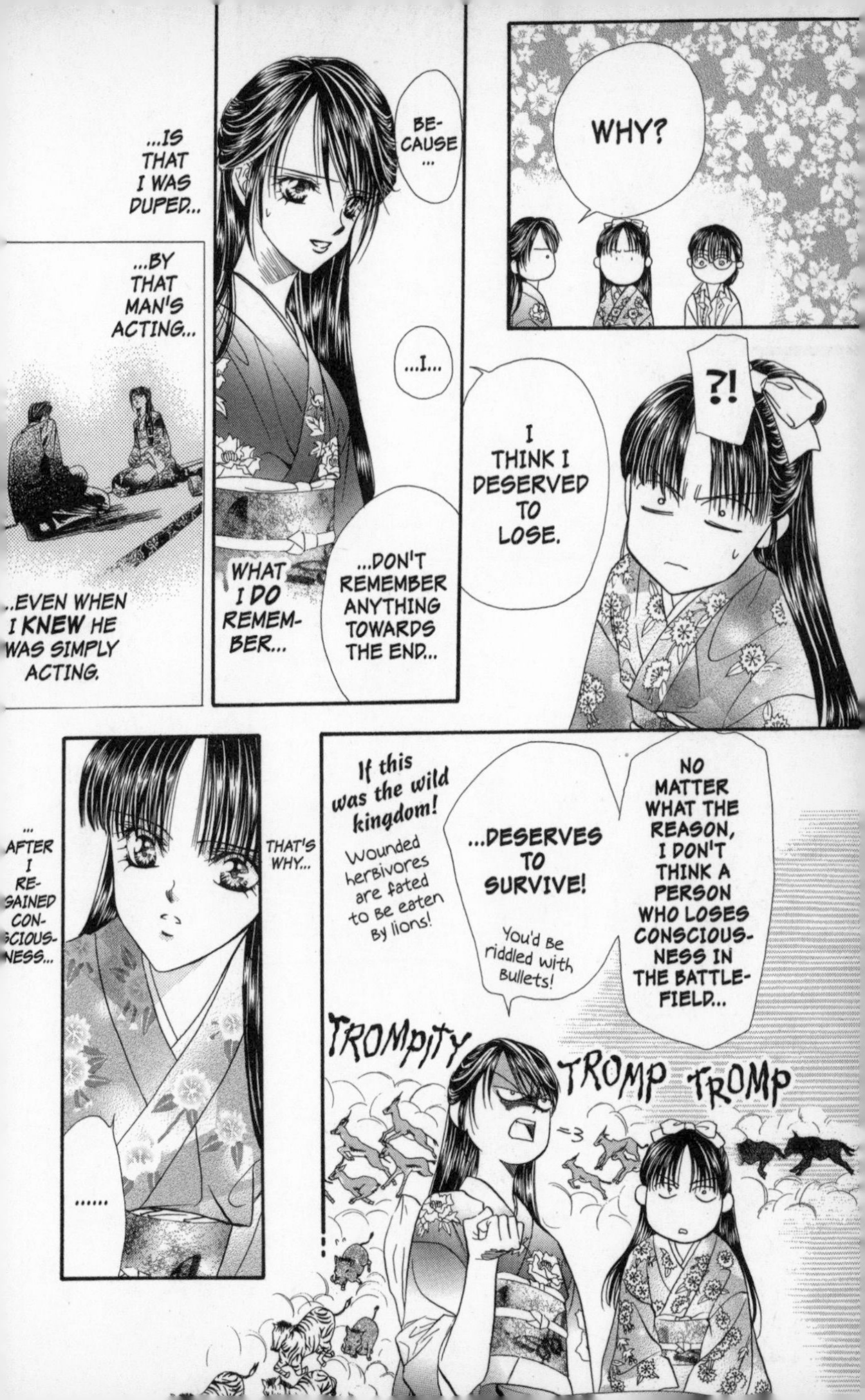
WHY?
?!
I THINK I DESERVED TO LOSE.
BE-CAUSE...
...I...
...DON'T REMEMBER ANYTHING TOWARDS THE END...
WHAT I DO REMEMBER...
...IS THAT I WAS DUPED...
...BY THAT MAN'S ACTING...
...EVEN WHEN I KNEW HE WAS SIMPLY ACTING.
NO MATTER WHAT THE REASON, I DON'T THINK A PERSON WHO LOSES CONSCIOUS-NESS IN THE BATTLE-FIELD...
...DESERVES TO SURVIVE!
You'd be riddled with bullets!
If this was the wild kingdom!
Wounded herbivores are fated to be eaten by lions!
TROMPITY
TROMP TROMP
THAT'S WHY...
...AFTER I RE-GAINED CON-SCIOUS-NESS...
......

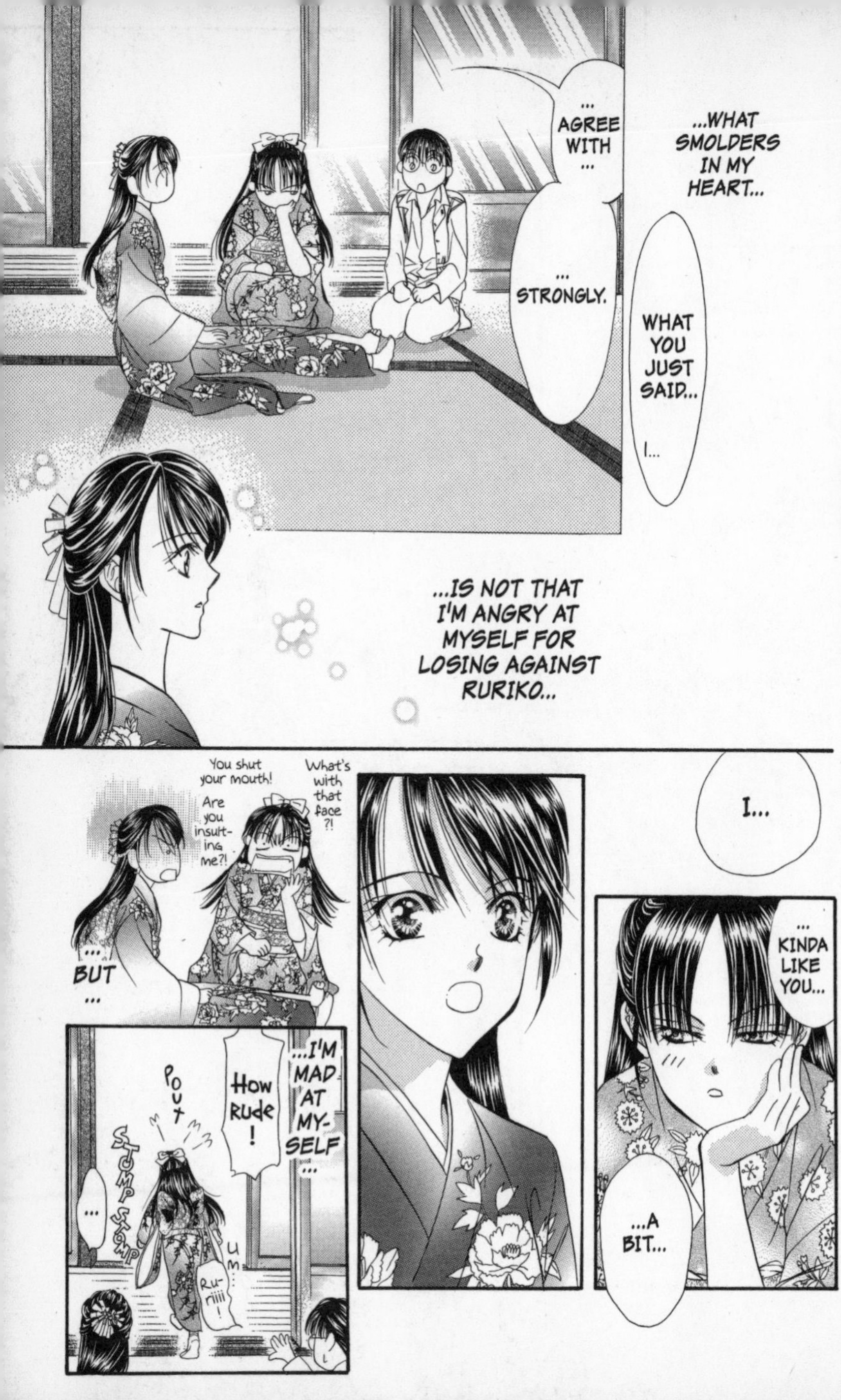

...WHAT SMOLDERS IN MY HEART...
WHAT YOU JUST SAID... I...
... AGREE WITH ...
... STRONGLY.
...IS NOT THAT I'M ANGRY AT MYSELF FOR LOSING AGAINST RURIKO...
I...
... KINDA LIKE YOU...
...A BIT...
What's with that face?!
You shut your mouth!
Are you insulting me?!
... BUT ...
...I'M MAD AT MYSELF...
How rude!
Pout
STOMP STOMP
...
Um... Ru-riiii!

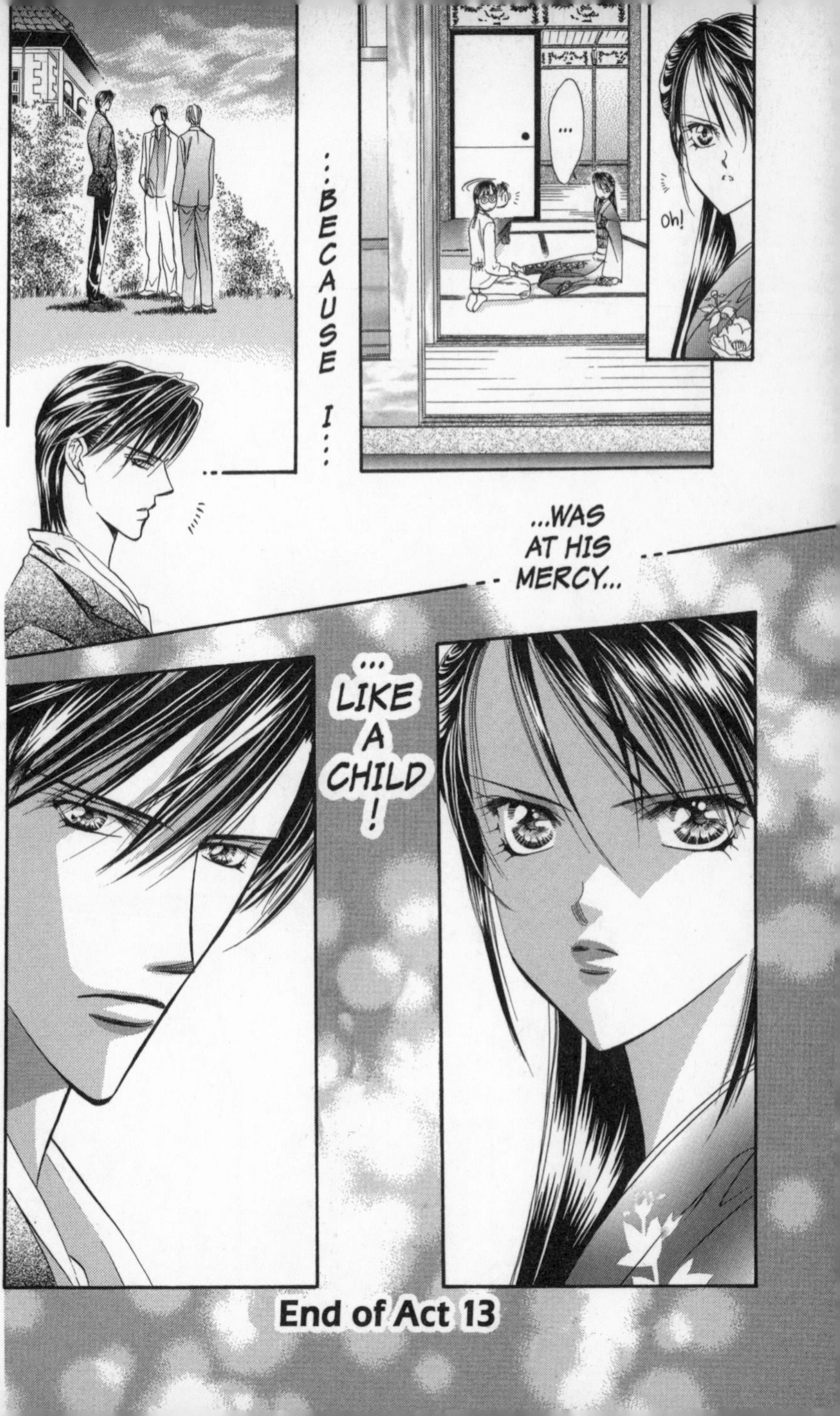
Oh!
...
...BECAUSE I...
...WAS AT HIS MERCY...
...LIKE A CHILD!
End of Act 13

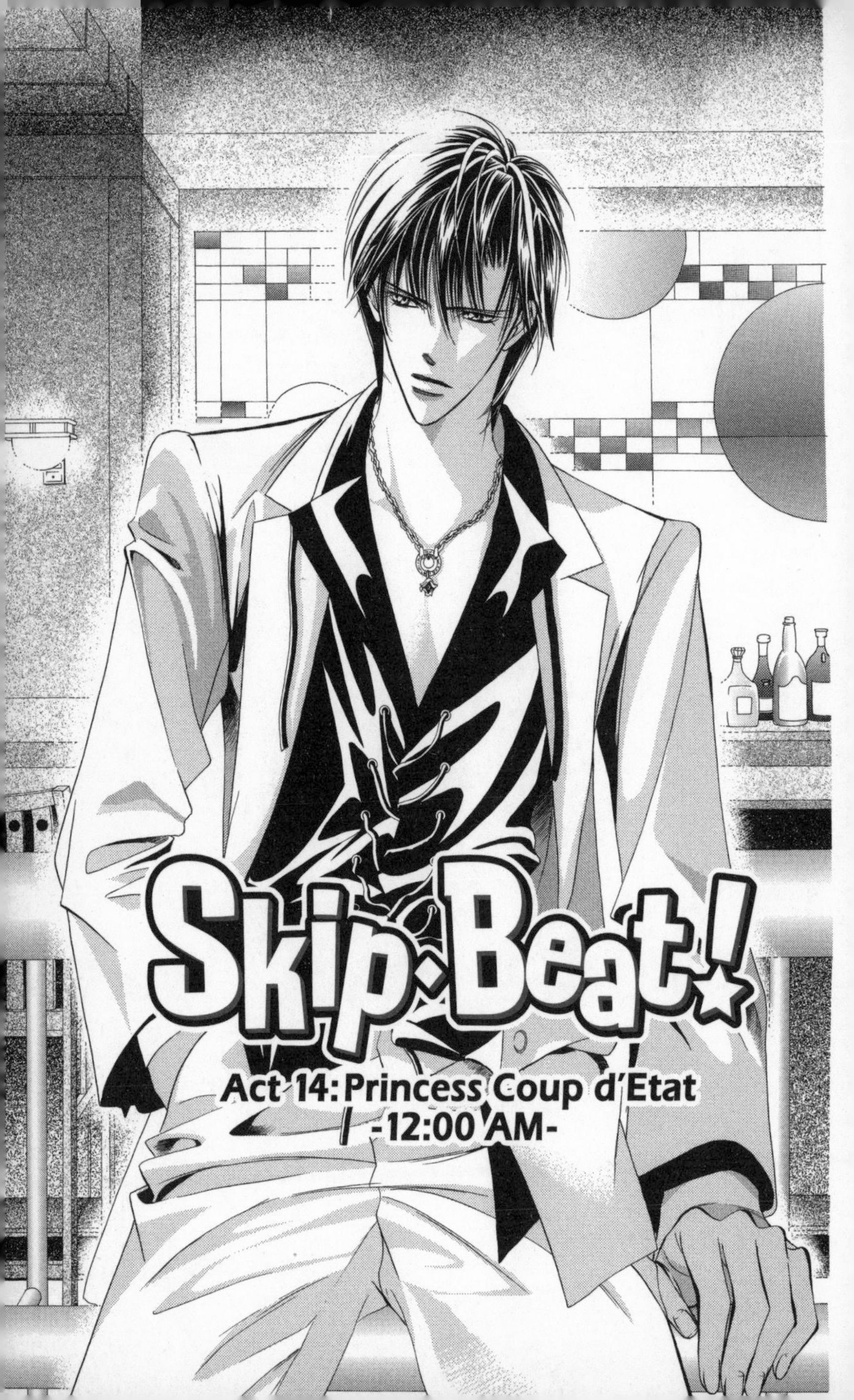
Skip·Beat!
Act 14: Princess Coup d'Etat
-12:00 AM-

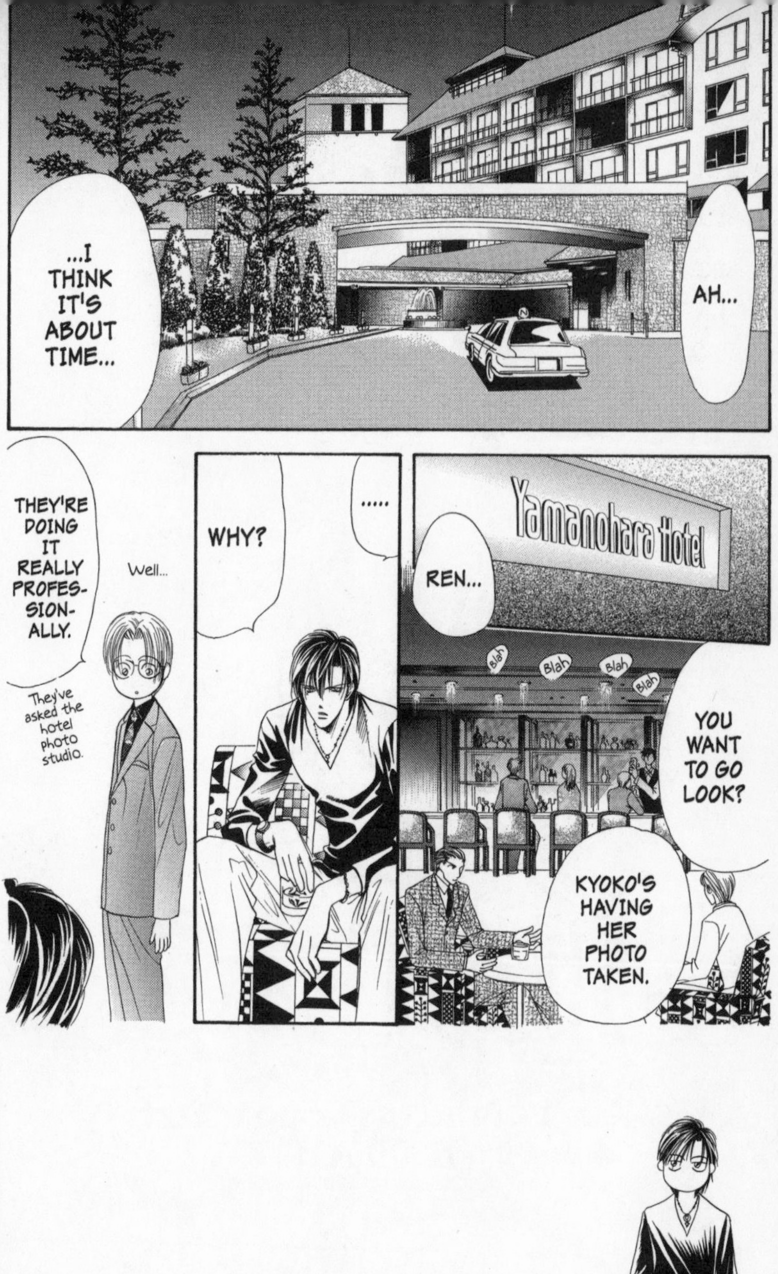
AH...
...I THINK IT'S ABOUT TIME...
Yamanohara Hotel
REN...
Blah
Blah
Blah
Blah
YOU WANT TO GO LOOK?
KYOKO'S HAVING HER PHOTO TAKEN.
.....
WHY?
THEY'RE DOING IT REALLY PROFES-SION-ALLY.
Well...
They've asked the hotel photo studio.

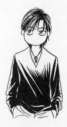

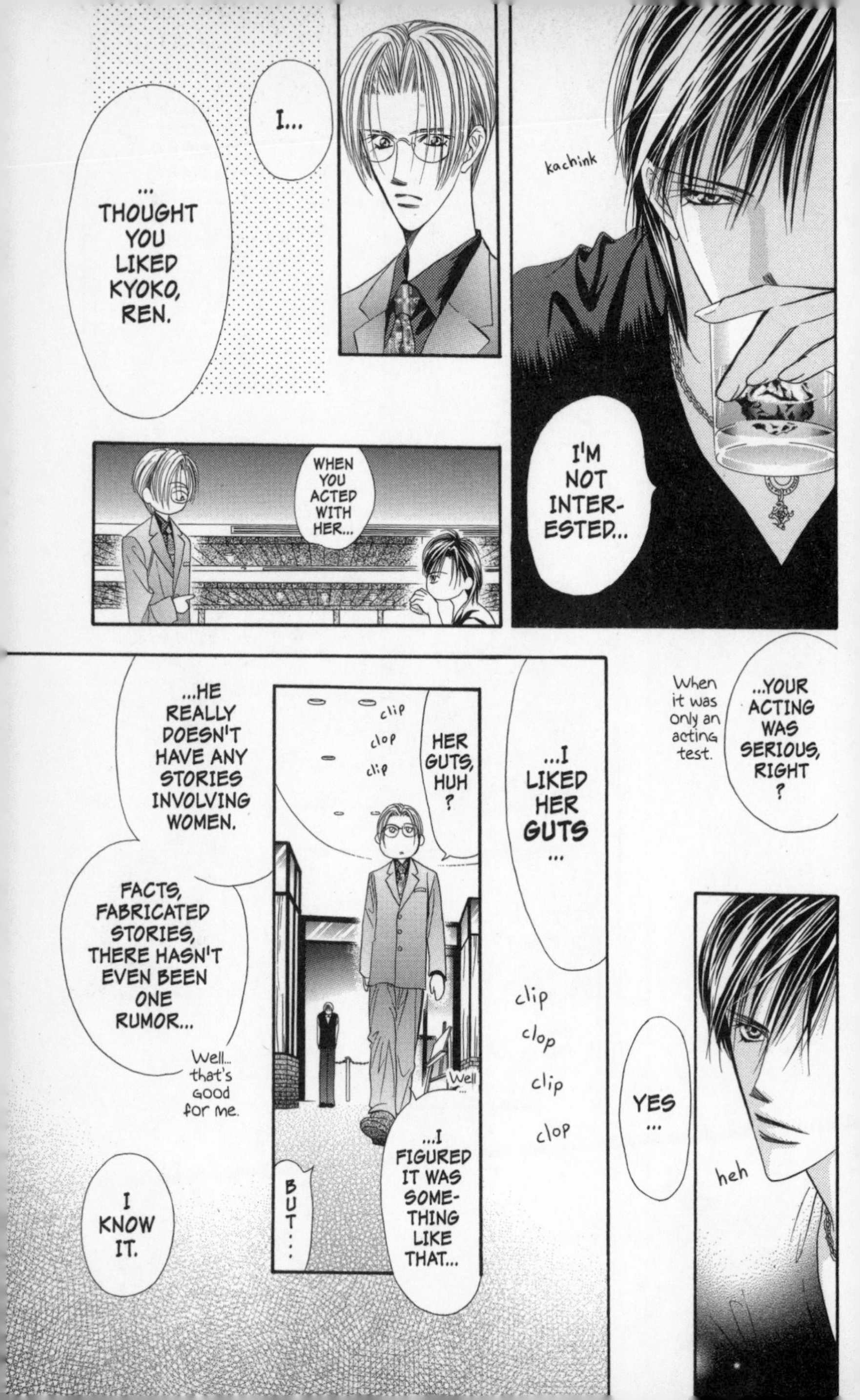
kachink
I'M NOT INTERESTED...
I...
...THOUGHT YOU LIKED KYOKO, REN.
WHEN YOU ACTED WITH HER...
...YOUR ACTING WAS SERIOUS, RIGHT?
When it was only an acting test.
YES...
heh
...I LIKED HER GUTS...
clip
clop
clip
clop
clip
clop
clip
HER GUTS, HUH?
Well...
...I FIGURED IT WAS SOMETHING LIKE THAT...
BUT...
...HE REALLY DOESN'T HAVE ANY STORIES INVOLVING WOMEN.
FACTS, FABRICATED STORIES, THERE HASN'T EVEN BEEN ONE RUMOR...
Well... that's good for me.
I KNOW IT.

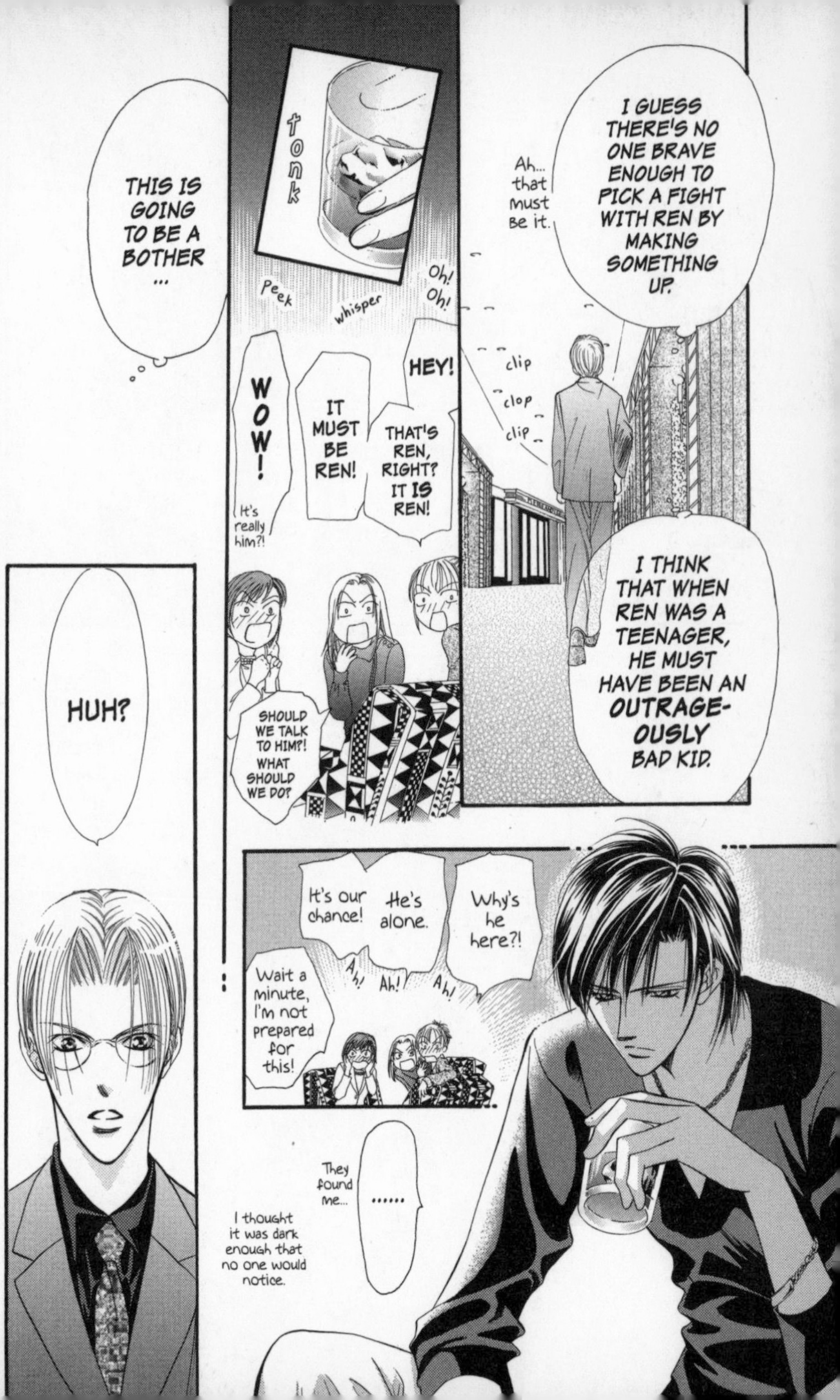
I GUESS THERE'S NO ONE BRAVE ENOUGH TO PICK A FIGHT WITH REN BY MAKING SOMETHING UP.
Ah... that must be it.
clip
clop
clip
I THINK THAT WHEN REN WAS A TEENAGER, HE MUST HAVE BEEN AN OUTRAGE-OUSLY BAD KID.
tonk
Oh! Oh!
whisper
Peek
HEY!
THAT'S REN, RIGHT? IT IS REN!
IT MUST BE REN!
WOW!
It's really him?!
SHOULD WE TALK TO HIM?! WHAT SHOULD WE DO?
Why's he here?!
He's alone.
It's our chance!
Ah! Ah! Ah!
Wait a minute, I'm not prepared for this!
......
They found me...
I thought it was dark enough that no one would notice.
THIS IS GOING TO BE A BOTHER ...
HUH?

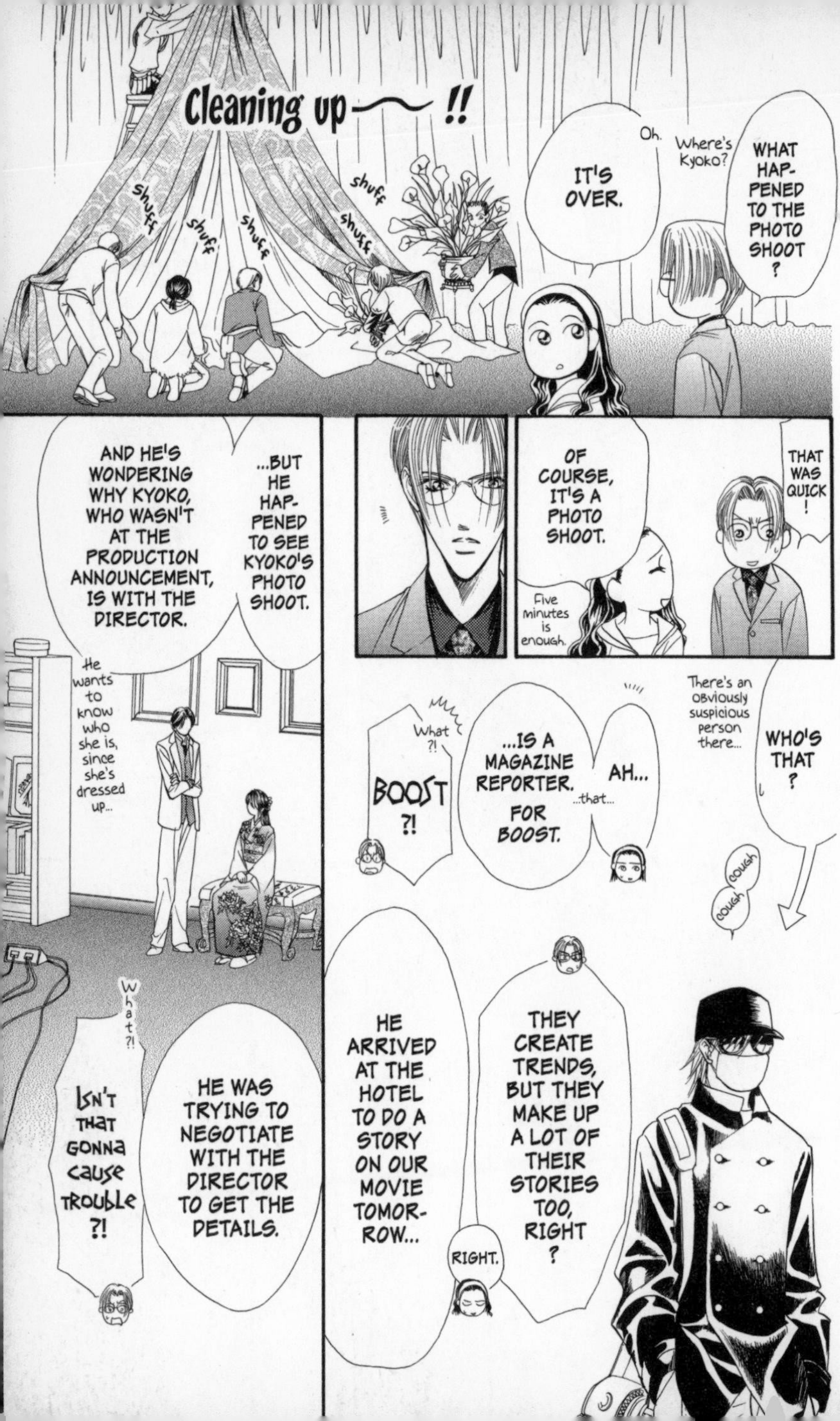
WHAT HAPPENED TO THE PHOTO SHOOT?
Where's Kyoko?
Oh.
IT'S OVER.
shuff
shuff
shuff
shuff
shuff
Cleaning up~~!!
THAT WAS QUICK!
OF COURSE, IT'S A PHOTO SHOOT.
Five minutes is enough.
WHO'S THAT?
There's an obviously suspicious person there...
AH...
...that...
...IS A MAGAZINE REPORTER. FOR BOOST.
What?!
BOOST?!
cough
cough
THEY CREATE TRENDS, BUT THEY MAKE UP A LOT OF THEIR STORIES TOO, RIGHT?
RIGHT.
HE ARRIVED AT THE HOTEL TO DO A STORY ON OUR MOVIE TOMORROW...
...BUT HE HAPPENED TO SEE KYOKO'S PHOTO SHOOT.
AND HE'S WONDERING WHY KYOKO, WHO WASN'T AT THE PRODUCTION ANNOUNCEMENT, IS WITH THE DIRECTOR.
He wants to know who she is, since she's dressed up...
HE WAS TRYING TO NEGOTIATE WITH THE DIRECTOR TO GET THE DETAILS.
What?!
ISN'T THAT GONNA CAUSE TROUBLE?!

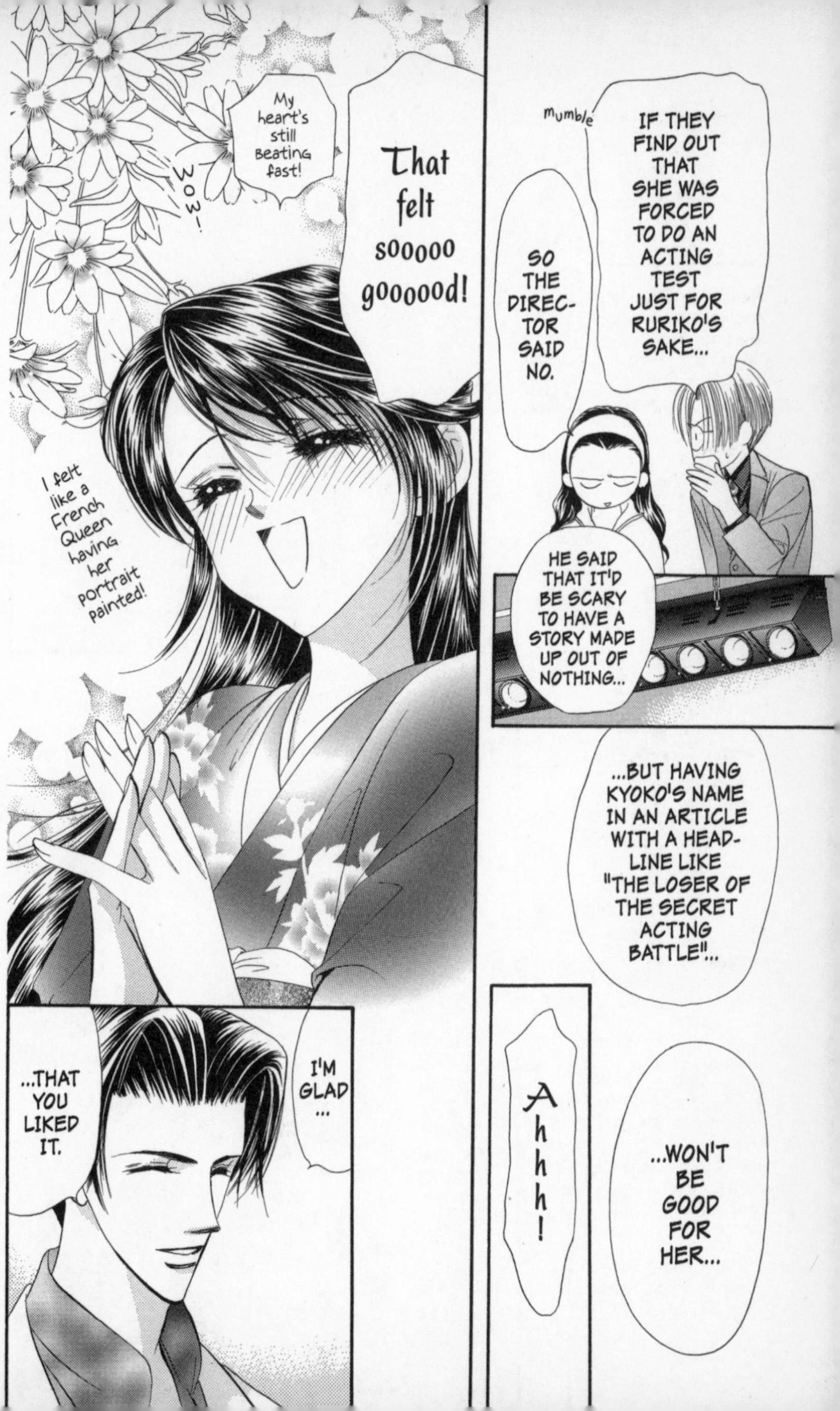
IF THEY FIND OUT THAT SHE WAS FORCED TO DO AN ACTING TEST JUST FOR RURIKO'S SAKE...
mumble
SO THE DIRECTOR SAID NO.
HE SAID THAT IT'D BE SCARY TO HAVE A STORY MADE UP OUT OF NOTHING...
...BUT HAVING KYOKO'S NAME IN AN ARTICLE WITH A HEADLINE LIKE "THE LOSER OF THE SECRET ACTING BATTLE"...
...WON'T BE GOOD FOR HER...
Ahhh!
That felt sooooo goooood!
My heart's still Beating fast!
WOW!
I felt like a French Queen having her portrait painted!
I'M GLAD...
...THAT YOU LIKED IT.

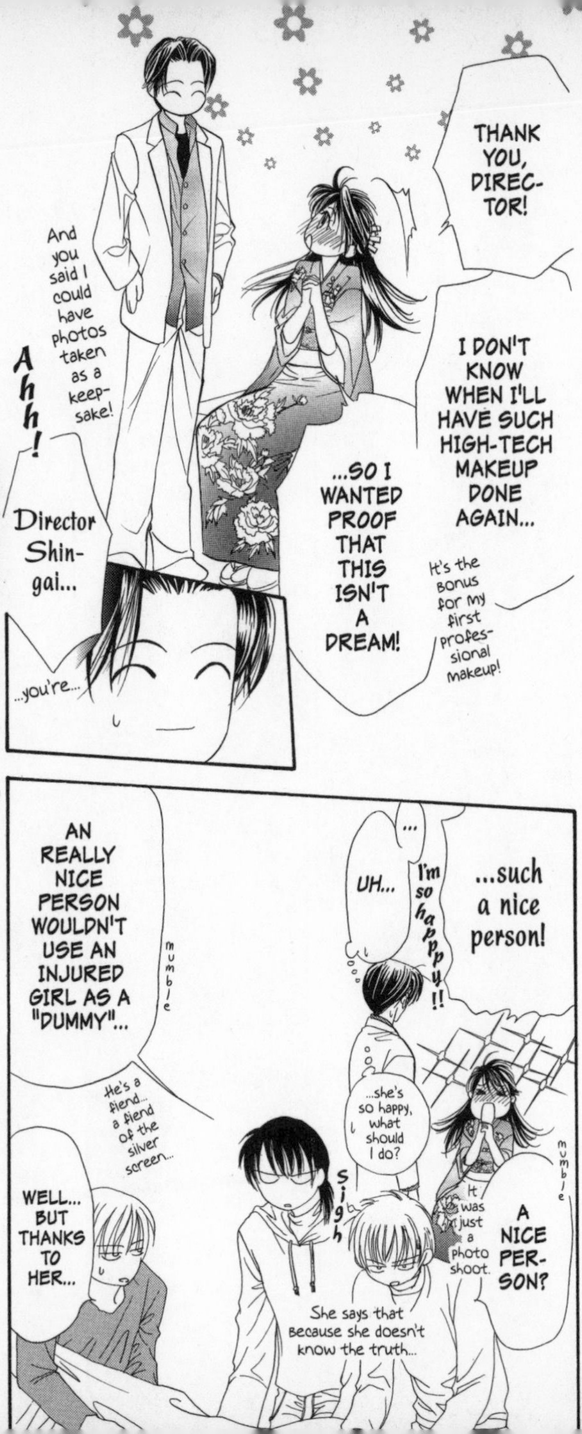
THANK YOU, DIRECTOR!
I DON'T KNOW WHEN I'LL HAVE SUCH HIGH-TECH MAKEUP DONE AGAIN...
...SO I WANTED PROOF THAT THIS ISN'T A DREAM!
It's the bonus for my first professional makeup!
And you said I could have photos taken as a keepsake!
Ahh!
Director Shingai...
...you're...
...such a nice person!
I'm so happy!!
...
UH...
...she's so happy, what should I do?
AN REALLY NICE PERSON WOULDN'T USE AN INJURED GIRL AS A "DUMMY"...
mumble
A NICE PERSON?
It was just a photo shoot.
mumble
sigh
He's a fiend... a fiend of the silver screen...
WELL... BUT THANKS TO HER...
She says that because she doesn't know the truth...

Seiji Shingai

Difficulty level

☆☆☆ ③

He was originally a cool looking middle-aged guy, like an "amazing director must look like this"...

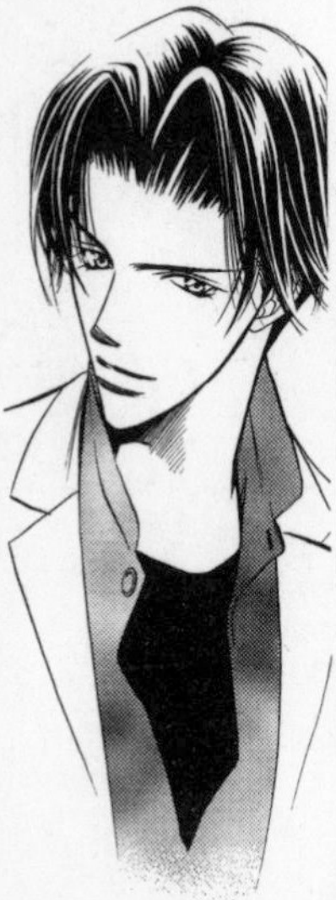

Well...because if you think about it logically, you can't be young and be well-known as a great director... that was what I'd thought... But in shojo manga, it seems to be useless to think logically like that...my editor promptly told me "Don't make him middle-aged" and his character design turned out this way...

Drooping eyes...that may be rare in a Nakamura manga...?

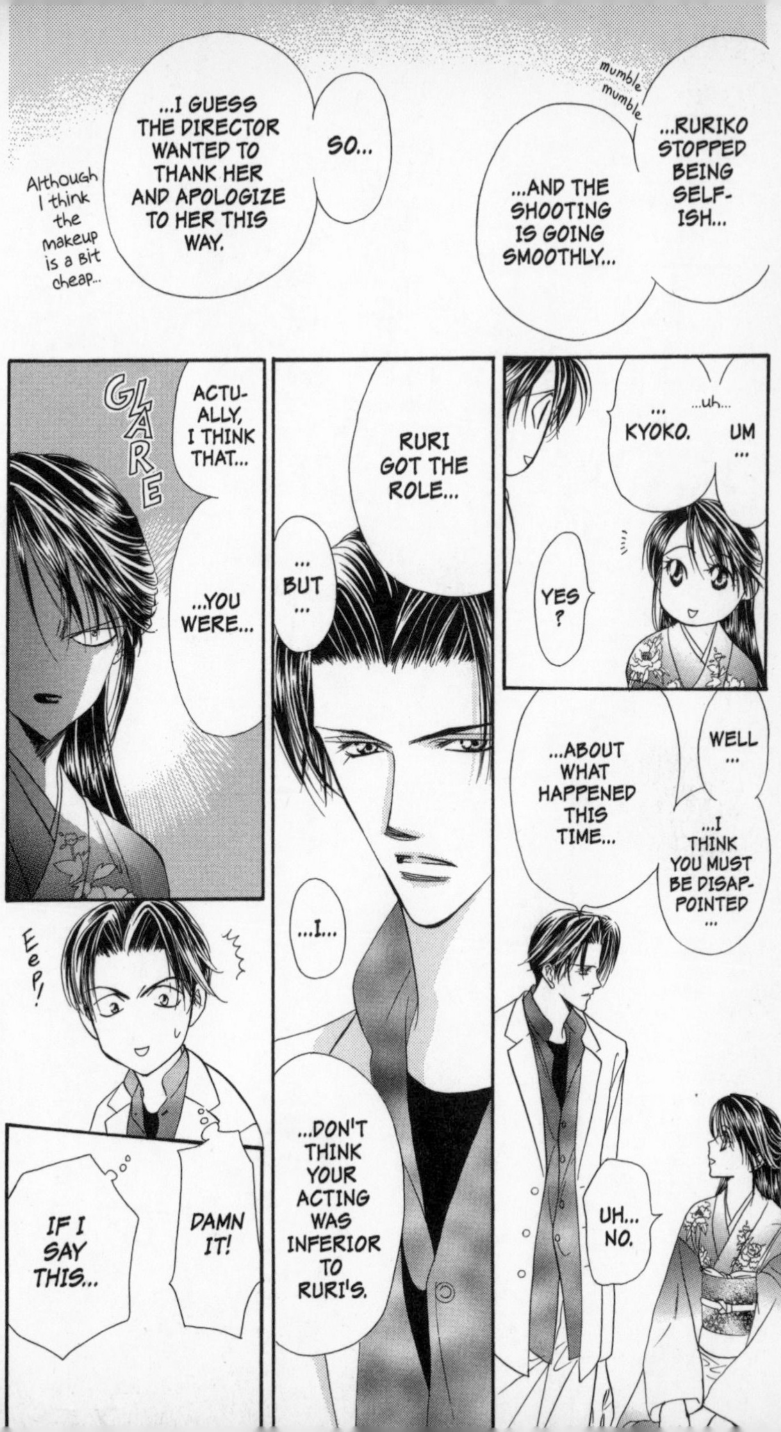
mumble mumble
...RURIKO STOPPED BEING SELF-ISH...
...AND THE SHOOTING IS GOING SMOOTHLY...
SO...
...I GUESS THE DIRECTOR WANTED TO THANK HER AND APOLOGIZE TO HER THIS WAY.
Although I think the makeup is a bit cheap...
...uh...
UM ...
... KYOKO.
YES ?
WELL ...
...I THINK YOU MUST BE DISAP-POINTED ...
...ABOUT WHAT HAPPENED THIS TIME...
UH... NO.
RURI GOT THE ROLE...
... BUT ...
...I...
...DON'T THINK YOUR ACTING WAS INFERIOR TO RURI'S.
ACTU-ALLY, I THINK THAT...
GLARE
...YOU WERE...
Eep!
DAMN IT!
IF I SAY THIS...

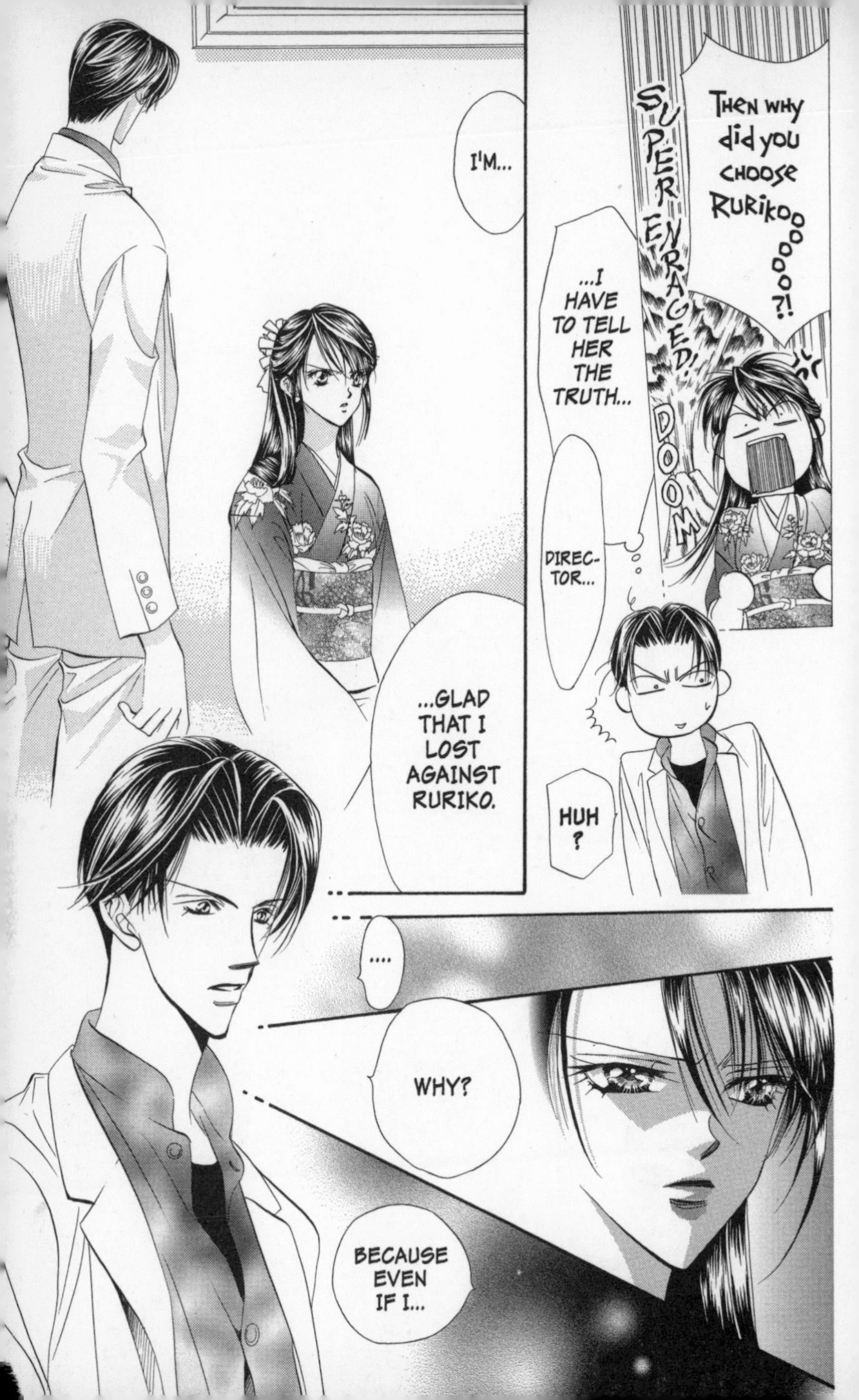
Then why did you choose Rurikoooooo?!
SUPER ENRAGED!
DOOM
...I HAVE TO TELL HER THE TRUTH...
DIRECTOR...
HUH?
I'M...
...GLAD THAT I LOST AGAINST RURIKO.
....
WHY?
BECAUSE EVEN IF I...

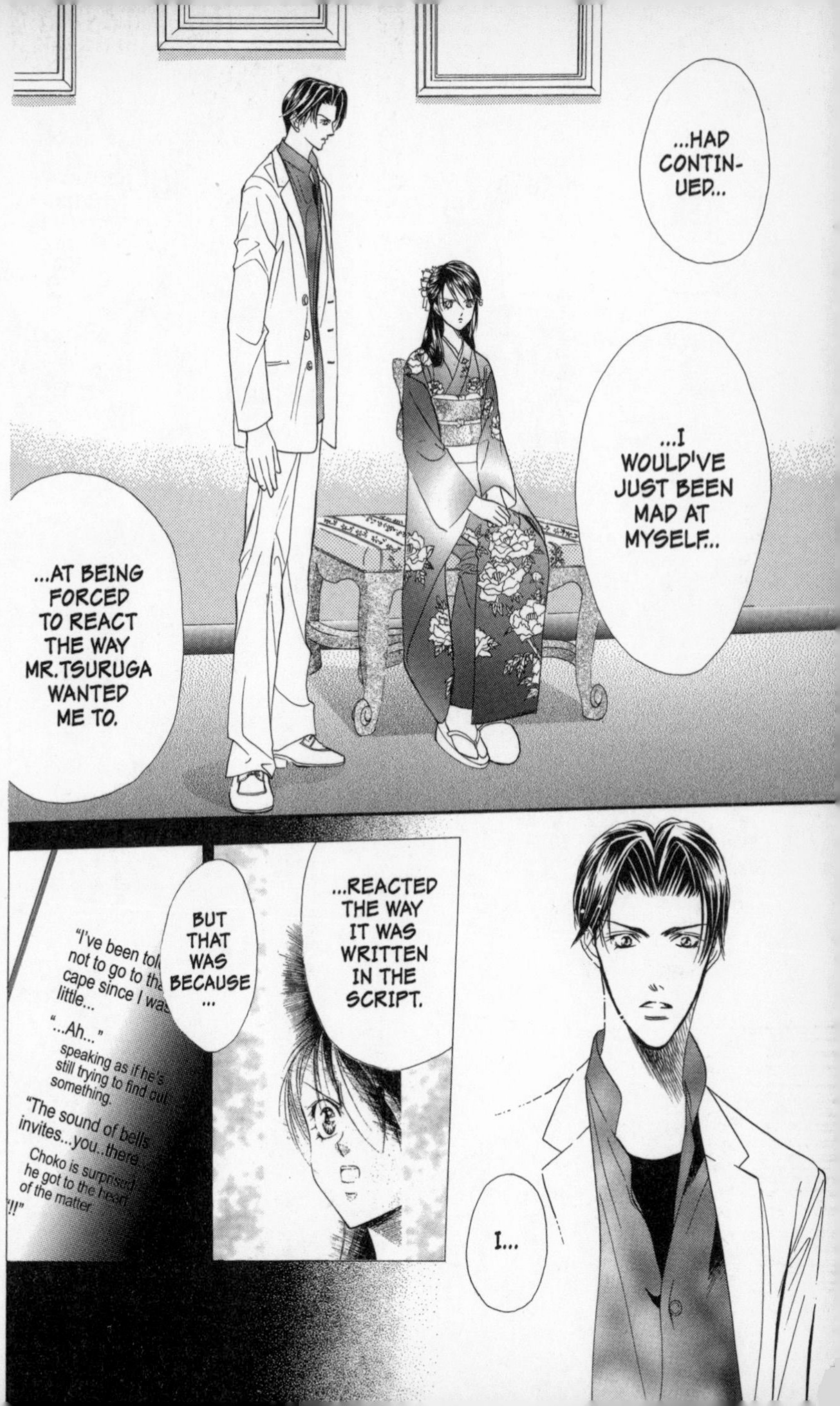
...HAD CONTIN-UED...
...I WOULD'VE JUST BEEN MAD AT MYSELF...
...AT BEING FORCED TO REACT THE WAY MR.TSURUGA WANTED ME TO.
I...
...REACTED THE WAY IT WAS WRITTEN IN THE SCRIPT.
BUT THAT WAS BECAUSE ...
"I've been tol
not to go to tha
cape since I was
little...
"...Ah..."
speaking as if he's
still trying to find out
something.
"The sound of bells
invites...you..there..
Choko is surprised
he got to the heart
of the matter
"!!"

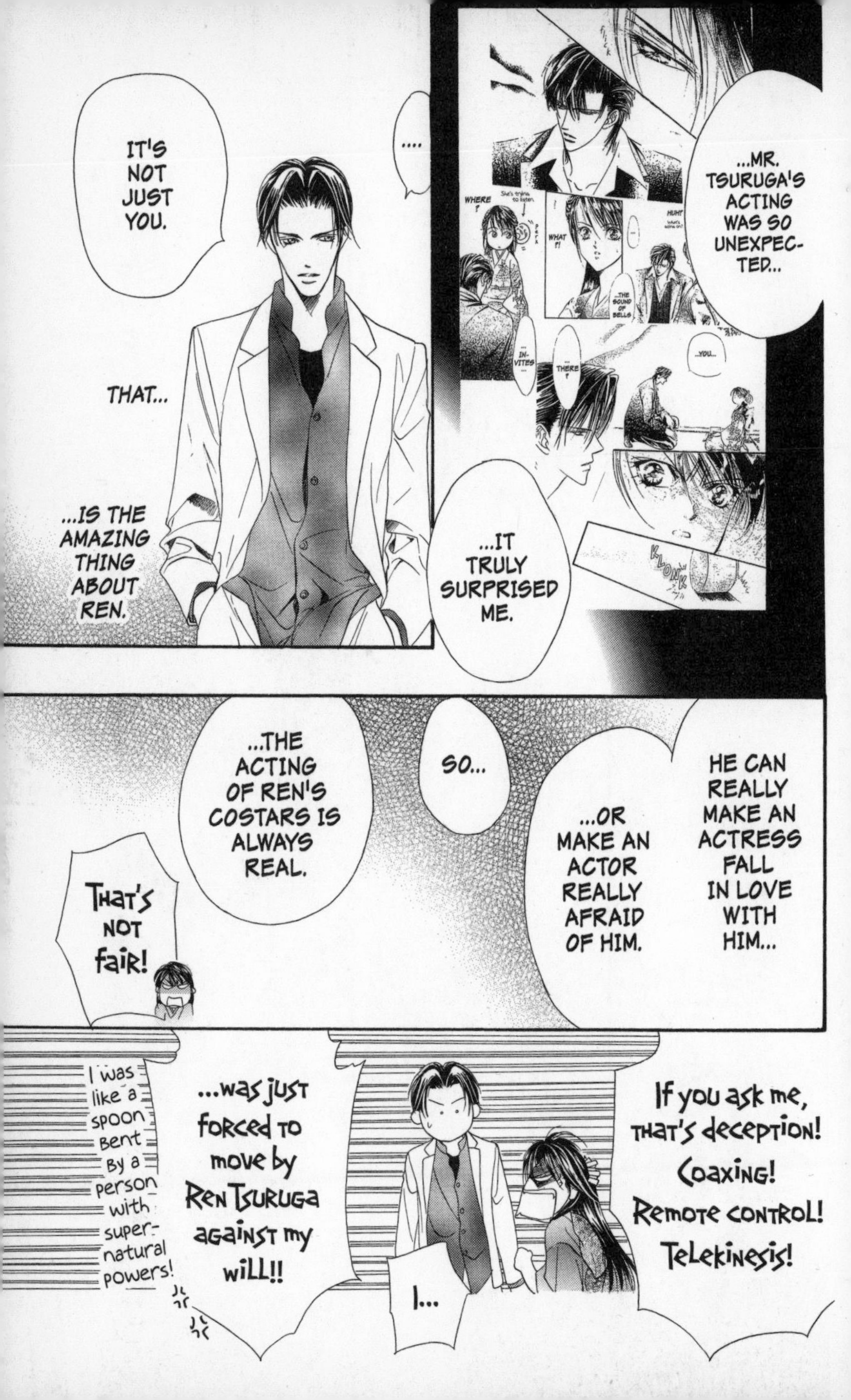
...MR. TSURUGA'S ACTING WAS SO UNEXPECTED...
WHERE ?
She's trying to listen.
WHAT !?
HUH? What's going on?
...THE SOUND OF BELLS
...INVITES...
...THERE ?
...YOU...
KVONK
...IT TRULY SURPRISED ME.
....
IT'S NOT JUST YOU.
THAT...
...IS THE AMAZING THING ABOUT REN.
HE CAN REALLY MAKE AN ACTRESS FALL IN LOVE WITH HIM...
...OR MAKE AN ACTOR REALLY AFRAID OF HIM.
SO...
...THE ACTING OF REN'S COSTARS IS ALWAYS REAL.
That's not fair!
If you ask me, that's deception! Coaxing! Remote control! Telekinesis!
I...
...was just forced to move by Ren Tsuruga against my will!!
I was like a spoon bent by a person with super-natural powers!

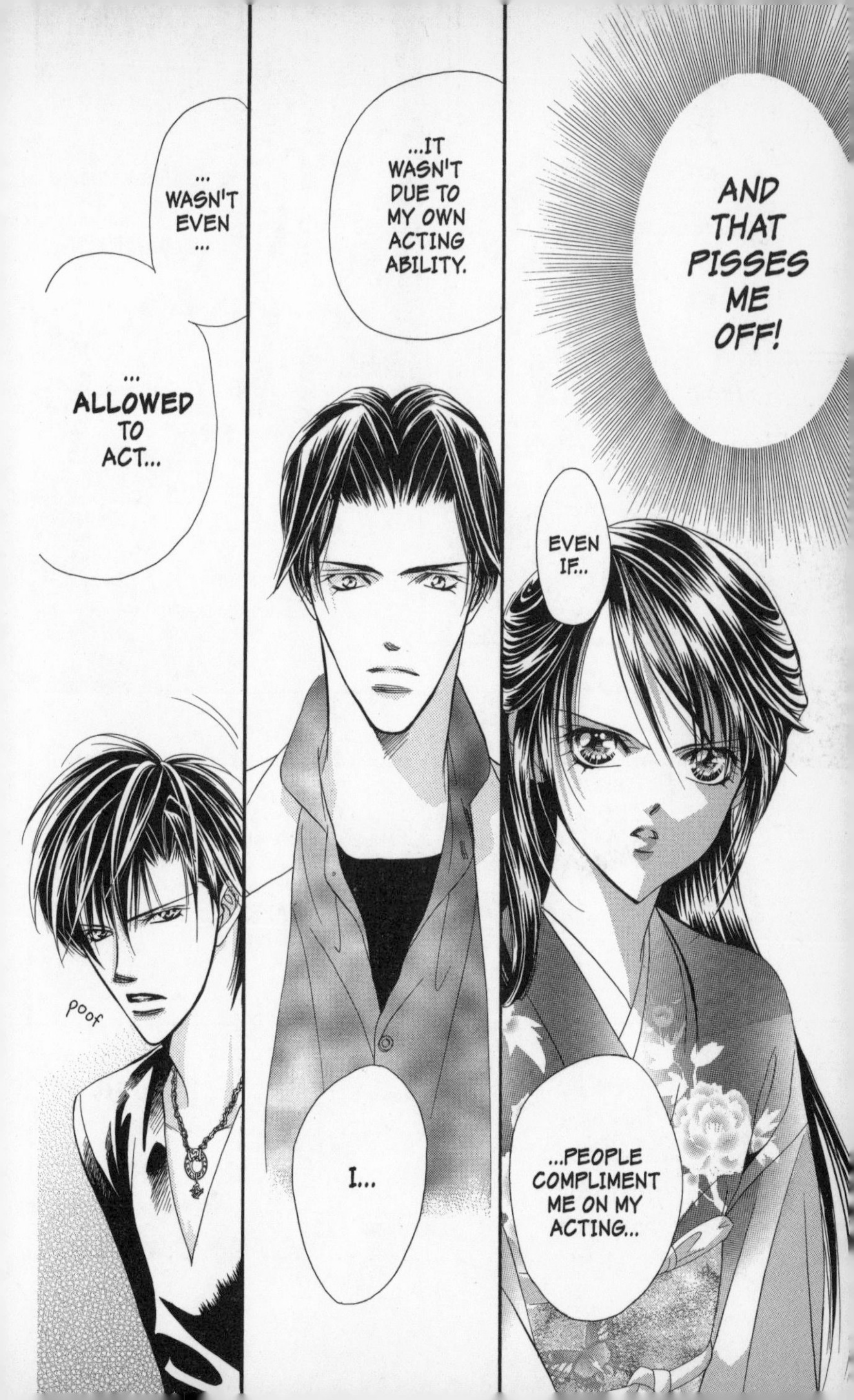

AND THAT PISSES ME OFF!
EVEN IF...
...PEOPLE COMPLIMENT ME ON MY ACTING...
...IT WASN'T DUE TO MY OWN ACTING ABILITY.
I...
... WASN'T EVEN ...
... ALLOWED TO ACT...
poof

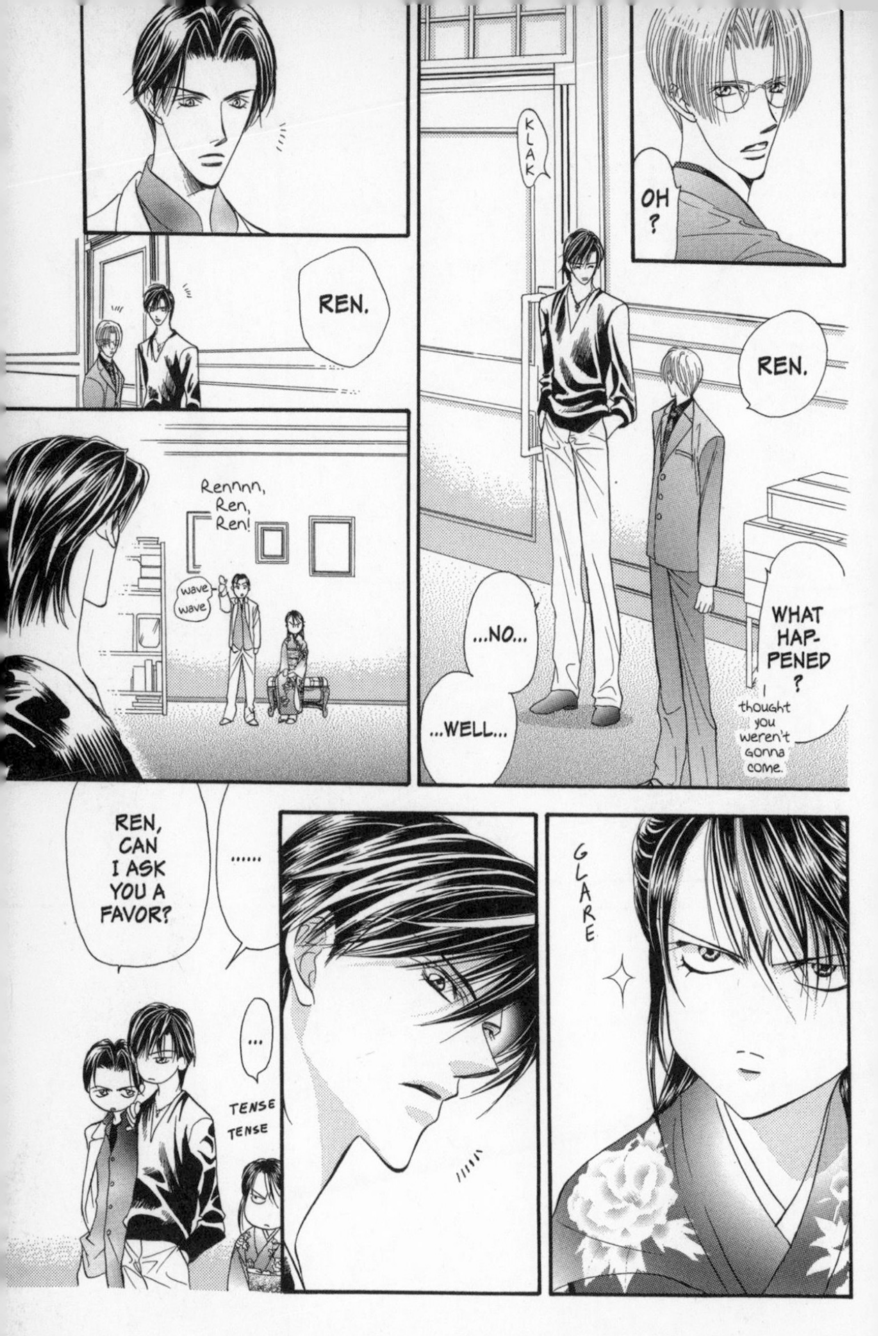
OH?
KLAK
REN.
WHAT HAPPENED? I thought you weren't gonna come.
...NO...
...WELL...
REN.
Rennnn, Ren, Ren!
wave wave
GLARE
REN, CAN I ASK YOU A FAVOR?
......
...
TENSE TENSE

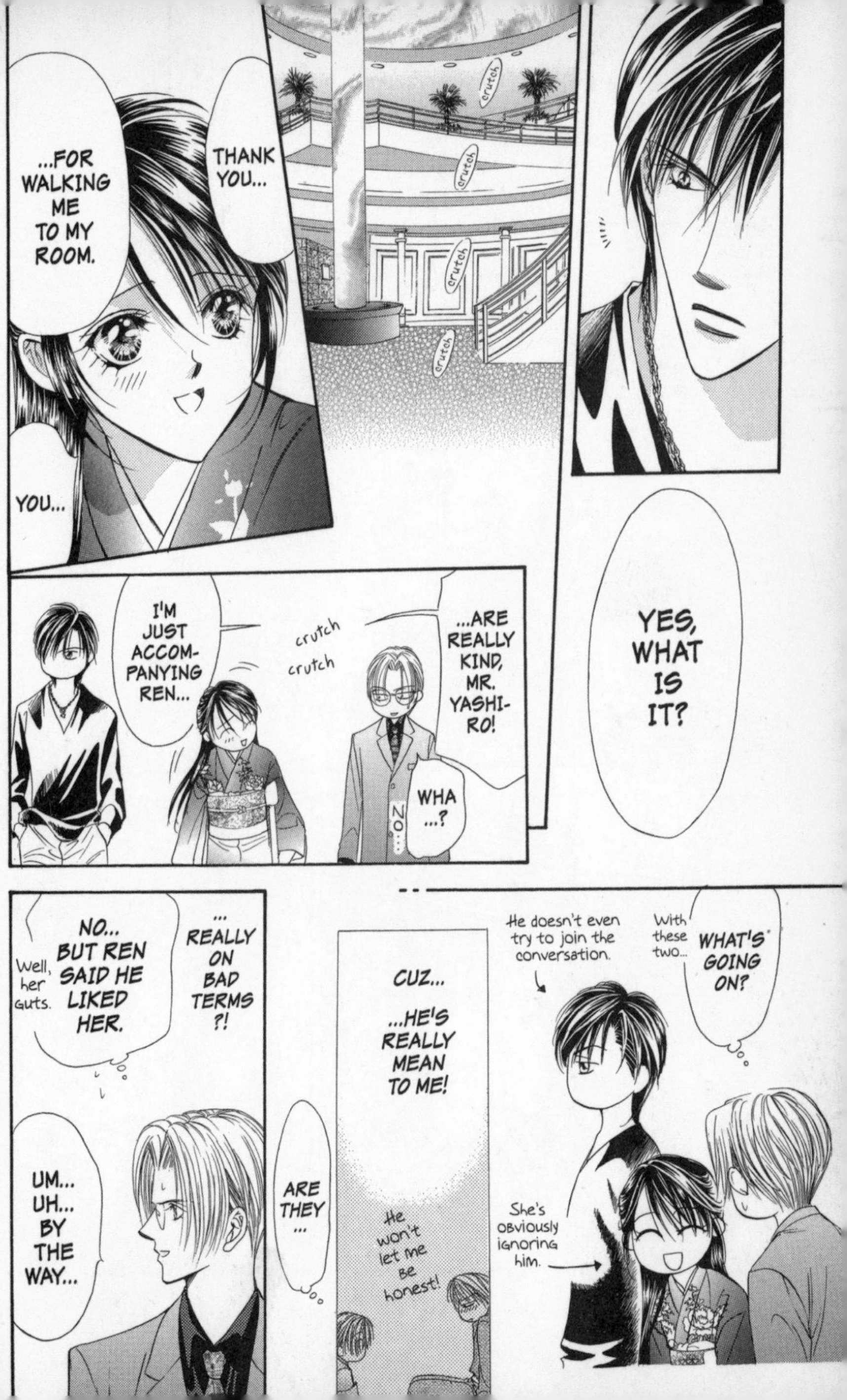
crutch
crutch
crutch
crutch
THANK YOU...
...FOR WALKING ME TO MY ROOM.
YOU...
YES, WHAT IS IT?
...ARE REALLY KIND, MR. YASHIRO!
WHA ...?
NO...
crutch
crutch
I'M JUST ACCOMPANYING REN...
WHAT'S GOING ON?
With these two...
He doesn't even try to join the conversation.
She's obviously ignoring him.
CUZ...
...HE'S REALLY MEAN TO ME!
He won't let me be honest!
ARE THEY ...
... REALLY ON BAD TERMS ?!
NO... BUT REN SAID HE LIKED HER.
Well, her guts.
UM... UH... BY THE WAY...

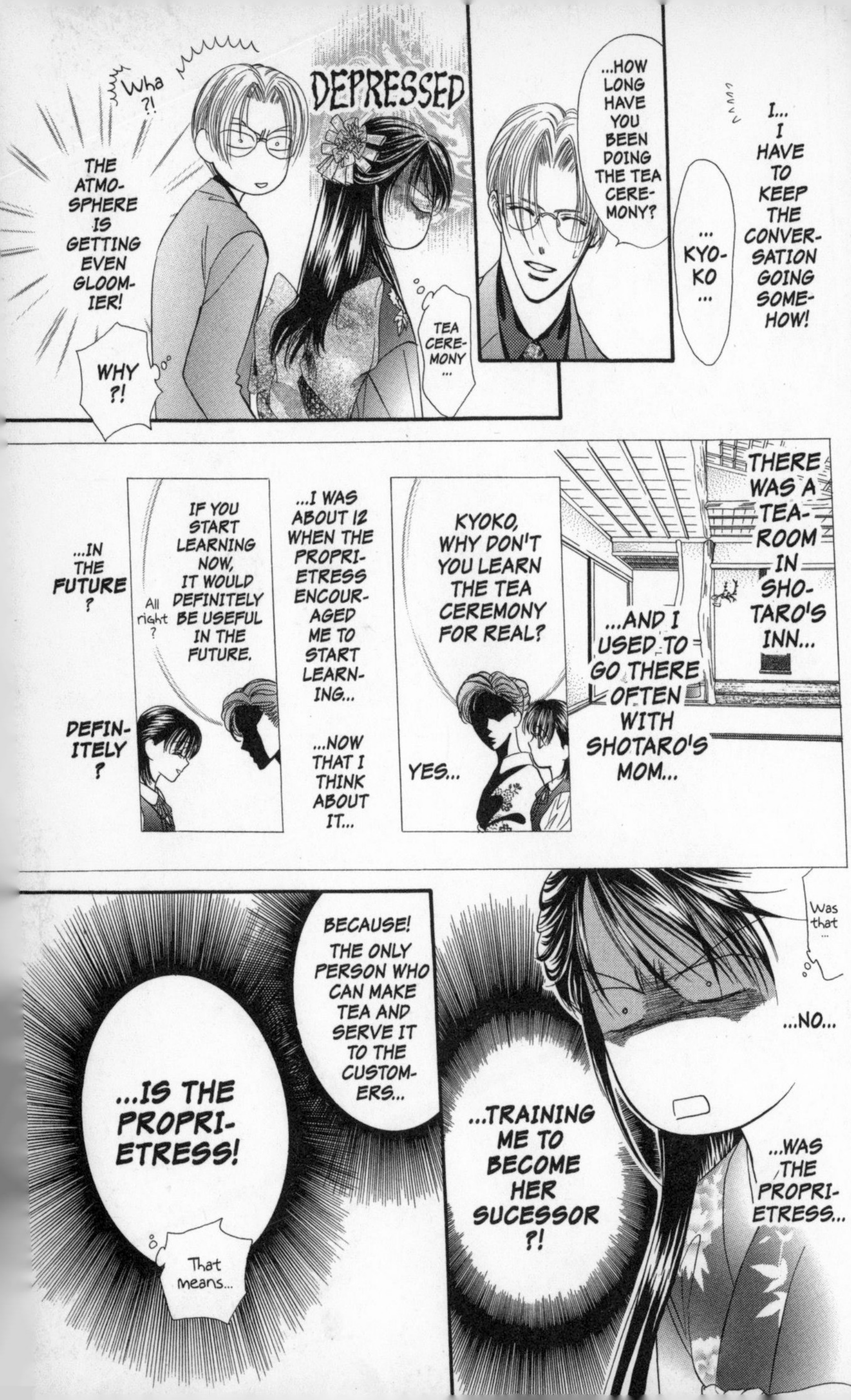

I... I HAVE TO KEEP THE CONVERSATION GOING SOMEHOW!
... KYOKO ...
...HOW LONG HAVE YOU BEEN DOING THE TEA CEREMONY?
TEA CEREMONY ...
DEPRESSED
Wha ?!
THE ATMOSPHERE IS GETTING EVEN GLOOMIER!
WHY ?!
THERE WAS A TEAROOM IN SHOTARO'S INN...
...AND I USED TO GO THERE OFTEN WITH SHOTARO'S MOM...
KYOKO, WHY DON'T YOU LEARN THE TEA CEREMONY FOR REAL?
YES...
...I WAS ABOUT 12 WHEN THE PROPRIETRESS ENCOURAGED ME TO START LEARNING...
...NOW THAT I THINK ABOUT IT...
IF YOU START LEARNING NOW, IT WOULD DEFINITELY BE USEFUL IN THE FUTURE.
All right?
DEFINITELY?
...IN THE FUTURE?
Was that ...
...NO...
...WAS THE PROPRIETRESS...
...TRAINING ME TO BECOME HER SUCESSOR?!
BECAUSE! THE ONLY PERSON WHO CAN MAKE TEA AND SERVE IT TO THE CUSTOMERS...
...IS THE PROPRIETRESS!
That means...

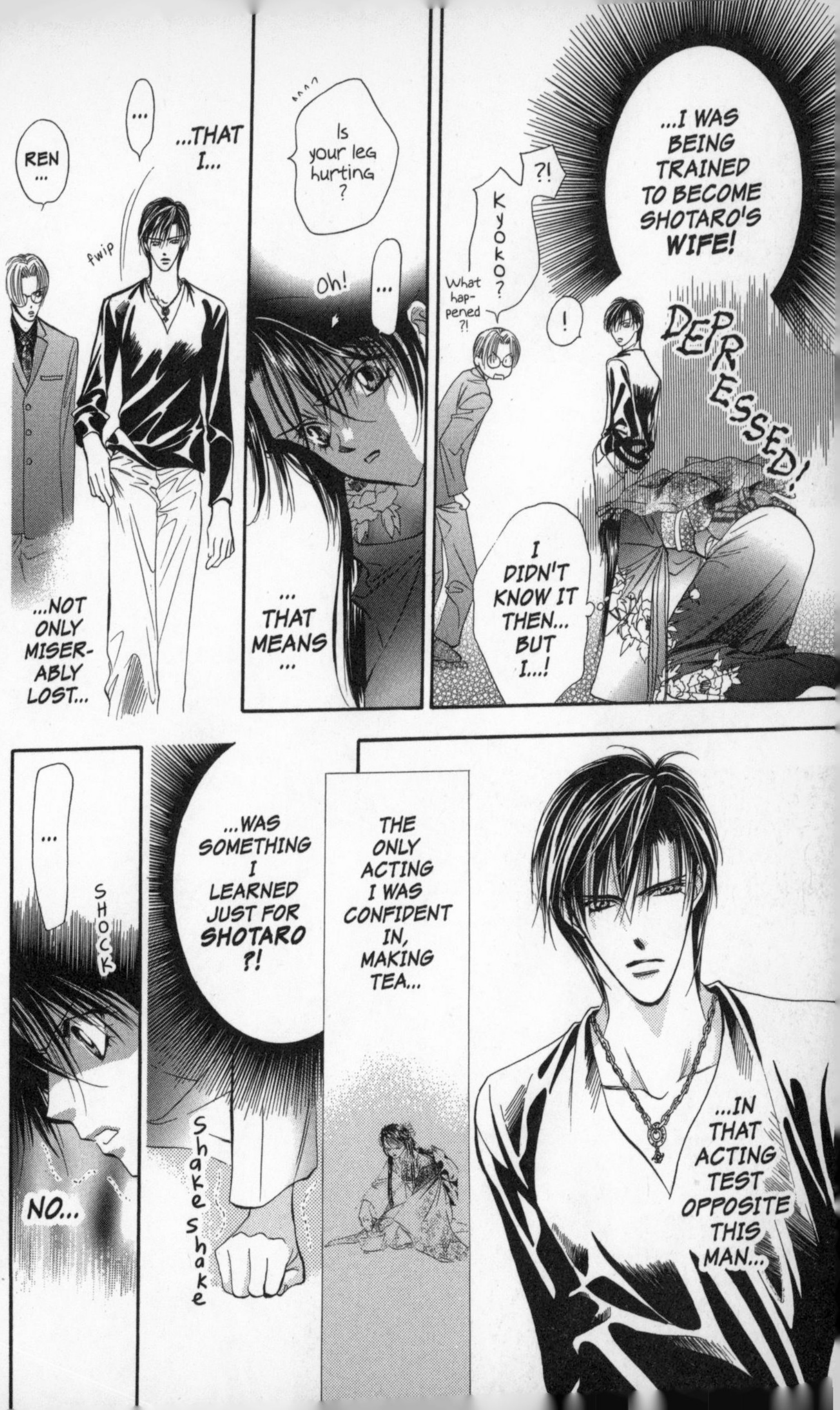
...I WAS BEING TRAINED TO BECOME SHOTARO'S WIFE!
DEPRESSED!
?!
KYOKO?
What happened ?!
!
I DIDN'T KNOW IT THEN... BUT I...!
Is your leg hurting ?
Oh!
...
...THAT MEANS...
...THAT I...
...
REN...
fwip
...NOT ONLY MISERABLY LOST...
...IN THAT ACTING TEST OPPOSITE THIS MAN...
THE ONLY ACTING I WAS CONFIDENT IN, MAKING TEA...
...WAS SOMETHING I LEARNED JUST FOR SHOTARO ?!
Shake shake
...
SHOCK
NO...

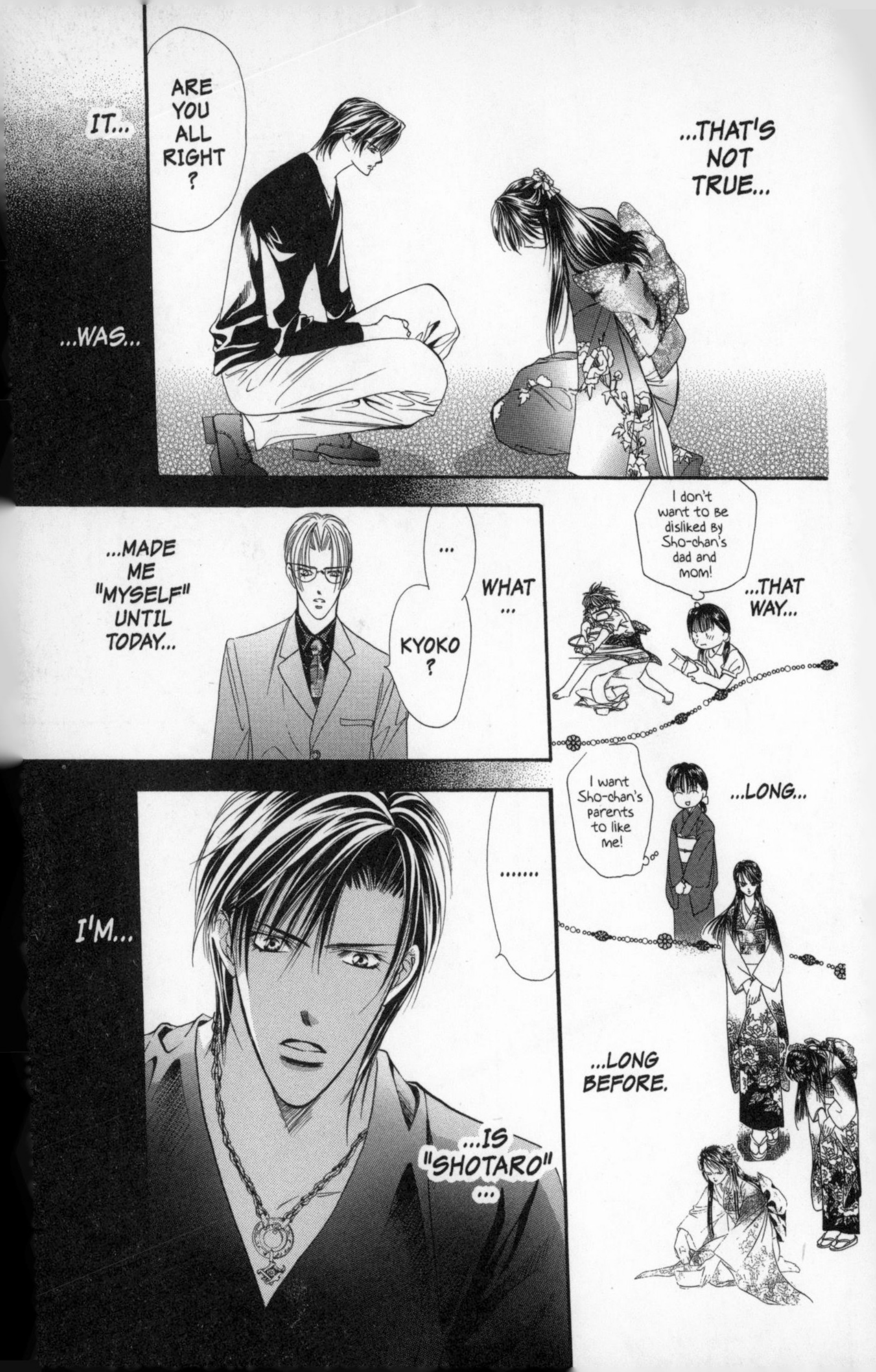
...THAT'S NOT TRUE...
ARE YOU ALL RIGHT?
IT...
...WAS...
I don't want to be disliked by Sho-chan's dad and mom!
...THAT WAY...
I want Sho-chan's parents to like me!
...LONG...
...LONG BEFORE.
...
WHAT... KYOKO?
...MADE ME "MYSELF" UNTIL TODAY...
....
I'M...
...IS "SHOTARO"...

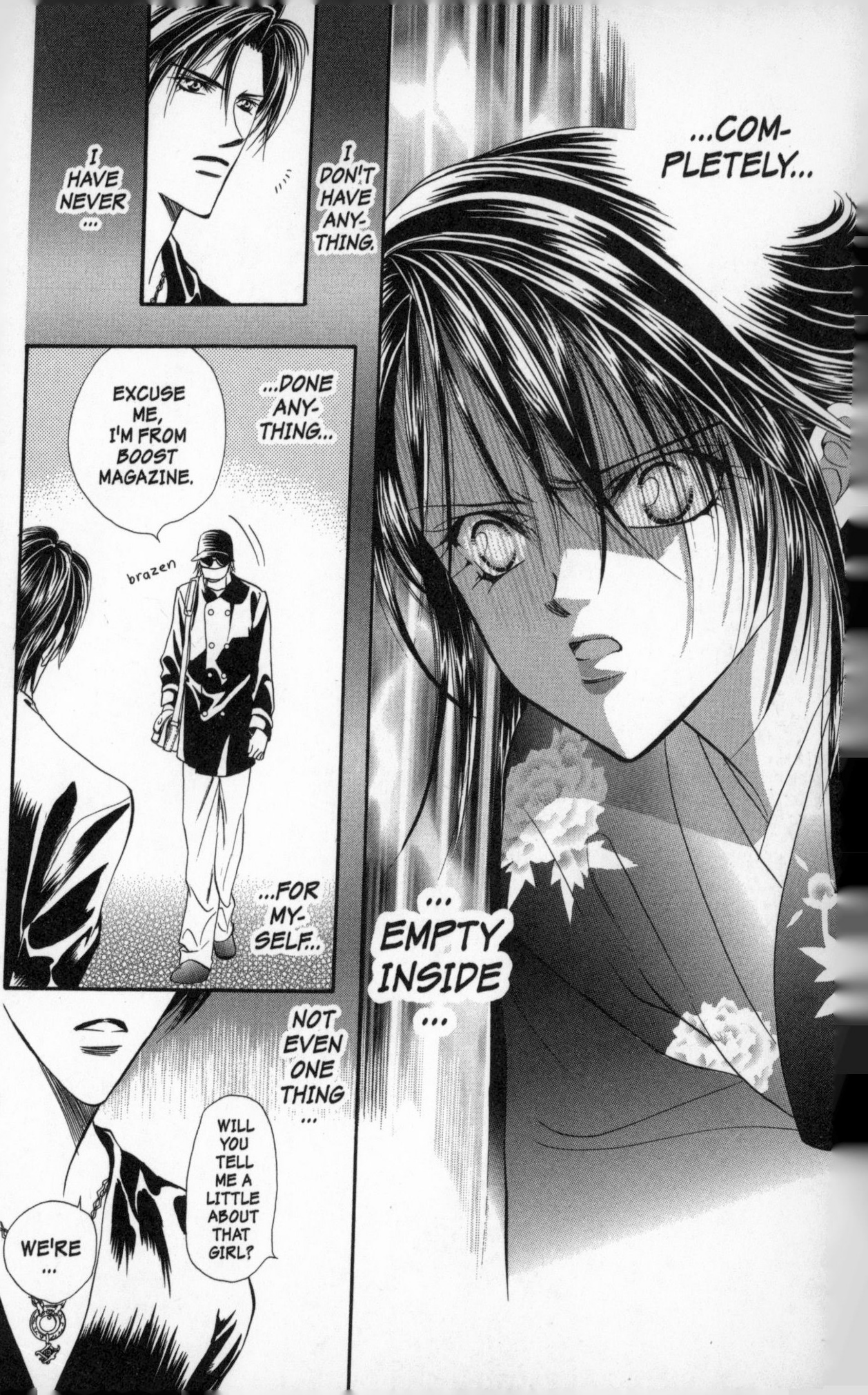
...COMPLETELY...
...EMPTY INSIDE...
I DON'T HAVE ANYTHING.
I HAVE NEVER...
...DONE ANYTHING...
EXCUSE ME, I'M FROM BOOST MAGAZINE.
brazen
...FOR MYSELF...
NOT EVEN ONE THING...
WILL YOU TELL ME A LITTLE ABOUT THAT GIRL?
WE'RE...

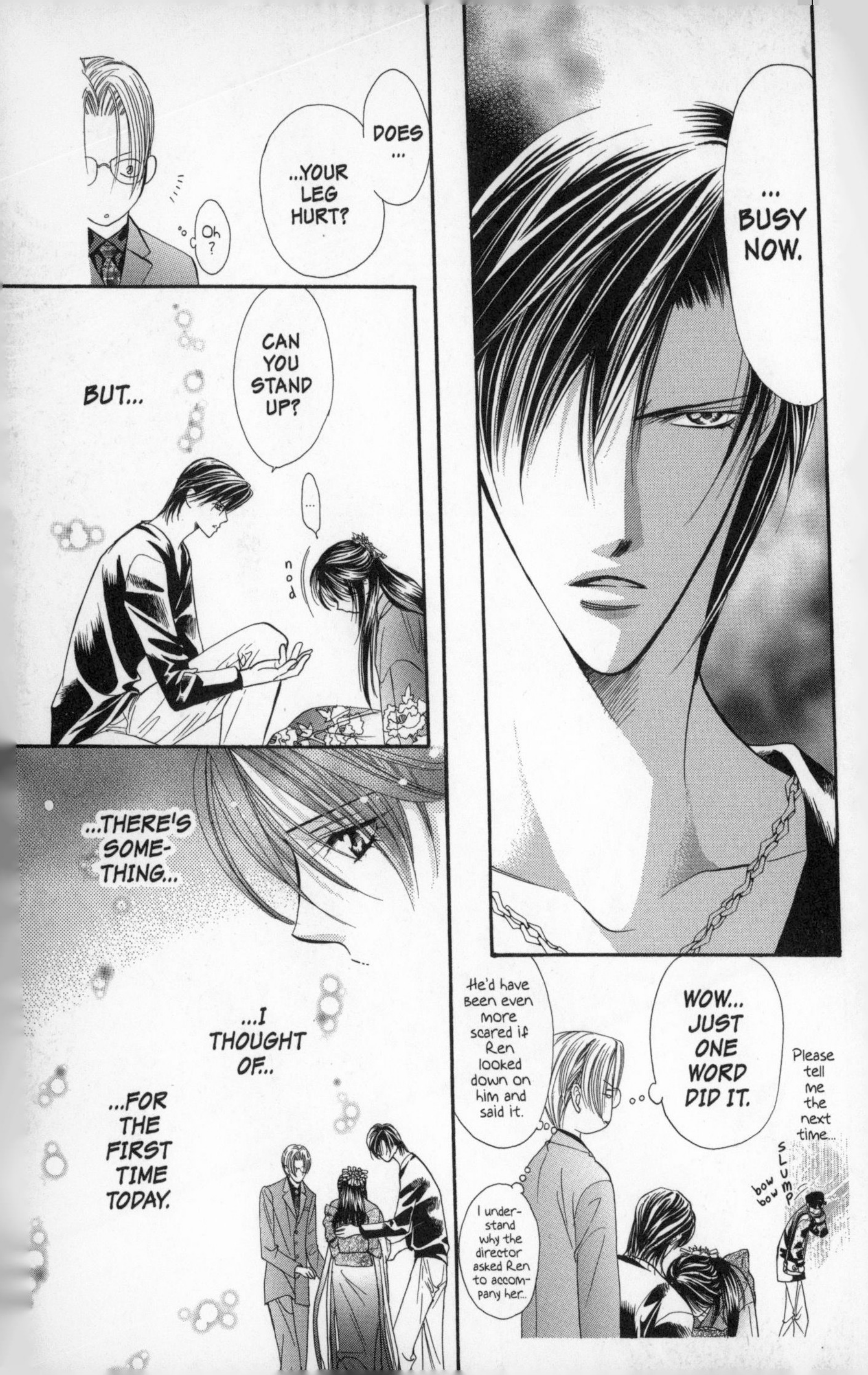
... BUSY NOW.
Please tell me the next time...
SLUMP
bow bow
WOW... JUST ONE WORD DID IT.
He'd have been even more scared if Ren looked down on him and said it.
I under-stand why the director asked Ren to accom-pany her...
DOES ...
...YOUR LEG HURT?
Oh ?
CAN YOU STAND UP?
BUT...
...
nod
...THERE'S SOME-THING...
...I THOUGHT OF...
...FOR THE FIRST TIME TODAY.

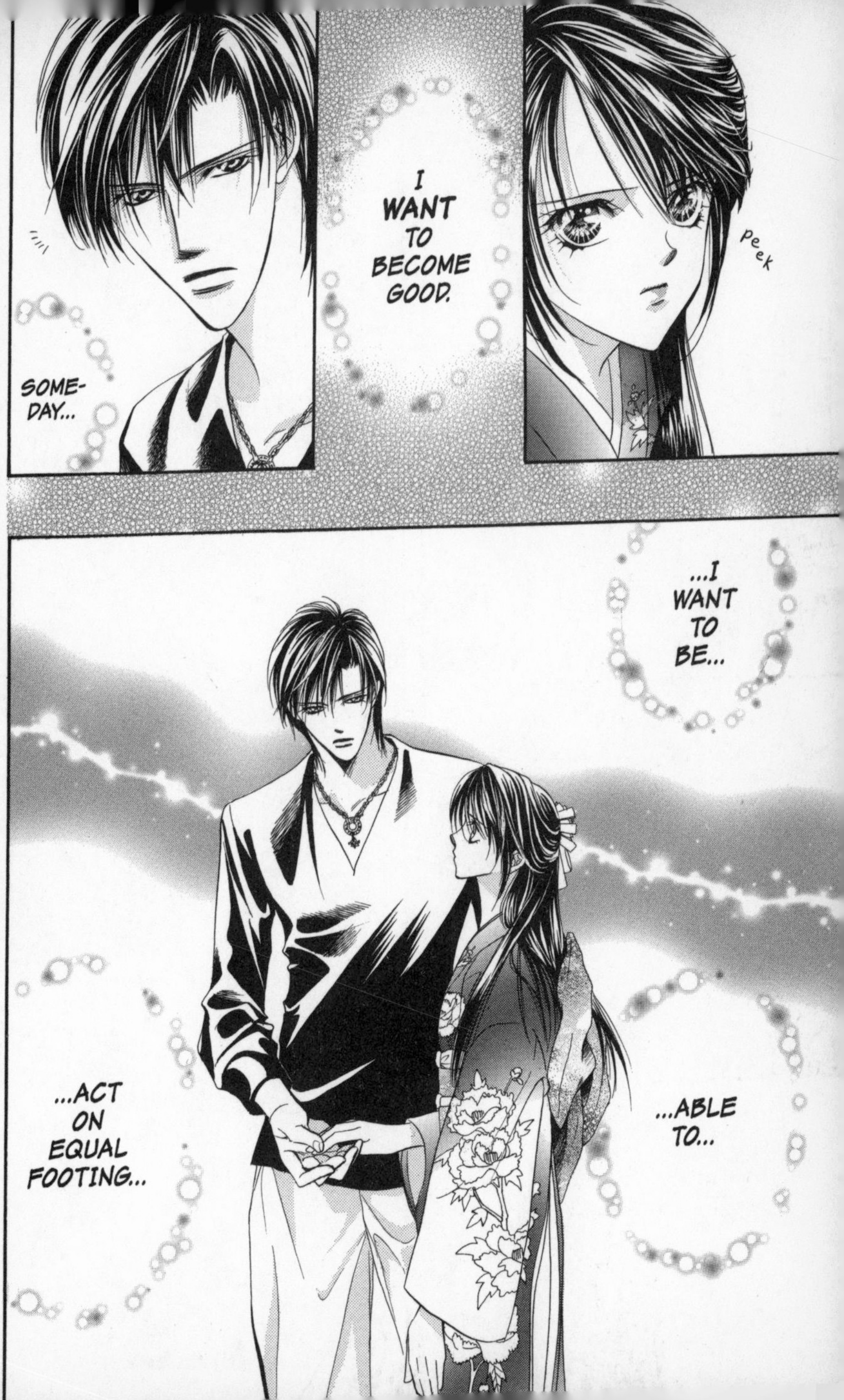
peek
I WANT TO BECOME GOOD.
SOME-DAY...
...I WANT TO BE...
...ABLE TO...
...ACT ON EQUAL FOOTING...

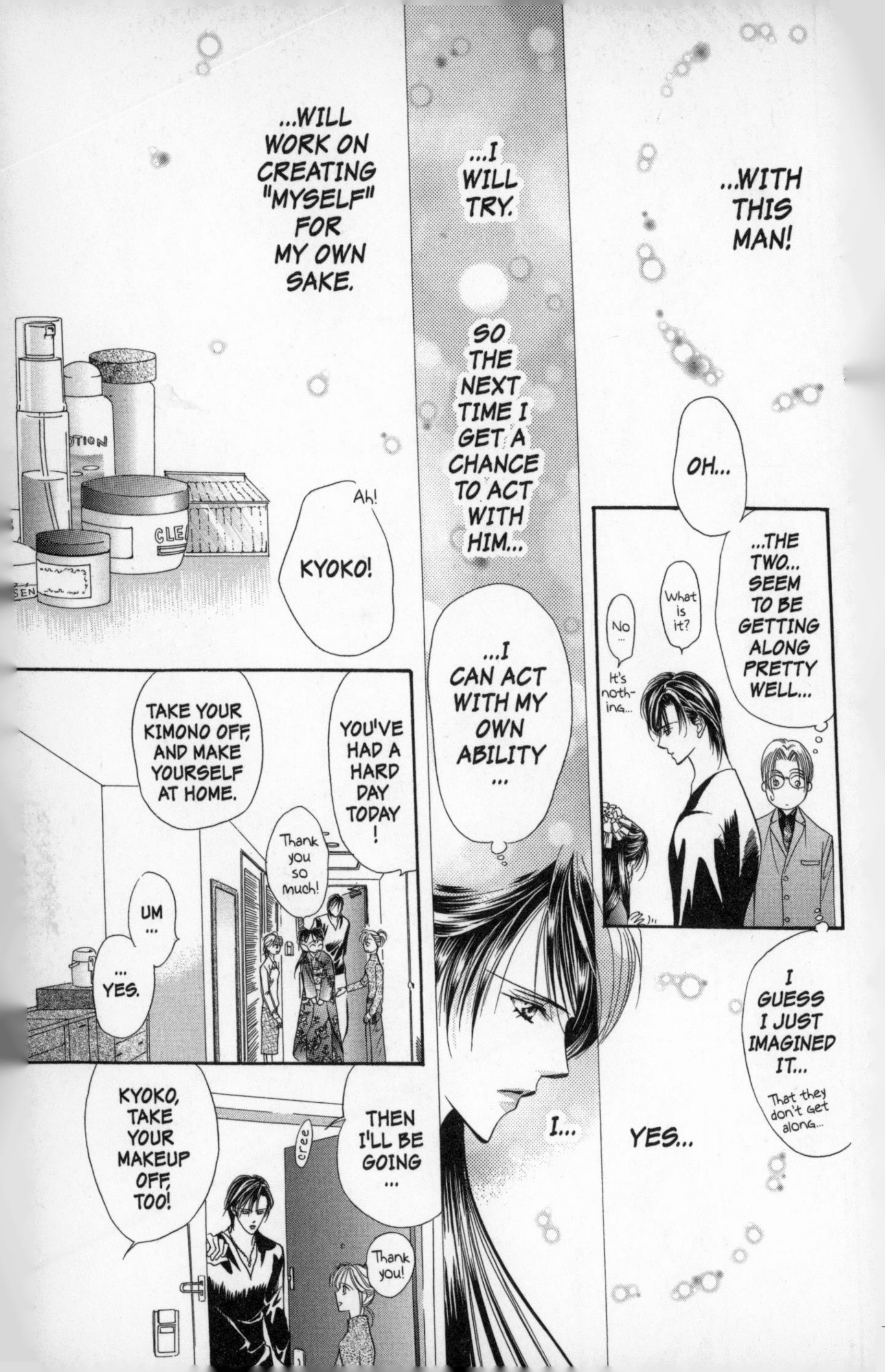
...WITH THIS MAN!
OH...
...THE TWO... SEEM TO BE GETTING ALONG PRETTY WELL...
What is it?
No... It's nothing...
I GUESS I JUST IMAGINED IT...
That they don't get along...
YES...
...I WILL TRY.
SO THE NEXT TIME I GET A CHANCE TO ACT WITH HIM...
...I CAN ACT WITH MY OWN ABILITY...
I...
...WILL WORK ON CREATING "MYSELF" FOR MY OWN SAKE.
Ah!
KYOKO!
YOU'VE HAD A HARD DAY TODAY!
TAKE YOUR KIMONO OFF, AND MAKE YOURSELF AT HOME.
Thank you so much!
UM...
...YES.
THEN I'LL BE GOING...
cree
KYOKO, TAKE YOUR MAKEUP OFF, TOO!
Thank you!

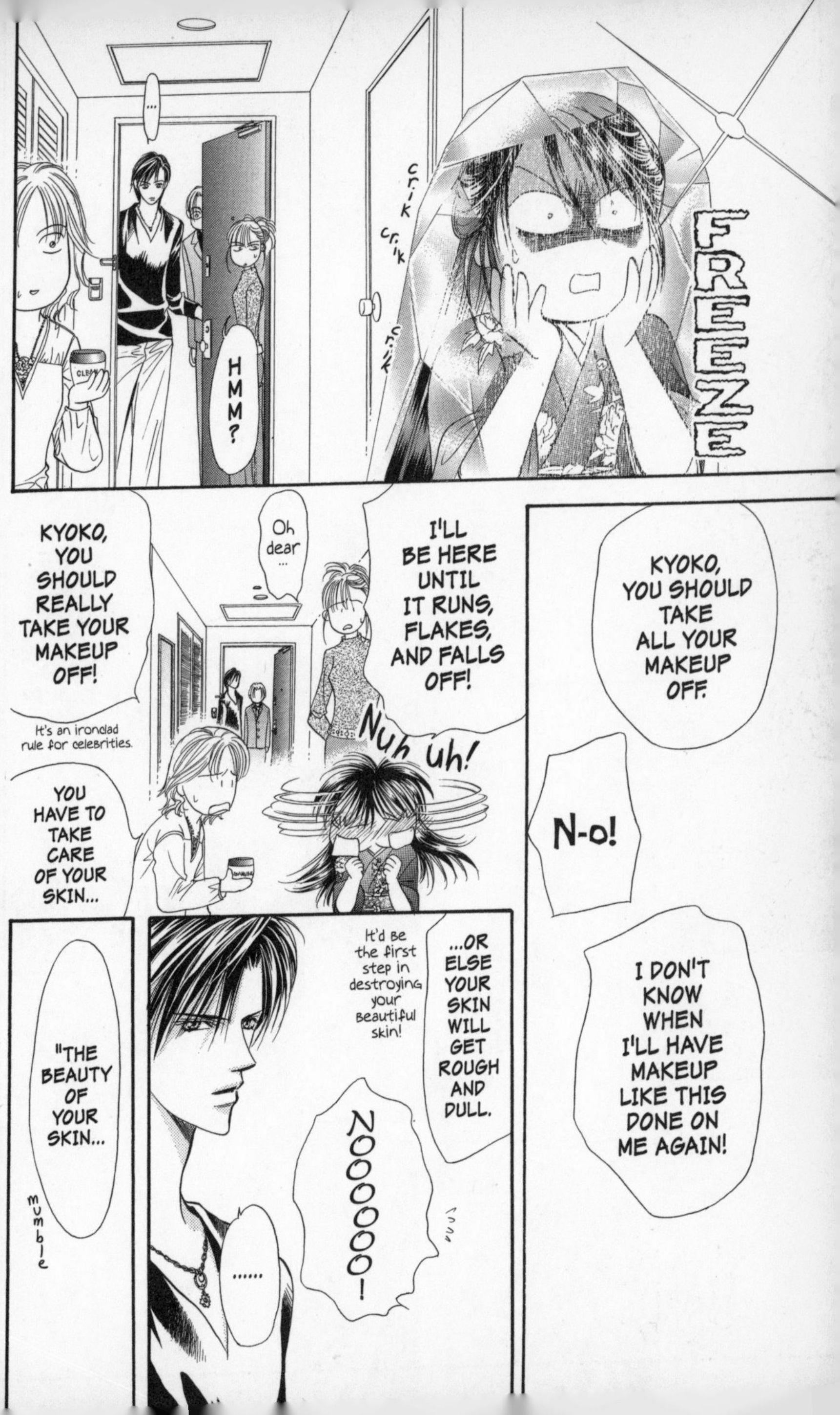

crik
crik
crik
FREEZE
...
HMM?
KYOKO, YOU SHOULD TAKE ALL YOUR MAKEUP OFF.
N-o!
I DON'T KNOW WHEN I'LL HAVE MAKEUP LIKE THIS DONE ON ME AGAIN!
I'LL BE HERE UNTIL IT RUNS, FLAKES, AND FALLS OFF!
Oh dear...
KYOKO, YOU SHOULD REALLY TAKE YOUR MAKEUP OFF!
It's an ironclad rule for celebrities.
Nuh uh!
YOU HAVE TO TAKE CARE OF YOUR SKIN...
...OR ELSE YOUR SKIN WILL GET ROUGH AND DULL.
It'd be the first step in destroying your beautiful skin!
NOOOOOO!
......
"THE BEAUTY OF YOUR SKIN...
mumble

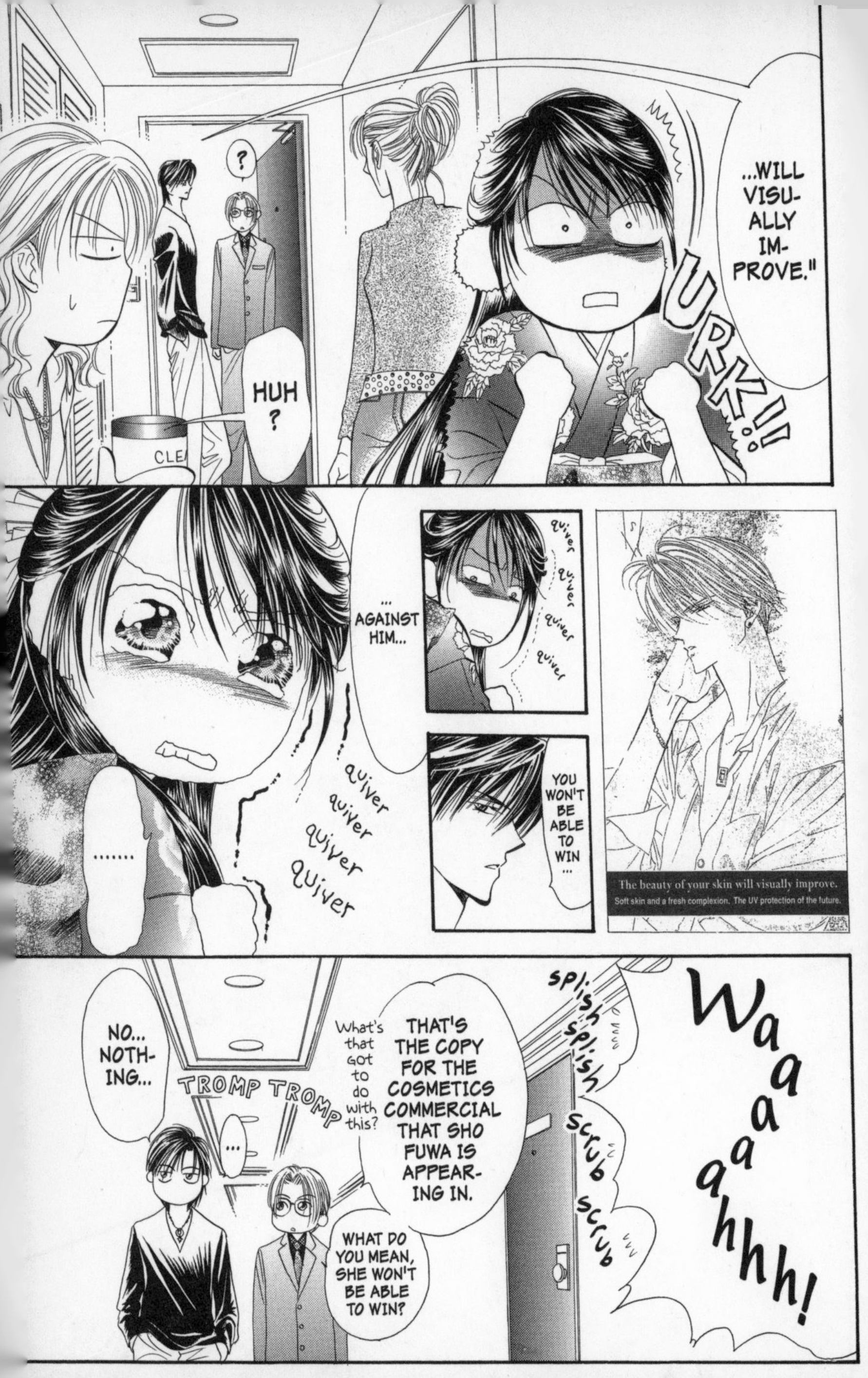
...WILL VISUALLY IMPROVE."
URK!!
?
HUH?
CLE
The beauty of your skin will visually improve.
Soft skin and a fresh complexion. The UV protection of the future.
quiver quiver quiver quiver
YOU WON'T BE ABLE TO WIN...
...AGAINST HIM...
quiver quiver quiver quiver
....
Waaaaaahhhh!
splish splish splish scrub scrub
THAT'S THE COPY FOR THE COSMETICS COMMERCIAL THAT SHO FUWA IS APPEARING IN.
What's that got to do with this?
NO... NOTHING...
TROMP TROMP
...
WHAT DO YOU MEAN, SHE WON'T BE ABLE TO WIN?

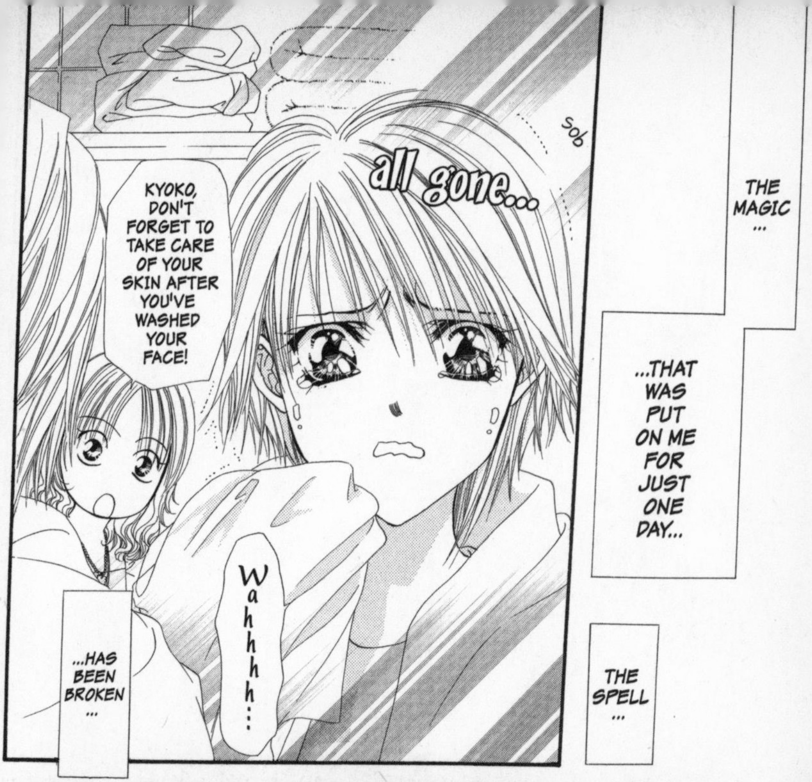
THE MAGIC ...
...THAT WAS PUT ON ME FOR JUST ONE DAY...
sob
all gone...
THE SPELL ...
KYOKO, DON'T FORGET TO TAKE CARE OF YOUR SKIN AFTER YOU'VE WASHED YOUR FACE!
Wahhhh...
...HAS BEEN BROKEN ...
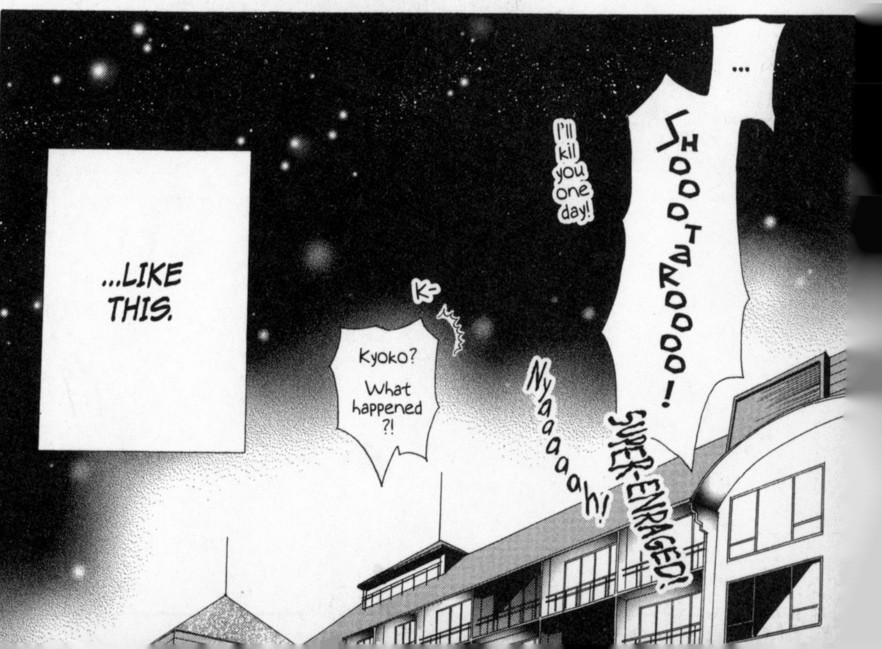
...
SHOOOTAROOOO!
I'll kil you one day!
SUPER-ENRAGED!
Nyaaaaah!
K-
Kyoko? What happened?!
...LIKE THIS.

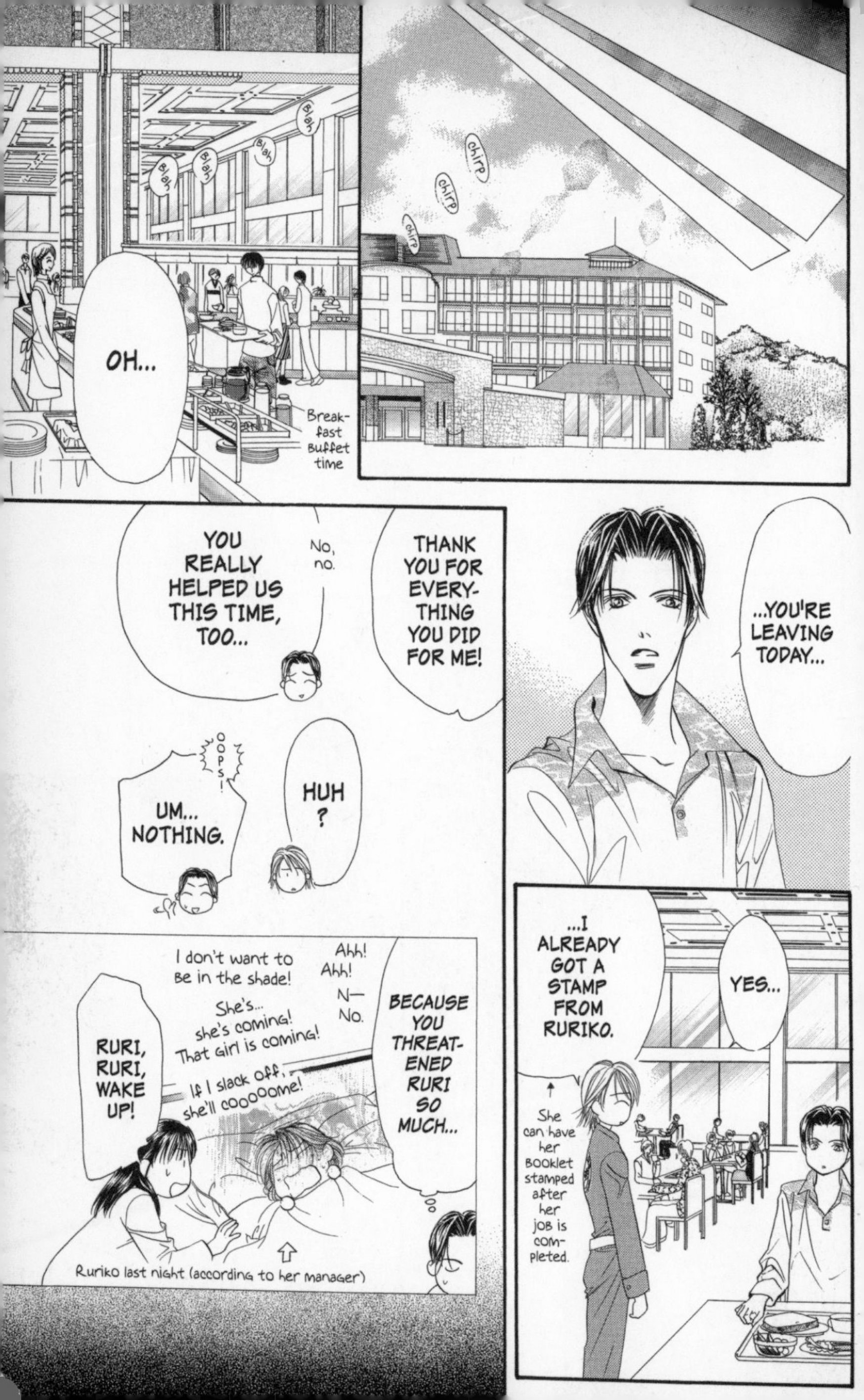
chirp
chirp
chirp
Blah
Blah
Blah
Blah
OH...
Break-fast Buffet time
...YOU'RE LEAVING TODAY...
YES...
...I ALREADY GOT A STAMP FROM RURIKO.
She can have her booklet stamped after her job is completed.
THANK YOU FOR EVERY-THING YOU DID FOR ME!
No, no.
YOU REALLY HELPED US THIS TIME, TOO...
HUH?
OOPS!
UM... NOTHING.
BECAUSE YOU THREAT-ENED RURI SO MUCH...
Ahh! Ahh! N— No.
I don't want to be in the shade!
She's... she's coming! That girl is coming!
If I slack off, she'll coooome!
RURI, RURI, WAKE UP!
Ruriko last night (according to her manager)

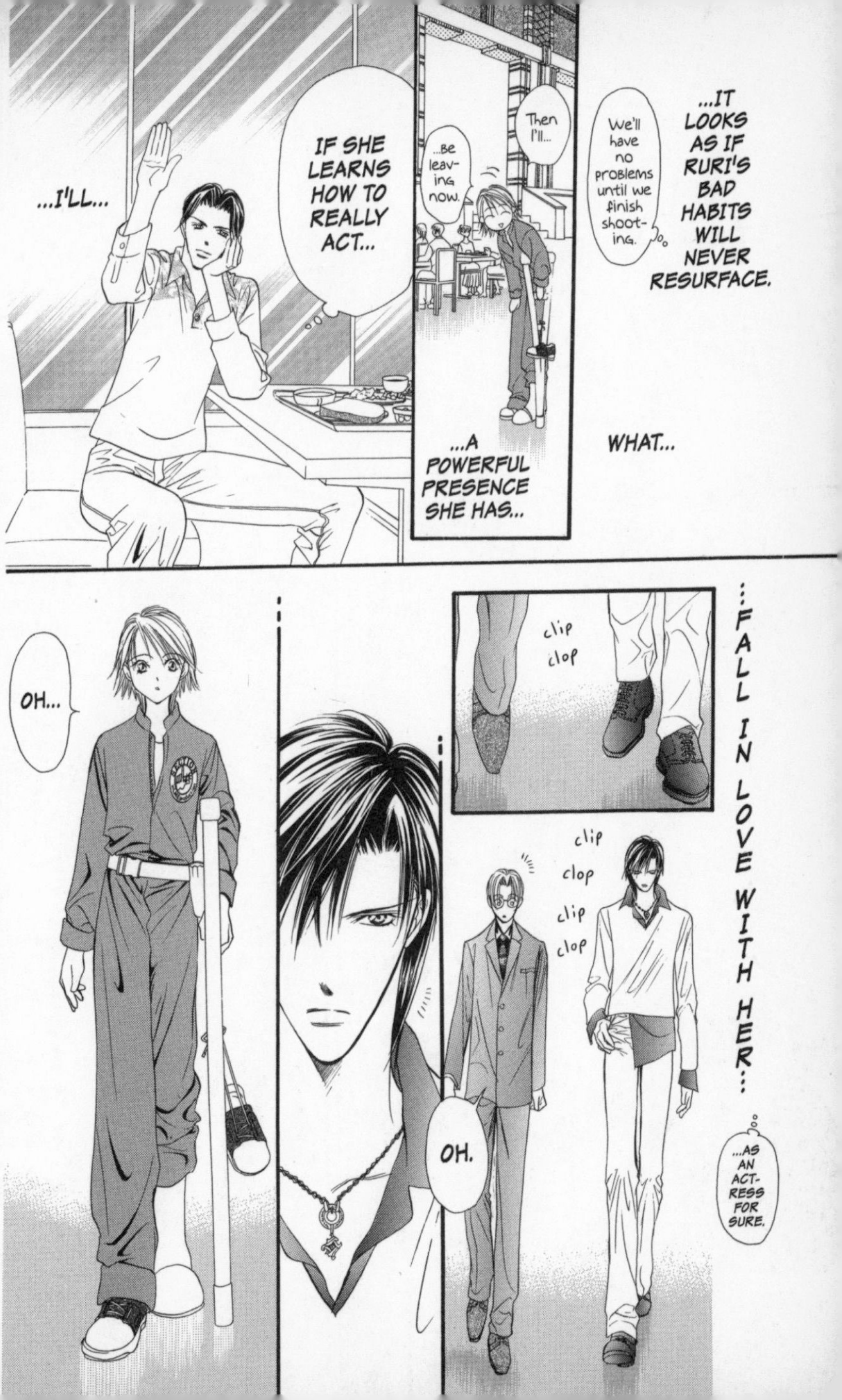
...IT LOOKS AS IF RURI'S BAD HABITS WILL NEVER RESURFACE.
We'll have no problems until we finish shoot-ing.
Then I'll...
...Be leav-ing now.
WHAT...
...A POWERFUL PRESENCE SHE HAS...
IF SHE LEARNS HOW TO REALLY ACT...
...I'LL...
...FALL IN LOVE WITH HER...
clip
clop
clip
clop
clip
clop
...AS AN ACT-RESS FOR SURE.
OH.
OH...

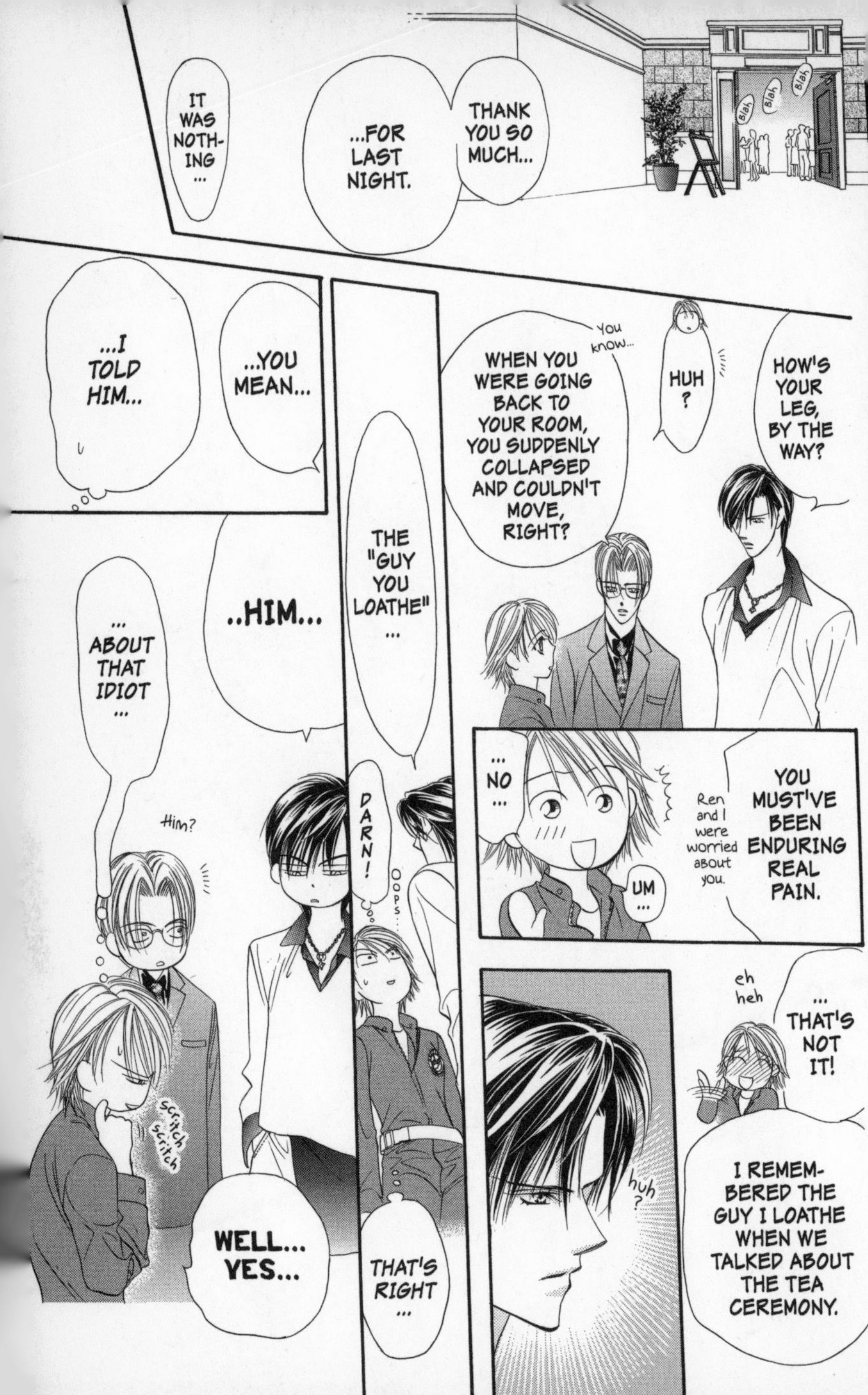
Blah
Blah
Blah
Blah
THANK YOU SO MUCH...
...FOR LAST NIGHT.
IT WAS NOTH-ING...
HOW'S YOUR LEG, BY THE WAY?
HUH?
You know...
WHEN YOU WERE GOING BACK TO YOUR ROOM, YOU SUDDENLY COLLAPSED AND COULDN'T MOVE, RIGHT?
YOU MUST'VE BEEN ENDURING REAL PAIN.
Ren and I were worried about you.
UM...
...NO...
...THAT'S NOT IT!
eh heh
I REMEM-BERED THE GUY I LOATHE WHEN WE TALKED ABOUT THE TEA CEREMONY.
huh?
THE "GUY YOU LOATHE"...
DARN!
Oops...
THAT'S RIGHT...
...YOU MEAN...
...I TOLD HIM...
..HIM...
...ABOUT THAT IDIOT...
Him?
scritch scritch
WELL... YES...

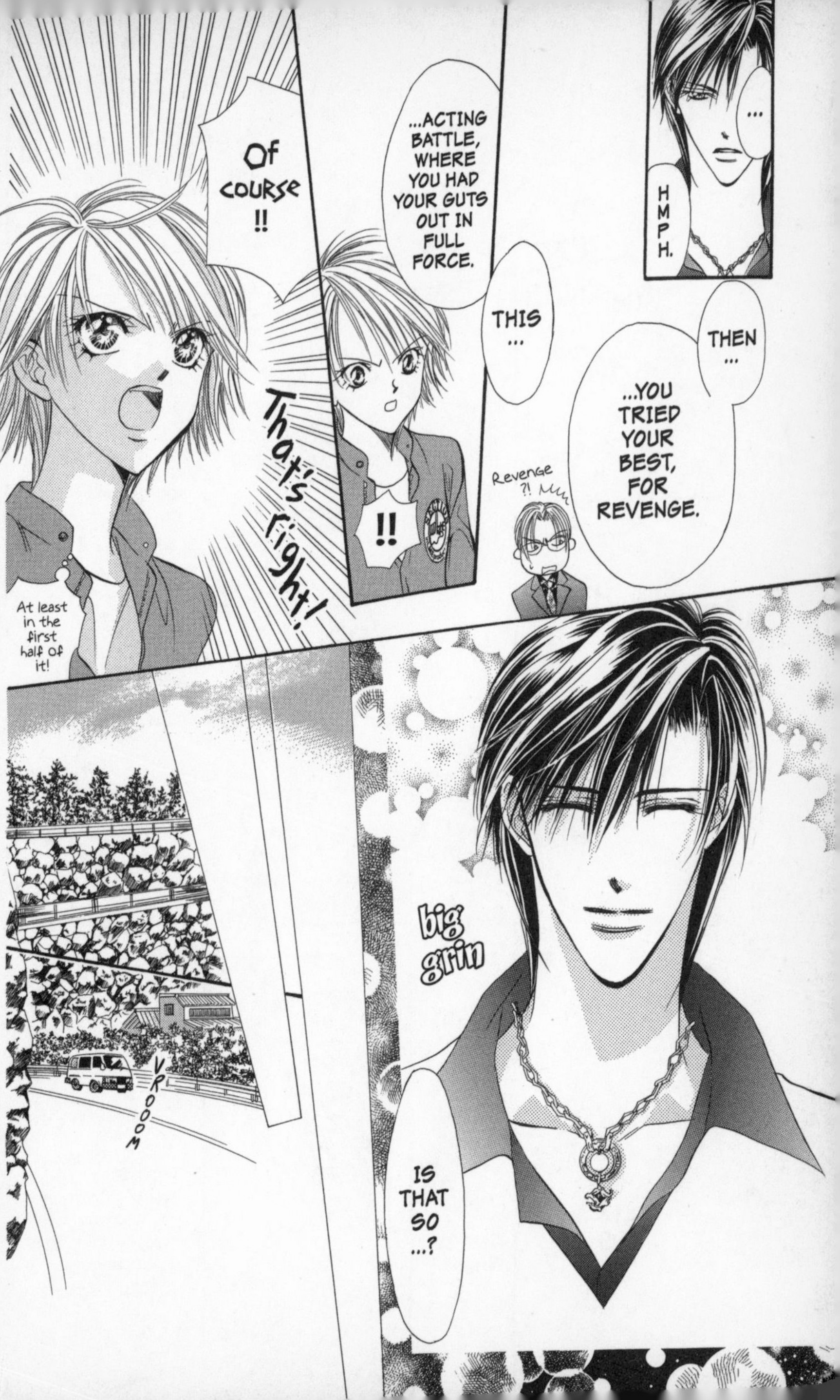
...
HMPH.
THEN ...
...YOU TRIED YOUR BEST, FOR REVENGE.
Revenge ?!
THIS ...
...ACTING BATTLE, WHERE YOU HAD YOUR GUTS OUT IN FULL FORCE.
!!
Of course !!
That's right!
At least in the first half of it!
big grin
IS THAT SO ...?
VROOOOM

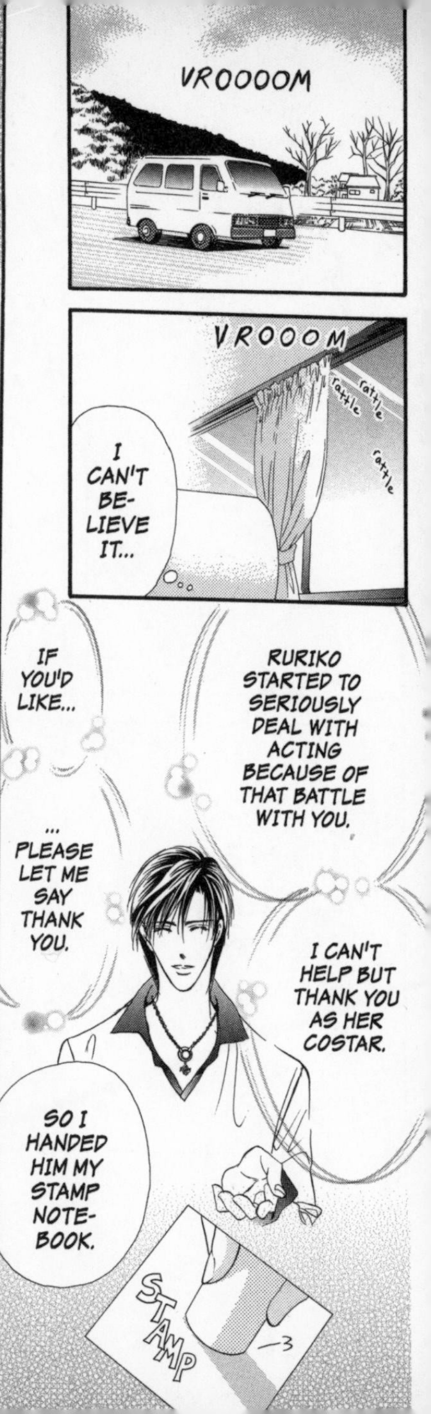
VROOOOM
VROOOM
rattle rattle
rattle
I CAN'T BE-LIEVE IT...
RURIKO STARTED TO SERIOUSLY DEAL WITH ACTING BECAUSE OF THAT BATTLE WITH YOU.
I CAN'T HELP BUT THANK YOU AS HER COSTAR.
IF YOU'D LIKE...
... PLEASE LET ME SAY THANK YOU.
SO I HANDED HIM MY STAMP NOTE-BOOK.
STAMP
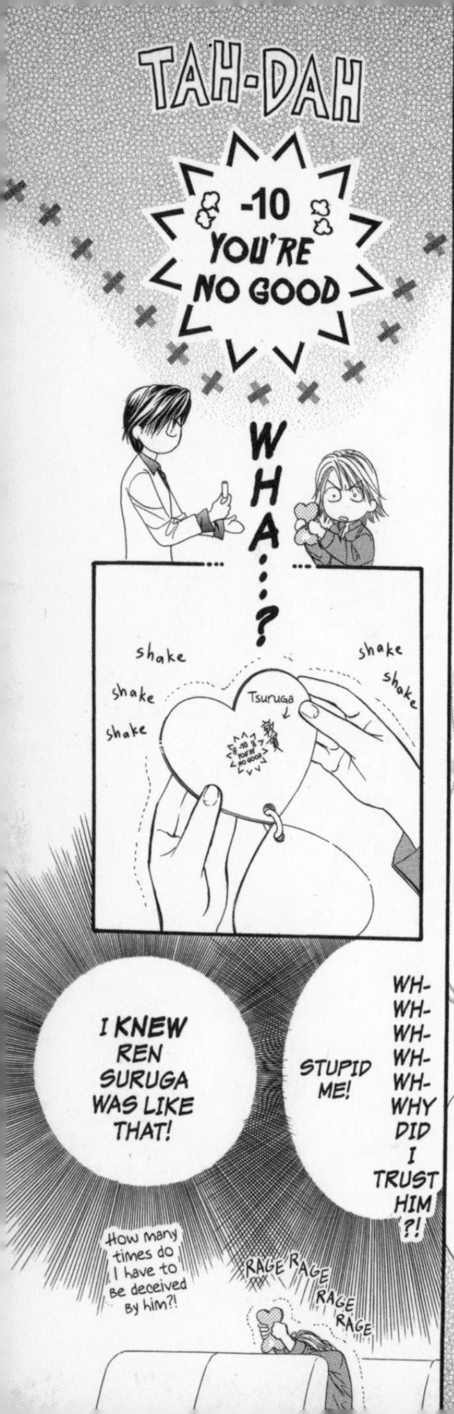
TAH-DAH
-10 YOU'RE NO GOOD
WHA...?
shake
shake
shake
shake
shake
Tsuruga
WH-WH-WH-WH-WH-WH-WHY DID I TRUST HIM?!
STUPID ME!
I KNEW REN SURUGA WAS LIKE THAT!
How many times do I have to be deceived by him?!
RAGE RAGE RAGE RAGE

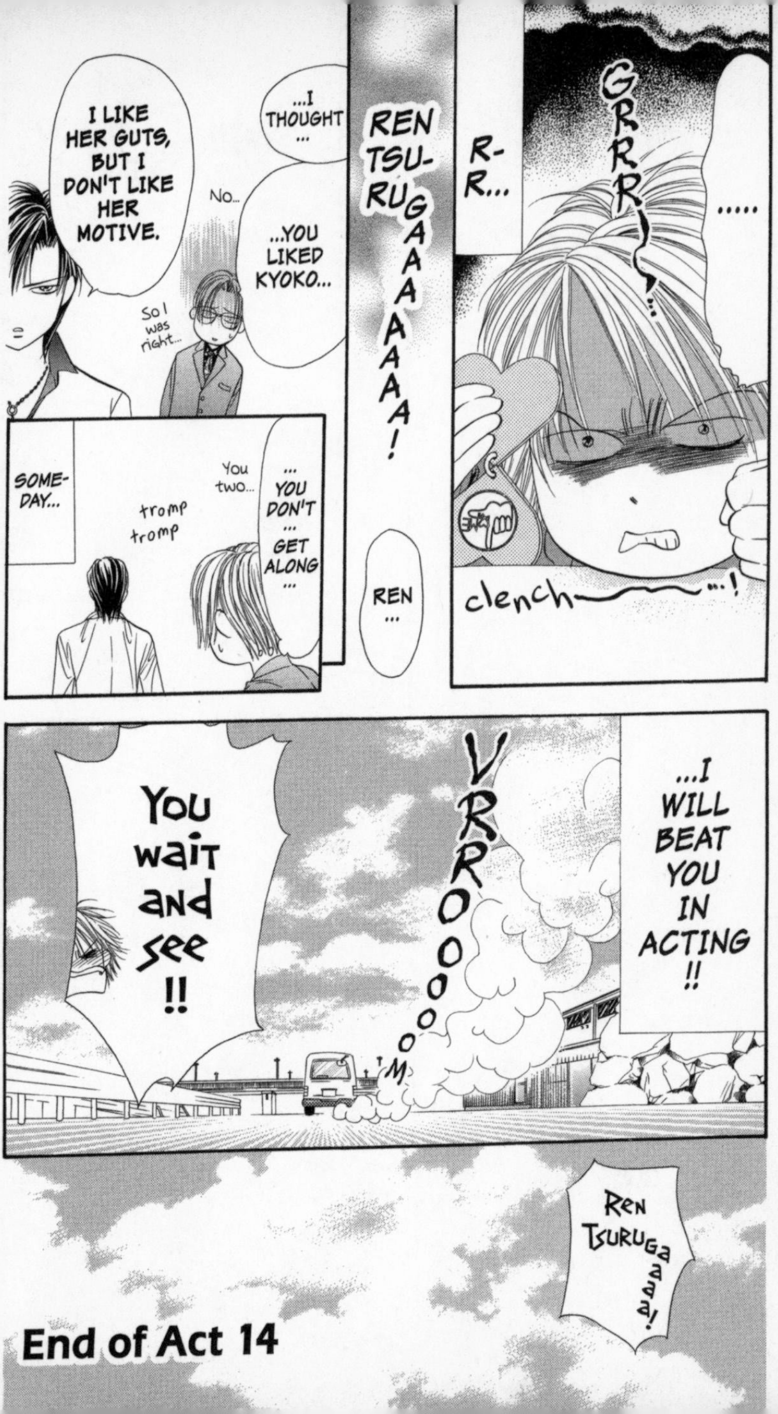
GRRR...
R-R...
.....
clench...!
REN TSURUGAAAAAAAAA!
REN...
...I THOUGHT...
...YOU LIKED KYOKO...
No...
I LIKE HER GUTS, BUT I DON'T LIKE HER MOTIVE.
So I was right...
...YOU DON'T ... GET ALONG ...
You two...
tromp tromp
SOMEDAY...
...I WILL BEAT YOU IN ACTING!!
VRROOOOOOOM
You wait and see!!
Ren Tsurugaaaa!

End of Act 14

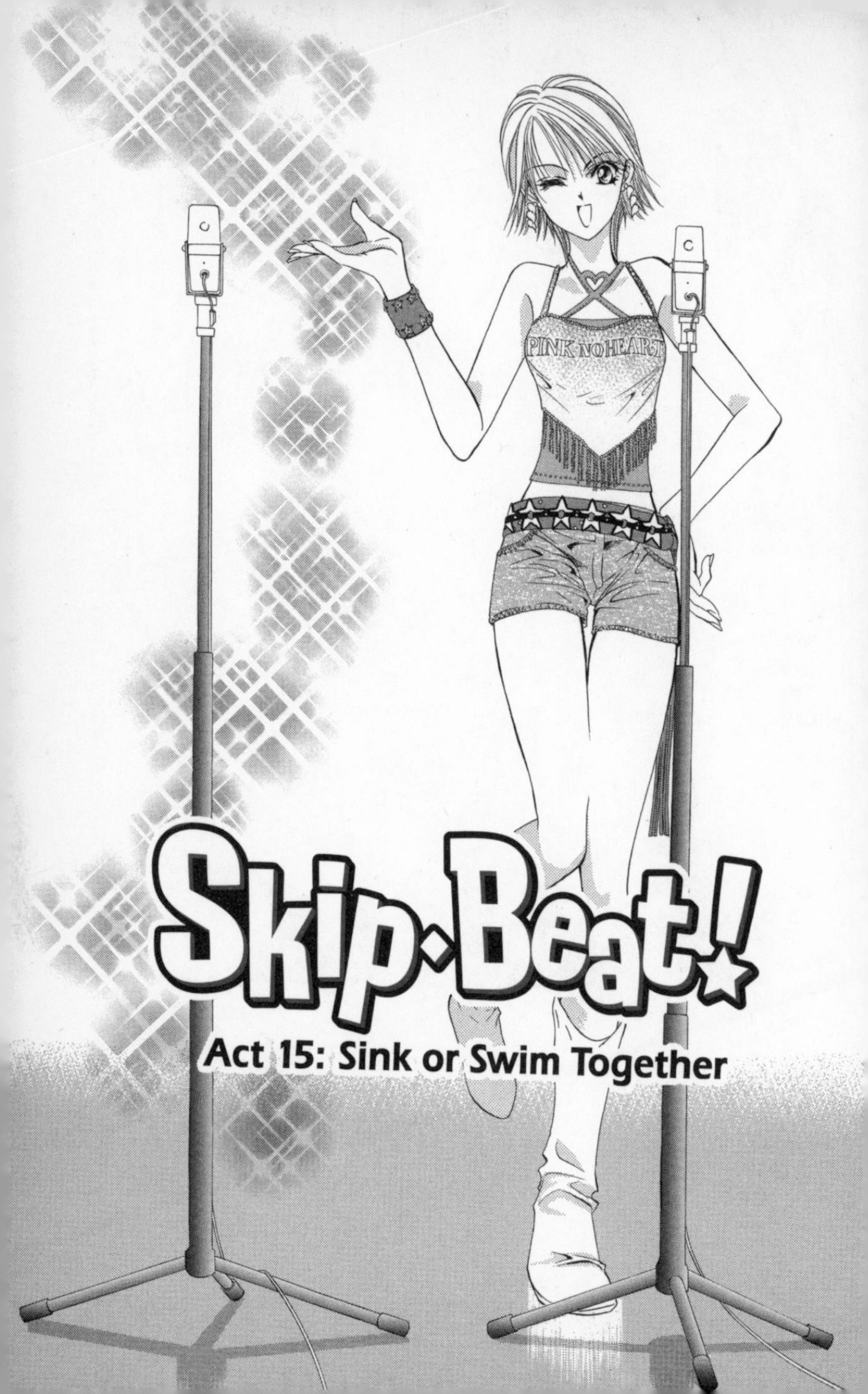
PINK NO HEART
Skip·Beat!
Act 15: Sink or Swim Together

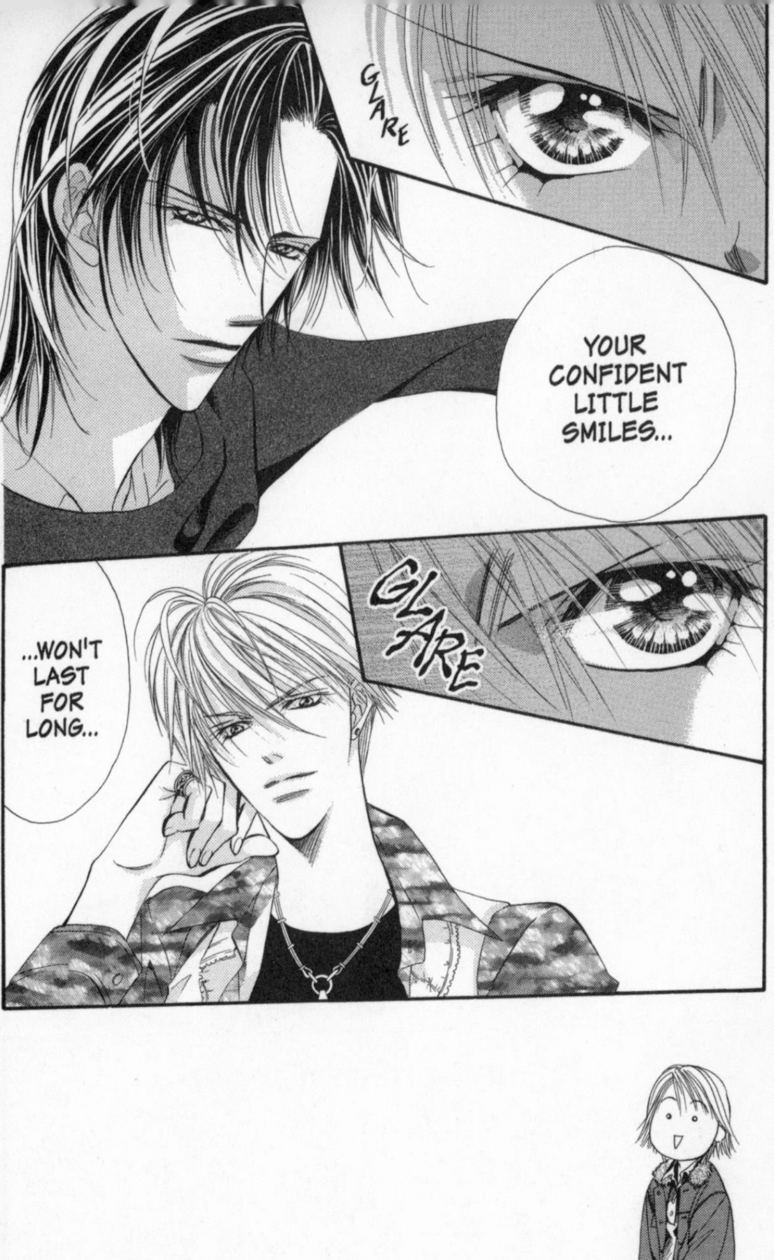
GLARE
YOUR CONFIDENT LITTLE SMILES...
GLARE
...WON'T LAST FOR LONG...

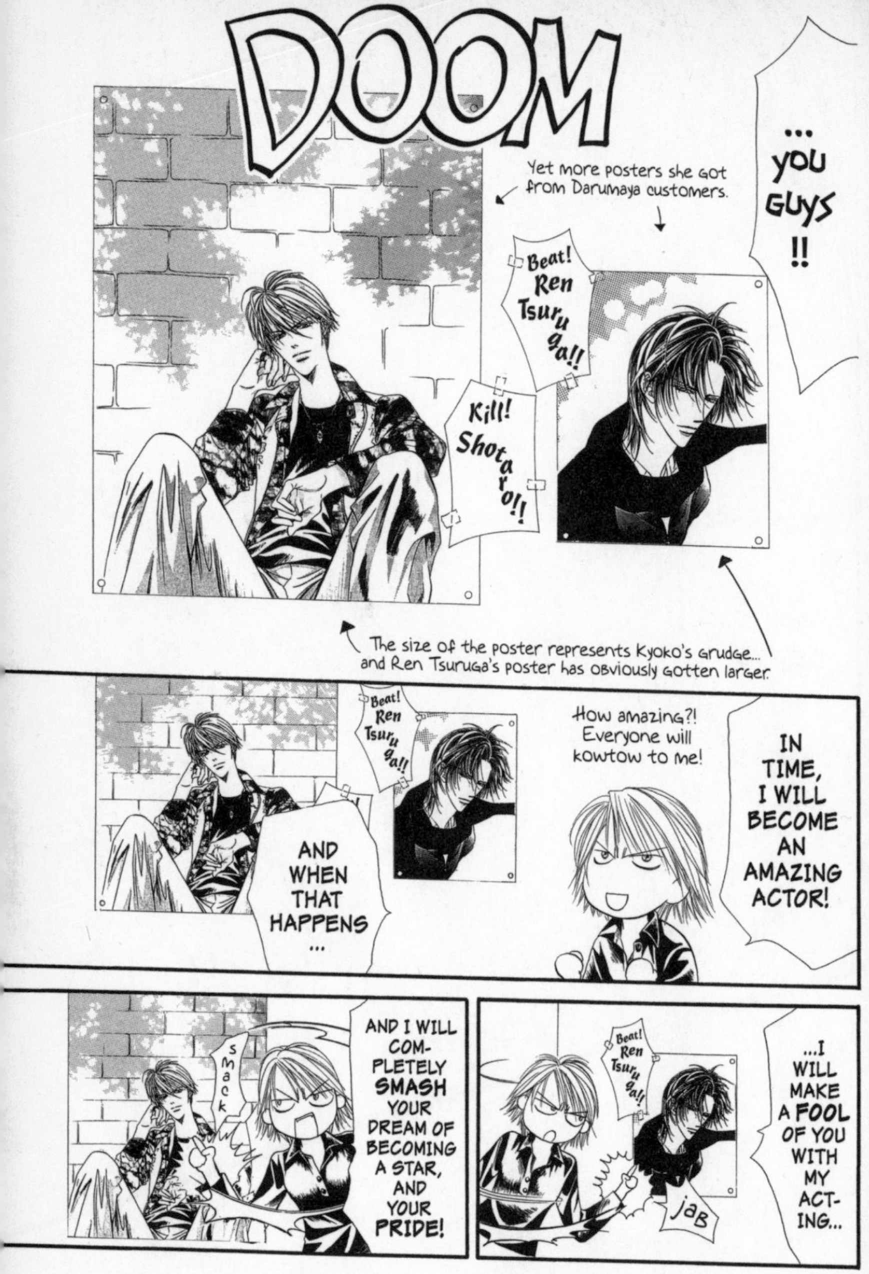
...YOU GUYS !!
DOOM
Yet more posters she got from Darumaya customers.
Beat! Ren Tsuruga!!
Kill! Shotaro!!
The size of the poster represents Kyoko's grudge... and Ren Tsuruga's poster has obviously gotten larger.
IN TIME, I WILL BECOME AN AMAZING ACTOR!
How amazing?! Everyone will kowtow to me!
Beat! Ren Tsuruga!!
AND WHEN THAT HAPPENS...
...I WILL MAKE A FOOL OF YOU WITH MY ACT-ING...
Beat! Ren Tsuruga!!
jab
AND I WILL COM-PLETELY SMASH YOUR DREAM OF BECOMING A STAR, AND YOUR PRIDE!
smack

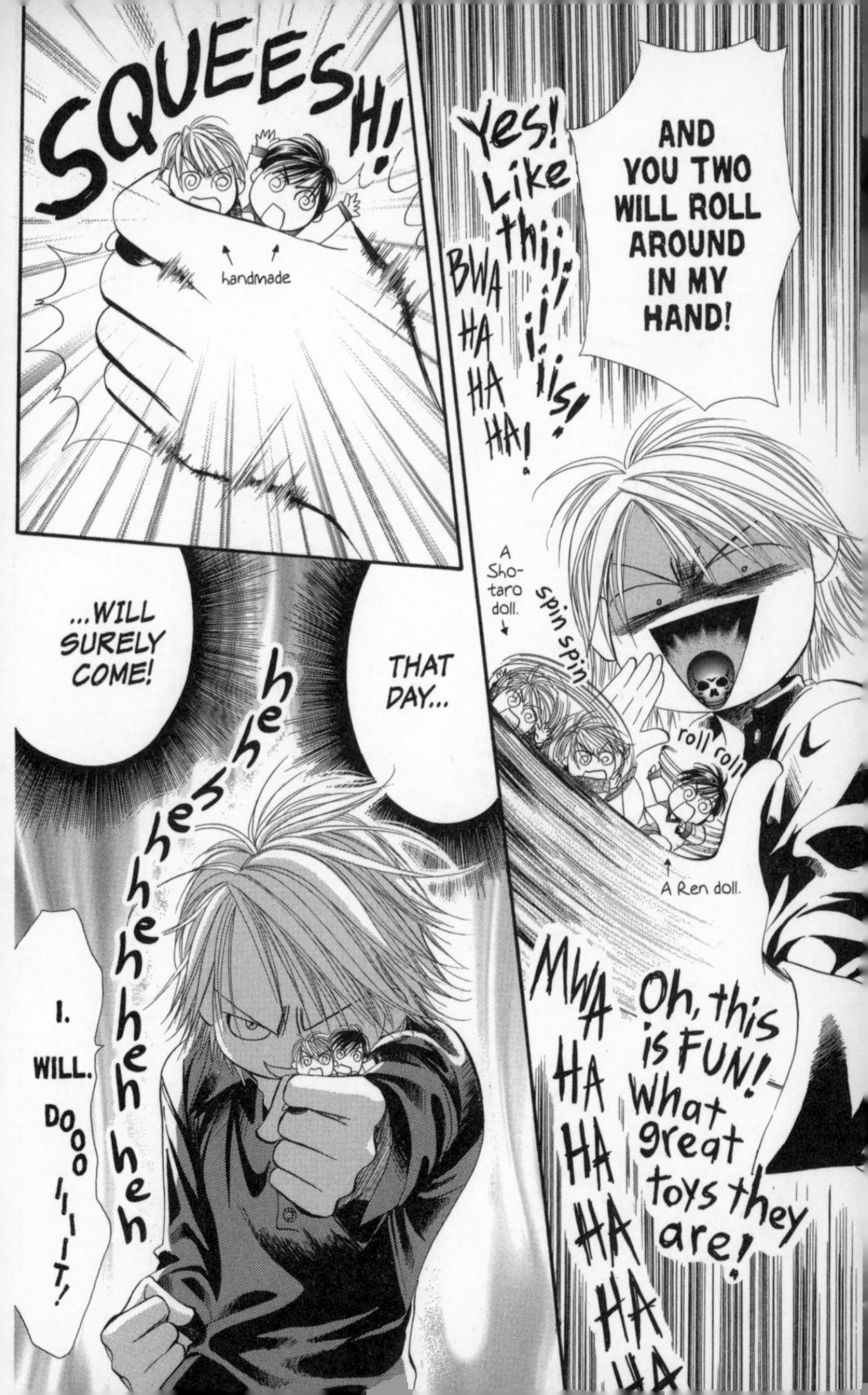
AND YOU TWO WILL ROLL AROUND IN MY HAND!
Yes! Like thiiiiiiis!
BWA HA HA HA HA!
A Sho-taro doll.
spin spin
roll roll
A Ren doll.
Oh, this is FUN! What great toys they are!
MWA HA HA HA HA HA HA
SQUEESH!
handmade
THAT DAY...
...WILL SURELY COME!
heh heh heh heh heh heh heh
I. WILL. DOOOIIIIT!

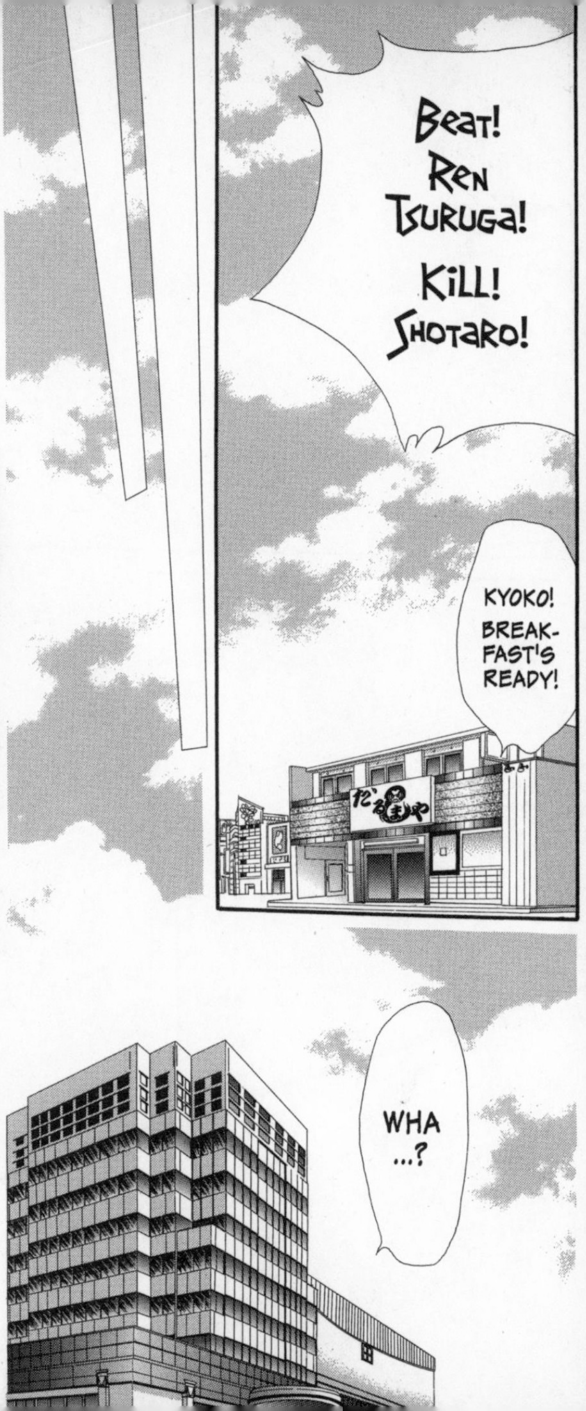
Beat! Ren Tsuruga!
Kill! Shotaro!
KYOKO! BREAK-FAST'S READY!
WHA ...?

Kanae Kotonami

Difficulty level

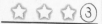

☆☆☆ ③

When Kanae appeared, she was close to Kyoko's age, but she looked more mature than Kyoko.

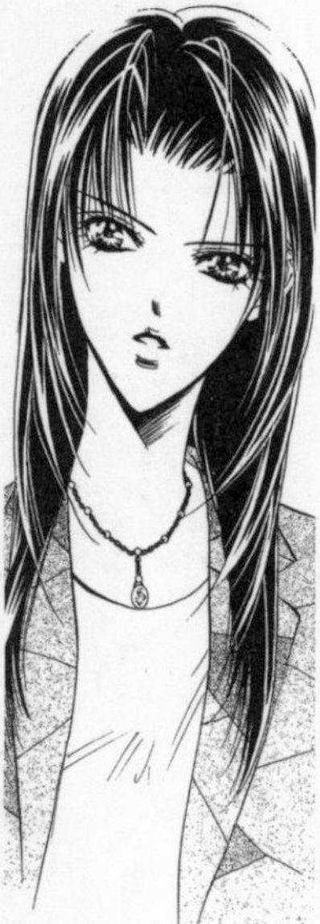

This should still be the case, but the more she appears, the more her face kinda looks younger. She's becoming the easiest girl to draw, and that's not good... When I draw Kanae, I should pay more attention to making her look **mature**... especially when she's with Kyoko. I've got to be careful from now on, too...

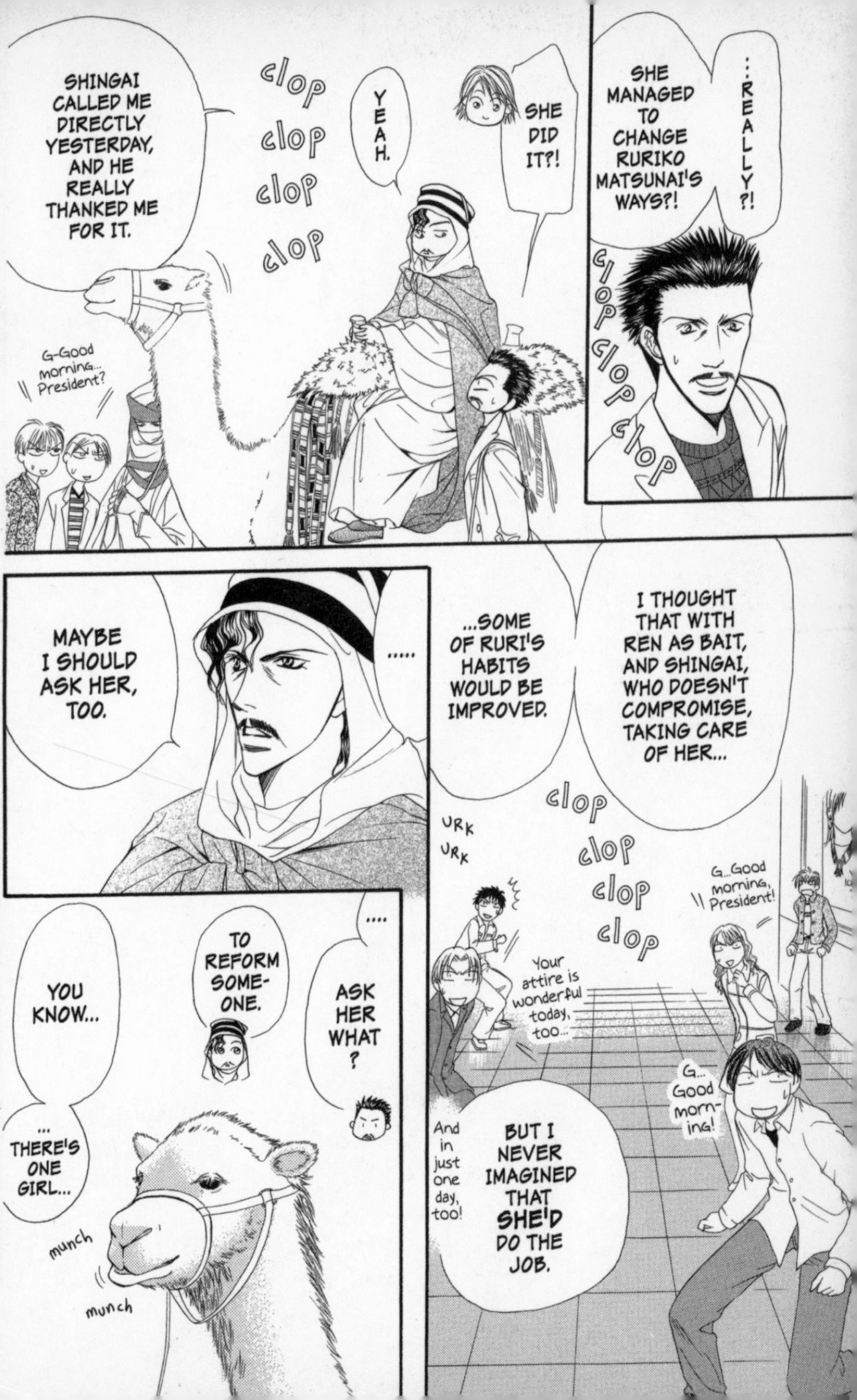
...REALLY?!
SHE MANAGED TO CHANGE RURIKO MATSUNAI'S WAYS?!
CLOP CLOP CLOP CLOP
SHE DID IT?!
YEAH.
clop clop clop clop
SHINGAI CALLED ME DIRECTLY YESTERDAY, AND HE REALLY THANKED ME FOR IT.
G-Good morning... President?
I THOUGHT THAT WITH REN AS BAIT, AND SHINGAI, WHO DOESN'T COMPROMISE, TAKING CARE OF HER...
...SOME OF RURI'S HABITS WOULD BE IMPROVED.
clop clop clop clop
G...Good morning, President!
URK URK
Your attire is wonderful today, too...
G... Good morn-ing!
BUT I NEVER IMAGINED THAT SHE'D DO THE JOB.
And in just one day, too!
.....
MAYBE I SHOULD ASK HER, TOO.
....
ASK HER WHAT?
TO REFORM SOME-ONE.
YOU KNOW...
... THERE'S ONE GIRL...
munch
munch

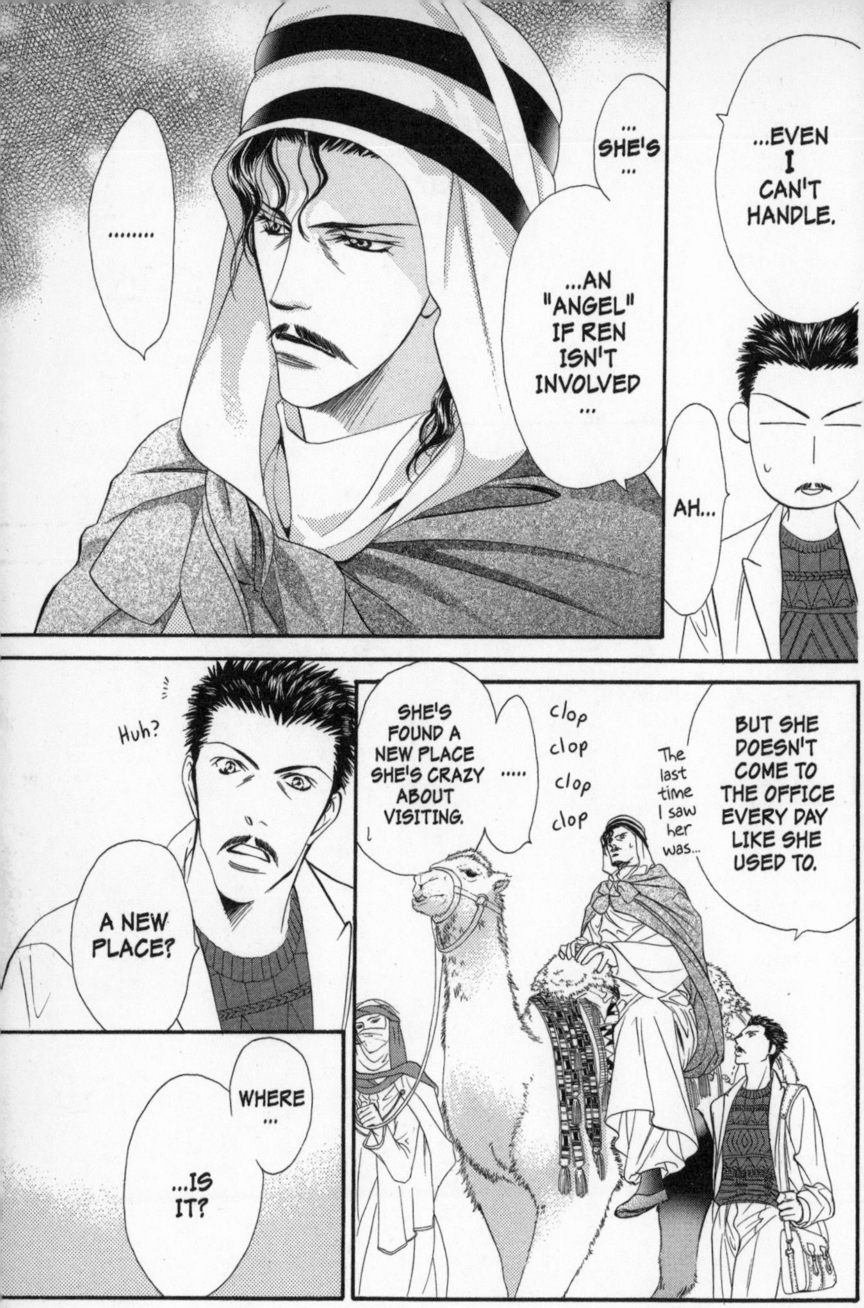

...EVEN I CAN'T HANDLE.
AH...
... SHE'S ...
...AN "ANGEL" IF REN ISN'T INVOLVED ...
....
BUT SHE DOESN'T COME TO THE OFFICE EVERY DAY LIKE SHE USED TO.
The last time I saw her was...
clop clop clop clop
SHE'S FOUND A NEW PLACE SHE'S CRAZY ABOUT VISITING.
.....
Huh?
A NEW PLACE?
WHERE ...
...IS IT?

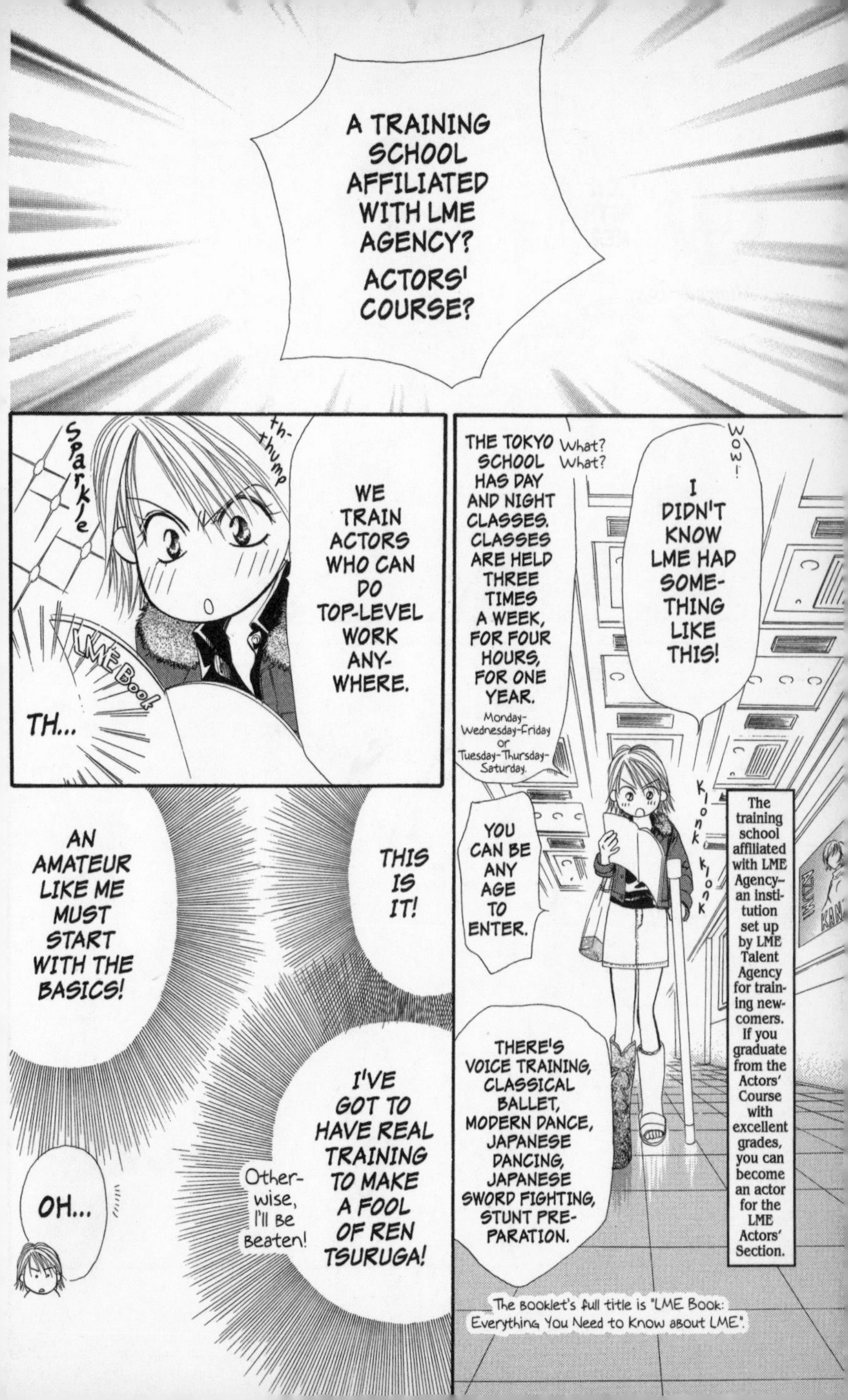
A TRAINING SCHOOL AFFILIATED WITH LME AGENCY? ACTORS' COURSE?
WOW!
I DIDN'T KNOW LME HAD SOME-THING LIKE THIS!
What? What?
THE TOKYO SCHOOL HAS DAY AND NIGHT CLASSES. CLASSES ARE HELD THREE TIMES A WEEK, FOR FOUR HOURS, FOR ONE YEAR.
Monday-Wednesday-Friday or Tuesday-Thursday-Saturday.
The training school affiliated with LME Agency—an institution set up by LME Talent Agency for training newcomers. If you graduate from the Actors' Course with excellent grades, you can become an actor for the LME Actors' Section.
Klonk klonk
YOU CAN BE ANY AGE TO ENTER.
THERE'S VOICE TRAINING, CLASSICAL BALLET, MODERN DANCE, JAPANESE DANCING, JAPANESE SWORD FIGHTING, STUNT PRE-PARATION.
The booklet's full title is "LME Book: Everything You Need to Know about LME".
th-thump
WE TRAIN ACTORS WHO CAN DO TOP-LEVEL WORK ANY-WHERE.
Sparkle
LME Book
TH...
THIS IS IT!
AN AMATEUR LIKE ME MUST START WITH THE BASICS!
I'VE GOT TO HAVE REAL TRAINING TO MAKE A FOOL OF REN TSURUGA!
Other-wise, I'll be Beaten!
OH...

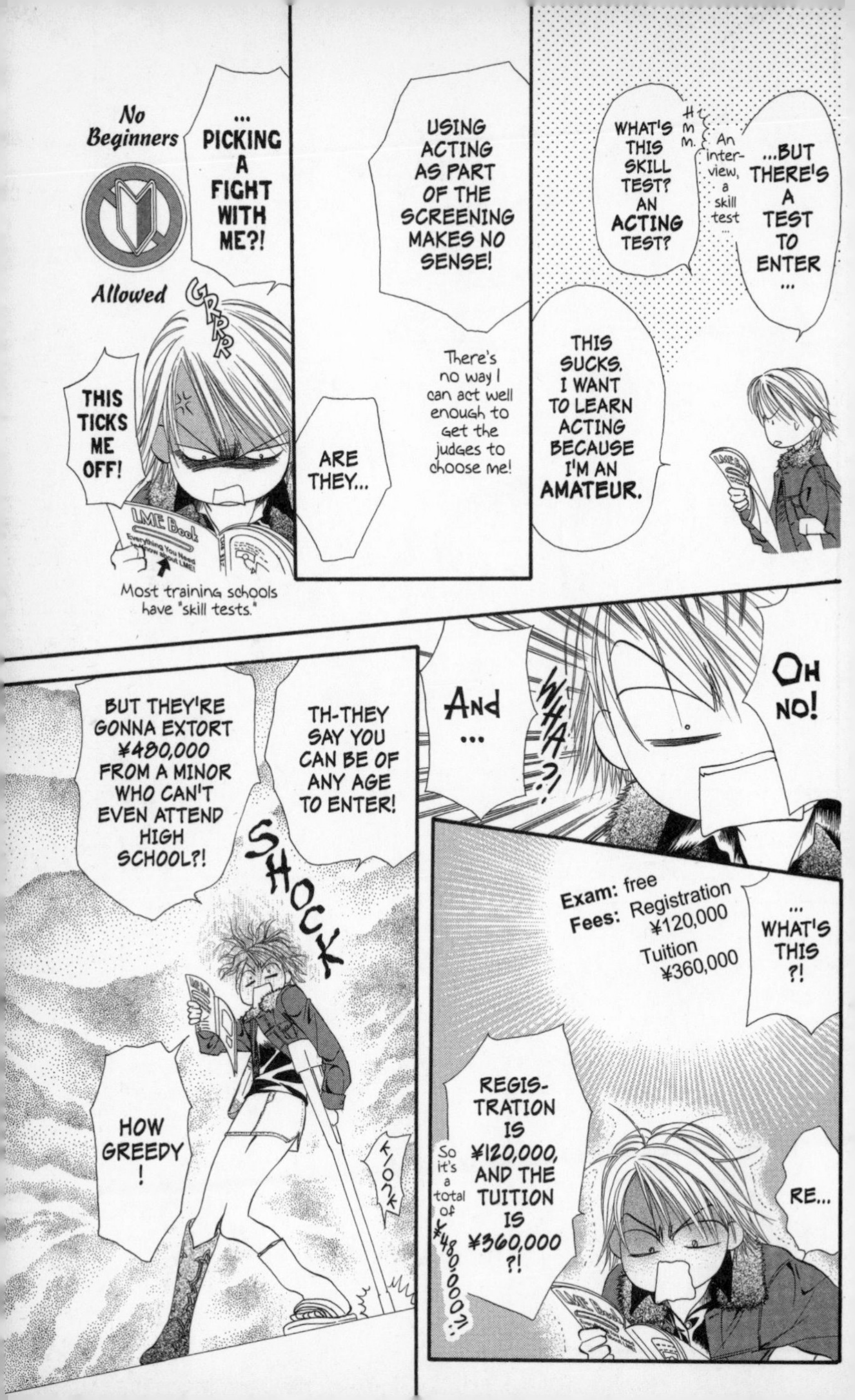

...BUT THERE'S A TEST TO ENTER...
An interview, a skill test...
HMM.
WHAT'S THIS SKILL TEST? AN ACTING TEST?
THIS SUCKS. I WANT TO LEARN ACTING BECAUSE I'M AN AMATEUR.
USING ACTING AS PART OF THE SCREENING MAKES NO SENSE!
There's no way I can act well enough to get the judges to choose me!
ARE THEY...
...PICKING A FIGHT WITH ME?!
No Beginners Allowed
GRRR
THIS TICKS ME OFF!
LME Book
Most training schools have "skill tests."
OH NO!
WHAA?!
And...
...WHAT'S THIS?!
Exam: free
Fees: Registration ¥120,000
Tuition ¥360,000
RE...
REGISTRATION IS ¥120,000, AND THE TUITION IS ¥360,000?!
So it's a total of ¥480,000?!
TH-THEY SAY YOU CAN BE OF ANY AGE TO ENTER!
BUT THEY'RE GONNA EXTORT ¥480,000 FROM A MINOR WHO CAN'T EVEN ATTEND HIGH SCHOOL?!
SHOCK
HOW GREEDY!
KLONK

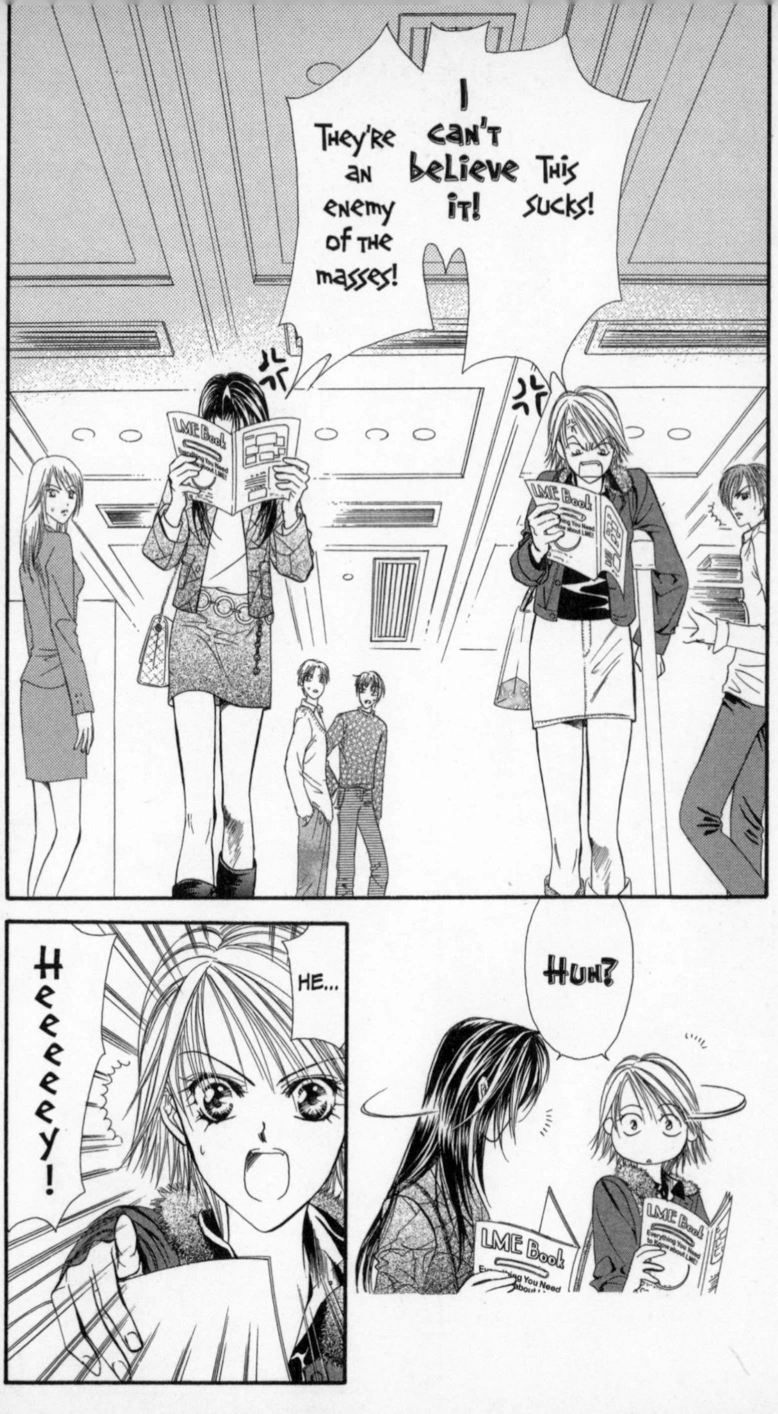
This sucks!
I can't believe it!
They're an enemy of the masses!
Huh?
He...
Heeeeeey!

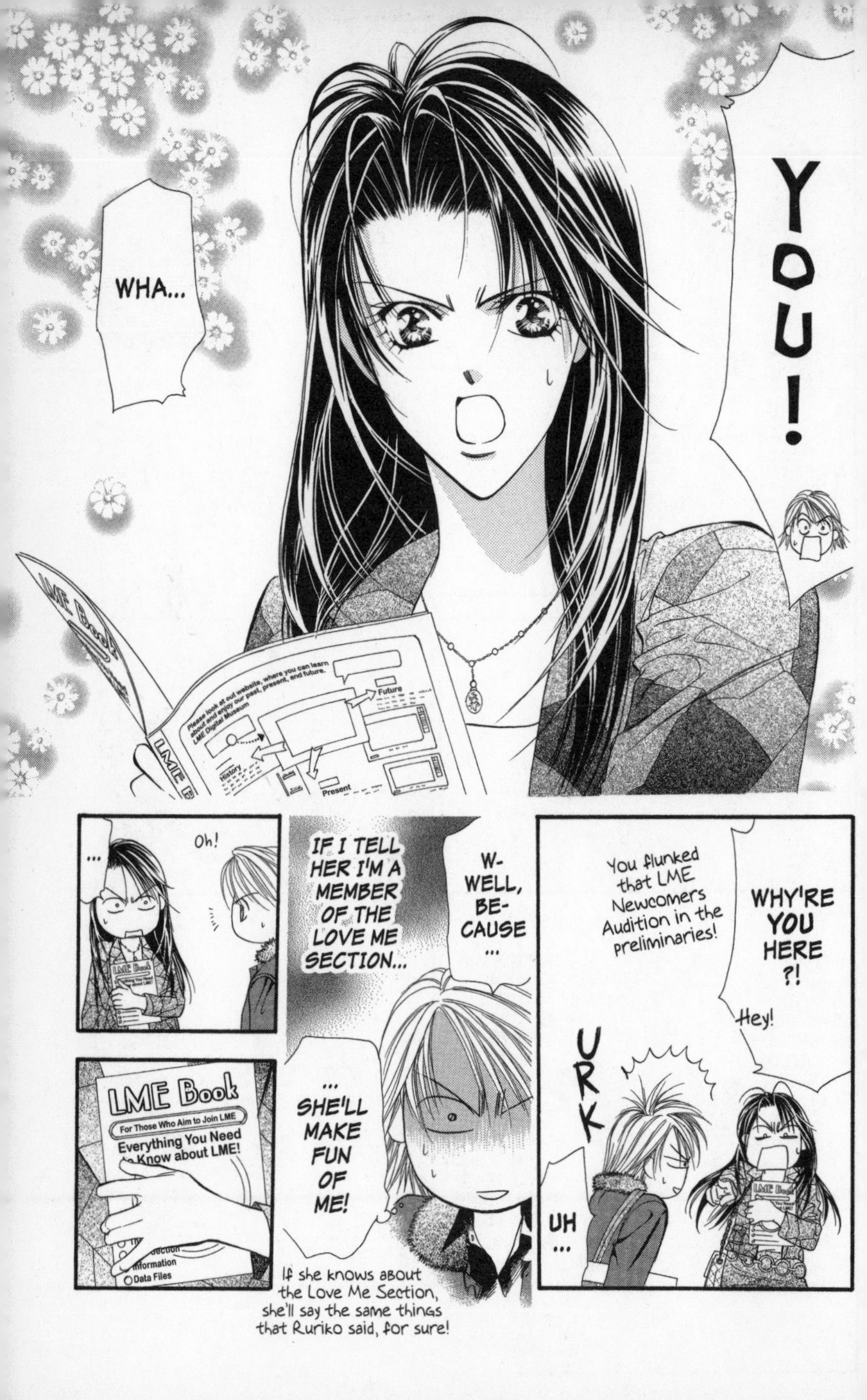
YOU!
WHA...
Please look at out website, where you can learn about and enjoy our past, present, and future.
LME Digital Museum
Future
History
Present
WHY'RE YOU HERE ?!
You flunked that LME Newcomers Audition in the preliminaries!
Hey!
URK
UH ...
W-WELL, BE-CAUSE ...
IF I TELL HER I'M A MEMBER OF THE LOVE ME SECTION...
... SHE'LL MAKE FUN OF ME!
If she knows about the Love Me Section, she'll say the same things that Ruriko said, for sure!
Oh!
...
LME Book
For Those Who Aim to Join LME
Everything You Need
Know about LME!
Information
Data Files

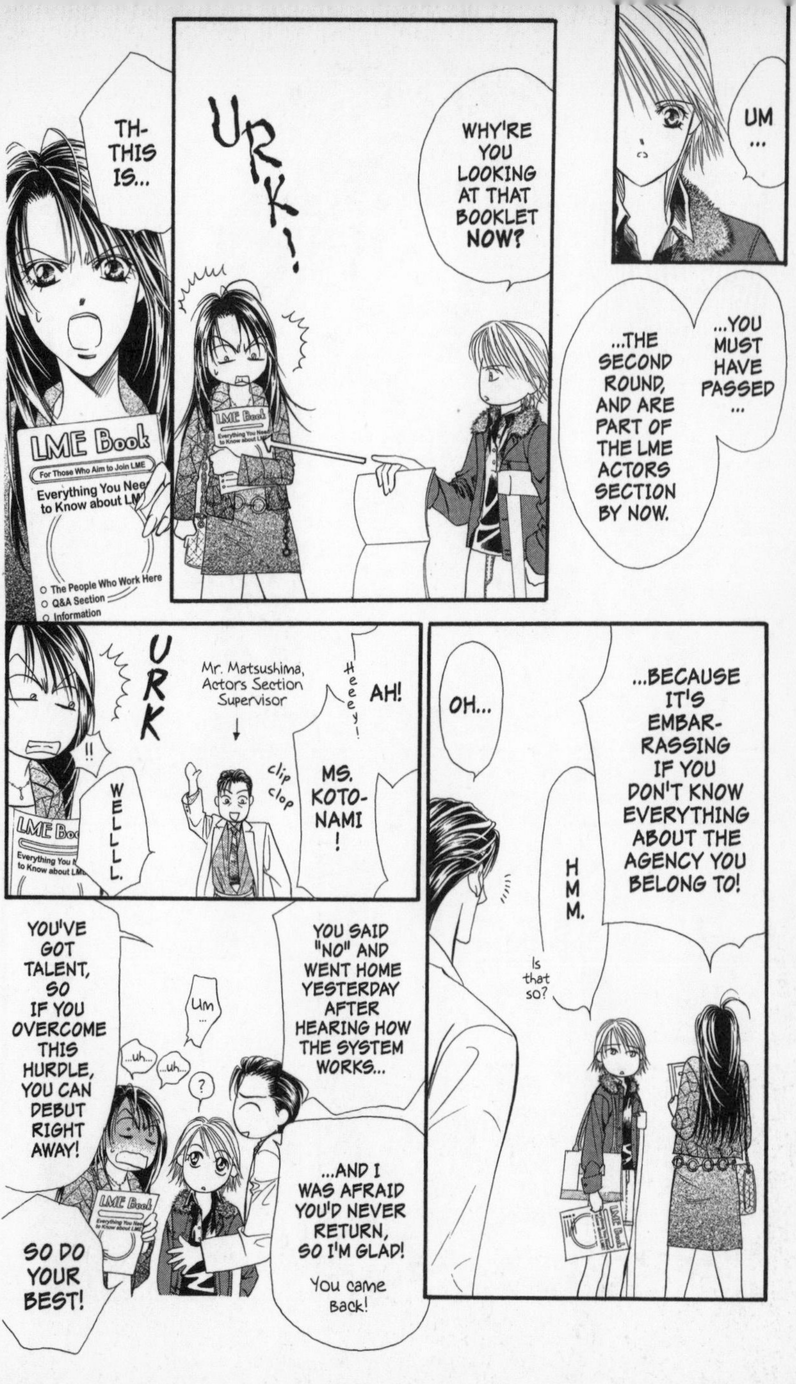
UM ...
...YOU MUST HAVE PASSED ...
...THE SECOND ROUND, AND ARE PART OF THE LME ACTORS SECTION BY NOW.
WHY'RE YOU LOOKING AT THAT BOOKLET NOW?
URK!
TH- THIS IS...
LME Book
For Those Who Aim to Join LME
Everything You Nee to Know about LM
The People Who Work Here
Q&A Section
Information
...BECAUSE IT'S EMBAR-RASSING IF YOU DON'T KNOW EVERYTHING ABOUT THE AGENCY YOU BELONG TO!
OH...
HMM.
Is that so?
AH!
Heeey!
MS. KOTO-NAMI!
Mr. Matsushima, Actors Section Supervisor
clip clop
URK
!!
WELLLL.
YOU SAID "NO" AND WENT HOME YESTERDAY AFTER HEARING HOW THE SYSTEM WORKS...
...AND I WAS AFRAID YOU'D NEVER RETURN, SO I'M GLAD!
You came back!
YOU'VE GOT TALENT, SO IF YOU OVERCOME THIS HURDLE, YOU CAN DEBUT RIGHT AWAY!
SO DO YOUR BEST!
Um ...
...uh...
...uh...
?

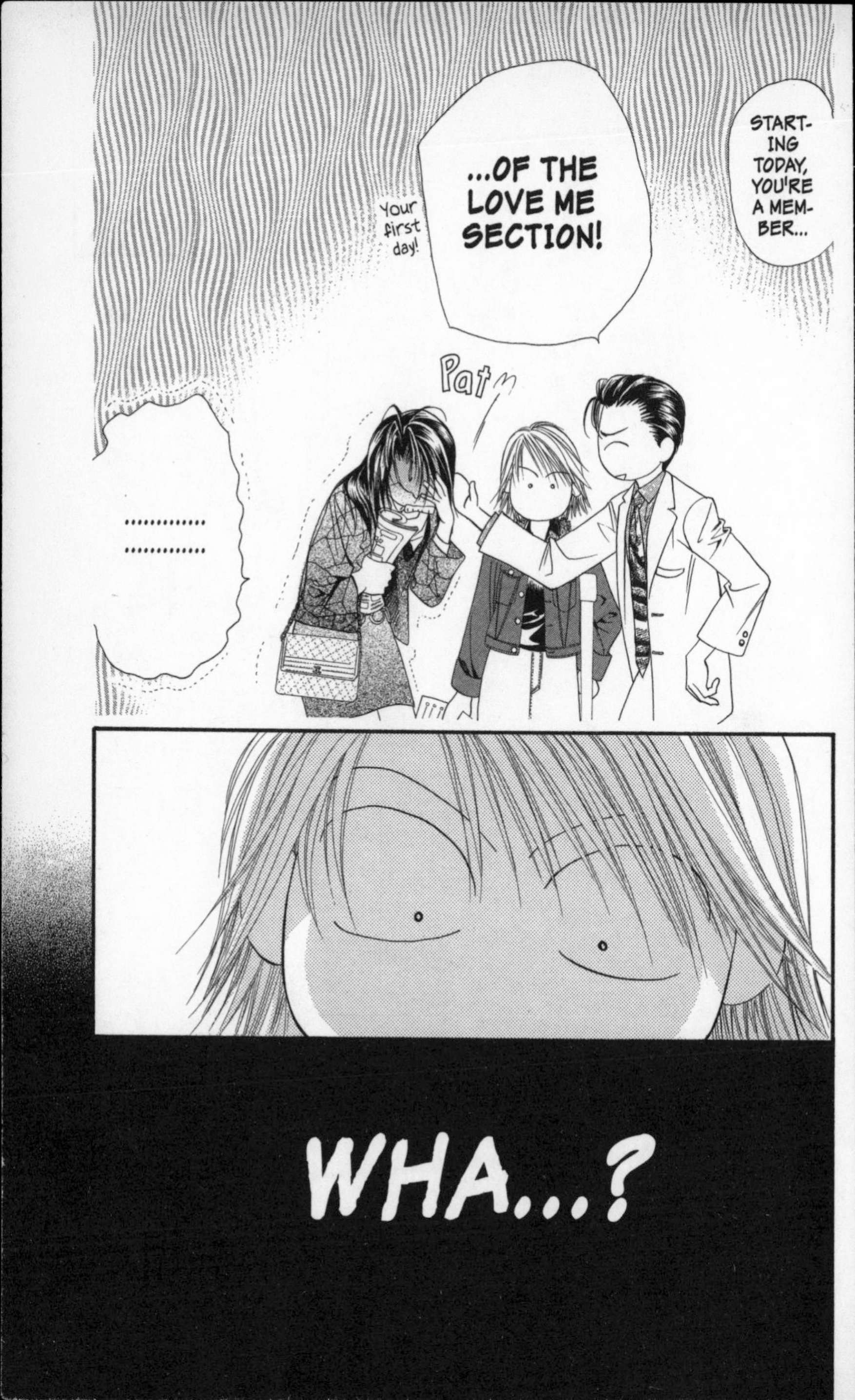
START-ING TODAY, YOU'RE A MEM-BER...
...OF THE LOVE ME SECTION!
Your first day!
Pat
....
....
WHA...?

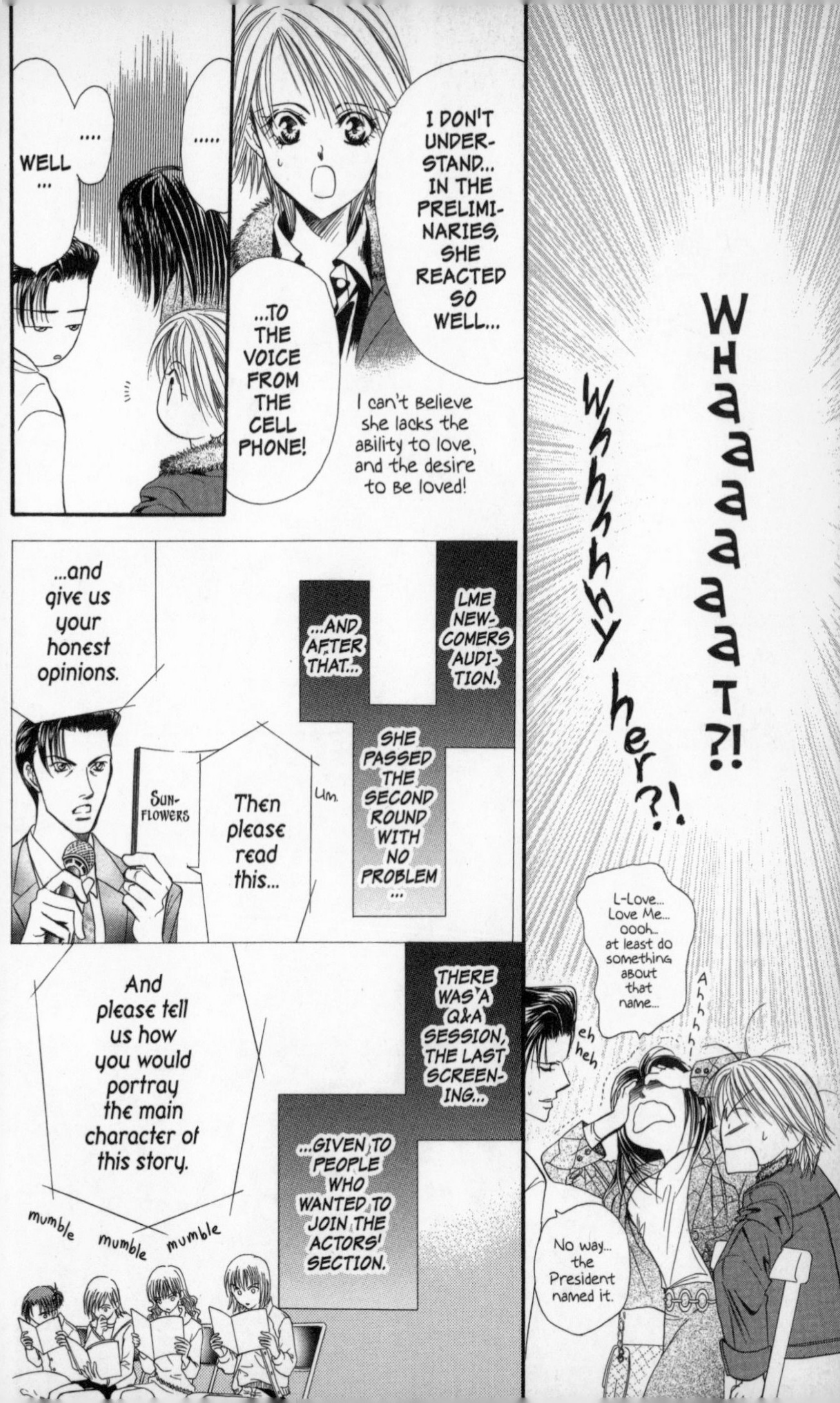
WHAAAAAT?!
Whhhhhy her?!
L-Love... Love Me... oooh... at least do something about that name...
Ahhhh!
eh heh
No way... the President named it.
I DON'T UNDERSTAND... IN THE PRELIMINARIES, SHE REACTED SO WELL...
...TO THE VOICE FROM THE CELL PHONE!
I can't believe she lacks the ability to love, and the desire to be loved!
.....
....
WELL...
LME NEWCOMERS AUDITION.
...AND AFTER THAT...
SHE PASSED THE SECOND ROUND WITH NO PROBLEM...
Um.
Then please read this...
SUNFLOWERS
...and give us your honest opinions.
THERE WAS A Q&A SESSION, THE LAST SCREENING...
...GIVEN TO PEOPLE WHO WANTED TO JOIN THE ACTORS' SECTION.
And please tell us how you would portray the main character of this story.
mumble mumble mumble

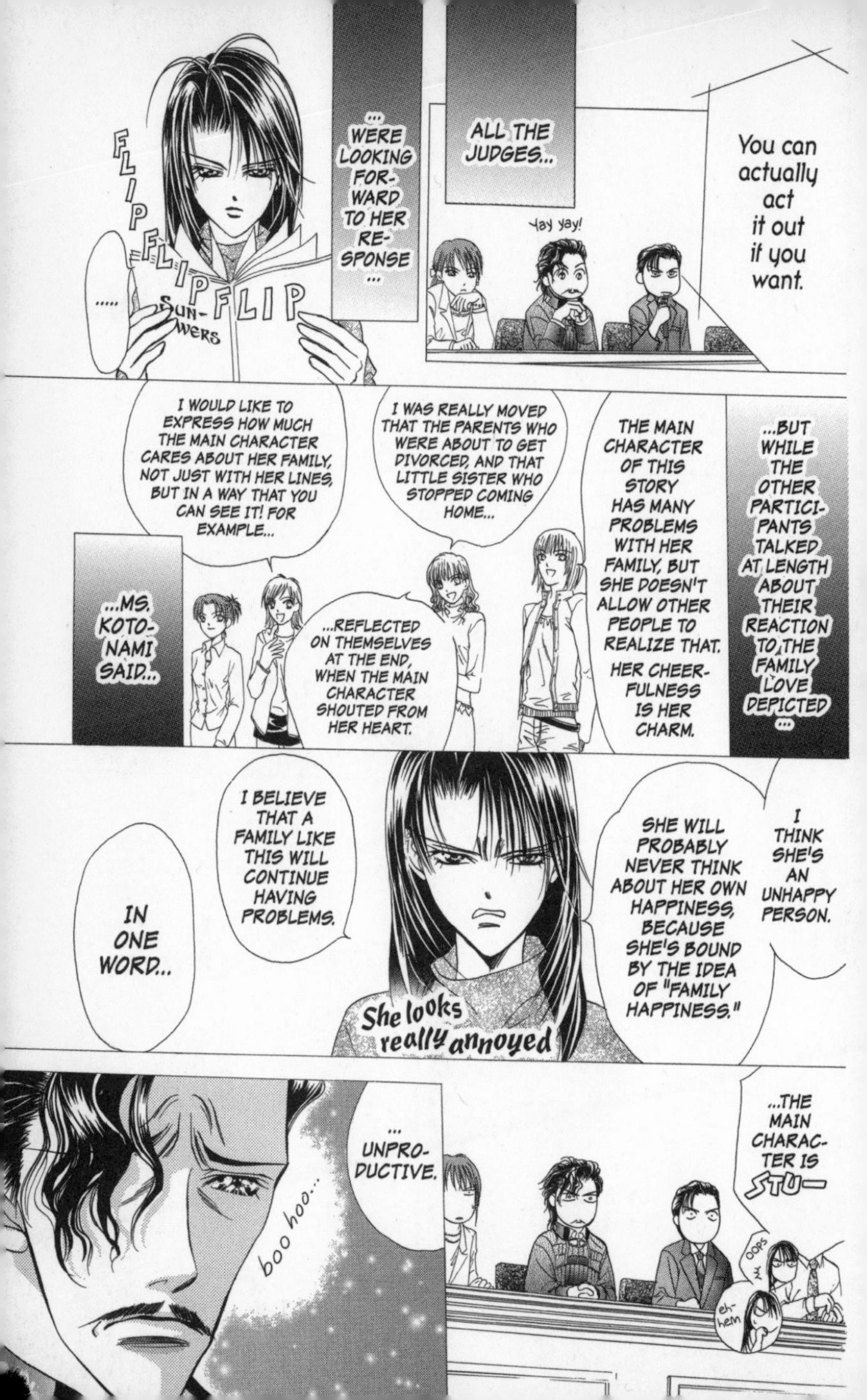
You can actually act it out if you want.
Yay yay!
ALL THE JUDGES...
...WERE LOOKING FORWARD TO HER RESPONSE...
FLIP FLIP FLIP FLIP
.....
...BUT WHILE THE OTHER PARTICIPANTS TALKED AT LENGTH ABOUT THEIR REACTION TO THE FAMILY LOVE DEPICTED...
THE MAIN CHARACTER OF THIS STORY HAS MANY PROBLEMS WITH HER FAMILY, BUT SHE DOESN'T ALLOW OTHER PEOPLE TO REALIZE THAT.
HER CHEERFULNESS IS HER CHARM.
I WAS REALLY MOVED THAT THE PARENTS WHO WERE ABOUT TO GET DIVORCED, AND THAT LITTLE SISTER WHO STOPPED COMING HOME...
...REFLECTED ON THEMSELVES AT THE END, WHEN THE MAIN CHARACTER SHOUTED FROM HER HEART.
I WOULD LIKE TO EXPRESS HOW MUCH THE MAIN CHARACTER CARES ABOUT HER FAMILY, NOT JUST WITH HER LINES, BUT IN A WAY THAT YOU CAN SEE IT! FOR EXAMPLE...
...MS. KOTONAMI SAID...
I THINK SHE'S AN UNHAPPY PERSON.
SHE WILL PROBABLY NEVER THINK ABOUT HER OWN HAPPINESS, BECAUSE SHE'S BOUND BY THE IDEA OF "FAMILY HAPPINESS."
She looks really annoyed
I BELIEVE THAT A FAMILY LIKE THIS WILL CONTINUE HAVING PROBLEMS.
IN ONE WORD...
...THE MAIN CHARACTER IS STU—
OOPS
eh-hem
...UNPRODUCTIVE.
boo hoo...

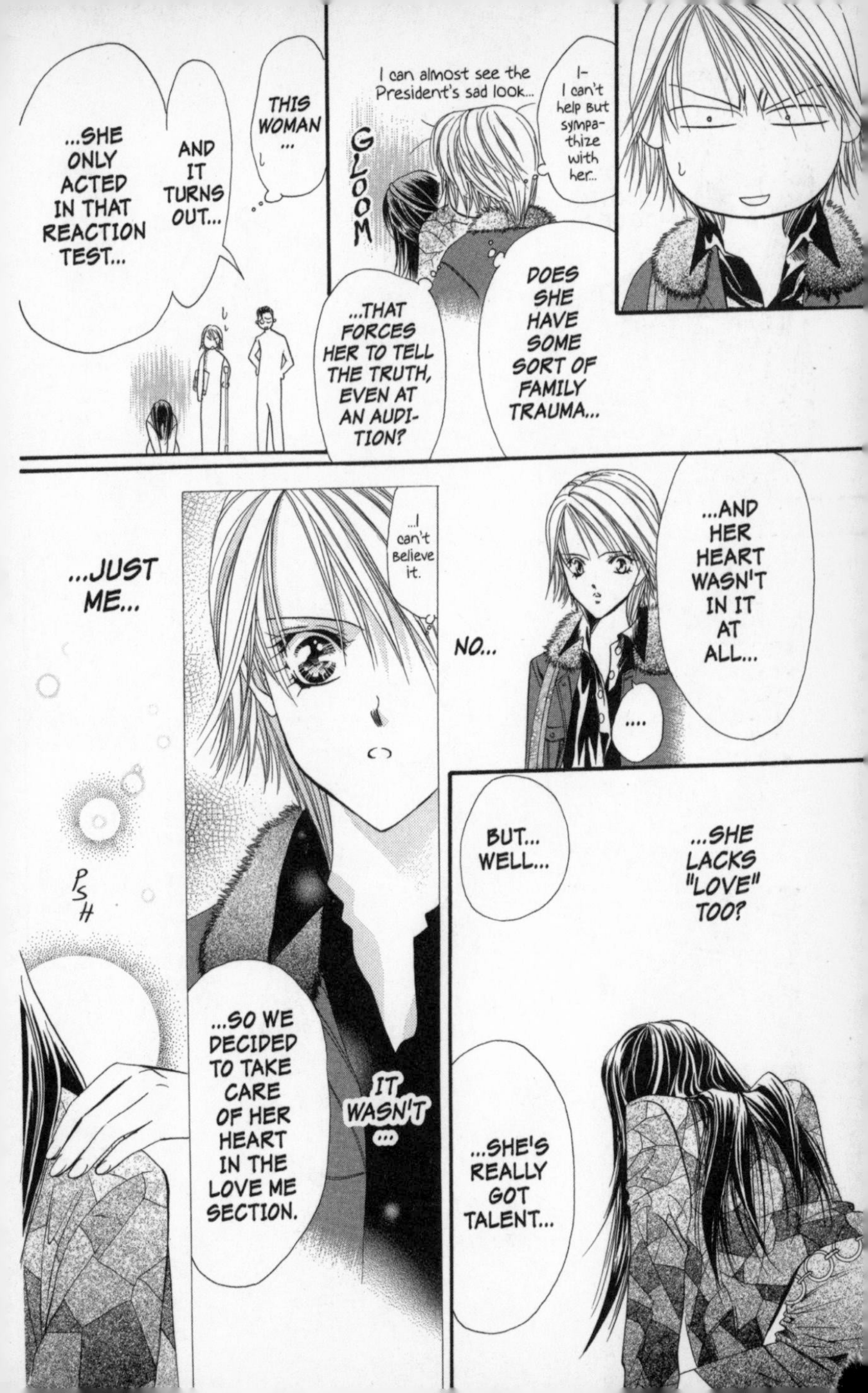
I- I can't help but sympathize with her...
I can almost see the President's sad look...
GLOOM
DOES SHE HAVE SOME SORT OF FAMILY TRAUMA...
...THAT FORCES HER TO TELL THE TRUTH, EVEN AT AN AUDITION?
THIS WOMAN...
AND IT TURNS OUT...
...SHE ONLY ACTED IN THAT REACTION TEST...
...AND HER HEART WASN'T IN IT AT ALL...
....
NO...
...I can't Believe it.
...SHE LACKS "LOVE" TOO?
BUT... WELL...
...SHE'S REALLY GOT TALENT...
IT WASN'T...
...SO WE DECIDED TO TAKE CARE OF HER HEART IN THE LOVE ME SECTION.
...JUST ME...
PSH

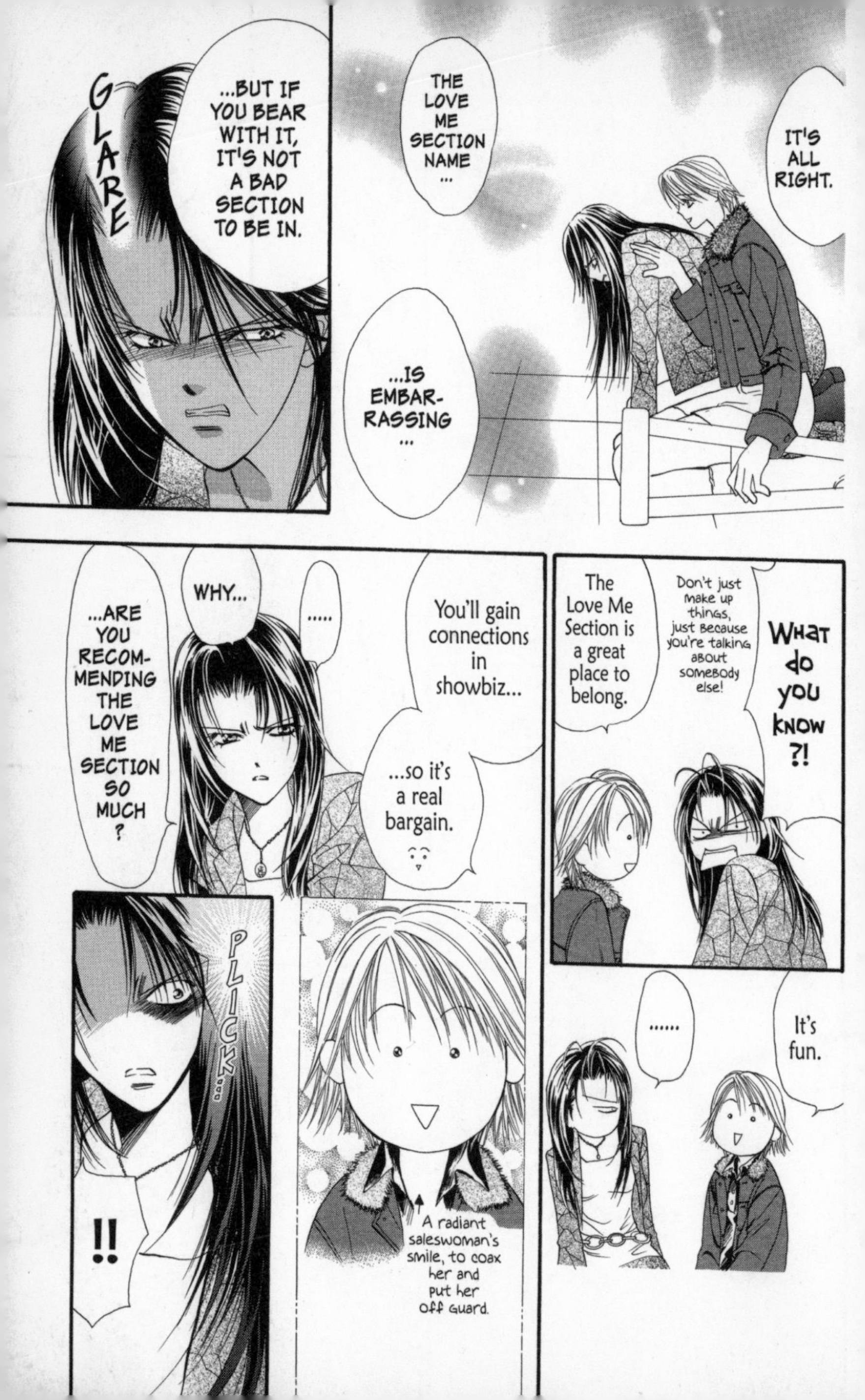
IT'S ALL RIGHT.
THE LOVE ME SECTION NAME...
...IS EMBARRASSING...
GLARE
...BUT IF YOU BEAR WITH IT, IT'S NOT A BAD SECTION TO BE IN.
WHAT do you know?!
Don't just make up things, just because you're talking about somebody else!
The Love Me Section is a great place to belong.
You'll gain connections in showbiz...
...so it's a real bargain.
.....
WHY...
...ARE YOU RECOMMENDING THE LOVE ME SECTION SO MUCH?
It's fun.
......
A radiant saleswoman's smile, to coax her and put her off guard.
PLICK...
!!

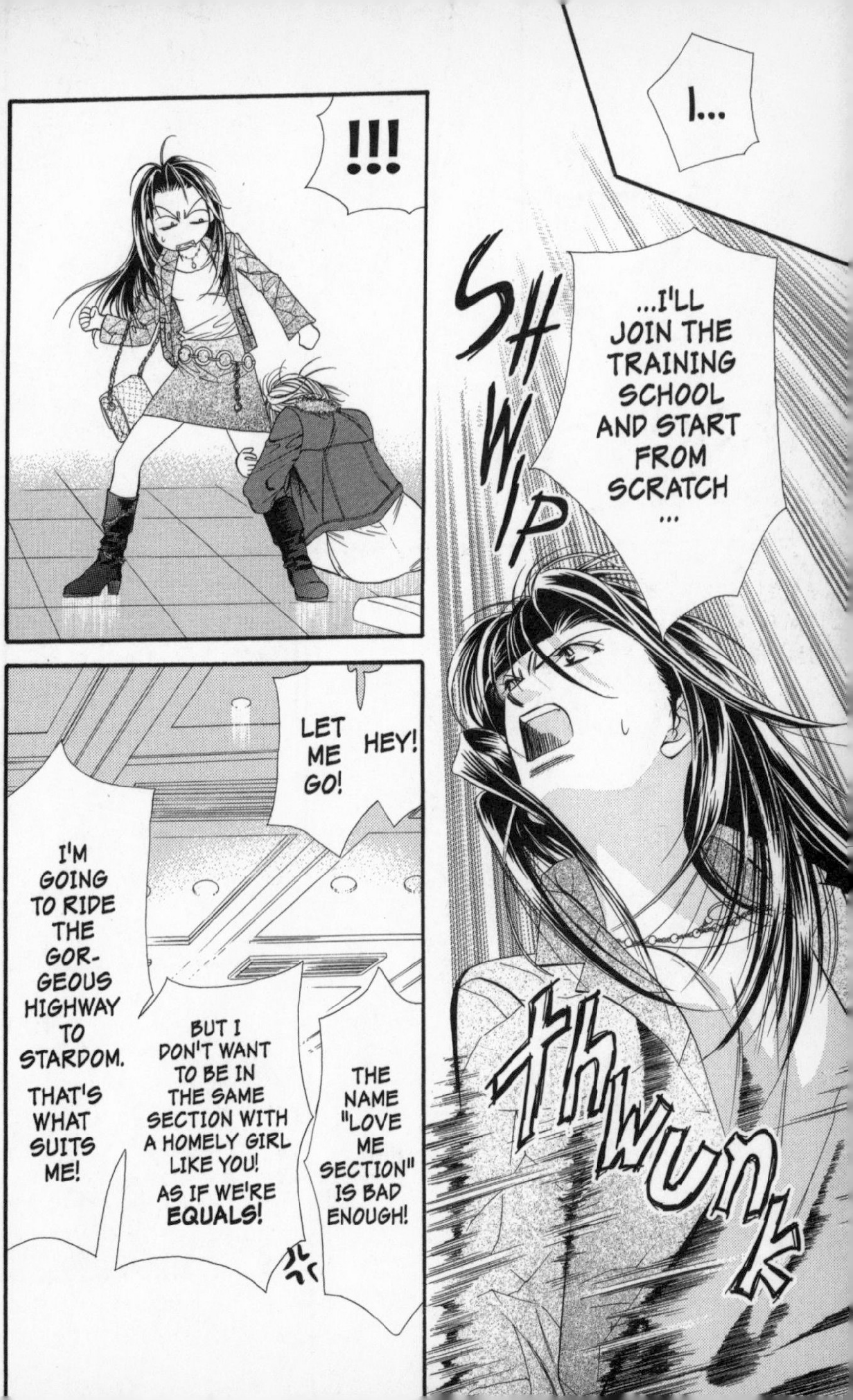
I...
...I'LL JOIN THE TRAINING SCHOOL AND START FROM SCRATCH ...
SHWIP
thwunk
!!!
HEY!
LET ME GO!
THE NAME "LOVE ME SECTION" IS BAD ENOUGH!
BUT I DON'T WANT TO BE IN THE SAME SECTION WITH A HOMELY GIRL LIKE YOU!
AS IF WE'RE EQUALS!
I'M GOING TO RIDE THE GOR-GEOUS HIGHWAY TO STARDOM.
THAT'S WHAT SUITS ME!

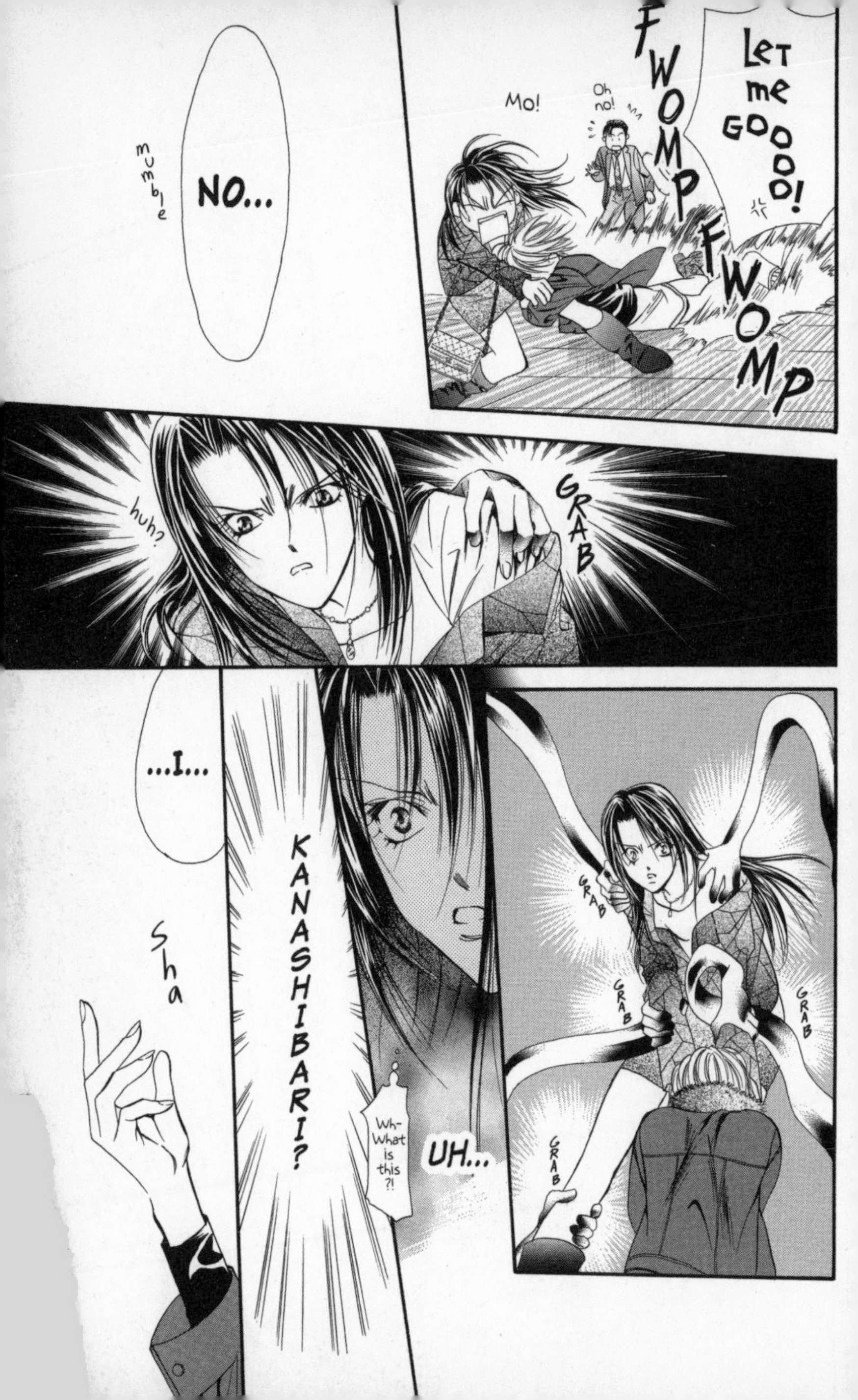
Let me GOOOOO!
FWOMP
FWOMP
Oh no!
Mo!
NO...
mumble
GRAB
huh?
GRAB
GRAB
GRAB
GRAB
KANASHIBARI?
Wh-What is this?!
UH...
...I...
Sha

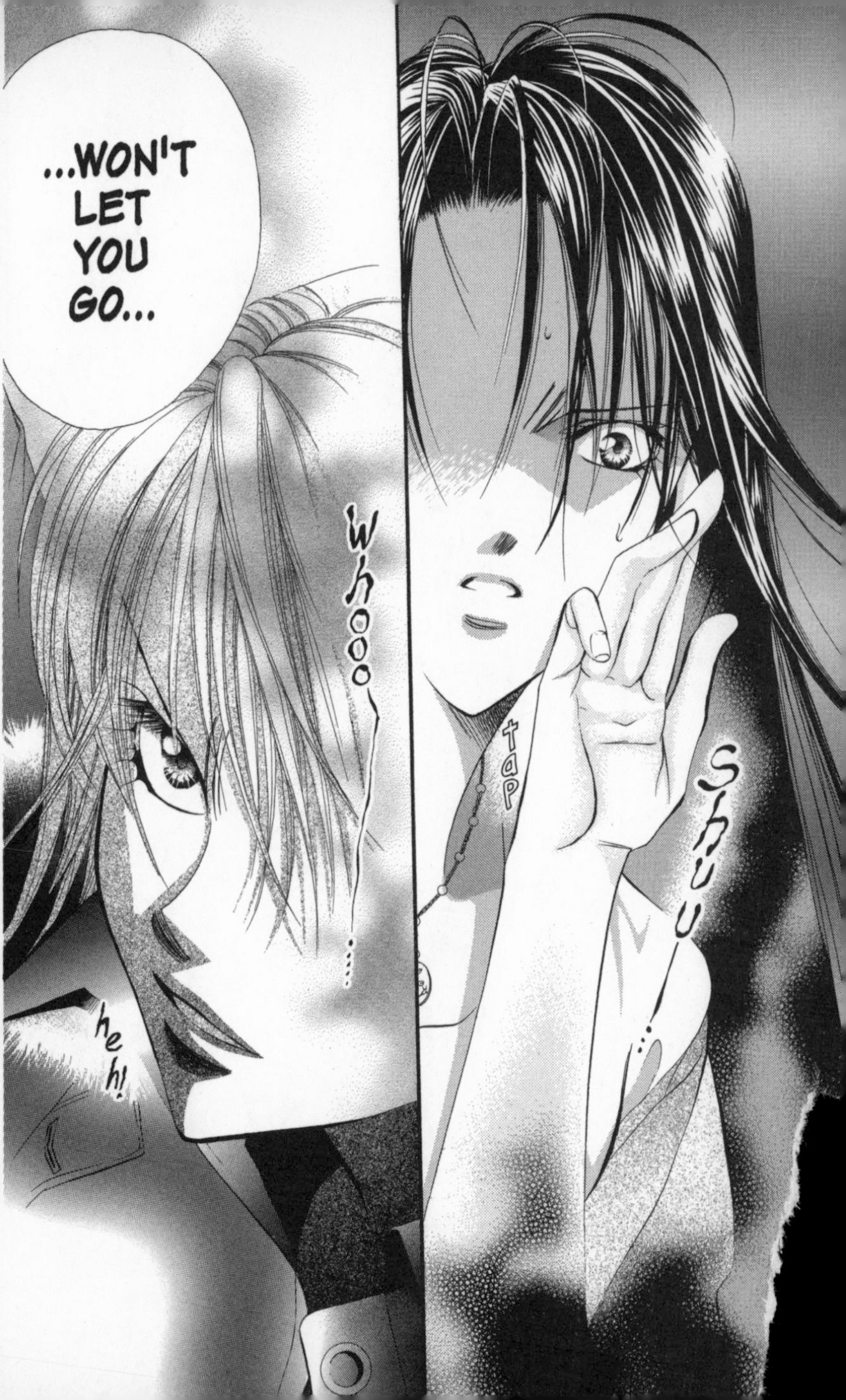
tap
Shuu...
...WON'T LET YOU GO...
Whoooo...
heh!

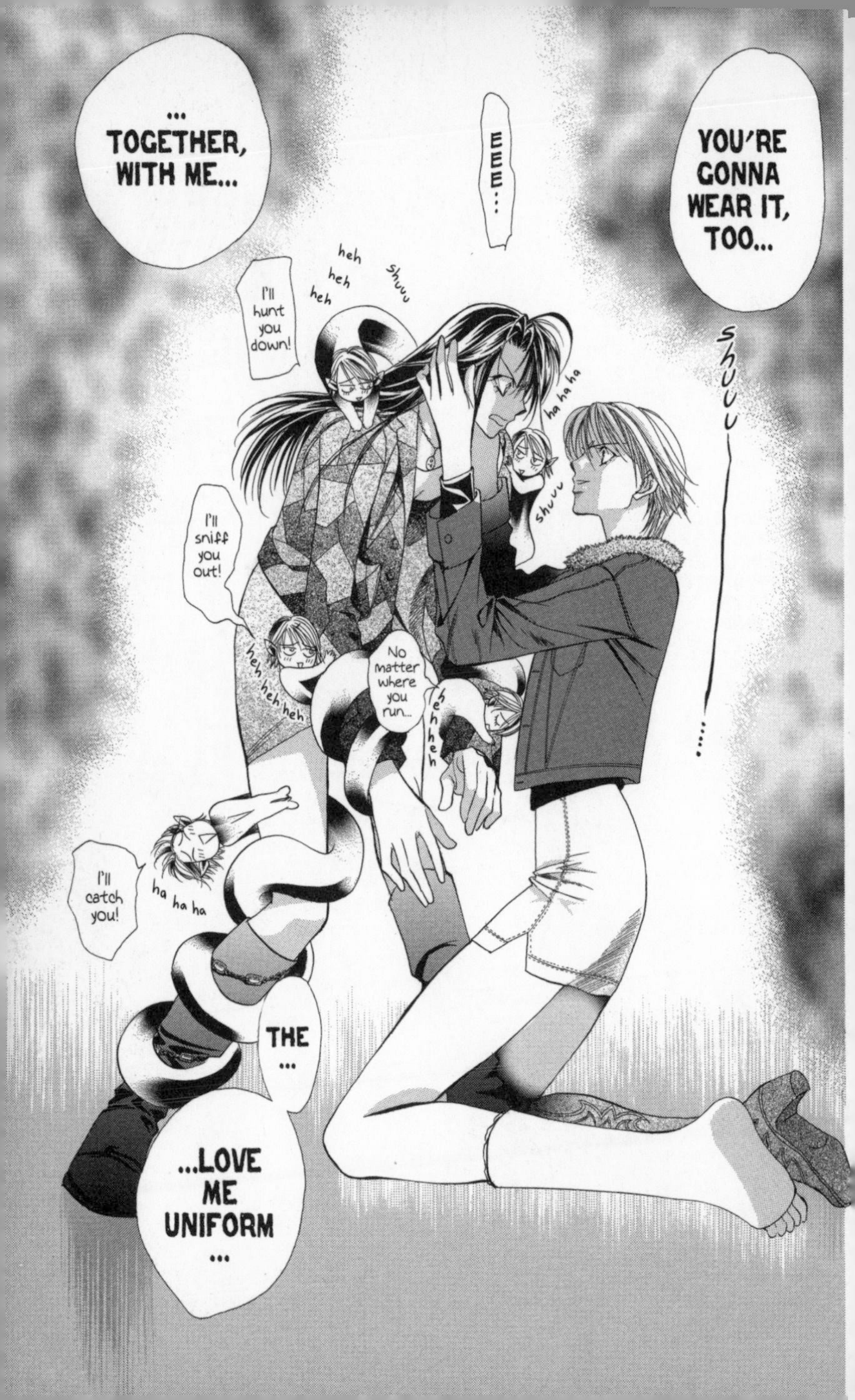
YOU'RE GONNA WEAR IT, TOO...
SHUUUU
......
EEE...
... TOGETHER, WITH ME...
shuuu
heh heh heh
I'll hunt you down!
ha ha ha
shuuu
I'll sniff you out!
heh heh heh
No matter where you run...
heh heh heh
I'll catch you!
ha ha ha
THE ...
...LOVE ME UNIFORM ...

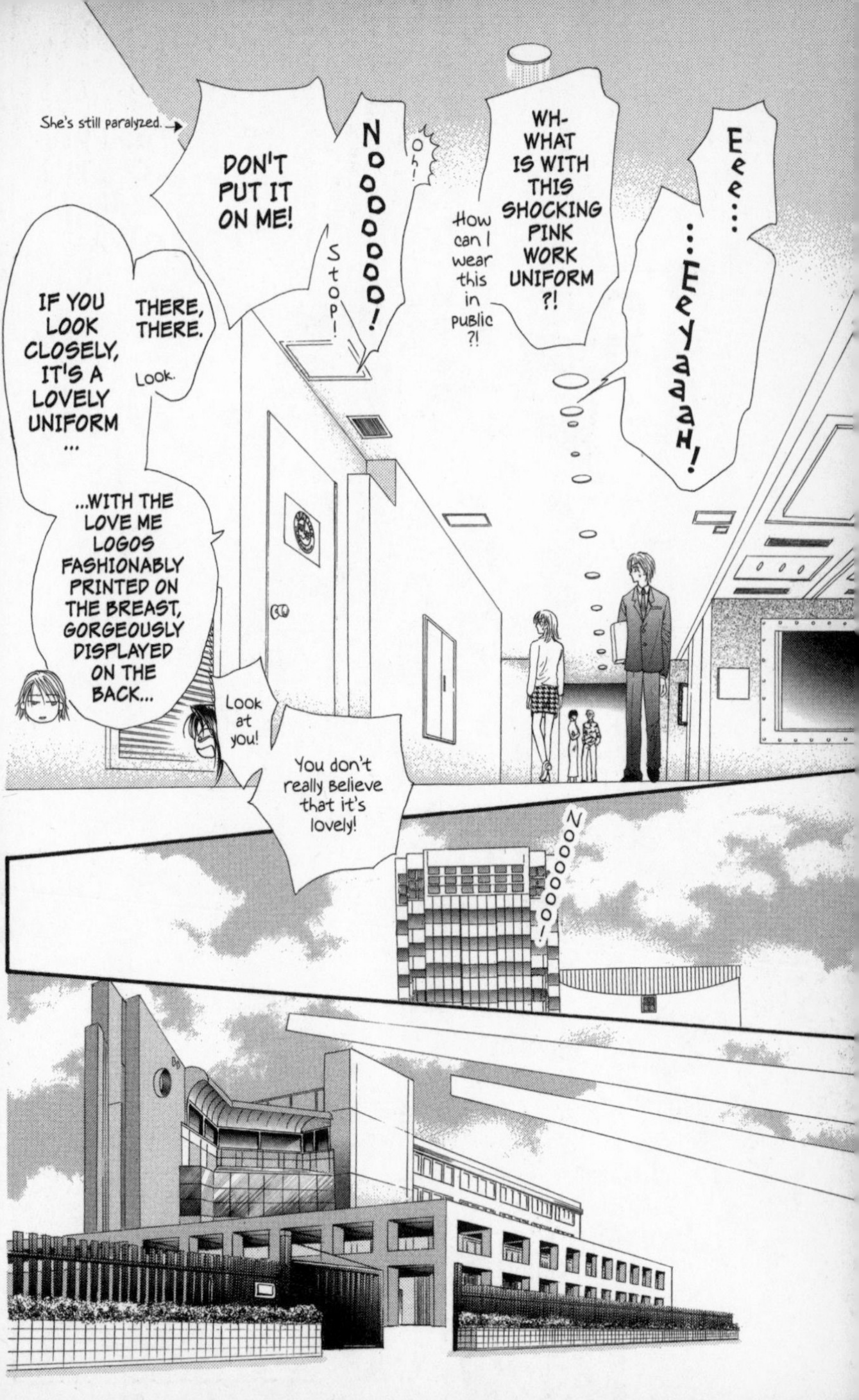
Eee...
...Eeyaaah!
WH-WHAT IS WITH THIS SHOCKING PINK WORK UNIFORM?!
How can I wear this in public?!
Oh!
NOOOOOOO!
Stop!
DON'T PUT IT ON ME!
She's still paralyzed.
THERE, THERE.
Look.
IF YOU LOOK CLOSELY, IT'S A LOVELY UNIFORM...
...WITH THE LOVE ME LOGOS FASHIONABLY PRINTED ON THE BREAST, GORGEOUSLY DISPLAYED ON THE BACK...
Look at you!
You don't really believe that it's lovely!
Nooooooo!

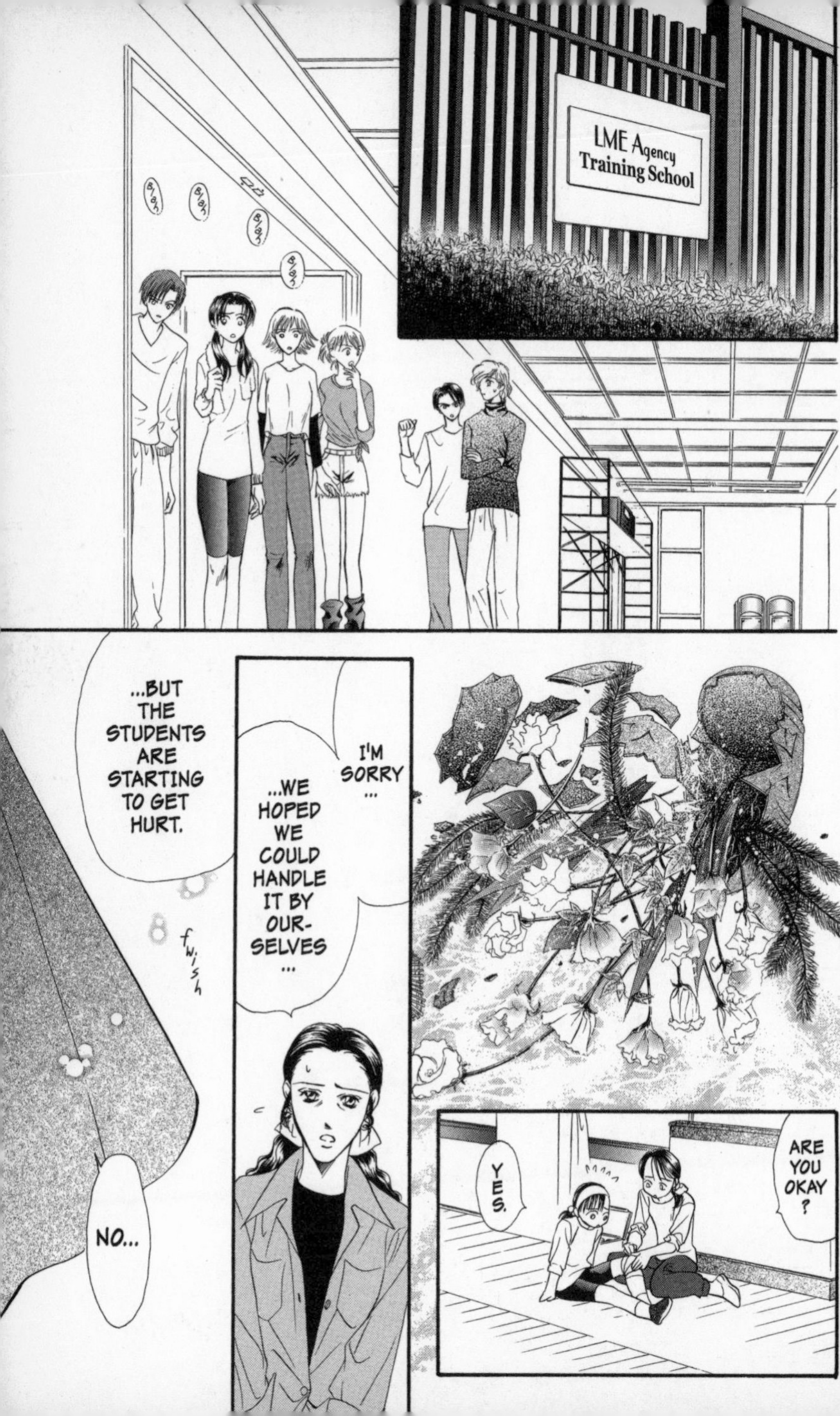

LME Agency Training School
Blah
Blah
Blah
Blah
ARE YOU OKAY?
YES.
I'M SORRY...
...WE HOPED WE COULD HANDLE IT BY OUR-SELVES...
...BUT THE STUDENTS ARE STARTING TO GET HURT.
fwish
NO...

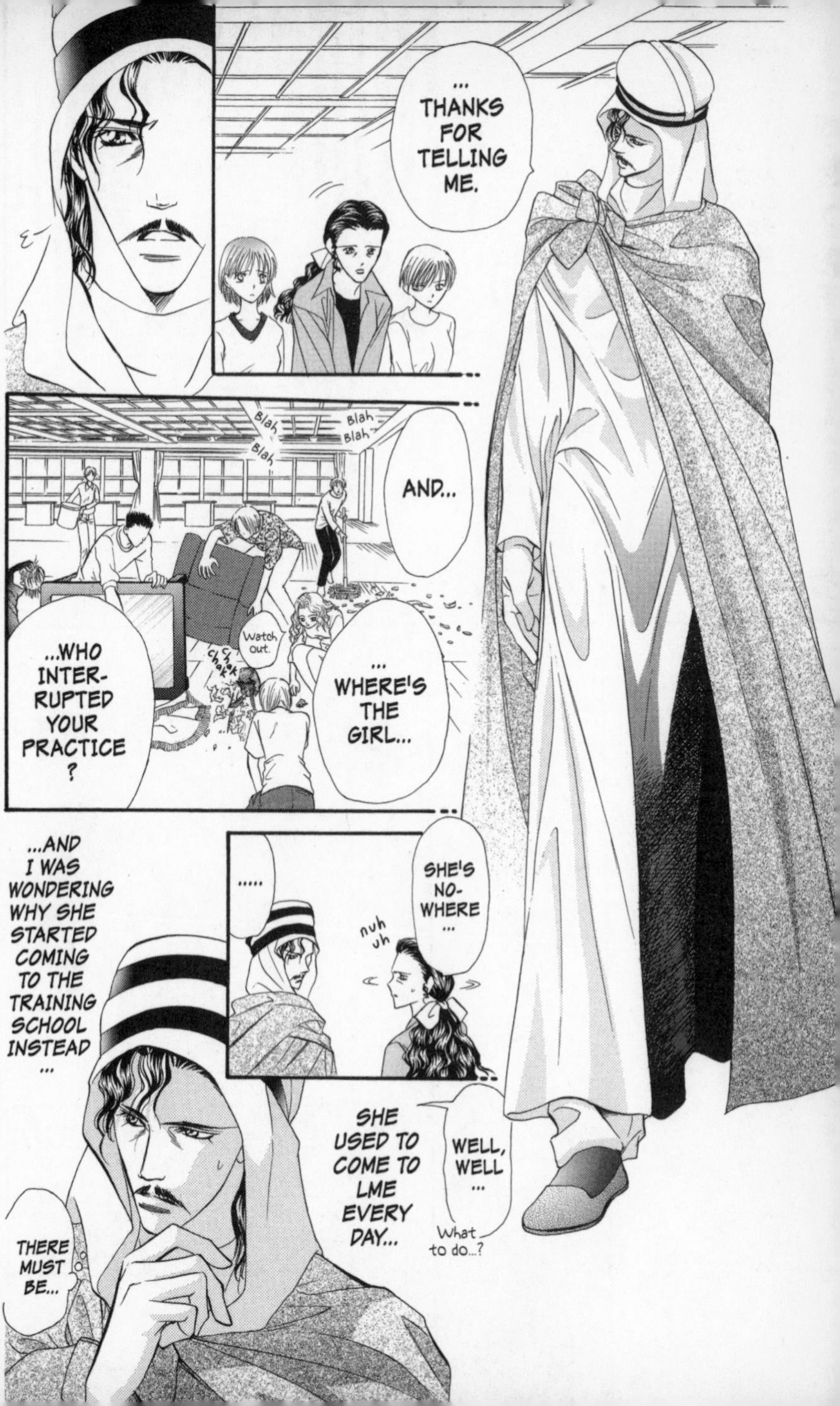

... THANKS FOR TELLING ME.
Blah Blah Blah Blah
AND...
... WHERE'S THE GIRL...
...WHO INTER-RUPTED YOUR PRACTICE?
Watch out.
Chak Chak
SHE'S NO-WHERE...
nuh uh
.....
...AND I WAS WONDERING WHY SHE STARTED COMING TO THE TRAINING SCHOOL INSTEAD...
WELL, WELL...
What to do...?
SHE USED TO COME TO LME EVERY DAY...
THERE MUST BE...

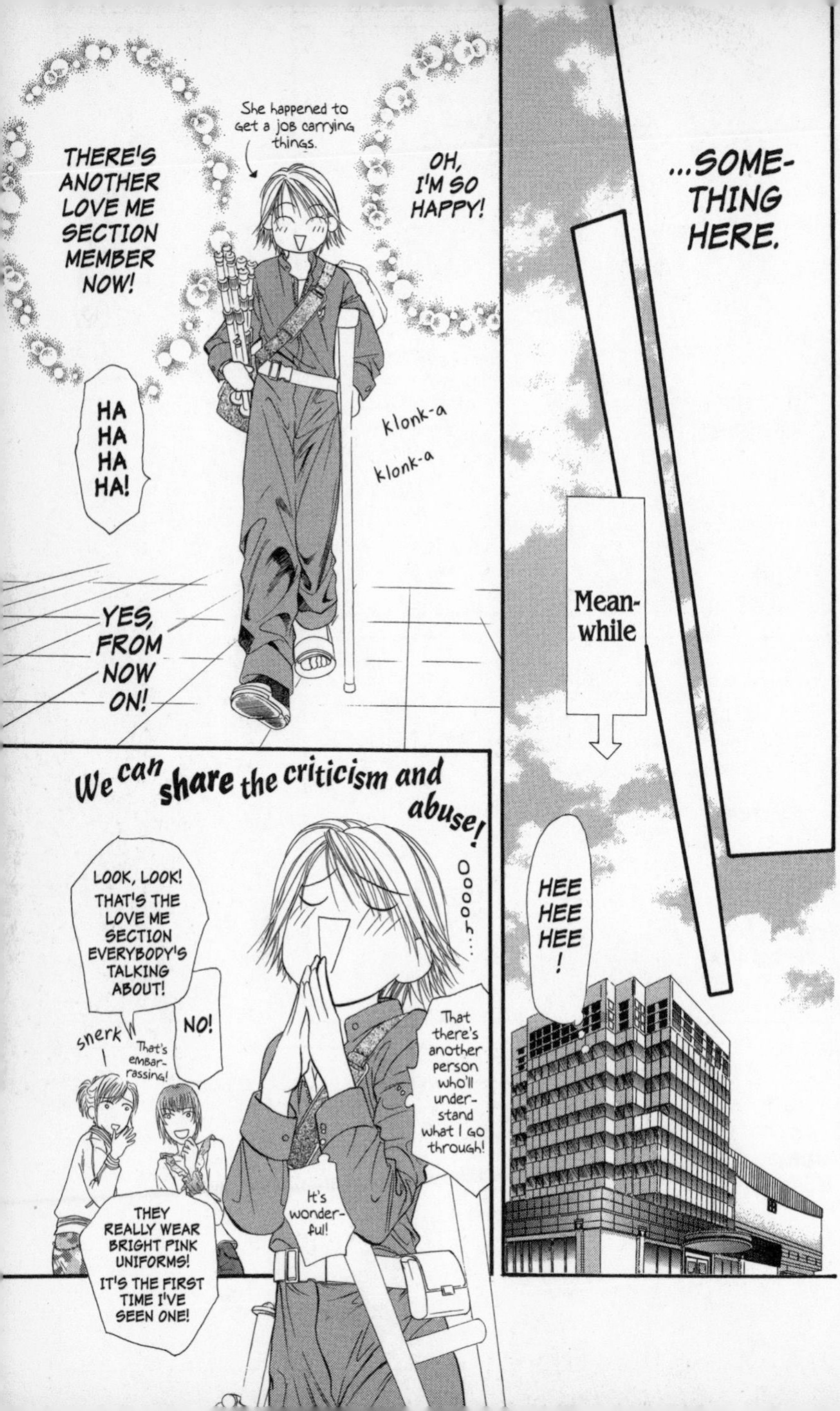
...SOMETHING HERE.
Meanwhile
HEE HEE HEE!
OH, I'M SO HAPPY!
She happened to get a job carrying things.
THERE'S ANOTHER LOVE ME SECTION MEMBER NOW!
klonk-a klonk-a
HA HA HA HA!
YES, FROM NOW ON!
We can share the criticism and abuse!
Ooooh...
That there's another person who'll understand what I go through!
It's wonderful!
LOOK, LOOK! THAT'S THE LOVE ME SECTION EVERYBODY'S TALKING ABOUT!
NO!
That's embarrassing!
snerk
THEY REALLY WEAR BRIGHT PINK UNIFORMS! IT'S THE FIRST TIME I'VE SEEN ONE!

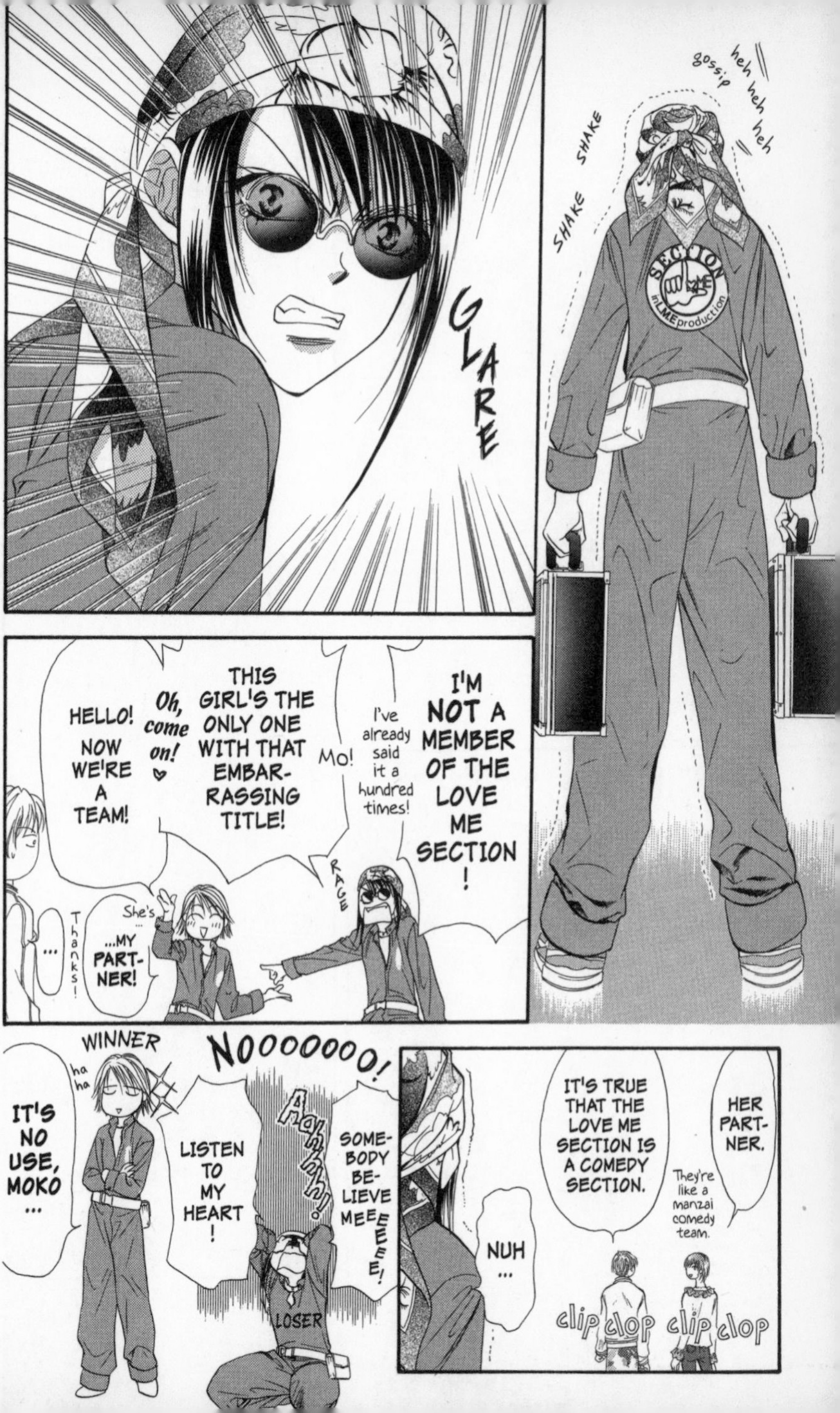
heh heh heh
gossip
SHAKE SHAKE
SECTION
inLMEproduction
GLARE
I'M NOT A MEMBER OF THE LOVE ME SECTION!
I've already said it a hundred times!
Mo!
RAGE
THIS GIRL'S THE ONLY ONE WITH THAT EMBARRASSING TITLE!
Oh, come on! ♡
HELLO! NOW WE'RE A TEAM!
She's ...
...MY PARTNER!
Thanks!
...
HER PARTNER.
They're like a manzai comedy team.
IT'S TRUE THAT THE LOVE ME SECTION IS A COMEDY SECTION.
NUH ...
clip clop clip clop
NOOOOOOO!
SOMEBODY BELIEVE MEEEEEE!
Aahhh!
LISTEN TO MY HEART!
LOSER
WINNER
ha ha
IT'S NO USE, MOKO ...

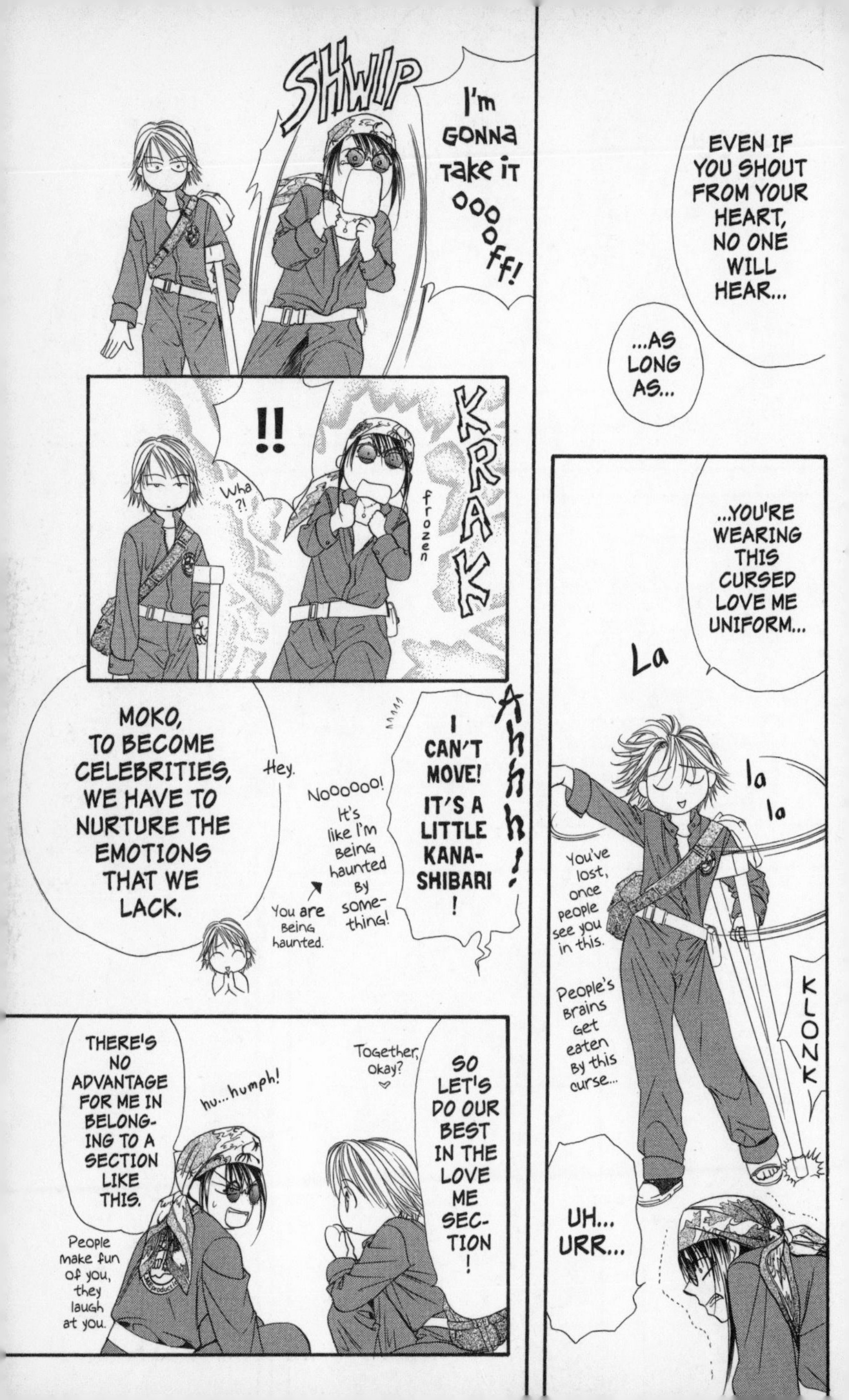
EVEN IF YOU SHOUT FROM YOUR HEART, NO ONE WILL HEAR...
...AS LONG AS...
...YOU'RE WEARING THIS CURSED LOVE ME UNIFORM...
La
la
la
You've lost, once people see you in this.
People's brains get eaten by this curse...
KLONK
UH... URR...
SHWIP
I'm gonna take it oooooff!
KRAK
!!
frozen
Wha?!
Ahhhh!
I CAN'T MOVE! IT'S A LITTLE KANA-SHIBARI!
Noooooo! It's like I'm being haunted by something!
You are being haunted.
Hey.
MOKO, TO BECOME CELEBRITIES, WE HAVE TO NURTURE THE EMOTIONS THAT WE LACK.
SO LET'S DO OUR BEST IN THE LOVE ME SECTION!
Together, okay? ♡
hu...humph!
THERE'S NO ADVANTAGE FOR ME IN BELONGING TO A SECTION LIKE THIS.
People make fun of you, they laugh at you.

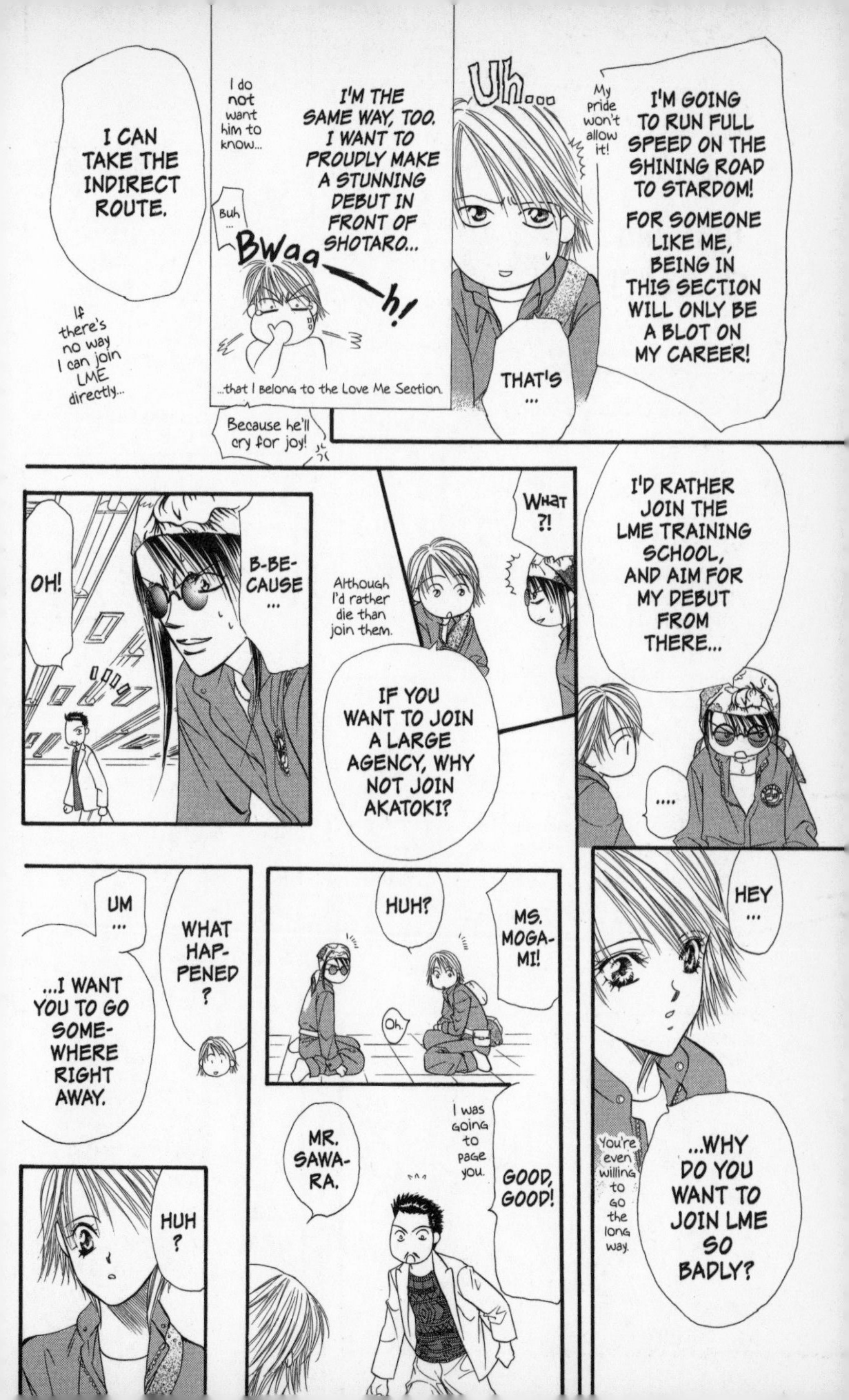

I'M GOING TO RUN FULL SPEED ON THE SHINING ROAD TO STARDOM!
FOR SOMEONE LIKE ME, BEING IN THIS SECTION WILL ONLY BE A BLOT ON MY CAREER!
Uh...
My pride won't allow it!
THAT'S ...
I'M THE SAME WAY, TOO. I WANT TO PROUDLY MAKE A STUNNING DEBUT IN FRONT OF SHOTARO...
I do not want him to know...
...that I belong to the Love Me Section.
Buh ...
Bwaa—h!
Because he'll cry for joy!
If there's no way I can join LME directly...
I CAN TAKE THE INDIRECT ROUTE.
I'D RATHER JOIN THE LME TRAINING SCHOOL, AND AIM FOR MY DEBUT FROM THERE...
....
WHAT?!
IF YOU WANT TO JOIN A LARGE AGENCY, WHY NOT JOIN AKATOKI?
Although I'd rather die than join them.
B-BE-CAUSE ...
OH!
HEY ...
...WHY DO YOU WANT TO JOIN LME SO BADLY?
You're even willing to go the long way.
MS. MOGA-MI!
HUH?
Oh.
GOOD, GOOD!
I was going to page you.
MR. SAWA-RA.
WHAT HAP-PENED?
UM ...
...I WANT YOU TO GO SOME-WHERE RIGHT AWAY.
HUH?

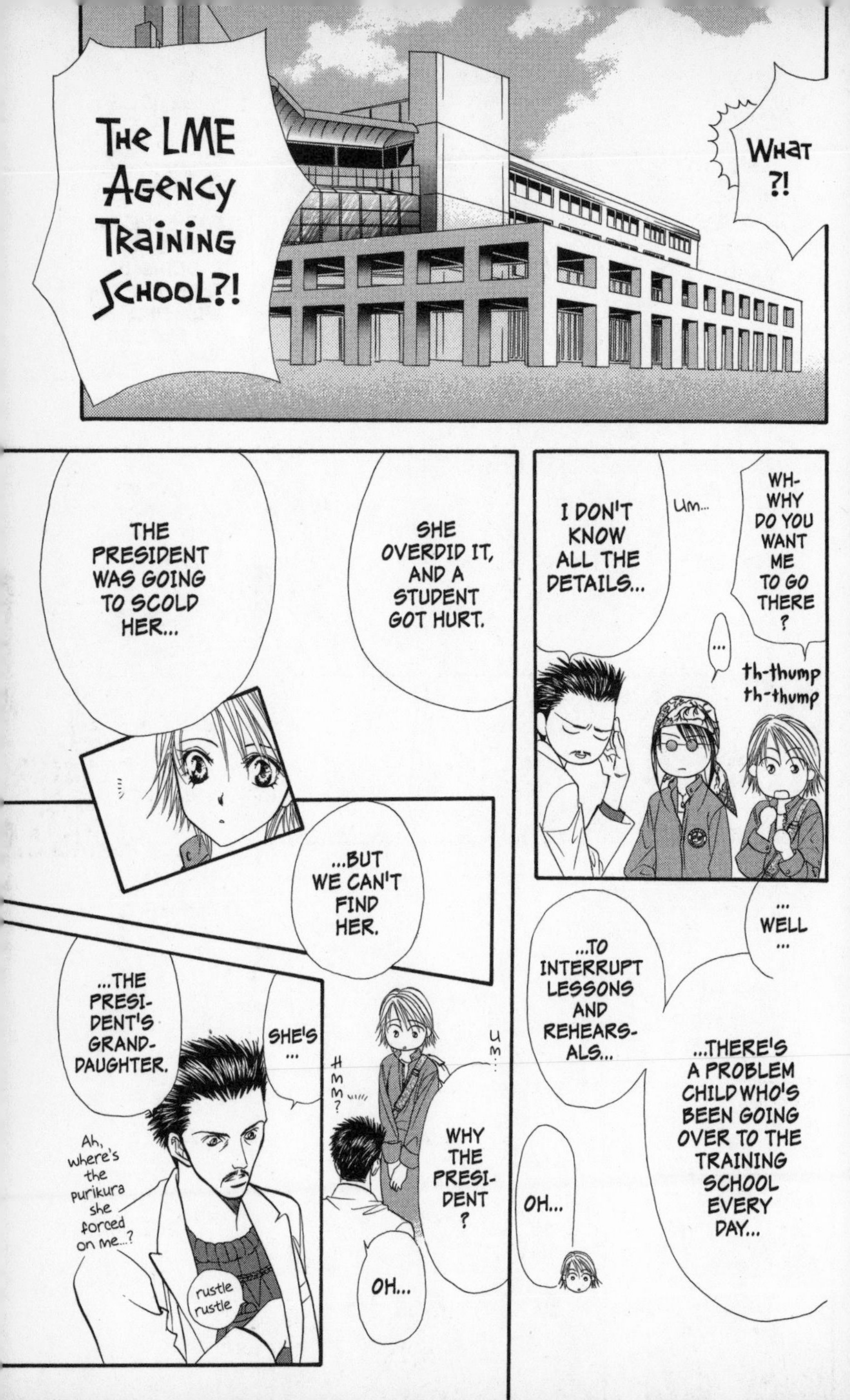
WHAT?!
THE LME AGENCY TRAINING SCHOOL?!
WH-WHY DO YOU WANT ME TO GO THERE?
th-thump th-thump
...
Um...
I DON'T KNOW ALL THE DETAILS...
...WELL...
...THERE'S A PROBLEM CHILD WHO'S BEEN GOING OVER TO THE TRAINING SCHOOL EVERY DAY...
...TO INTERRUPT LESSONS AND REHEARSALS...
OH...
SHE OVERDID IT, AND A STUDENT GOT HURT.
THE PRESIDENT WAS GOING TO SCOLD HER...
...BUT WE CAN'T FIND HER.
UM...
WHY THE PRESIDENT?
HMM?
OH...
SHE'S...
...THE PRESIDENT'S GRANDDAUGHTER.
Ah, where's the purikura she forced on me...?
rustle rustle

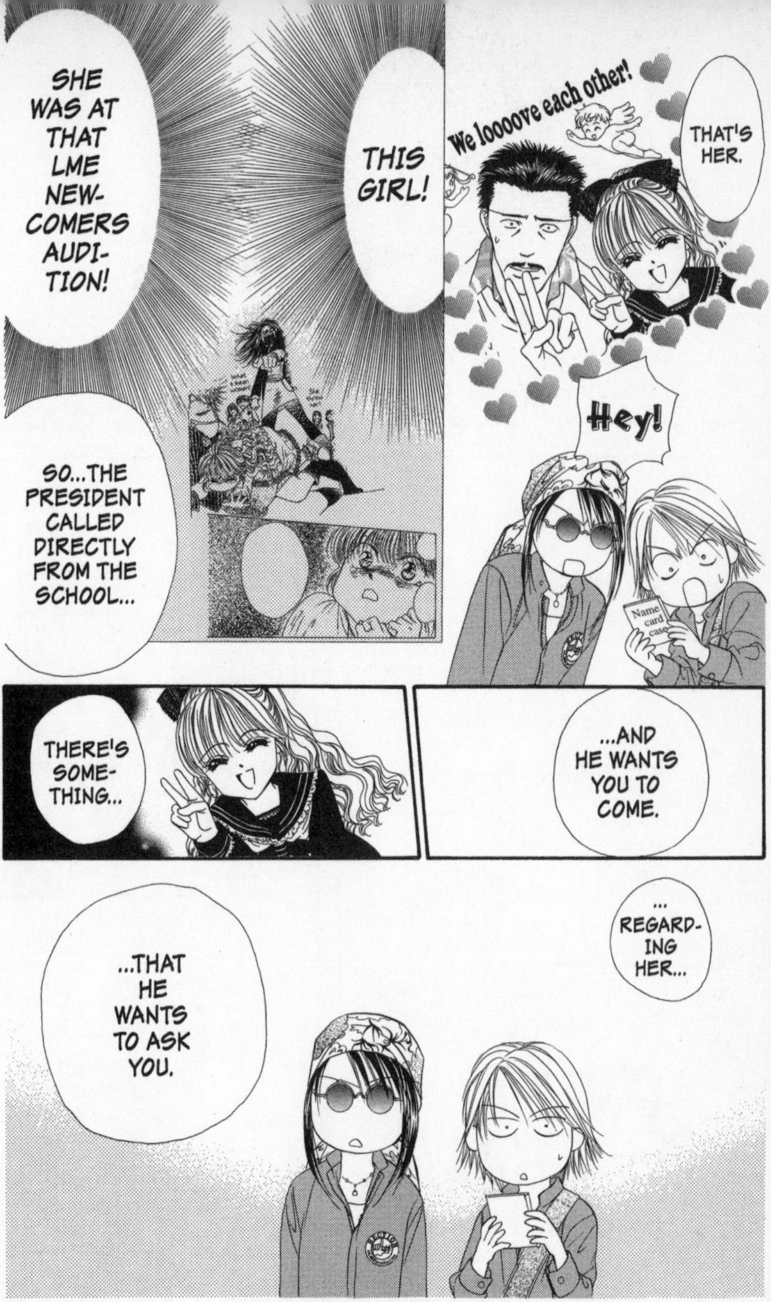
THAT'S HER.
We loooove each other!
Hey!
Name card case
THIS GIRL!
SHE WAS AT THAT LME NEW-COMERS AUDI-TION!
SO...THE PRESIDENT CALLED DIRECTLY FROM THE SCHOOL...
...AND HE WANTS YOU TO COME.
THERE'S SOME-THING...
...REGARD-ING HER...
...THAT HE WANTS TO ASK YOU.

End of Act 15

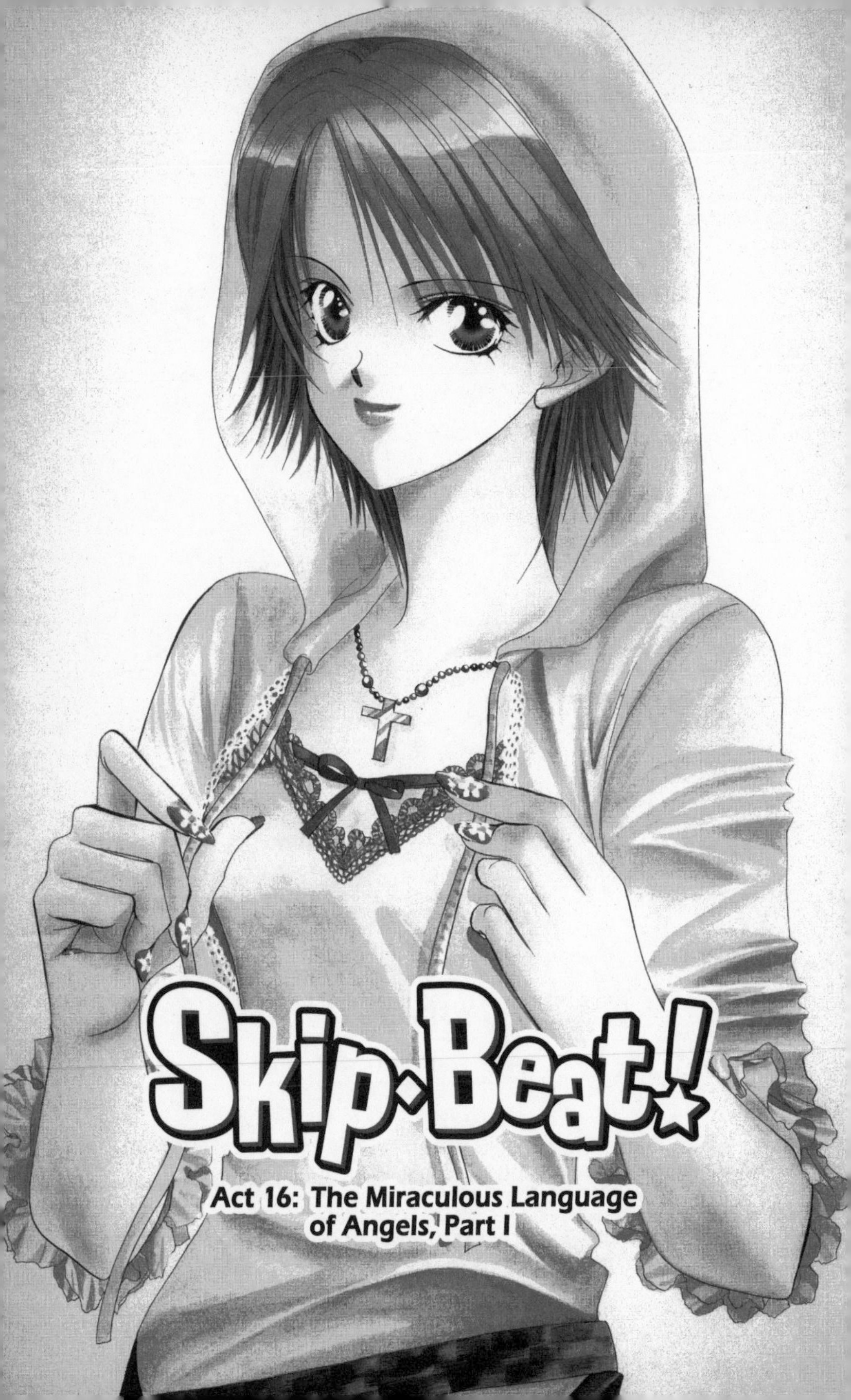
Skip·Beat!
Act 16: The Miraculous Language of Angels, Part I

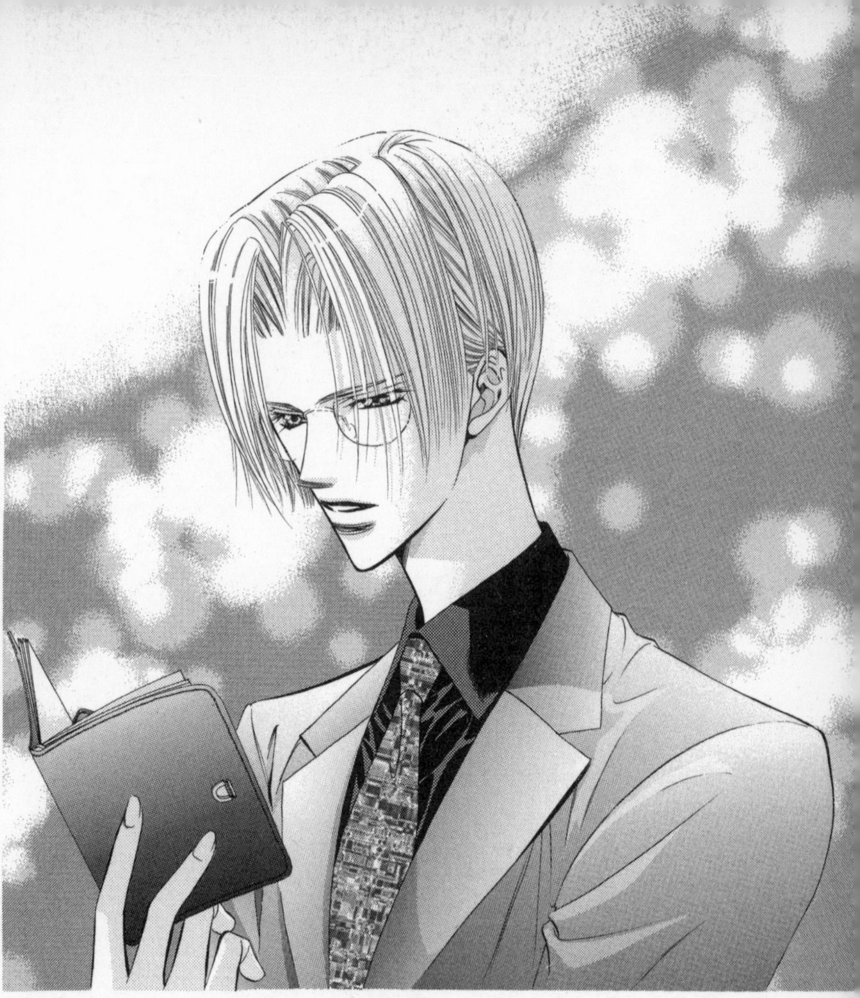

Yukihito Yashiro

Difficulty level ☆☆☆☆ (4)

It's his hair that's difficult... His expression is softer than it was in the beginning, and I'm not sure whether that's good or bad. I feel that the blurry image of Yashiro I had in my head has changed a little bit... But this Yashiro...he hasn't really done anything conspicuous, but somehow, secretly, the readers love him and I'm surprised...does that mean girls love guys who wear glasses...?

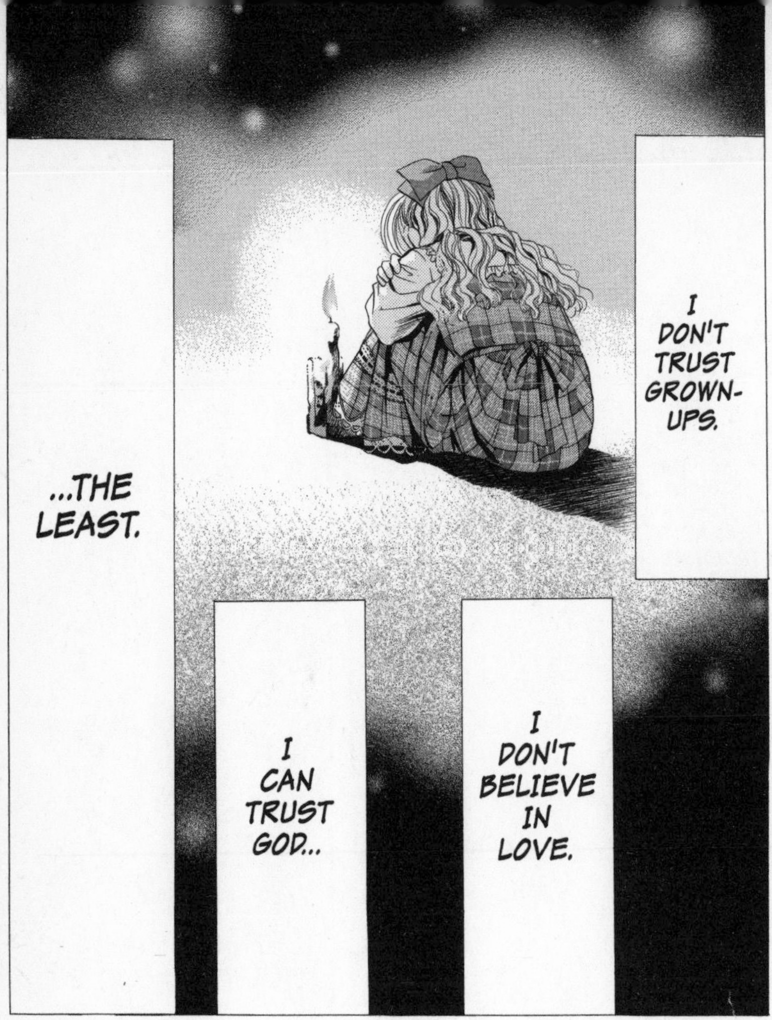
I DON'T TRUST GROWN-UPS.
I DON'T BELIEVE IN LOVE.
I CAN TRUST GOD...
...THE LEAST.

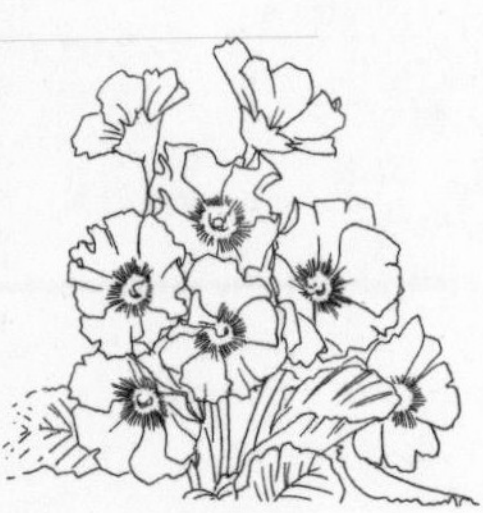

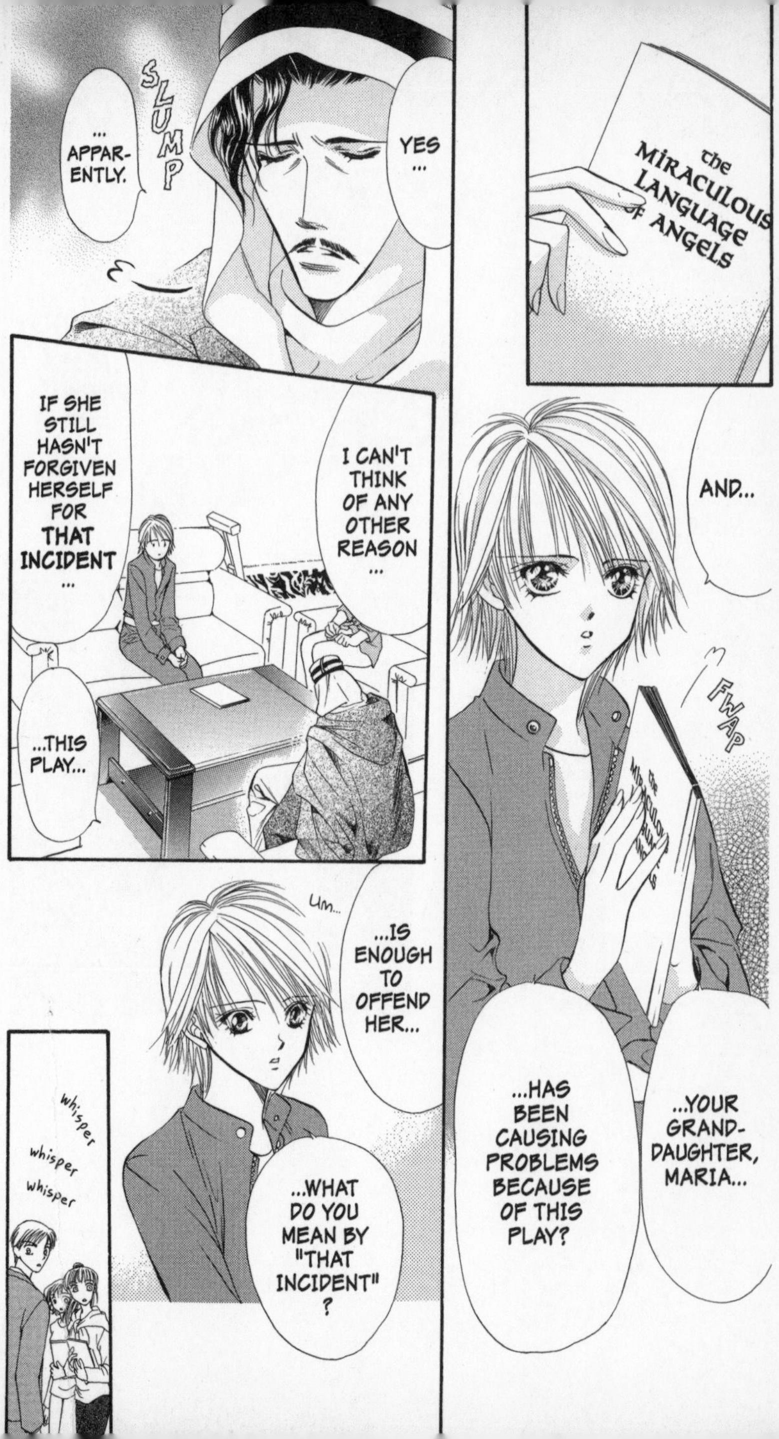
The Miraculous Language of Angels
YES ...
... APPARENTLY.
SLUMP
AND...
FWAP
The Miraculous Language of Angels
...YOUR GRAND-DAUGHTER, MARIA...
...HAS BEEN CAUSING PROBLEMS BECAUSE OF THIS PLAY?
I CAN'T THINK OF ANY OTHER REASON ...
IF SHE STILL HASN'T FORGIVEN HERSELF FOR THAT INCIDENT ...
...THIS PLAY...
Um...
...IS ENOUGH TO OFFEND HER...
...WHAT DO YOU MEAN BY "THAT INCIDENT" ?
whisper
whisper
whisper

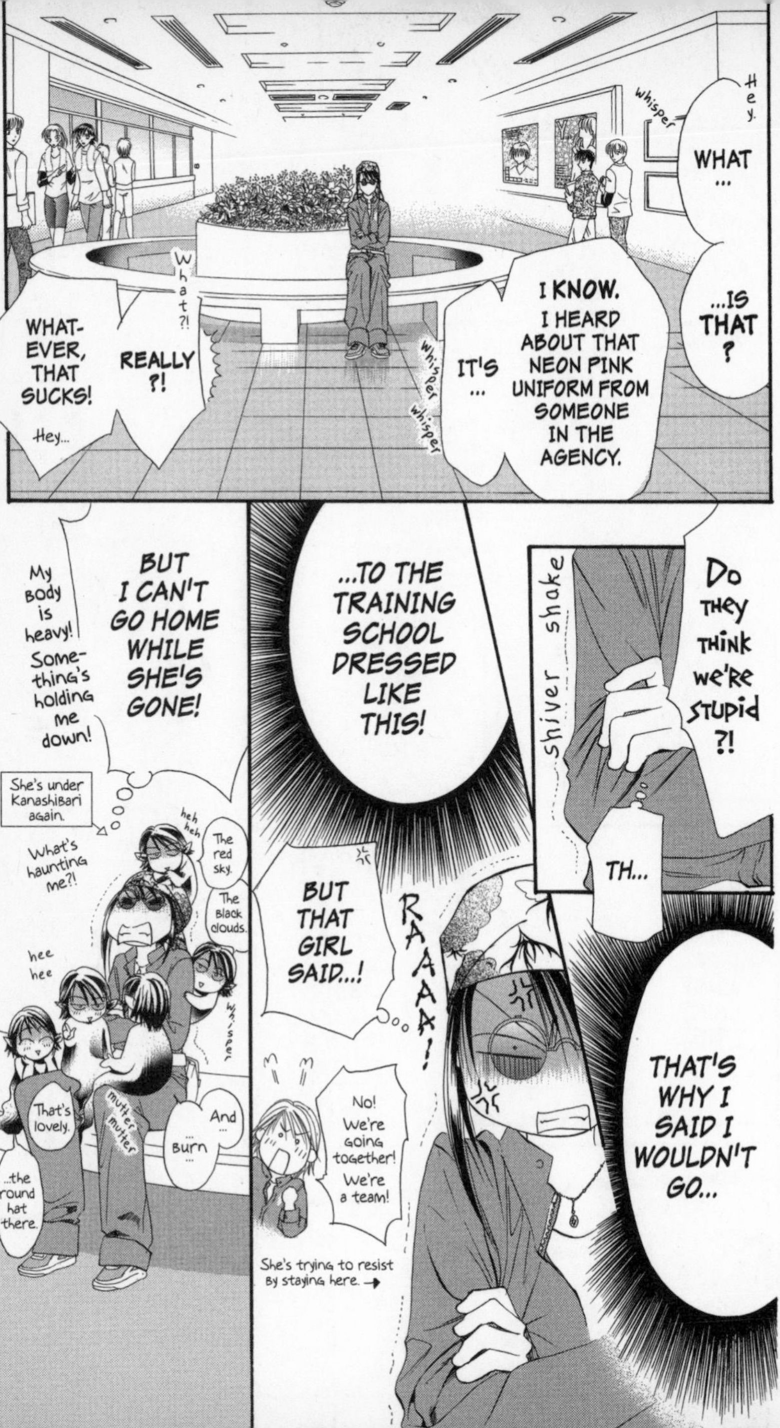
Hey.
WHAT...
...IS THAT?
whisper
I KNOW. I HEARD ABOUT THAT NEON PINK UNIFORM FROM SOMEONE IN THE AGENCY.
IT'S...
whisper whisper
What?!
REALLY?!
WHATEVER, THAT SUCKS!
Hey...
Do they think we're stupid?!
shiver shake
TH...
THAT'S WHY I SAID I WOULDN'T GO...
...TO THE TRAINING SCHOOL DRESSED LIKE THIS!
BUT THAT GIRL SAID...!
RAAAA!
No! We're going together! We're a team!
She's trying to resist by staying here.
BUT I CAN'T GO HOME WHILE SHE'S GONE!
My body is heavy! Something's holding me down!
She's under Kanashibari again.
What's haunting me?!
heh heh
The red sky.
The black clouds.
hee hee
whisper
That's lovely.
mutter mutter
And... Burn...
...the round hat there.

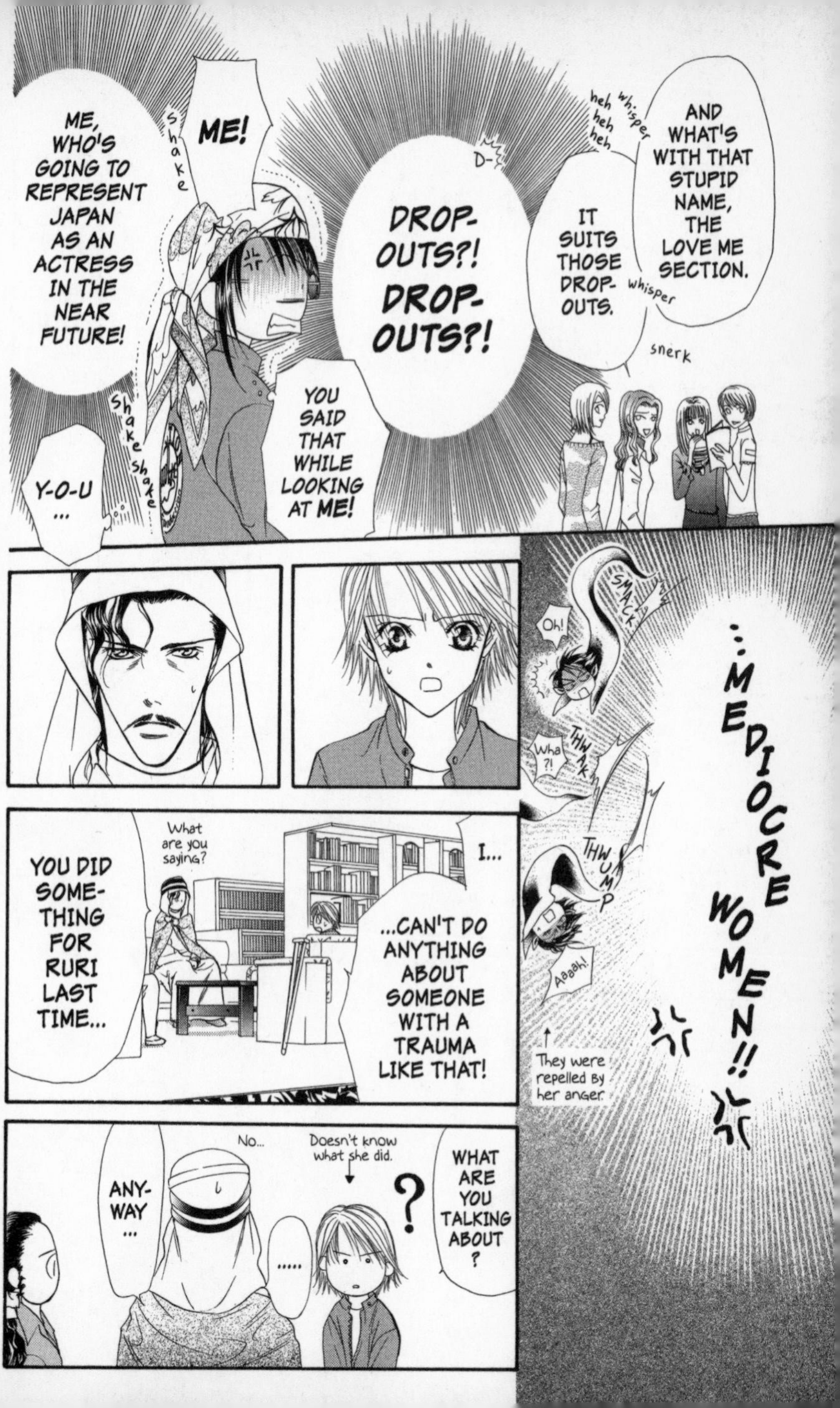
AND WHAT'S WITH THAT STUPID NAME, THE LOVE ME SECTION.
whisper
whisper
IT SUITS THOSE DROP-OUTS.
heh heh heh
snerk
D-
DROP-OUTS?! DROP-OUTS?!
YOU SAID THAT WHILE LOOKING AT ME!
ME!
shake
ME, WHO'S GOING TO REPRESENT JAPAN AS AN ACTRESS IN THE NEAR FUTURE!
shake shake
Y-O-U ...
...MEDIOCRE WOMEN!!
SMACK
Oh!
THWAK
Wha ?!
THWUMP
Aaaah!
They were repelled by her anger.
I...
...CAN'T DO ANYTHING ABOUT SOMEONE WITH A TRAUMA LIKE THAT!
What are you saying?
YOU DID SOME-THING FOR RURI LAST TIME...
WHAT ARE YOU TALKING ABOUT?
?
Doesn't know what she did.
.....
No...
ANY-WAY ...

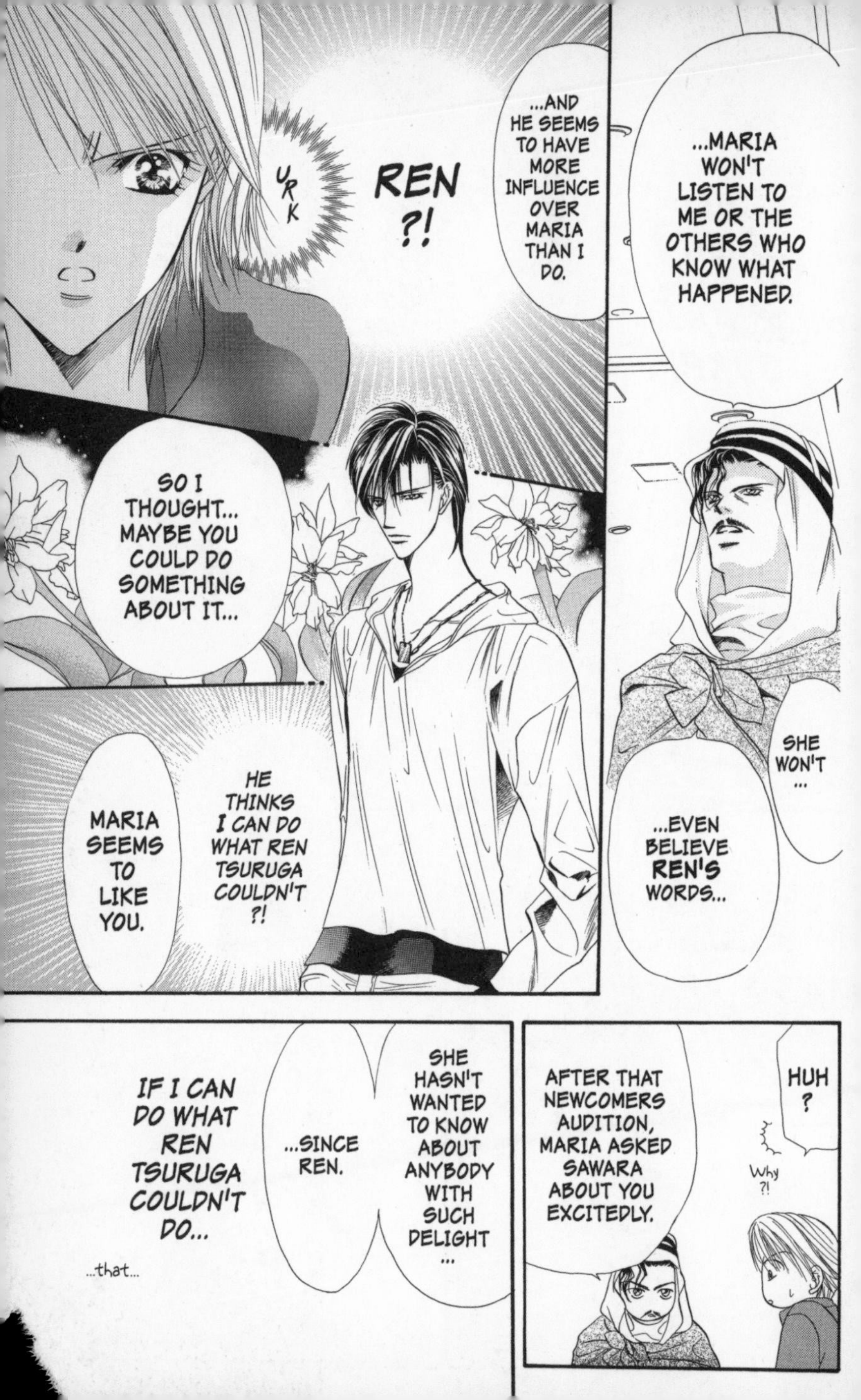
...MARIA WON'T LISTEN TO ME OR THE OTHERS WHO KNOW WHAT HAPPENED.
...AND HE SEEMS TO HAVE MORE INFLUENCE OVER MARIA THAN I DO.
REN ?!
URK
SHE WON'T ...
...EVEN BELIEVE REN'S WORDS...
SO I THOUGHT... MAYBE YOU COULD DO SOMETHING ABOUT IT...
HE THINKS I CAN DO WHAT REN TSURUGA COULDN'T ?!
MARIA SEEMS TO LIKE YOU.
HUH ?
Why ?!
AFTER THAT NEWCOMERS AUDITION, MARIA ASKED SAWARA ABOUT YOU EXCITEDLY.
SHE HASN'T WANTED TO KNOW ABOUT ANYBODY WITH SUCH DELIGHT ...
...SINCE REN.
IF I CAN DO WHAT REN TSURUGA COULDN'T DO...
...that...

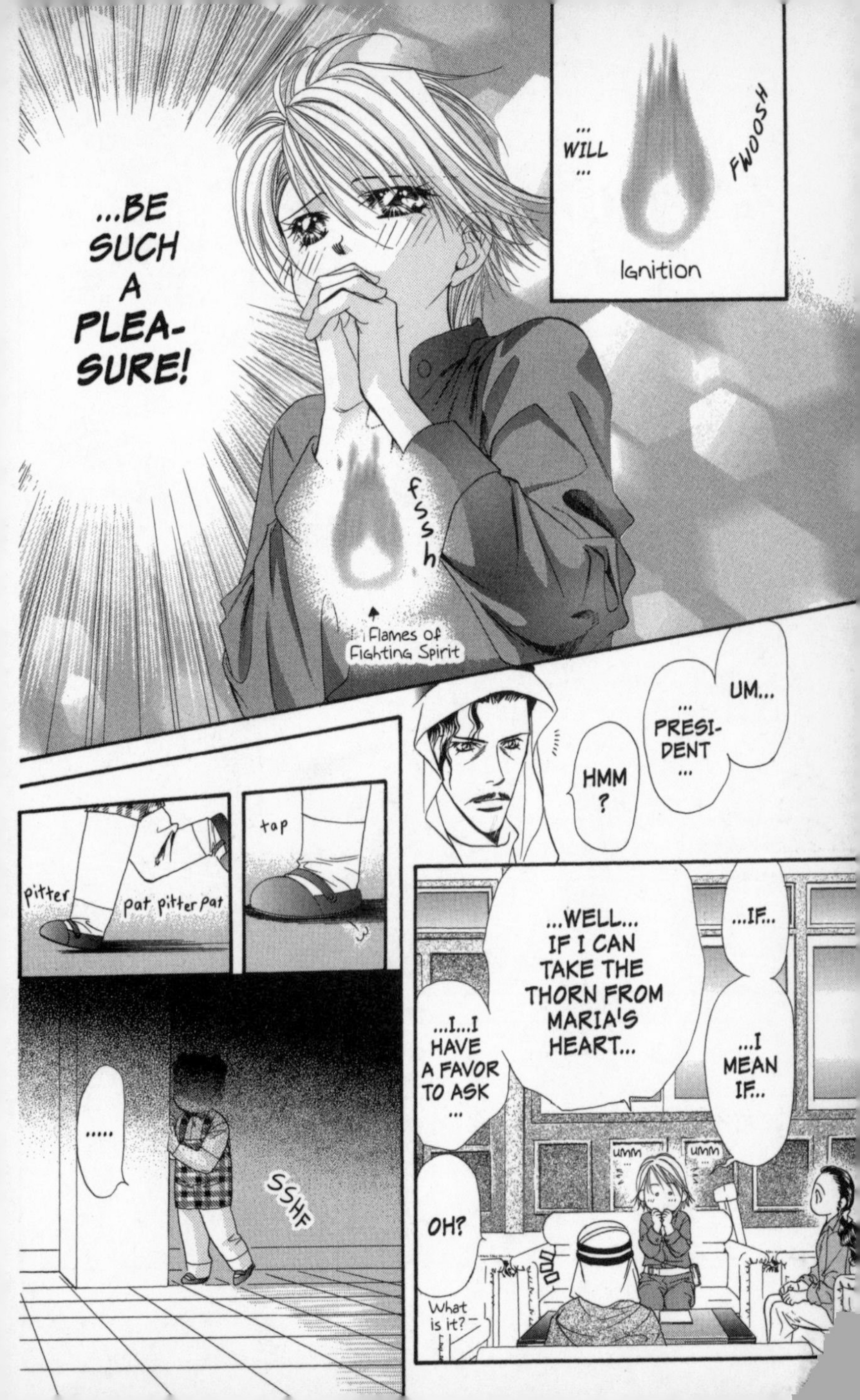
...WILL...
FWOOSH
Ignition
...BE SUCH A PLEA-SURE!
fssh
Flames of Fighting Spirit
UM...
...PRESI-DENT...
HMM?
tap
pitter
pat pitter pat
...IF...
...WELL... IF I CAN TAKE THE THORN FROM MARIA'S HEART...
...I MEAN IF...
...I...I HAVE A FAVOR TO ASK...
umm...
umm...
OH?
What is it?
.....
SSHF

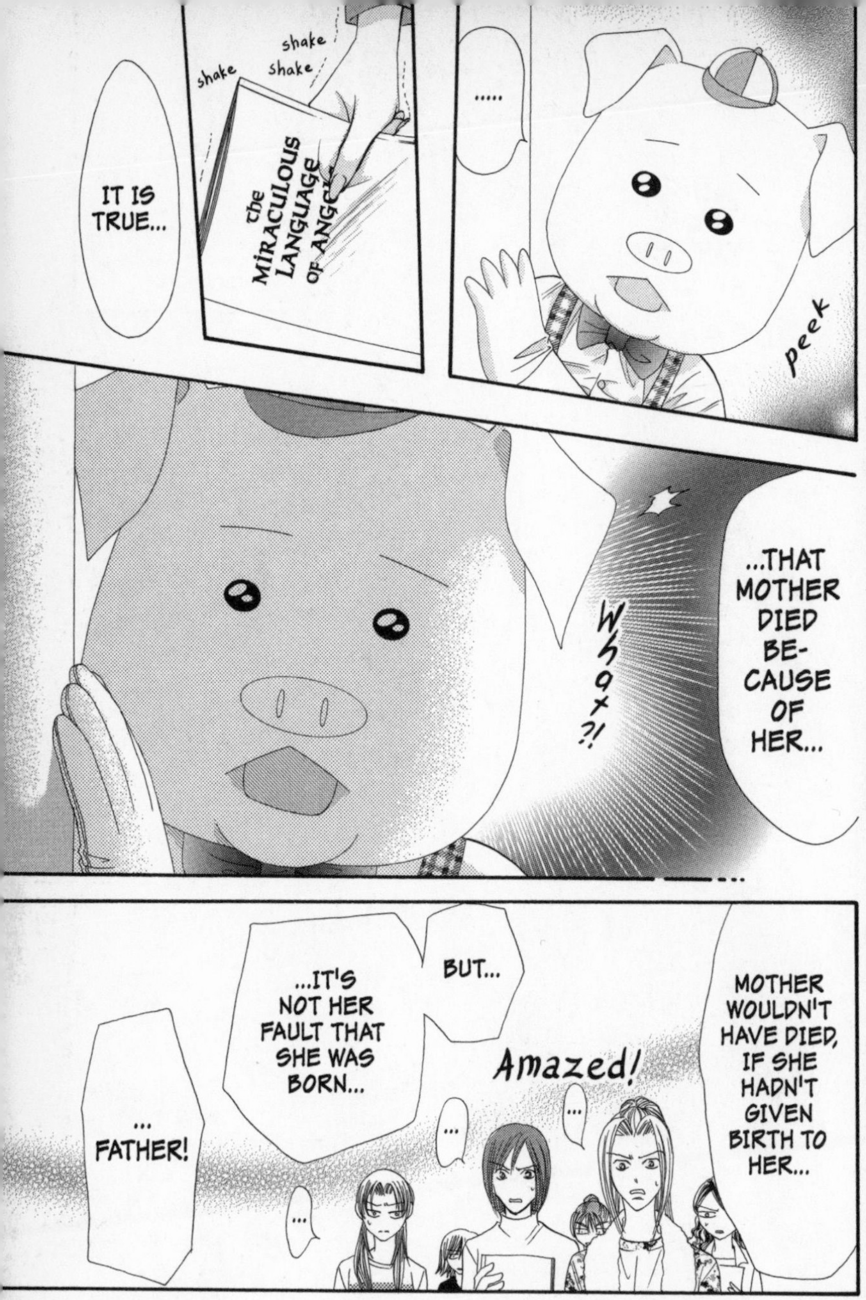
.....
peek
shake
shake
shake
the MiRACULOUS LANGUAGE OF ANGE
IT IS TRUE...
...THAT MOTHER DIED BE-CAUSE OF HER...
What?!
MOTHER WOULDN'T HAVE DIED, IF SHE HADN'T GIVEN BIRTH TO HER...
BUT...
...IT'S NOT HER FAULT THAT SHE WAS BORN...
Amazed!
...
...
...
... FATHER!

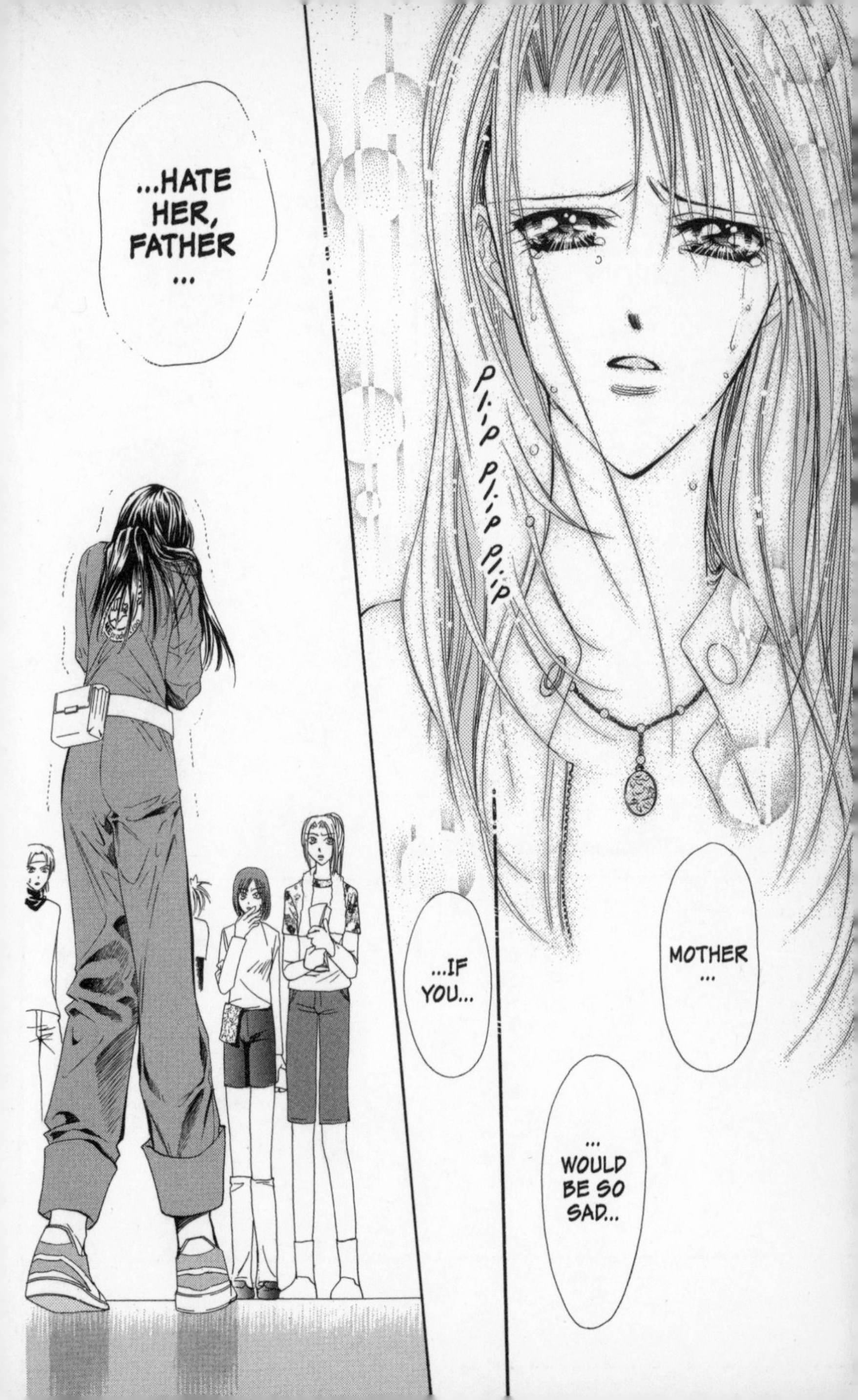
PLIP PLIP PLIP
MOTHER ...
...IF YOU...
... WOULD BE SO SAD...
...HATE HER, FATHER ...

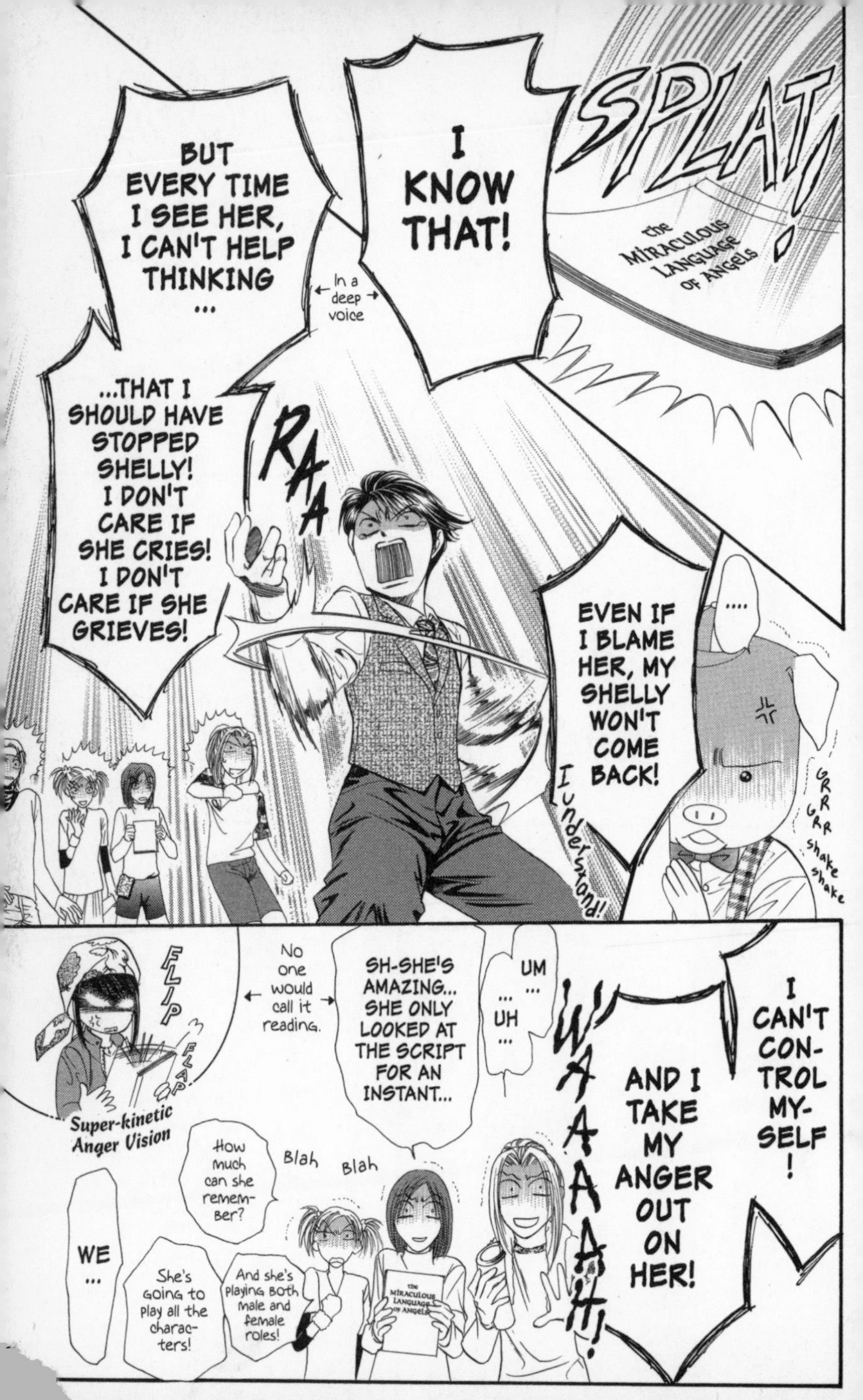
SPLAT!
the MIRACULOUS LANGUAGE OF ANGELS
I KNOW THAT!
In a deep voice
BUT EVERY TIME I SEE HER, I CAN'T HELP THINKING...
...THAT I SHOULD HAVE STOPPED SHELLY! I DON'T CARE IF SHE CRIES! I DON'T CARE IF SHE GRIEVES!
RAA
EVEN IF I BLAME HER, MY SHELLY WON'T COME BACK!
....
GRR GRR
shake shake
I understand!
I CAN'T CONTROL MYSELF!
AND I TAKE MY ANGER OUT ON HER!
WAAAAAH!
UM... ...UH...
SH-SHE'S AMAZING... SHE ONLY LOOKED AT THE SCRIPT FOR AN INSTANT...
No one would call it reading.
FLIP
FLAP
Super-kinetic Anger Vision
How much can she remember?
Blah Blah
THE MIRACULOUS LANGUAGE OF ANGELS
WE...
And she's playing both male and female roles!
She's going to play all the characters!

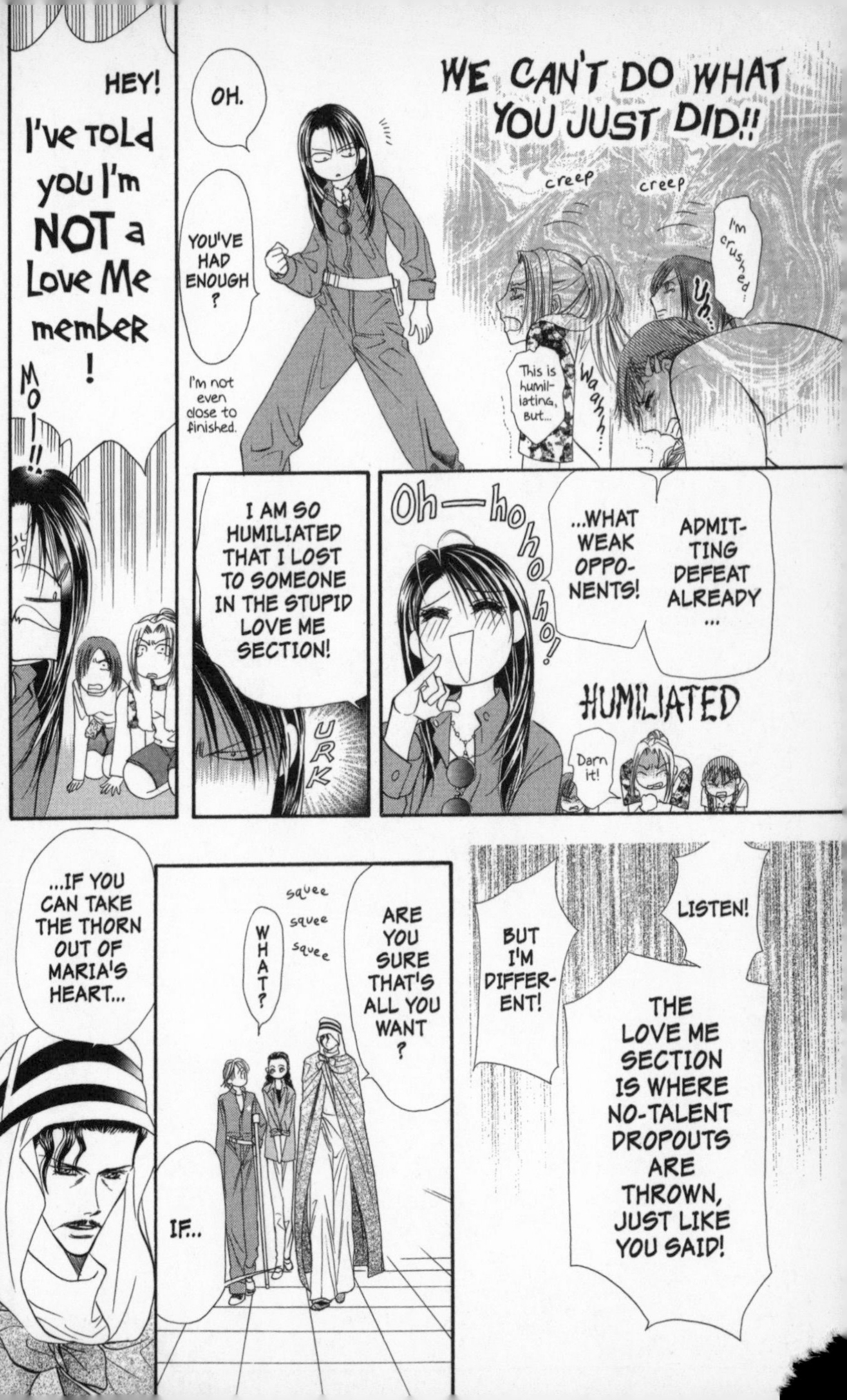
WE CAN'T DO WHAT YOU JUST DID!!
creep
creep
I'm crushed...
Uh...
This is humiliating, but...
Waahh...
OH.
YOU'VE HAD ENOUGH?
I'm not even close to finished.
HEY!
I've told you I'm NOT a Love Me member!
MO—!!
Oh—hohohoho!
ADMITTING DEFEAT ALREADY...
...WHAT WEAK OPPONENTS!
HUMILIATED
Darn it!
I AM SO HUMILIATED THAT I LOST TO SOMEONE IN THE STUPID LOVE ME SECTION!
URK
LISTEN!
BUT I'M DIFFERENT!
THE LOVE ME SECTION IS WHERE NO-TALENT DROPOUTS ARE THROWN, JUST LIKE YOU SAID!
ARE YOU SURE THAT'S ALL YOU WANT?
squee
squee
squee
WHAT?
IF...
...IF YOU CAN TAKE THE THORN OUT OF MARIA'S HEART...

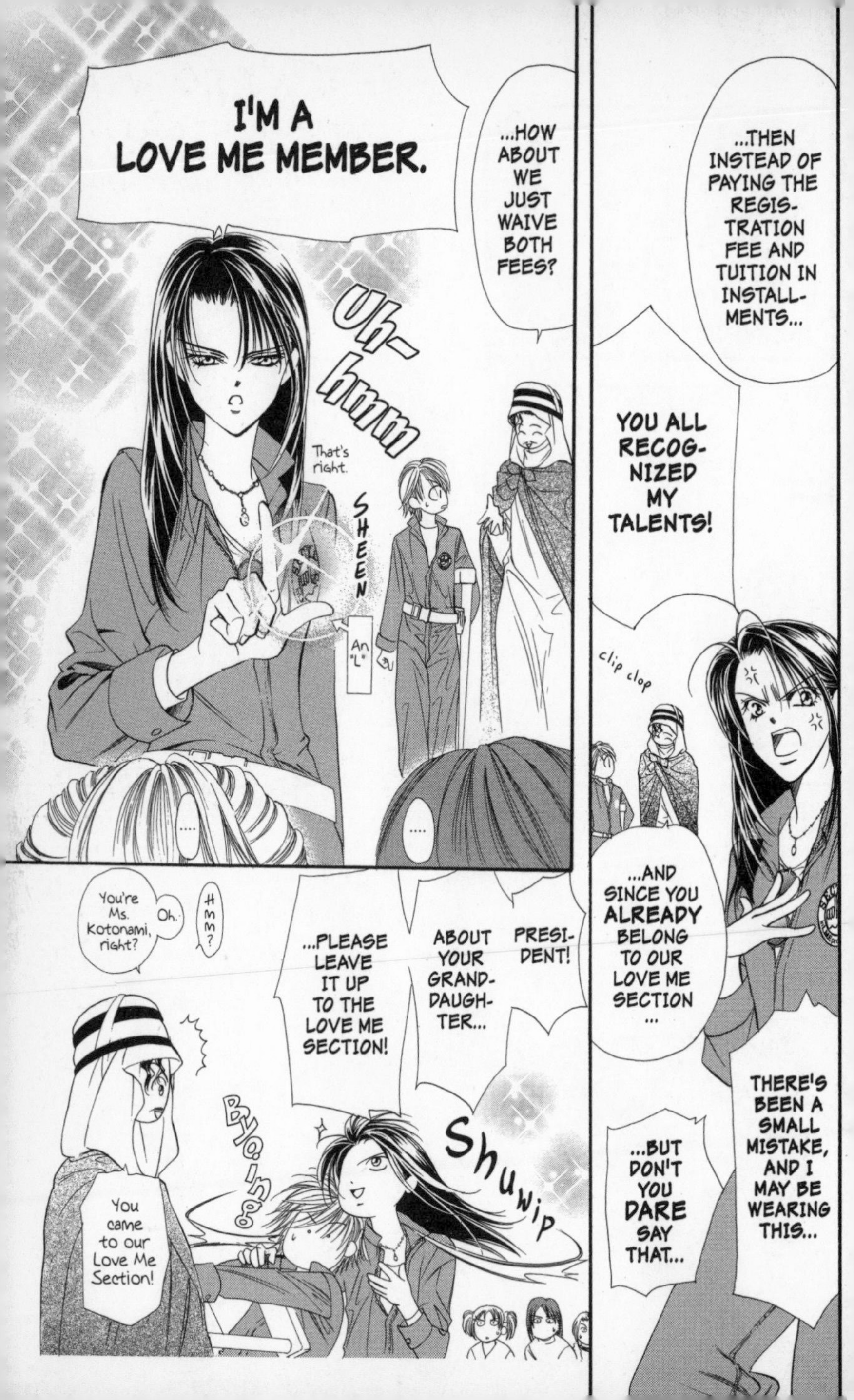

...THEN INSTEAD OF PAYING THE REGIS-TRATION FEE AND TUITION IN INSTALL-MENTS...
YOU ALL RECOG-NIZED MY TALENTS!
clip clop
...AND SINCE YOU ALREADY BELONG TO OUR LOVE ME SECTION ...
THERE'S BEEN A SMALL MISTAKE, AND I MAY BE WEARING THIS...
...BUT DON'T YOU DARE SAY THAT...
...HOW ABOUT WE JUST WAIVE BOTH FEES?
I'M A LOVE ME MEMBER.
Uh-hmm
That's right.
SHEEN
An "L"
....
....
PRESI-DENT!
ABOUT YOUR GRAND-DAUGH-TER...
...PLEASE LEAVE IT UP TO THE LOVE ME SECTION!
Hmm?
Oh.
You're Ms. Kotonami, right?
Shuwip
Byoing
You came to our Love Me Section!

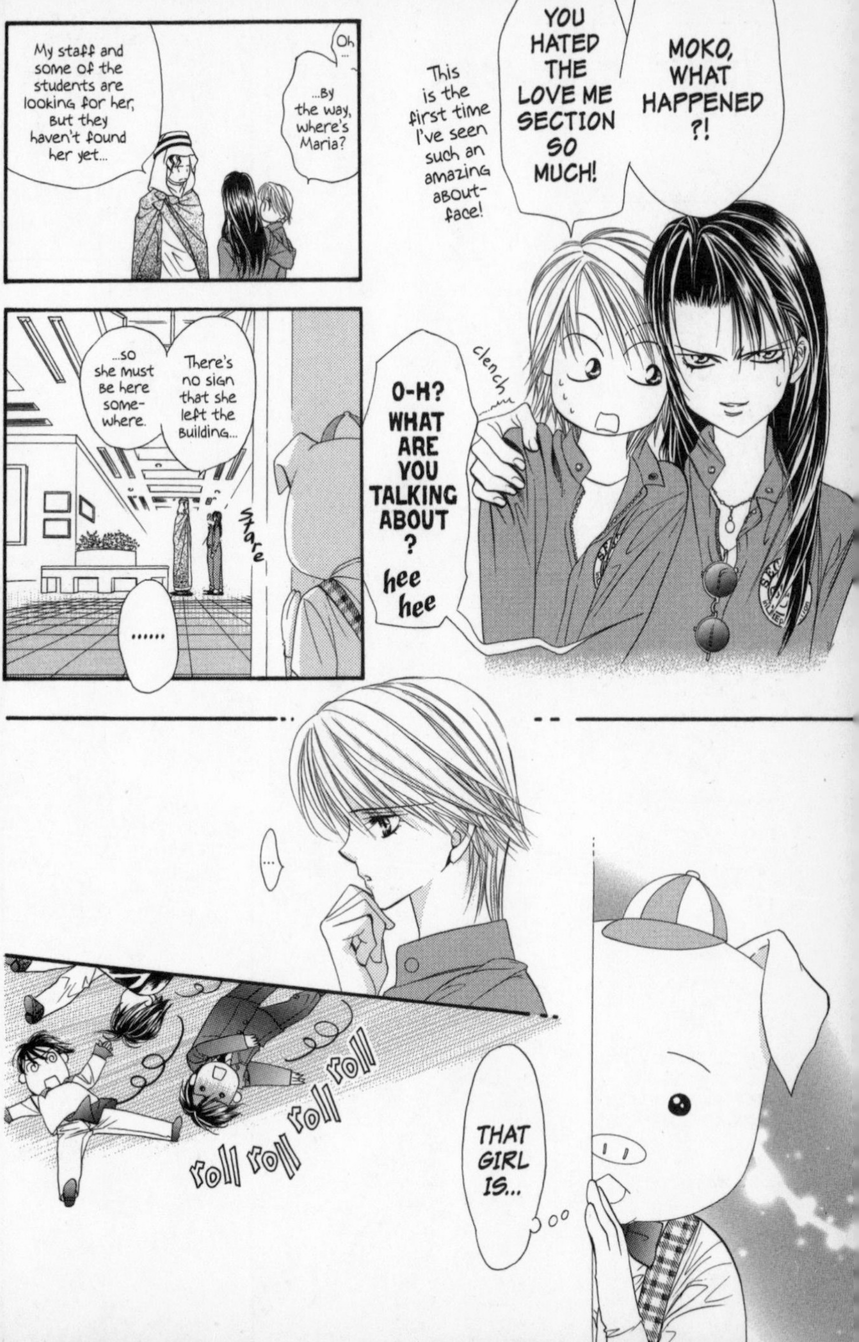

MOKO, WHAT HAPPENED?!
YOU HATED THE LOVE ME SECTION SO MUCH!
This is the first time I've seen such an amazing about-face!
clench
O-H? WHAT ARE YOU TALKING ABOUT?
hee hee
Oh...
...By the way, where's Maria?
My staff and some of the students are looking for her, but they haven't found her yet...
There's no sign that she left the building...
...so she must be here somewhere.
stare
......
THAT GIRL IS...
...
roll roll roll roll

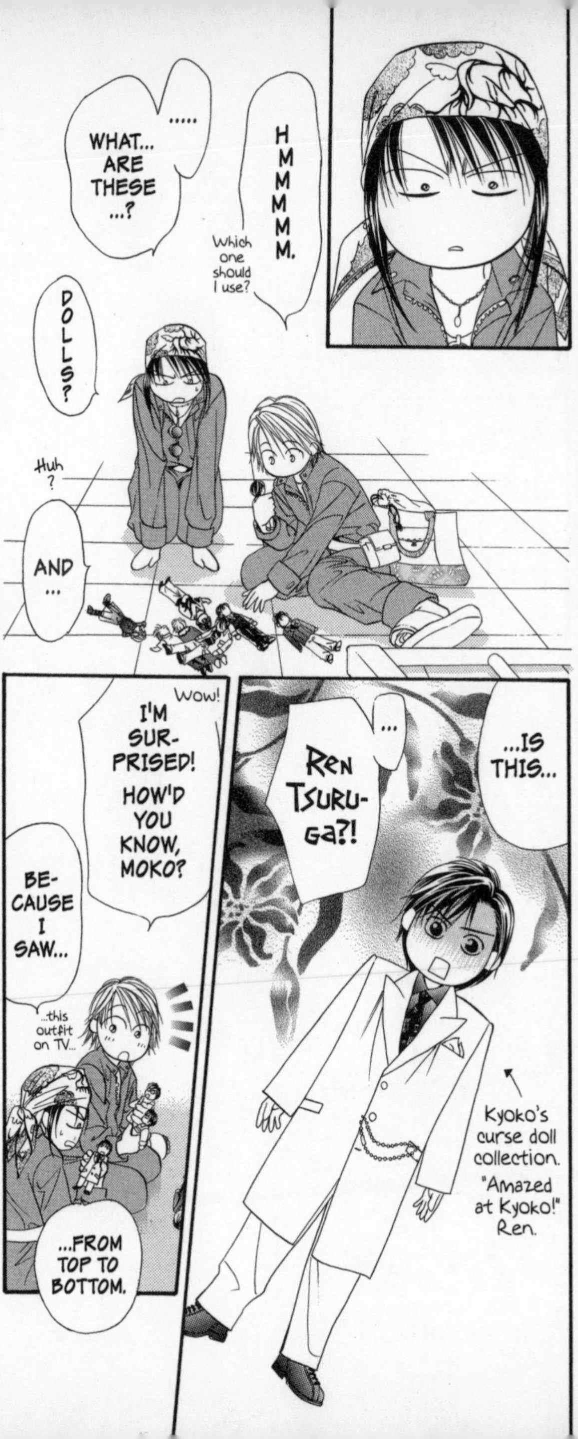
HMMMMM.
Which one should I use?
.....
WHAT... ARE THESE ...?
DOLLS?
Huh?
AND ...
...IS THIS...
...
Ren Tsuruga?!
Kyoko's curse doll collection. "Amazed at Kyoko!" Ren.
Wow!
I'M SURPRISED! HOW'D YOU KNOW, MOKO?
BECAUSE I SAW...
...this outfit on TV...
...FROM TOP TO BOTTOM.

Maria Takarada

...is her name...? I guess... ♪

Difficulty level

☆ ☆ ②

The difficulty level must be 5 for my assistants... ♪ (Because she's always wearing complicated clothes with frills... ♪) ...well...I put 2 stars for difficulty, but to tell the truth, drawing Maria's hair takes a lot of time, and I don't like that.

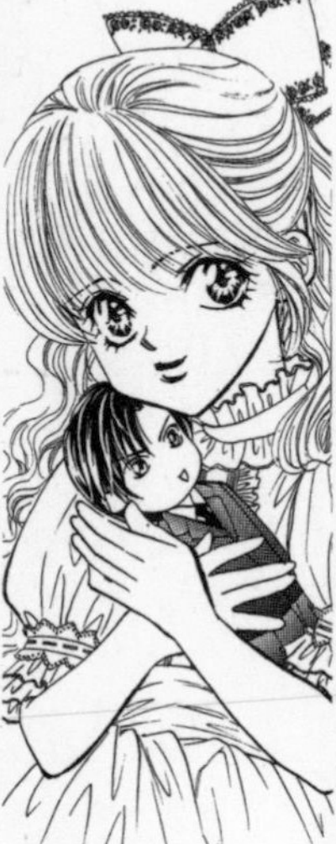

But you can't paint soft hair all black, because the picture would become heavy. And in any case, it's sad but...even though it's a bother, I like girls with this type of soft hair.. ♪

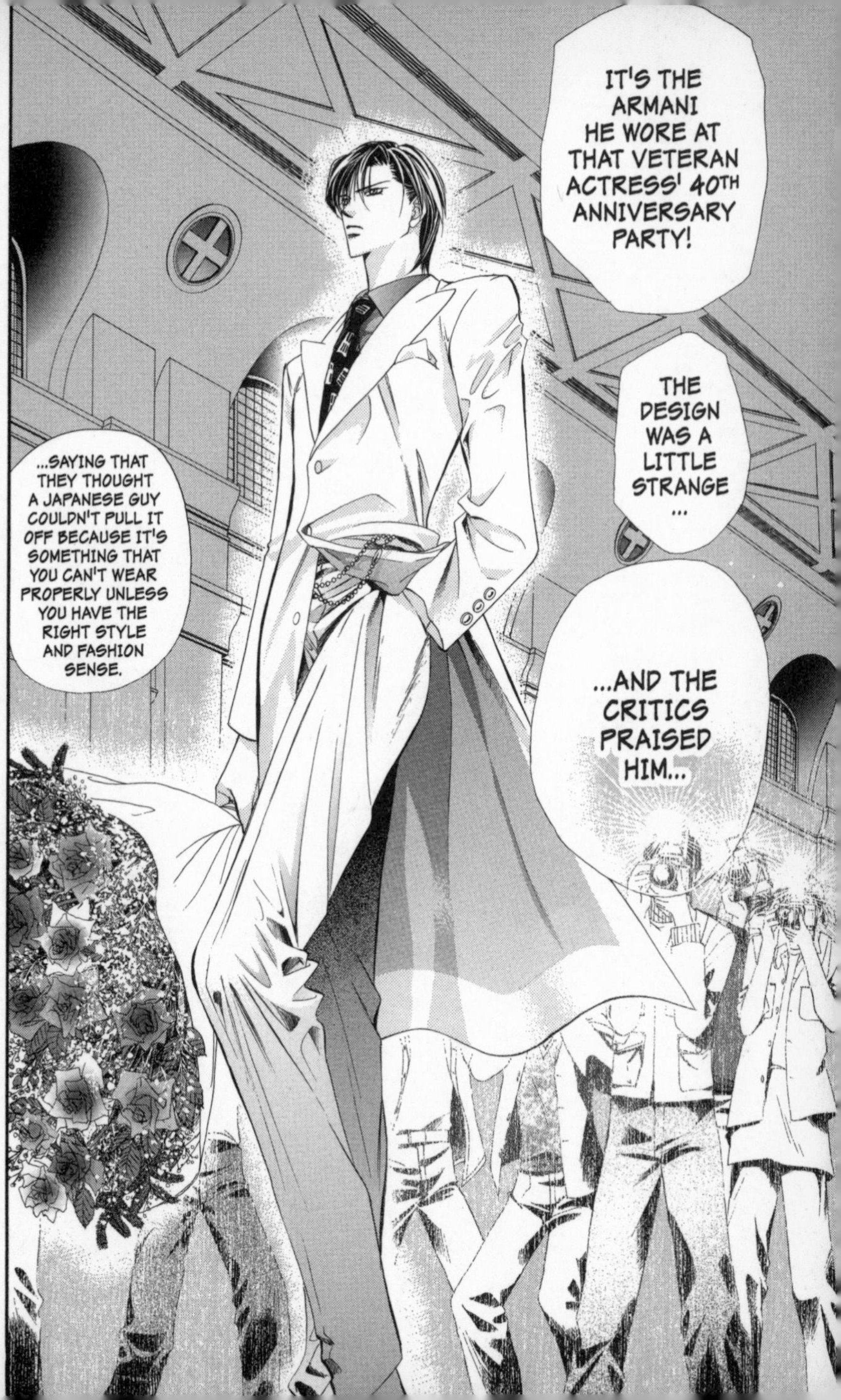
IT'S THE ARMANI HE WORE AT THAT VETERAN ACTRESS' 40TH ANNIVERSARY PARTY!
THE DESIGN WAS A LITTLE STRANGE ...
...AND THE CRITICS PRAISED HIM...
...SAYING THAT THEY THOUGHT A JAPANESE GUY COULDN'T PULL IT OFF BECAUSE IT'S SOMETHING THAT YOU CAN'T WEAR PROPERLY UNLESS YOU HAVE THE RIGHT STYLE AND FASHION SENSE.

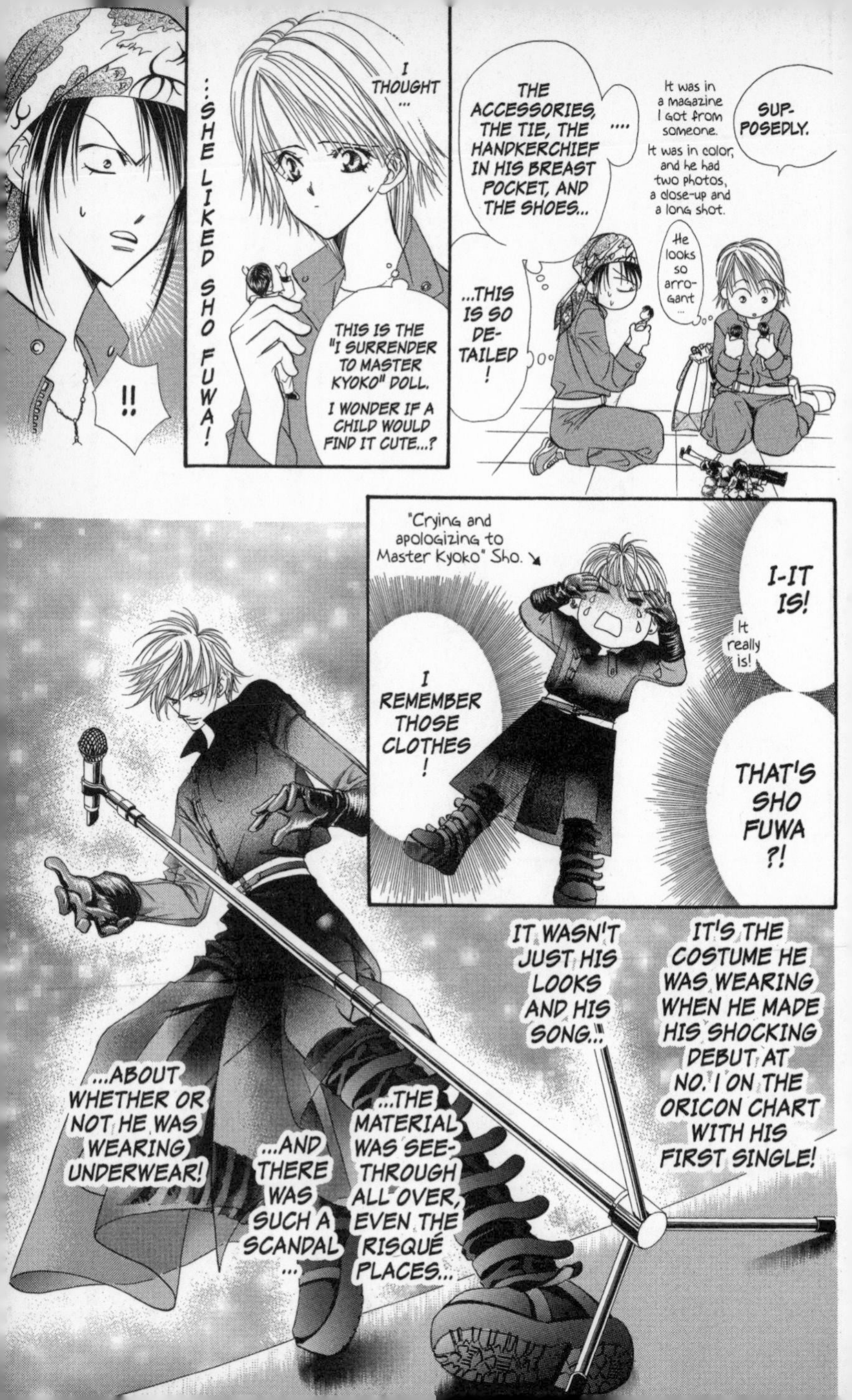
SUP-POSEDLY.
It was in a magazine I got from someone.
It was in color, and he had two photos, a close-up and a long shot.
THE ACCESSORIES, THE TIE, THE HANDKERCHIEF IN HIS BREAST POCKET, AND THE SHOES...
....
He looks so arro-gant...
...THIS IS SO DE-TAILED!
I THOUGHT...
THIS IS THE "I SURRENDER TO MASTER KYOKO" DOLL.
I WONDER IF A CHILD WOULD FIND IT CUTE...?
...SHE LIKED SHO FUWA!
!!
I-IT IS!
It really is!
THAT'S SHO FUWA?!
I REMEMBER THOSE CLOTHES!
"Crying and apologizing to Master Kyoko" Sho.
IT'S THE COSTUME HE WAS WEARING WHEN HE MADE HIS SHOCKING DEBUT AT NO. 1 ON THE ORICON CHART WITH HIS FIRST SINGLE!
IT WASN'T JUST HIS LOOKS AND HIS SONG...
...THE MATERIAL WAS SEE-THROUGH ALL OVER, EVEN THE RISQUÉ PLACES...
...AND THERE WAS SUCH A SCANDAL...
...ABOUT WHETHER OR NOT HE WAS WEARING UNDERWEAR!

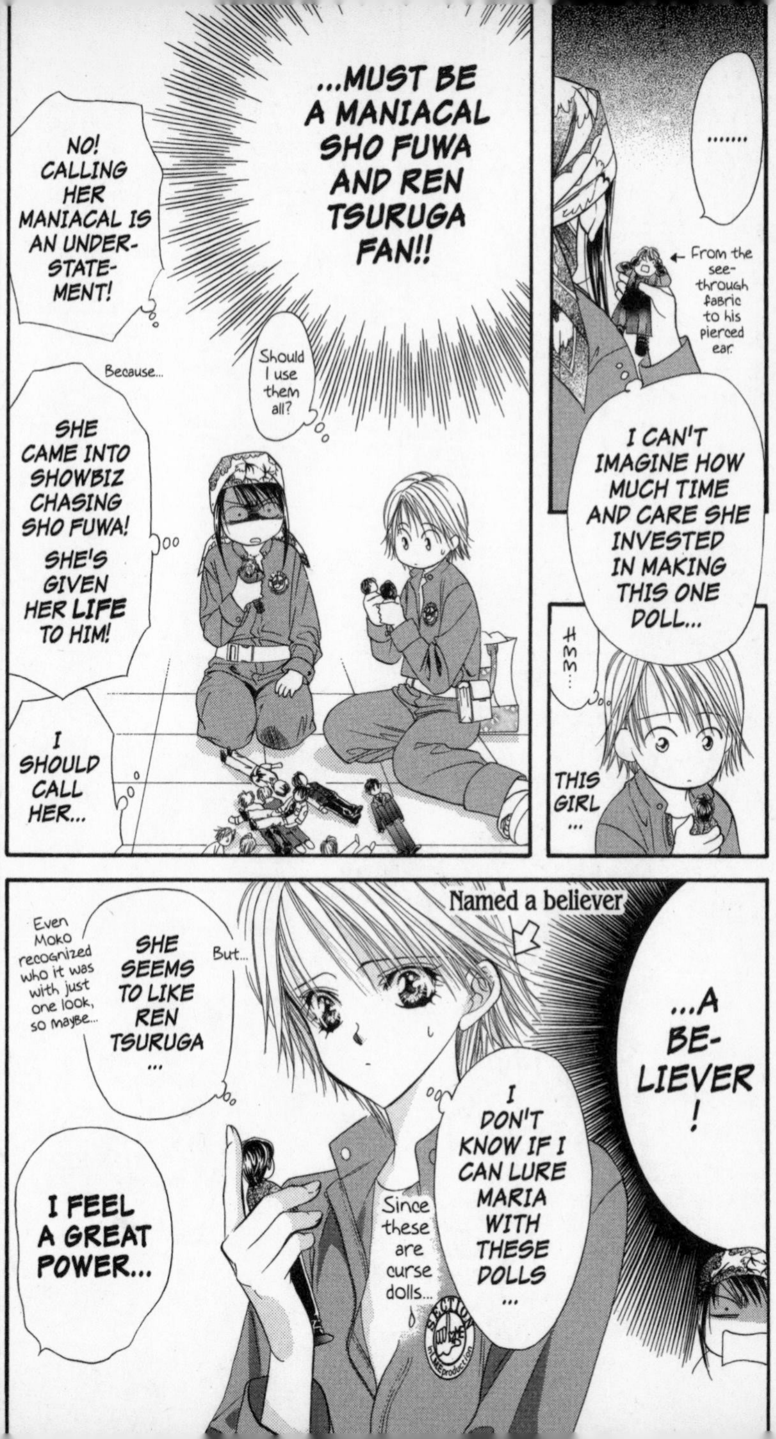

....
From the see-through fabric to his pierced ear.
I CAN'T IMAGINE HOW MUCH TIME AND CARE SHE INVESTED IN MAKING THIS ONE DOLL...
HMM...
THIS GIRL...
...MUST BE A MANIACAL SHO FUWA AND REN TSURUGA FAN!!
NO! CALLING HER MANIACAL IS AN UNDER-STATE-MENT!
Should I use them all?
Because...
SHE CAME INTO SHOWBIZ CHASING SHO FUWA! SHE'S GIVEN HER LIFE TO HIM!
I SHOULD CALL HER...
...A BE-LIEVER!
Named a believer
I DON'T KNOW IF I CAN LURE MARIA WITH THESE DOLLS...
Since these are curse dolls...
But...
SHE SEEMS TO LIKE REN TSURUGA...
Even Moko recognized who it was with just one look, so maybe...
I FEEL A GREAT POWER...

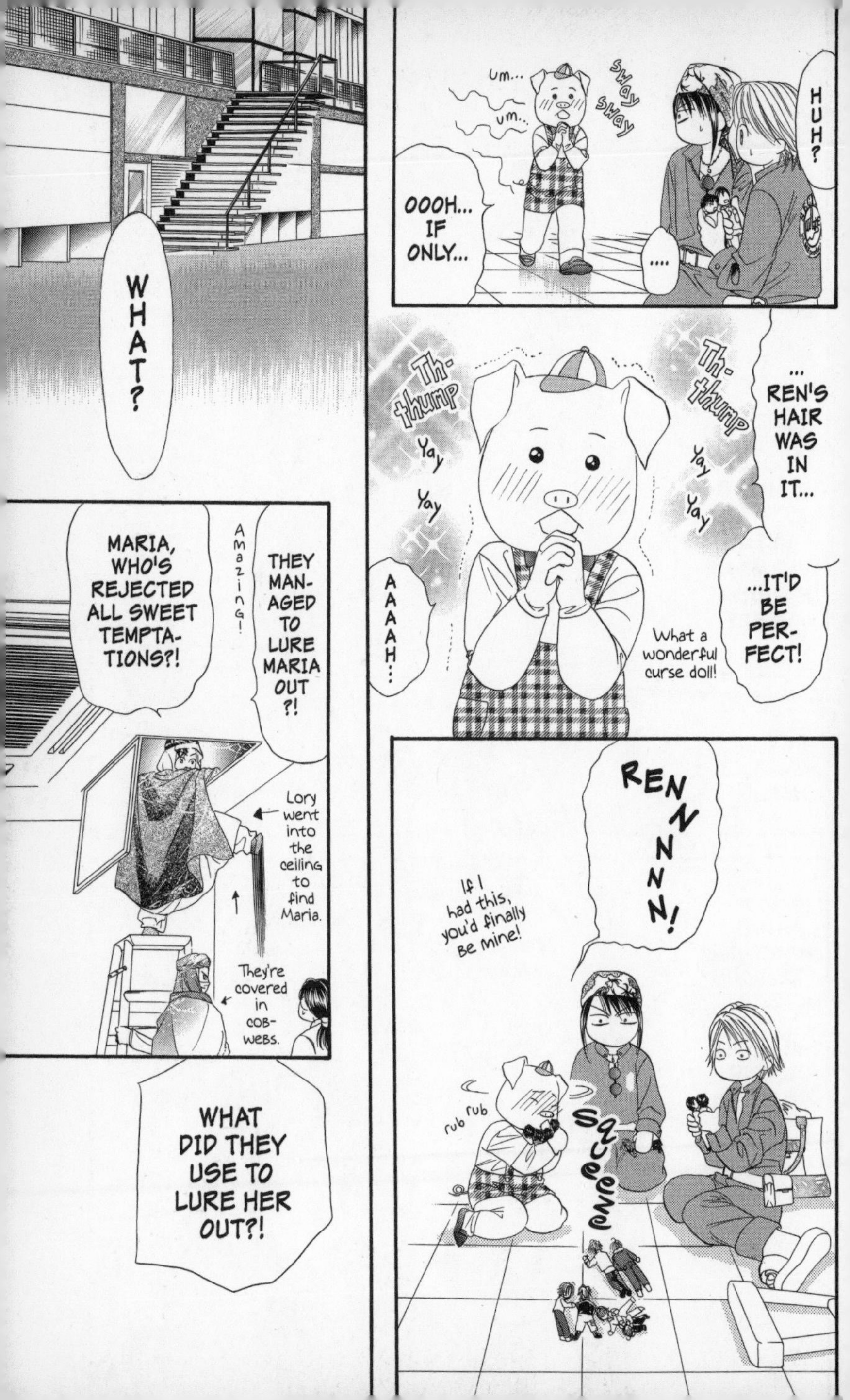
HUH?
Sway sway
um... um...
....
OOOH... IF ONLY...
...REN'S HAIR WAS IN IT...
Th-thump
Yay Yay
...IT'D BE PER-FECT!
What a wonderful curse doll!
Th-thump
Yay Yay
AAAAH...
RENNNNN!
If I had this, you'd finally be mine!
Squeeeze
rub rub
WHAT?
THEY MAN-AGED TO LURE MARIA OUT?!
Amazing!
MARIA, WHO'S REJECTED ALL SWEET TEMPTA-TIONS?!
Lory went into the ceiling to find Maria.
They're covered in cob-webs.
WHAT DID THEY USE TO LURE HER OUT?!

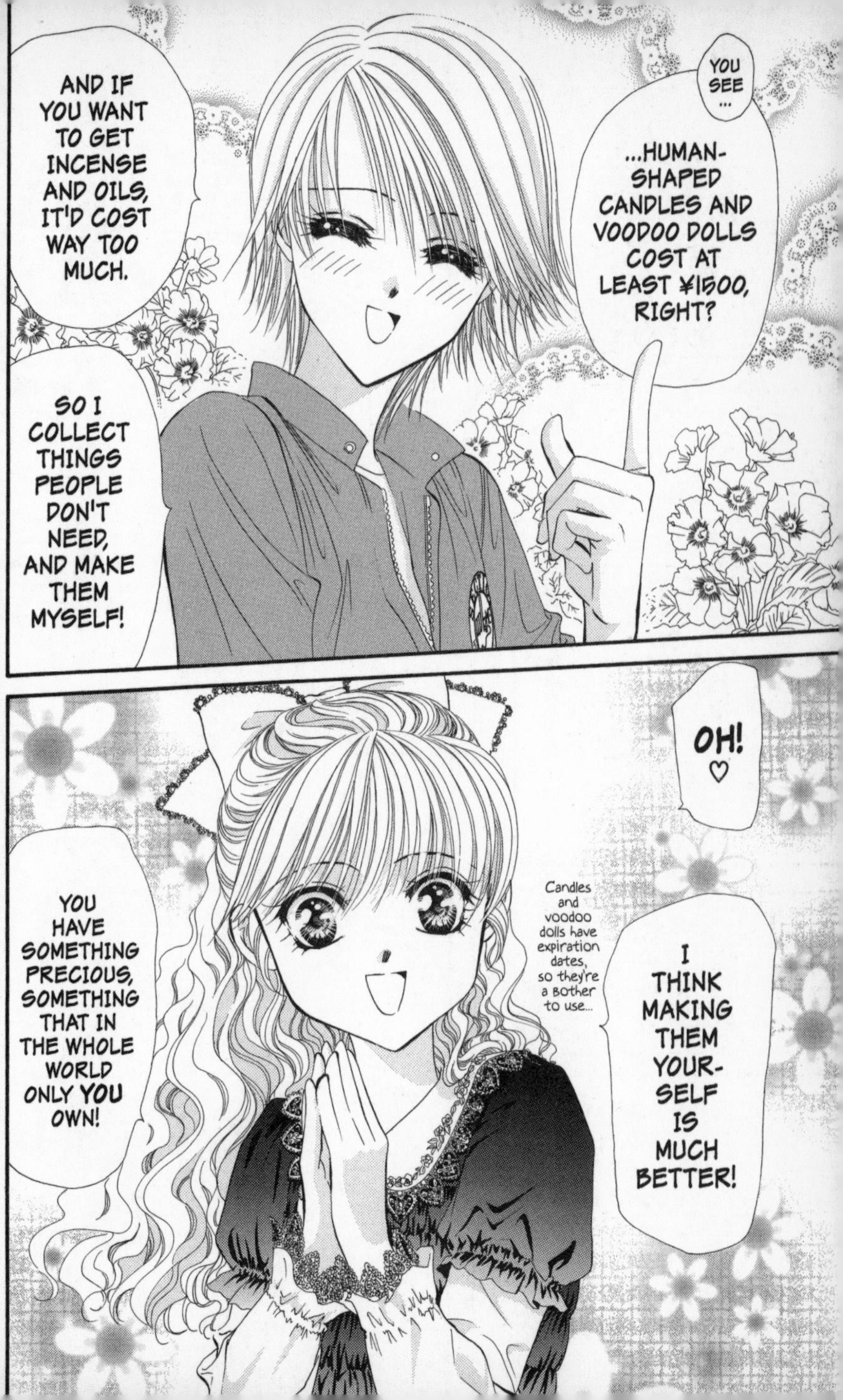
YOU SEE ...
...HUMAN-SHAPED CANDLES AND VOODOO DOLLS COST AT LEAST ¥1500, RIGHT?
AND IF YOU WANT TO GET INCENSE AND OILS, IT'D COST WAY TOO MUCH.
SO I COLLECT THINGS PEOPLE DON'T NEED, AND MAKE THEM MYSELF!
OH! ♡
Candles and voodoo dolls have expiration dates, so they're a bother to use...
I THINK MAKING THEM YOUR-SELF IS MUCH BETTER!
YOU HAVE SOMETHING PRECIOUS, SOMETHING THAT IN THE WHOLE WORLD ONLY YOU OWN!

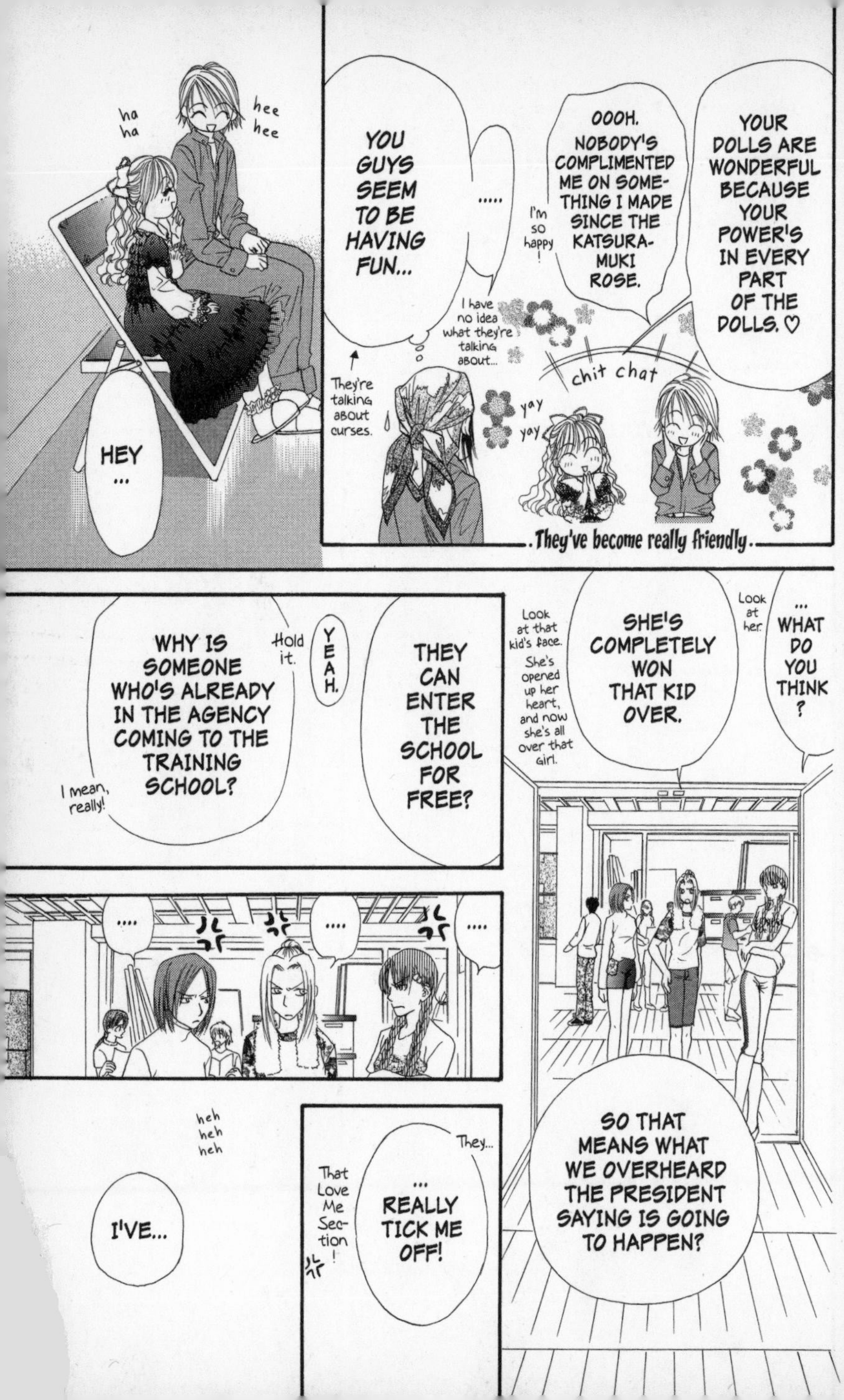
YOUR DOLLS ARE WONDERFUL BECAUSE YOUR POWER'S IN EVERY PART OF THE DOLLS. ♡
OOOH. NOBODY'S COMPLIMENTED ME ON SOMETHING I MADE SINCE THE KATSURA-MUKI ROSE.
I'm so happy!
.....
YOU GUYS SEEM TO BE HAVING FUN...
I have no idea what they're talking about...
chit chat
yay yay
They're talking about curses.
They've become really friendly.
hee hee
ha ha
HEY ...
... WHAT DO YOU THINK?
Look at her.
SHE'S COMPLETELY WON THAT KID OVER.
Look at that kid's face. She's opened up her heart, and now she's all over that girl.
SO THAT MEANS WHAT WE OVERHEARD THE PRESIDENT SAYING IS GOING TO HAPPEN?
THEY CAN ENTER THE SCHOOL FOR FREE?
YEAH.
Hold it.
WHY IS SOMEONE WHO'S ALREADY IN THE AGENCY COMING TO THE TRAINING SCHOOL?
I mean, really!
....
....
....
They...
... REALLY TICK ME OFF!
That Love Me Section!
heh heh heh
I'VE...

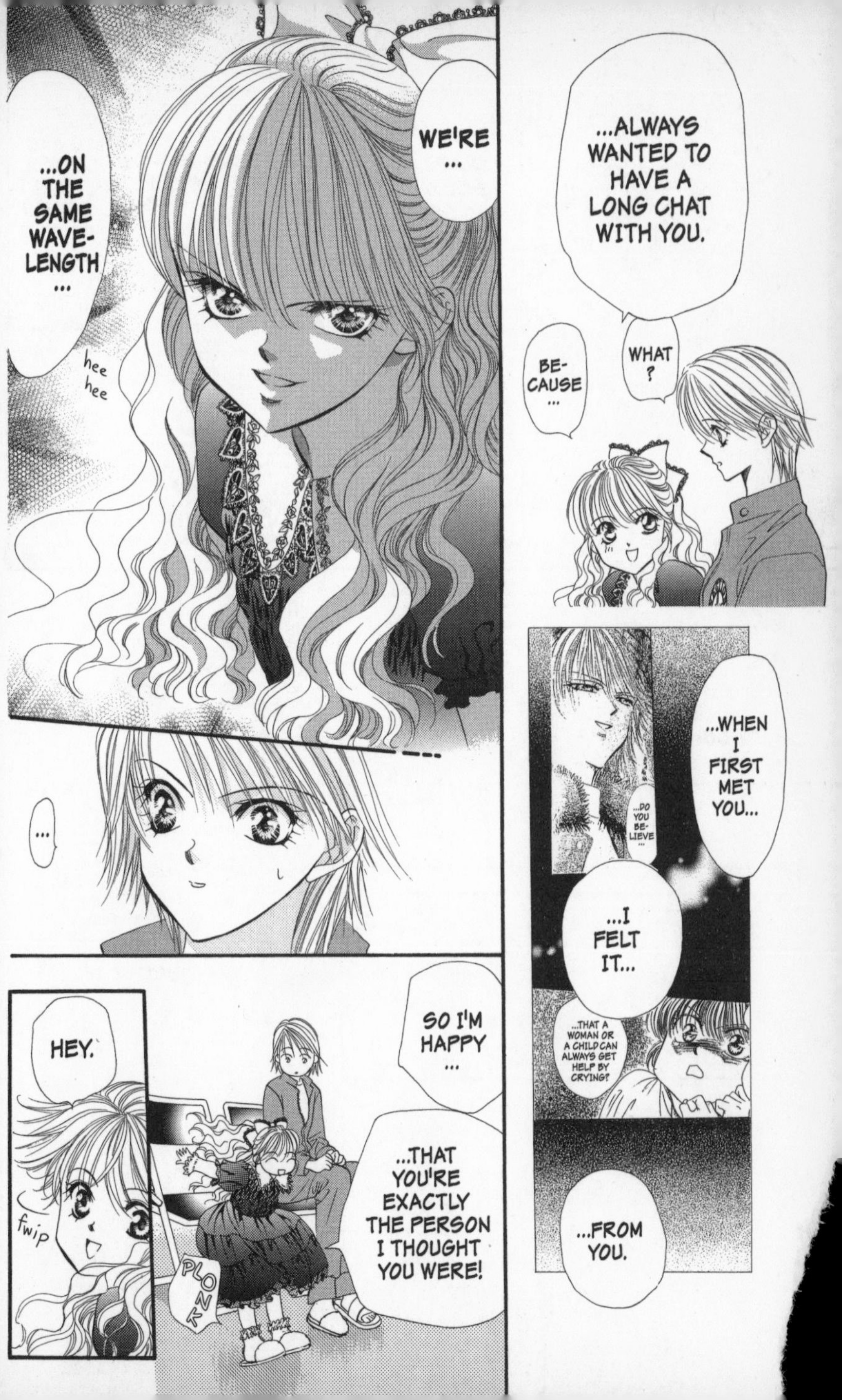
...ALWAYS WANTED TO HAVE A LONG CHAT WITH YOU.
WHAT?
BE-CAUSE...
...WHEN I FIRST MET YOU...
...DO YOU BE-LIEVE...
...I FELT IT...
...THAT A WOMAN OR A CHILD CAN ALWAYS GET HELP BY CRYING?
...FROM YOU.
WE'RE...
...ON THE SAME WAVE-LENGTH...
hee hee
...
SO I'M HAPPY...
...THAT YOU'RE EXACTLY THE PERSON I THOUGHT YOU WERE!
PLONK
HEY.
fwip

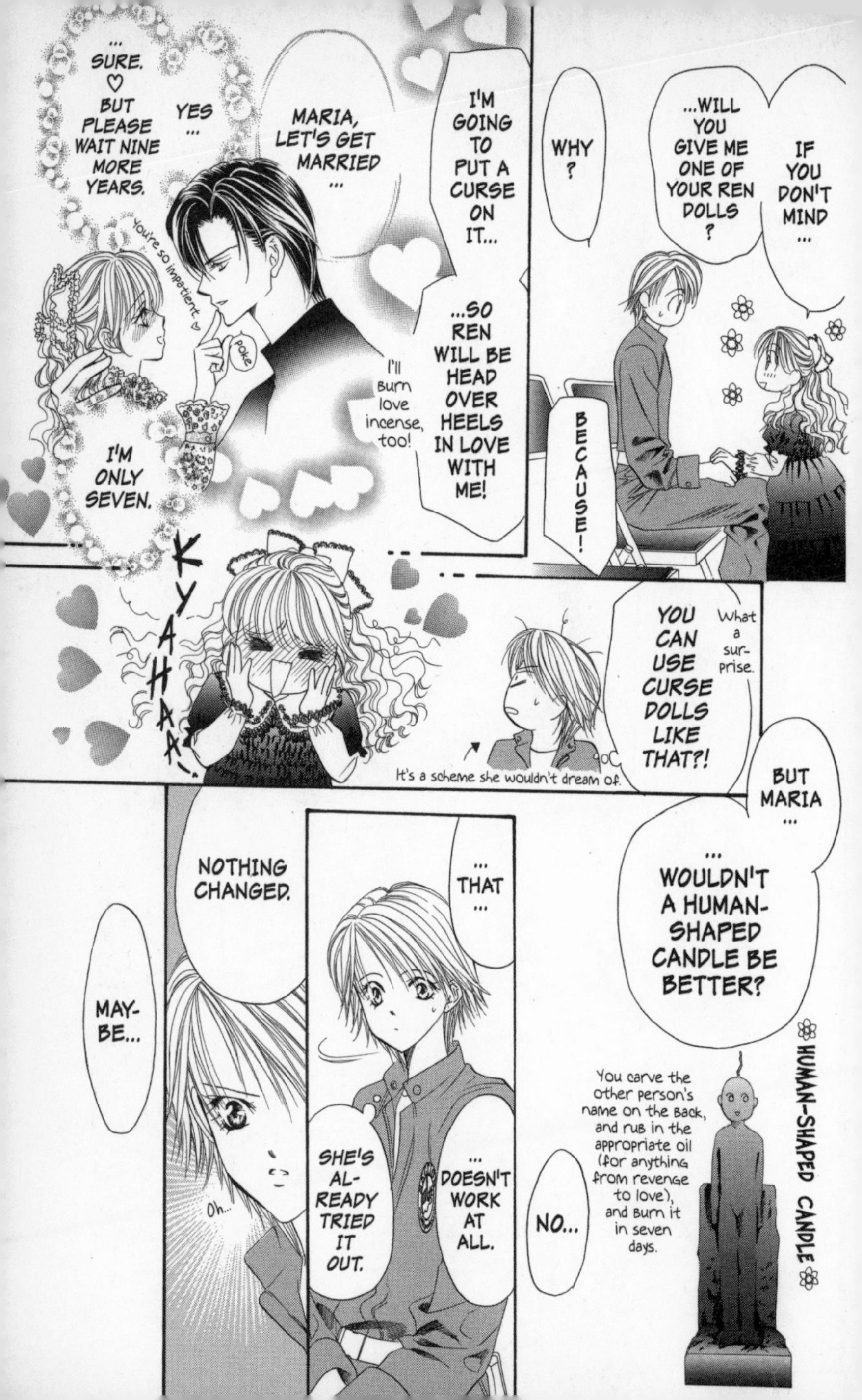
IF YOU DON'T MIND...
...WILL YOU GIVE ME ONE OF YOUR REN DOLLS?
WHY?
BECAUSE!
I'M GOING TO PUT A CURSE ON IT...
...SO REN WILL BE HEAD OVER HEELS IN LOVE WITH ME!
I'll burn love incense, too!
MARIA, LET'S GET MARRIED...
YES...
...SURE. ♡ BUT PLEASE WAIT NINE MORE YEARS.
You're so impatient ♡
poke
I'M ONLY SEVEN.
What a sur-prise.
YOU CAN USE CURSE DOLLS LIKE THAT?!
It's a scheme she wouldn't dream of.
KYAHAHA!
BUT MARIA...
...WOULDN'T A HUMAN-SHAPED CANDLE BE BETTER?
HUMAN-SHAPED CANDLE
You carve the other person's name on the back, and rub in the appropriate oil (for anything from revenge to love), and burn it in seven days.
NO...
...THAT...
...DOESN'T WORK AT ALL.
SHE'S AL-READY TRIED IT OUT.
NOTHING CHANGED.
MAY-BE...
Oh...

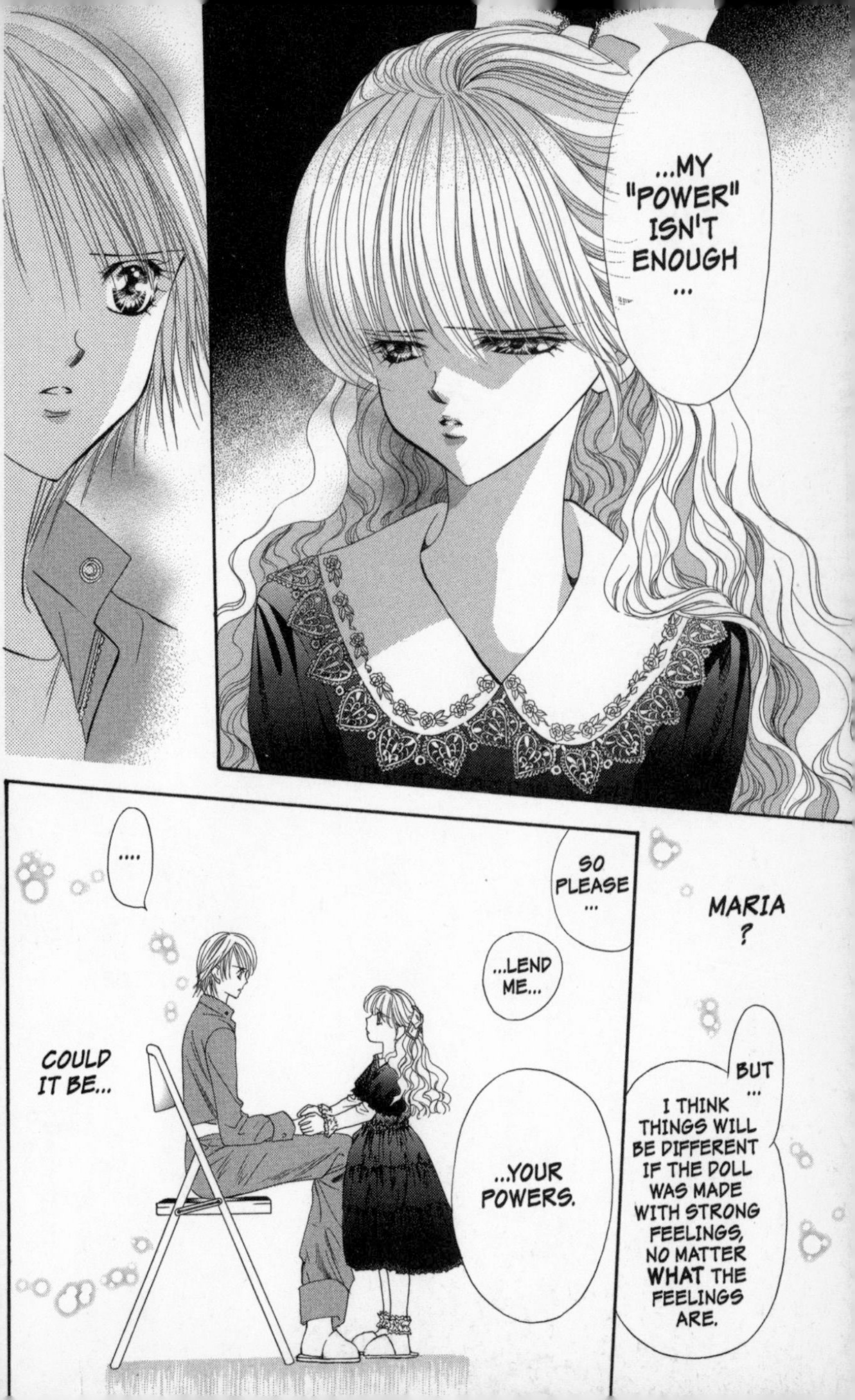
...MY "POWER" ISN'T ENOUGH ...
MARIA ?
BUT... I THINK THINGS WILL BE DIFFERENT IF THE DOLL WAS MADE WITH STRONG FEELINGS, NO MATTER WHAT THE FEELINGS ARE.
SO PLEASE ...
...LEND ME...
...YOUR POWERS.
....
COULD IT BE...

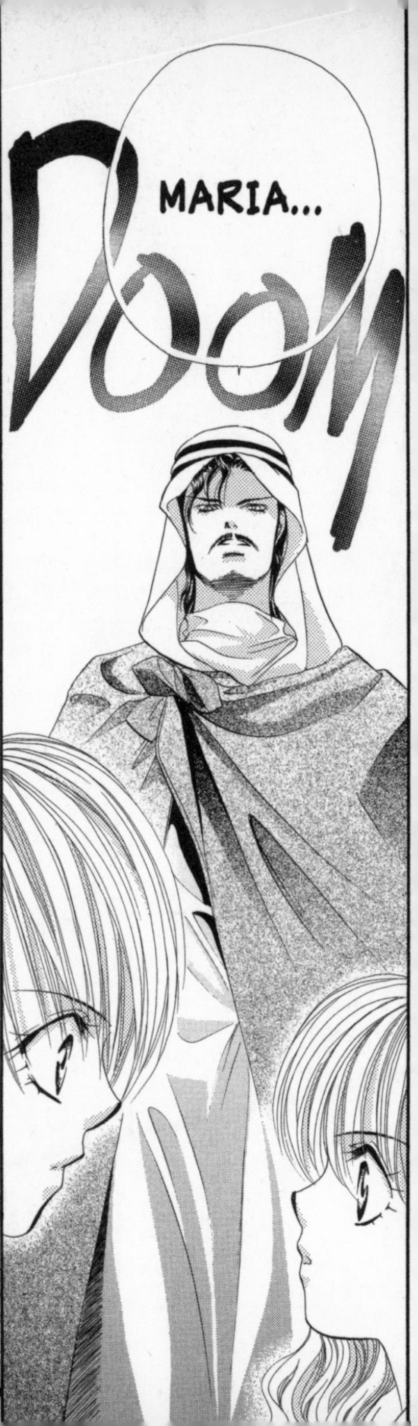
MARIA...
DOOM
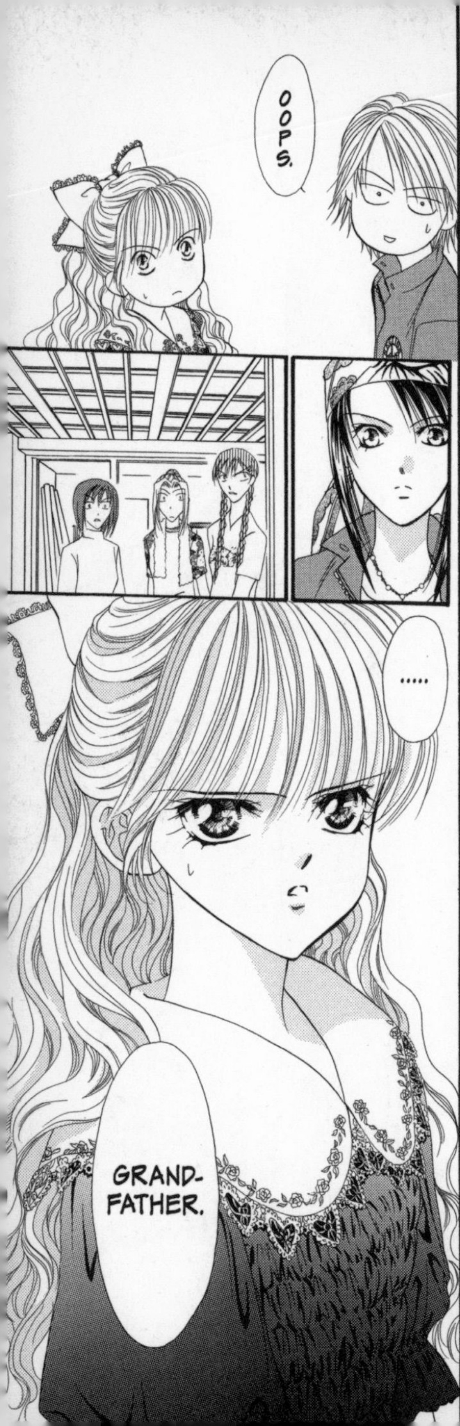
OOPS.
......
GRAND-FATHER.

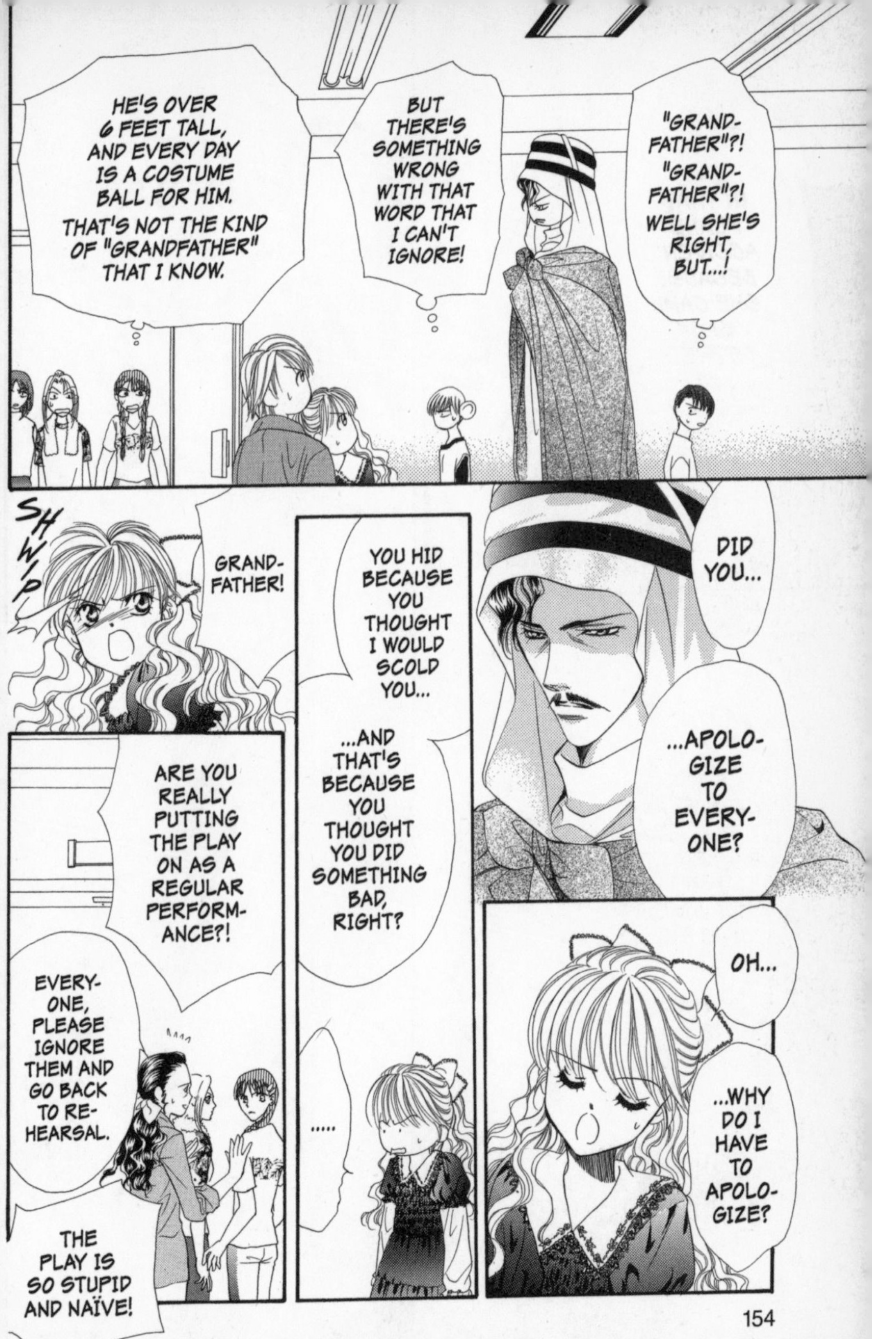
"GRAND-FATHER"?! "GRAND-FATHER"?! WELL SHE'S RIGHT, BUT...!
BUT THERE'S SOMETHING WRONG WITH THAT WORD THAT I CAN'T IGNORE!
HE'S OVER 6 FEET TALL, AND EVERY DAY IS A COSTUME BALL FOR HIM.
THAT'S NOT THE KIND OF "GRANDFATHER" THAT I KNOW.
SHWIP
GRAND-FATHER!
YOU HID BECAUSE YOU THOUGHT I WOULD SCOLD YOU...
...AND THAT'S BECAUSE YOU THOUGHT YOU DID SOMETHING BAD, RIGHT?
DID YOU...
...APOLO-GIZE TO EVERY-ONE?
OH...
...WHY DO I HAVE TO APOLO-GIZE?
.....
ARE YOU REALLY PUTTING THE PLAY ON AS A REGULAR PERFORM-ANCE?!
EVERY-ONE, PLEASE IGNORE THEM AND GO BACK TO RE-HEARSAL.
THE PLAY IS SO STUPID AND NAÏVE!

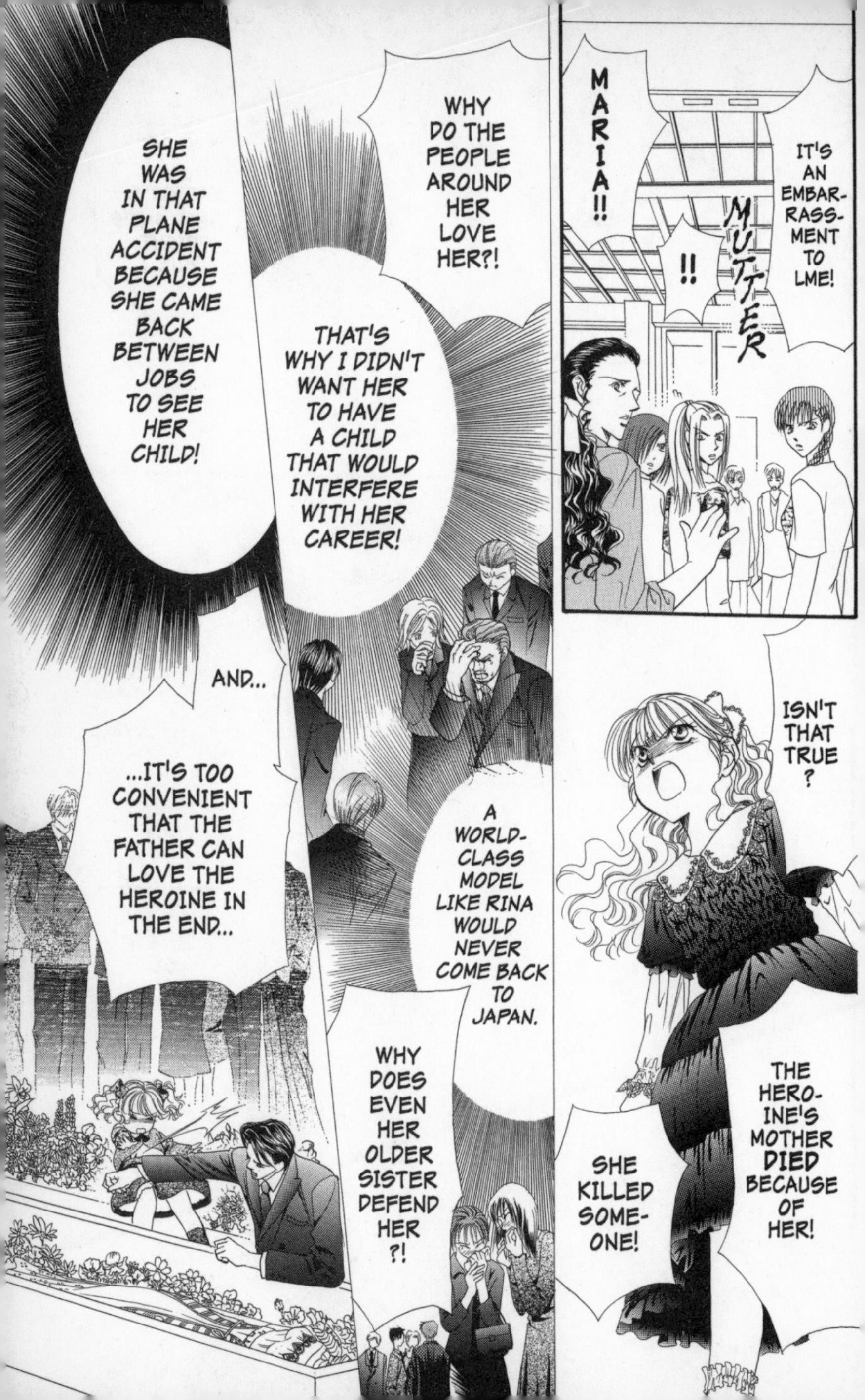

IT'S AN EMBARRASSMENT TO LME!
MARIA!!
MUTTER
!!
ISN'T THAT TRUE?
THE HEROINE'S MOTHER DIED BECAUSE OF HER!
SHE KILLED SOMEONE!
WHY DO THE PEOPLE AROUND HER LOVE HER?!
THAT'S WHY I DIDN'T WANT HER TO HAVE A CHILD THAT WOULD INTERFERE WITH HER CAREER!
SHE WAS IN THAT PLANE ACCIDENT BECAUSE SHE CAME BACK BETWEEN JOBS TO SEE HER CHILD!
AND...
...IT'S TOO CONVENIENT THAT THE FATHER CAN LOVE THE HEROINE IN THE END...
A WORLD-CLASS MODEL LIKE RINA WOULD NEVER COME BACK TO JAPAN.
WHY DOES EVEN HER OLDER SISTER DEFEND HER?!

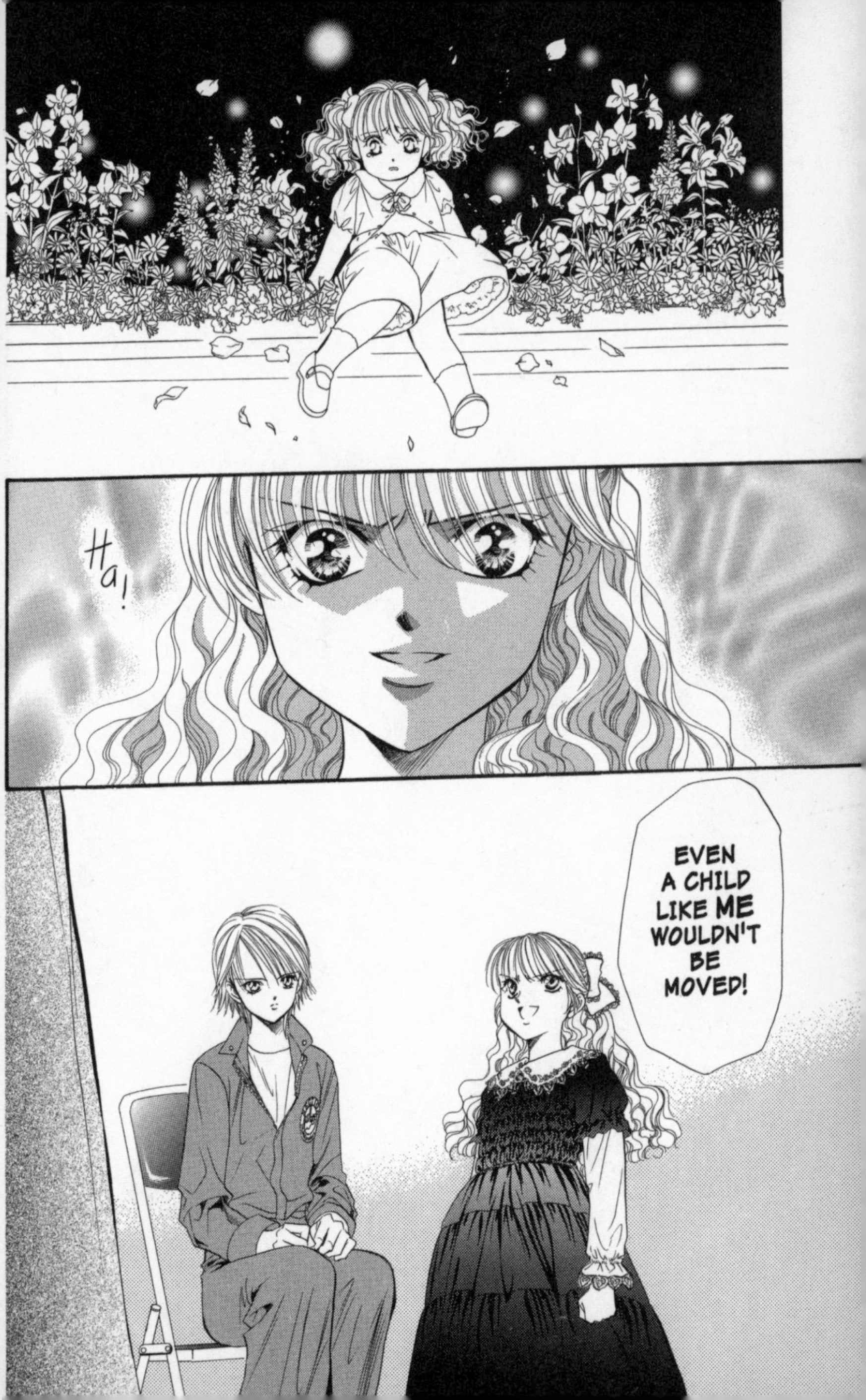
Ha!
EVEN A CHILD LIKE ME WOULDN'T BE MOVED!

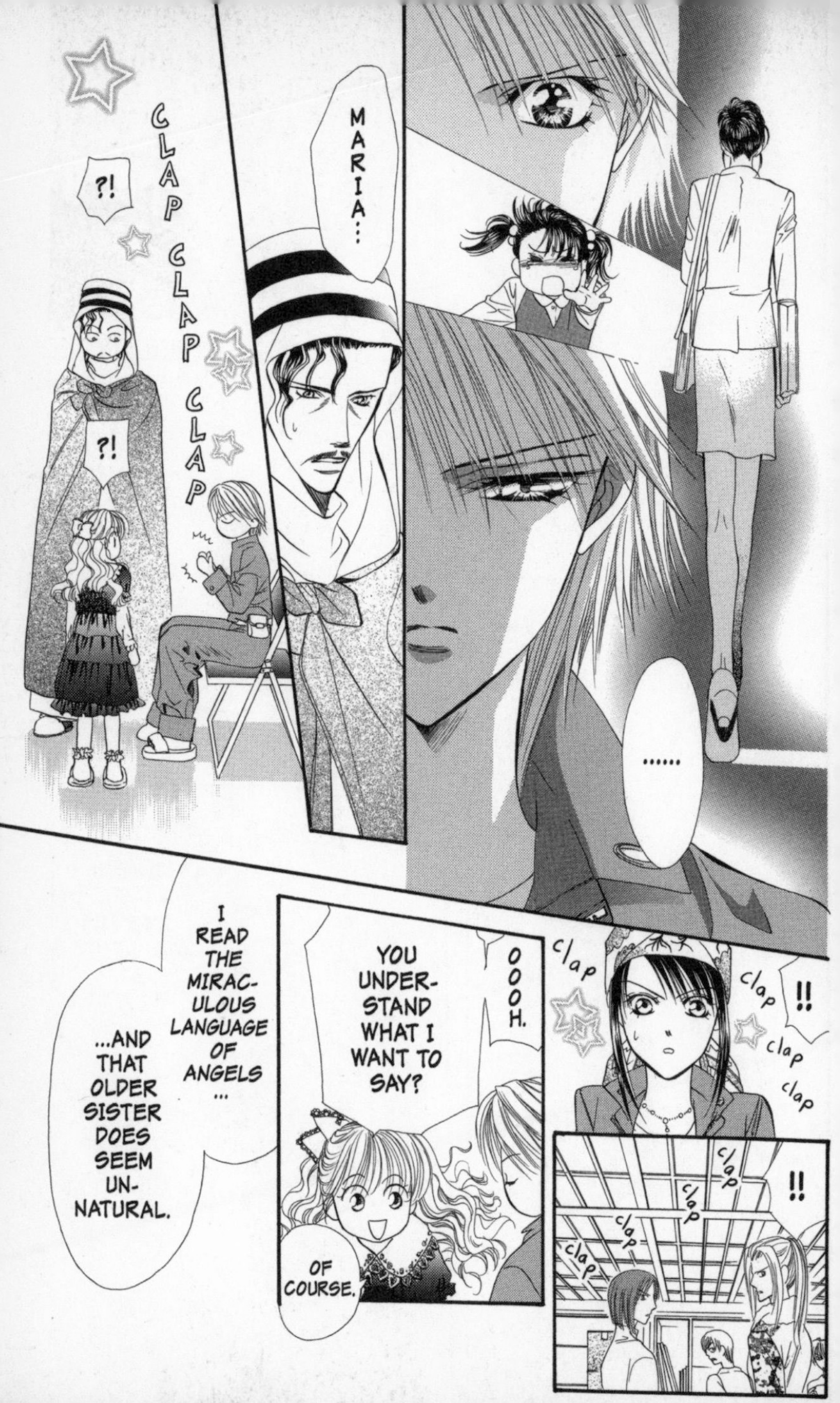
......
MARIA...
?!
CLAP CLAP CLAP CLAP
?!
clap clap clap clap
!!
clap clap clap clap
!!
OOOH.
YOU UNDER-STAND WHAT I WANT TO SAY?
OF COURSE.
I READ THE MIRAC-ULOUS LANGUAGE OF ANGELS...
...AND THAT OLDER SISTER DOES SEEM UN-NATURAL.

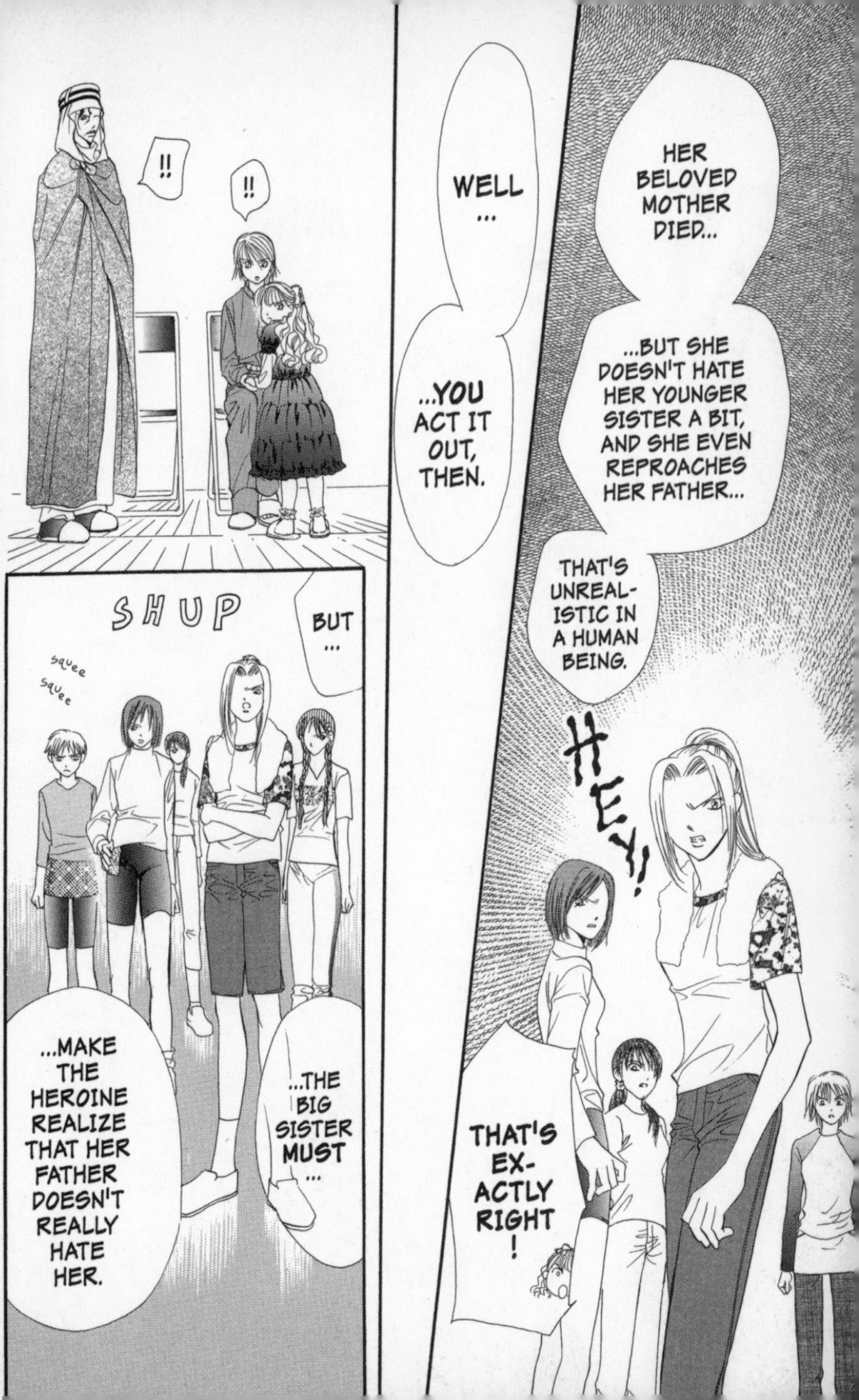
HER BELOVED MOTHER DIED...
...BUT SHE DOESN'T HATE HER YOUNGER SISTER A BIT, AND SHE EVEN REPROACHES HER FATHER...
THAT'S UNREAL-ISTIC IN A HUMAN BEING.
HEY!!
THAT'S EX-ACTLY RIGHT!
WELL...
...YOU ACT IT OUT, THEN.
!!
!!
SHUP
BUT...
squee
squee
...THE BIG SISTER MUST...
...MAKE THE HEROINE REALIZE THAT HER FATHER DOESN'T REALLY HATE HER.

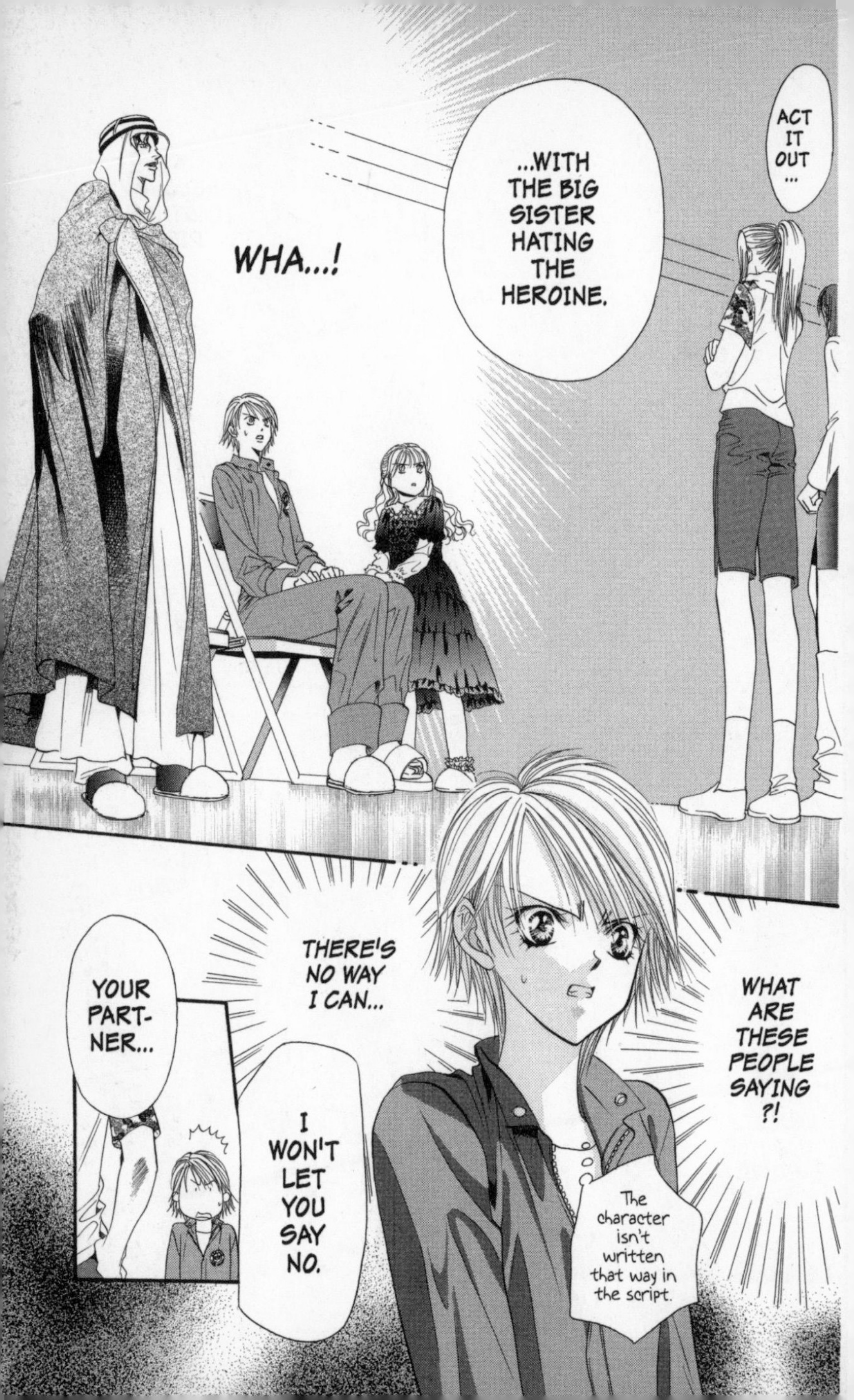
ACT IT OUT...
...WITH THE BIG SISTER HATING THE HEROINE.
WHA...!
WHAT ARE THESE PEOPLE SAYING?!
The character isn't written that way in the script.
THERE'S NO WAY I CAN...
YOUR PART-NER...
I WON'T LET YOU SAY NO.

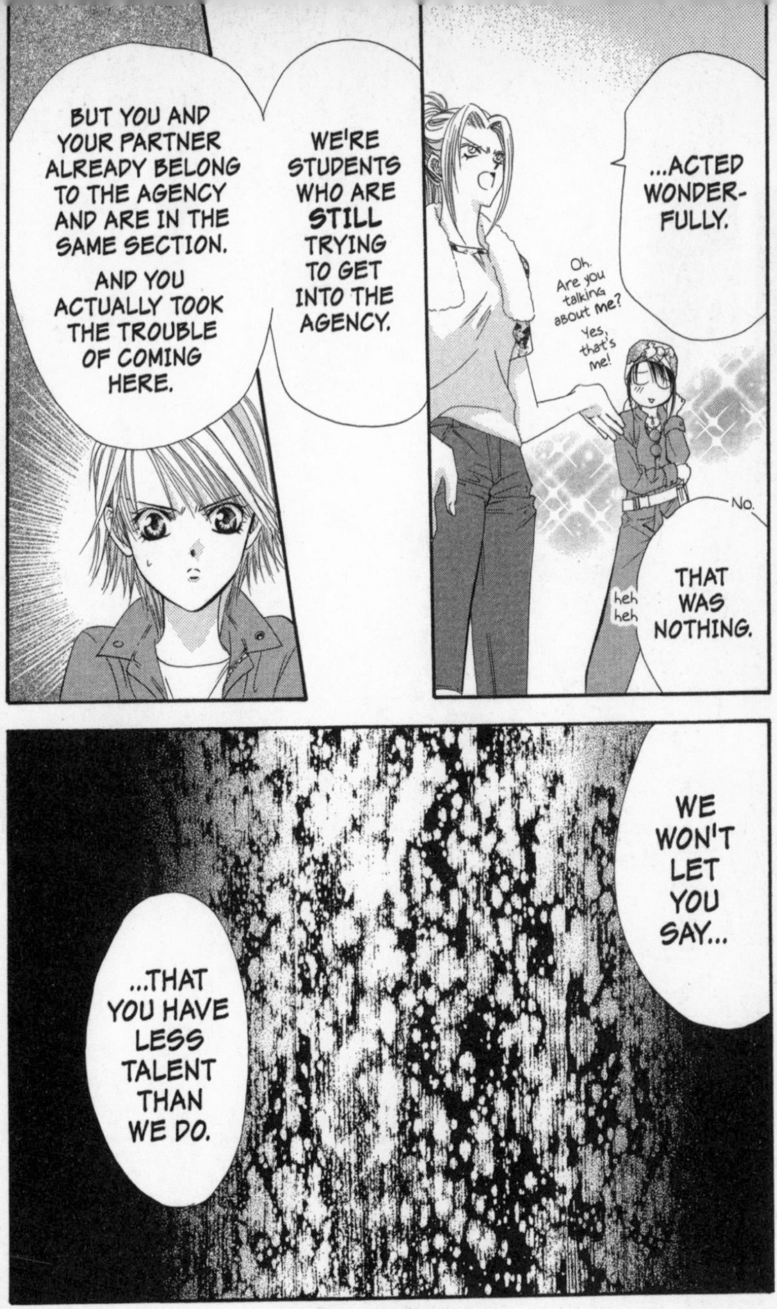
...ACTED WONDERFULLY.
Oh. Are you talking about me? Yes, that's me!
No.
THAT WAS NOTHING.
heh heh
WE'RE STUDENTS WHO ARE STILL TRYING TO GET INTO THE AGENCY.
BUT YOU AND YOUR PARTNER ALREADY BELONG TO THE AGENCY AND ARE IN THE SAME SECTION.
AND YOU ACTUALLY TOOK THE TROUBLE OF COMING HERE.
WE WON'T LET YOU SAY...
...THAT YOU HAVE LESS TALENT THAN WE DO.

End of Act 16

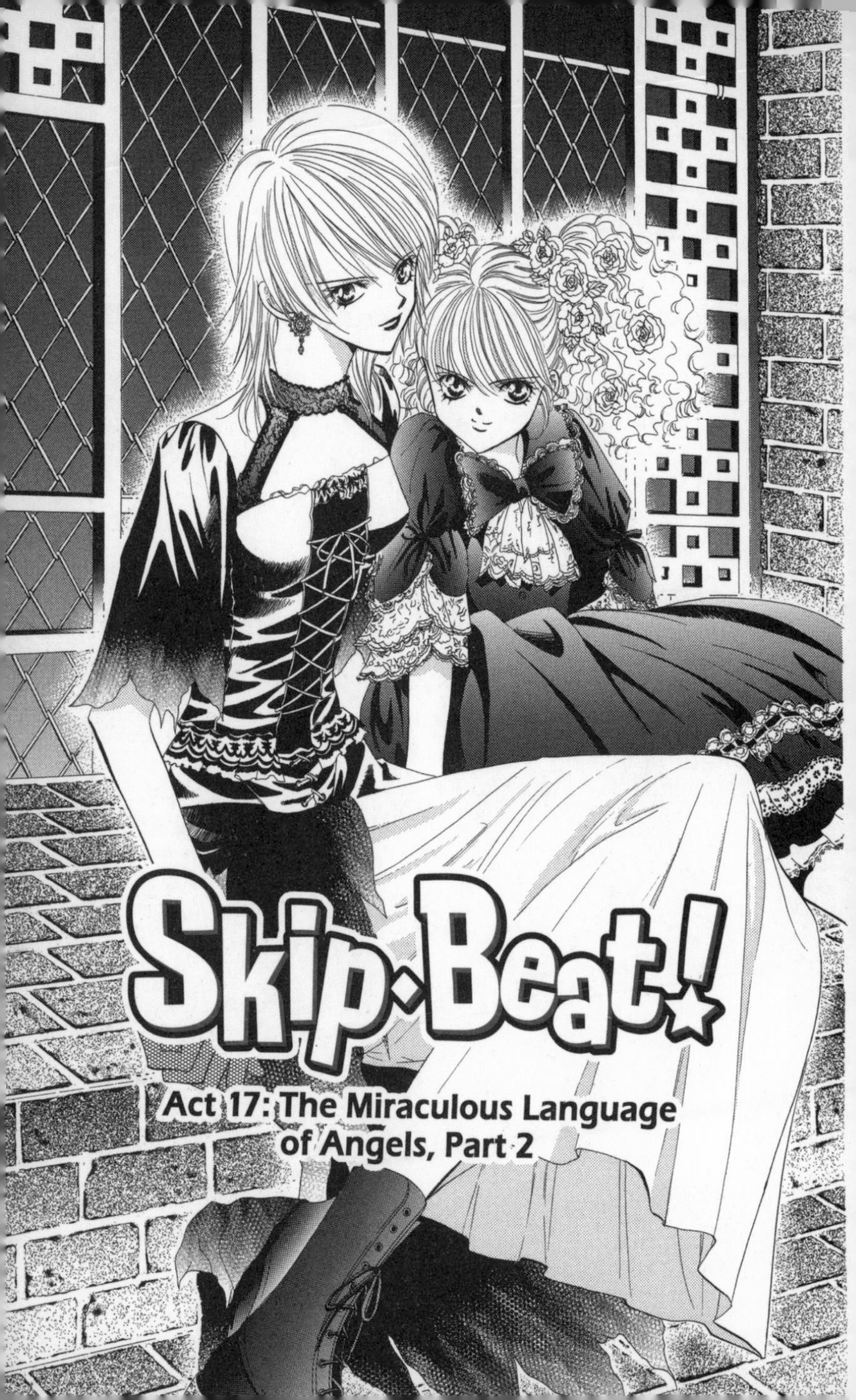
Skip·Beat!
Act 17: The Miraculous Language of Angels, Part 2

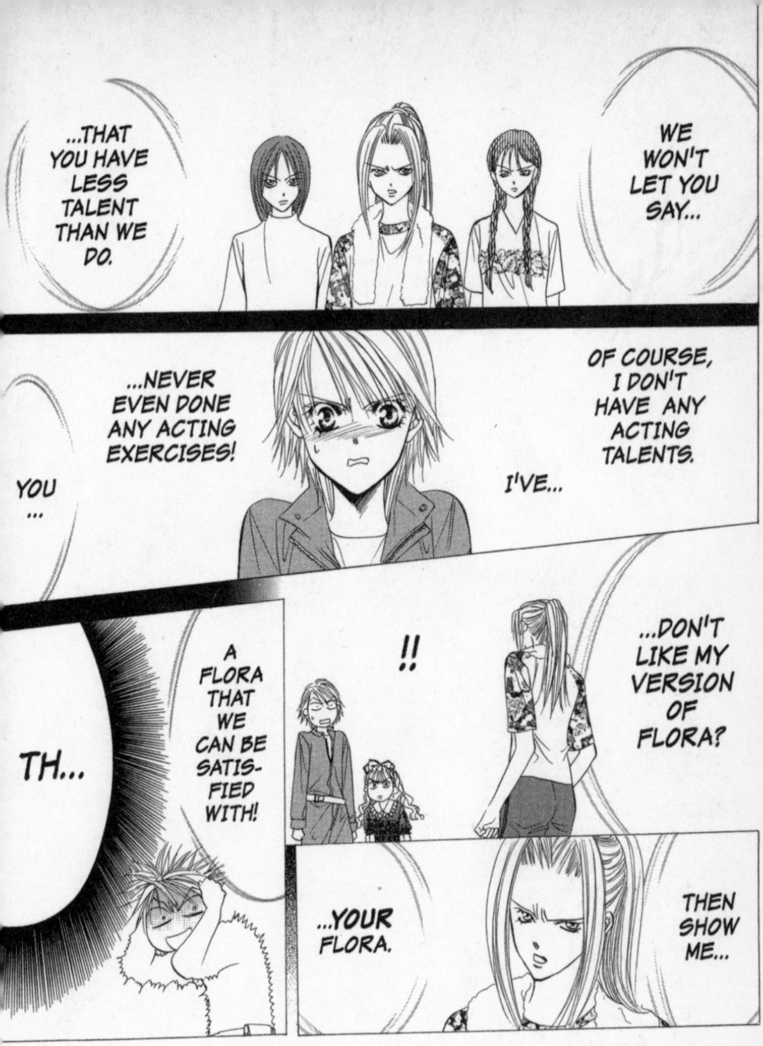
WE WON'T LET YOU SAY...
...THAT YOU HAVE LESS TALENT THAN WE DO.
OF COURSE, I DON'T HAVE ANY ACTING TALENTS.
I'VE...
...NEVER EVEN DONE ANY ACTING EXERCISES!
YOU ...
...DON'T LIKE MY VERSION OF FLORA?
!!
THEN SHOW ME...
...YOUR FLORA.
A FLORA THAT WE CAN BE SATISFIED WITH!
TH...

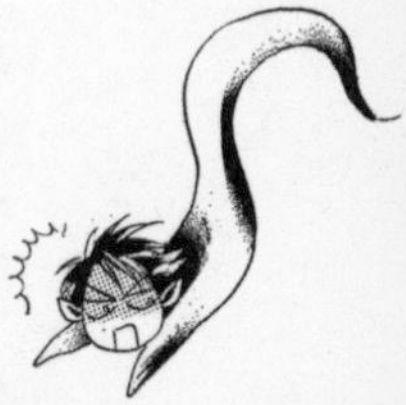

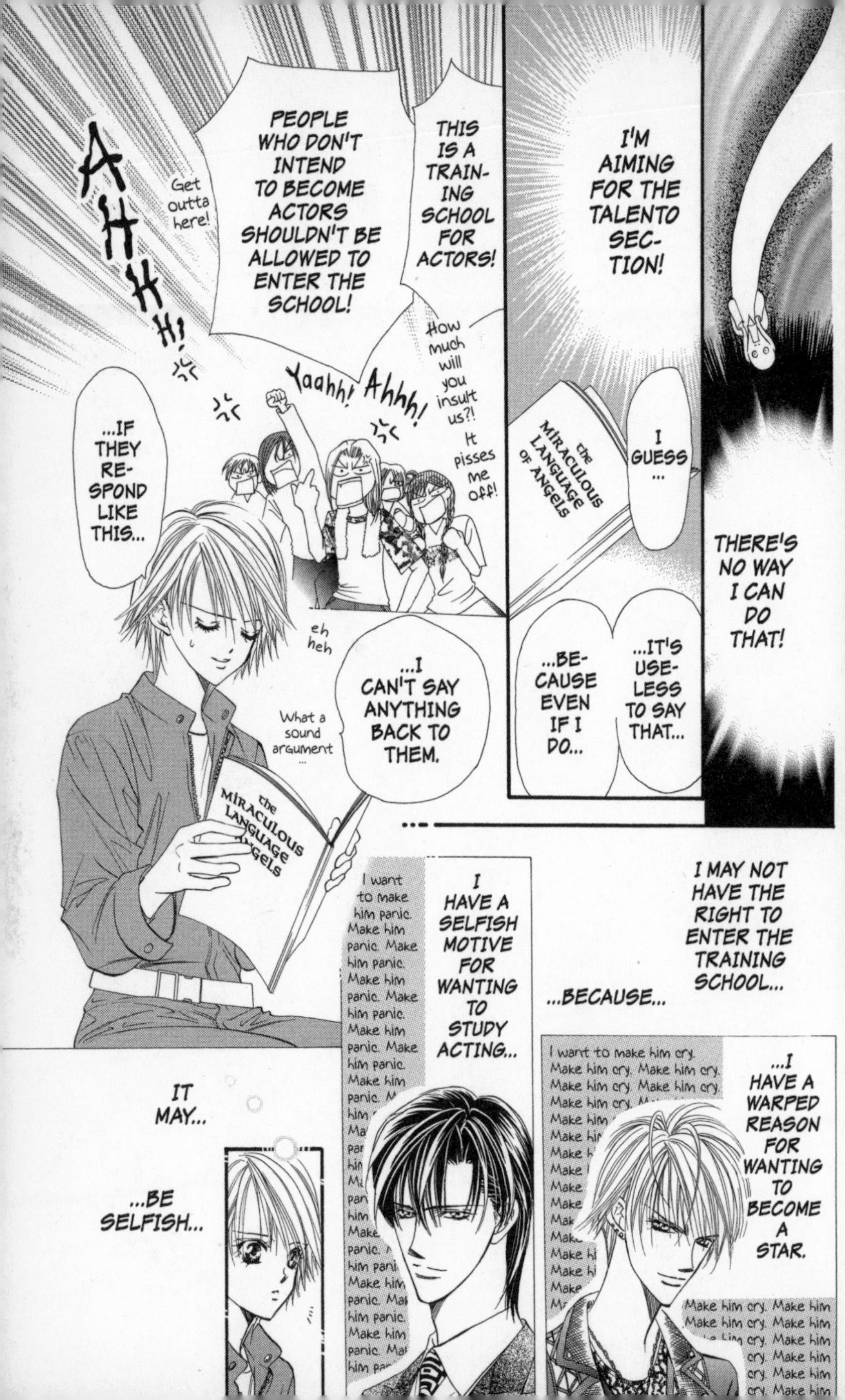
I'M AIMING FOR THE TALENTO SECTION!
I GUESS...
the MIRACULOUS LANGUAGE of ANGELS
THERE'S NO WAY I CAN DO THAT!
...IT'S USELESS TO SAY THAT...
...BECAUSE EVEN IF I DO...
THIS IS A TRAINING SCHOOL FOR ACTORS!
PEOPLE WHO DON'T INTEND TO BECOME ACTORS SHOULDN'T BE ALLOWED TO ENTER THE SCHOOL!
AHHH!
Get outta here!
How much will you insult us?!
It pisses me off!
Ahhh!
Yaahh!
...IF THEY RESPOND LIKE THIS...
...I CAN'T SAY ANYTHING BACK TO THEM.
eh heh
What a sound argument...
the MIRACULOUS LANGUAGE ANGELS
I MAY NOT HAVE THE RIGHT TO ENTER THE TRAINING SCHOOL...
...BECAUSE...
I want to make him cry. Make him cry. Make him cry. Make him cry. Make him cry.
...I HAVE A WARPED REASON FOR WANTING TO BECOME A STAR.
I HAVE A SELFISH MOTIVE FOR WANTING TO STUDY ACTING...
I want to make him panic. Make him panic. Make him panic.
IT MAY...
...BE SELFISH...

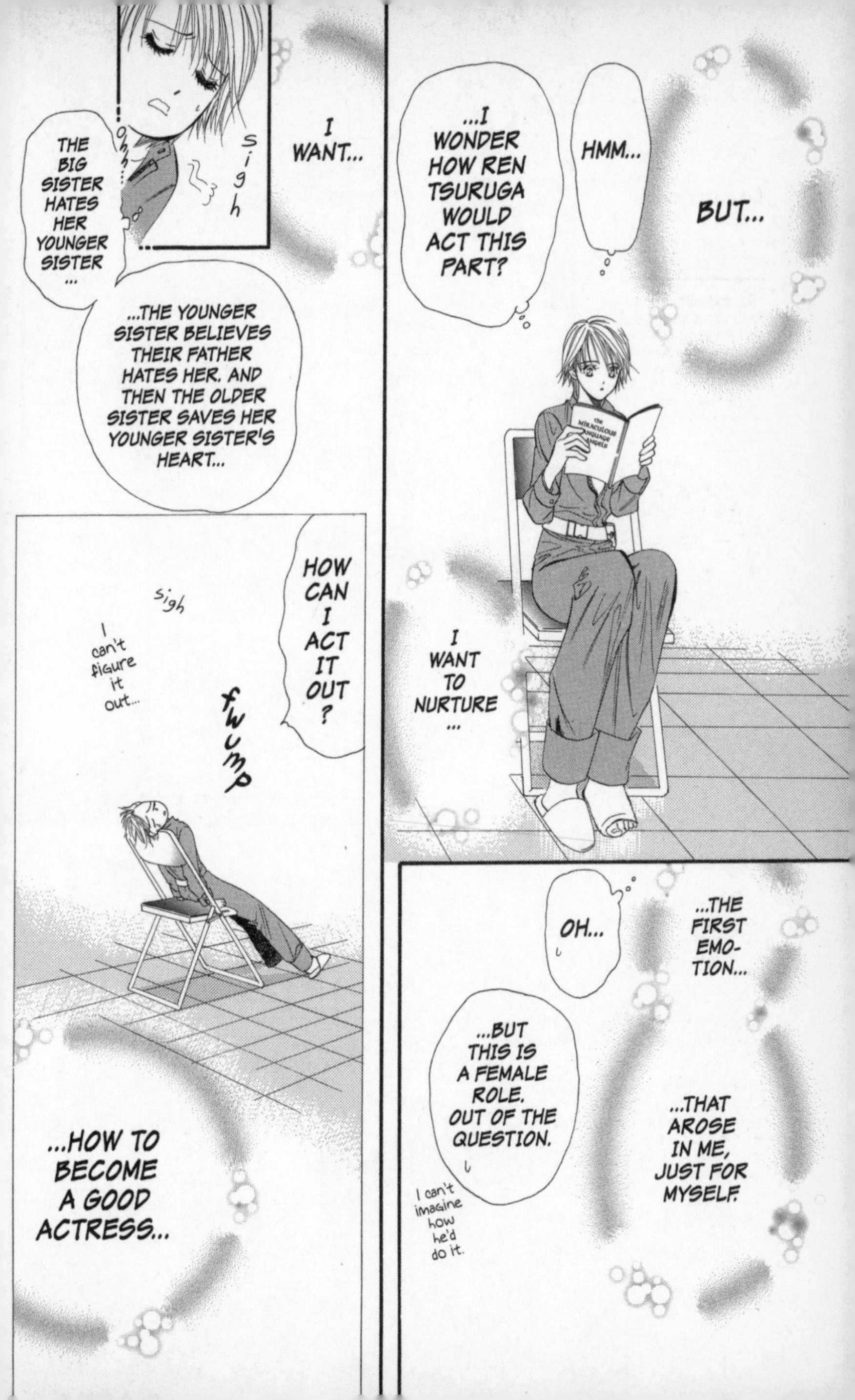
HMM...
...I WONDER HOW REN TSURUGA WOULD ACT THIS PART?
BUT...
the MIRACULOUS LANGUAGE ANGELS
I WANT TO NURTURE...
OH...
...BUT THIS IS A FEMALE ROLE. OUT OF THE QUESTION.
I can't imagine how he'd do it.
...THE FIRST EMO-TION...
...THAT AROSE IN ME, JUST FOR MYSELF.
I WANT...
sigh
Ohh...
THE BIG SISTER HATES HER YOUNGER SISTER...
...THE YOUNGER SISTER BELIEVES THEIR FATHER HATES HER. AND THEN THE OLDER SISTER SAVES HER YOUNGER SISTER'S HEART...
HOW CAN I ACT IT OUT?
sigh
I can't figure it out...
fwump
...HOW TO BECOME A GOOD ACTRESS...

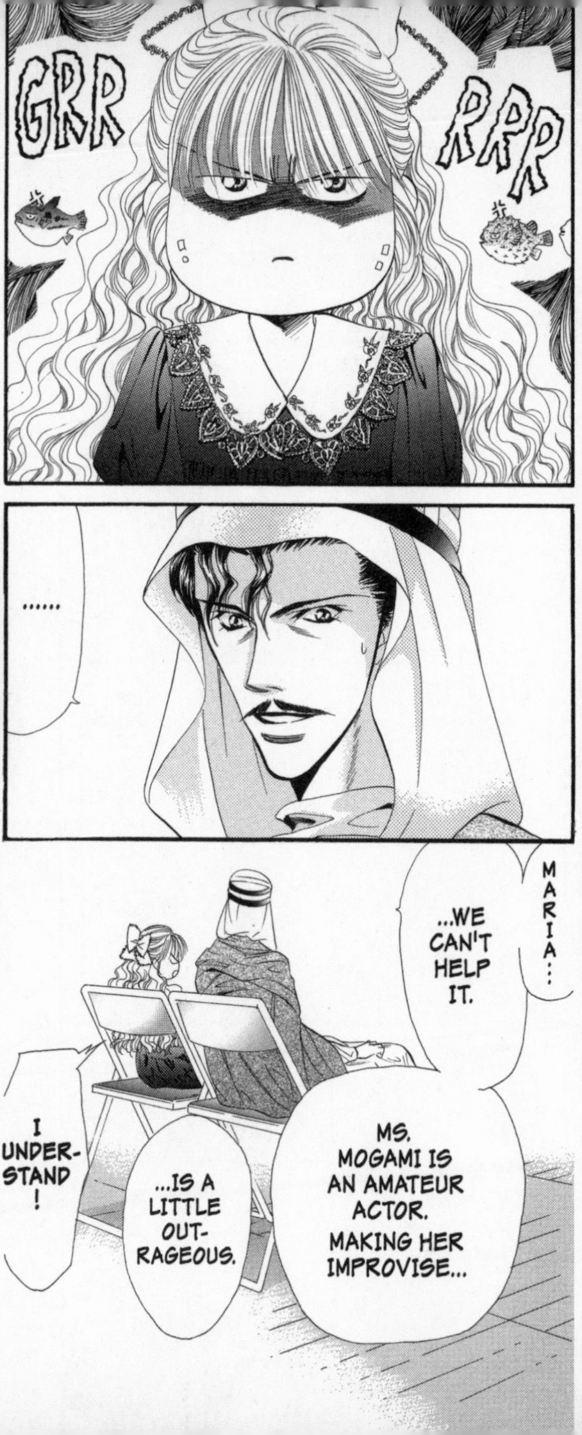
GRR
RRR
......
MARIA...
...WE CAN'T HELP IT.
MS. MOGAMI IS AN AMATEUR ACTOR. MAKING HER IMPROVISE...
...IS A LITTLE OUTRAGEOUS.
I UNDERSTAND!

Lory Takarada

Difficulty level

☆ ☆ 2

The difficulty for my assistants must be a 4...♭ (Because he's always wearing ethnic costumes that aren't coordinated at all...♭) Moreover, he sometimes comes with dancers or a camel...

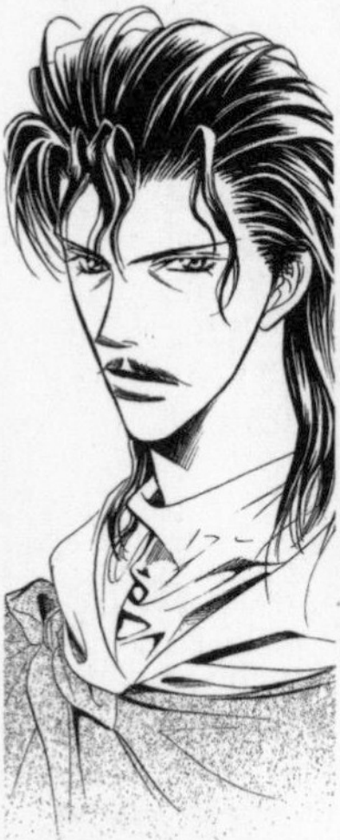

Lory should be a character that I draw without thinking, but there were lots of faces in the pages of this volume that I didn't like, and I didn't know what to do...

There is a reason Lory's name is spelled in Japanese with a small "i" at the end instead of with a dash. It is because...well...I'll talk about it...sometime in the future...so...that's it...

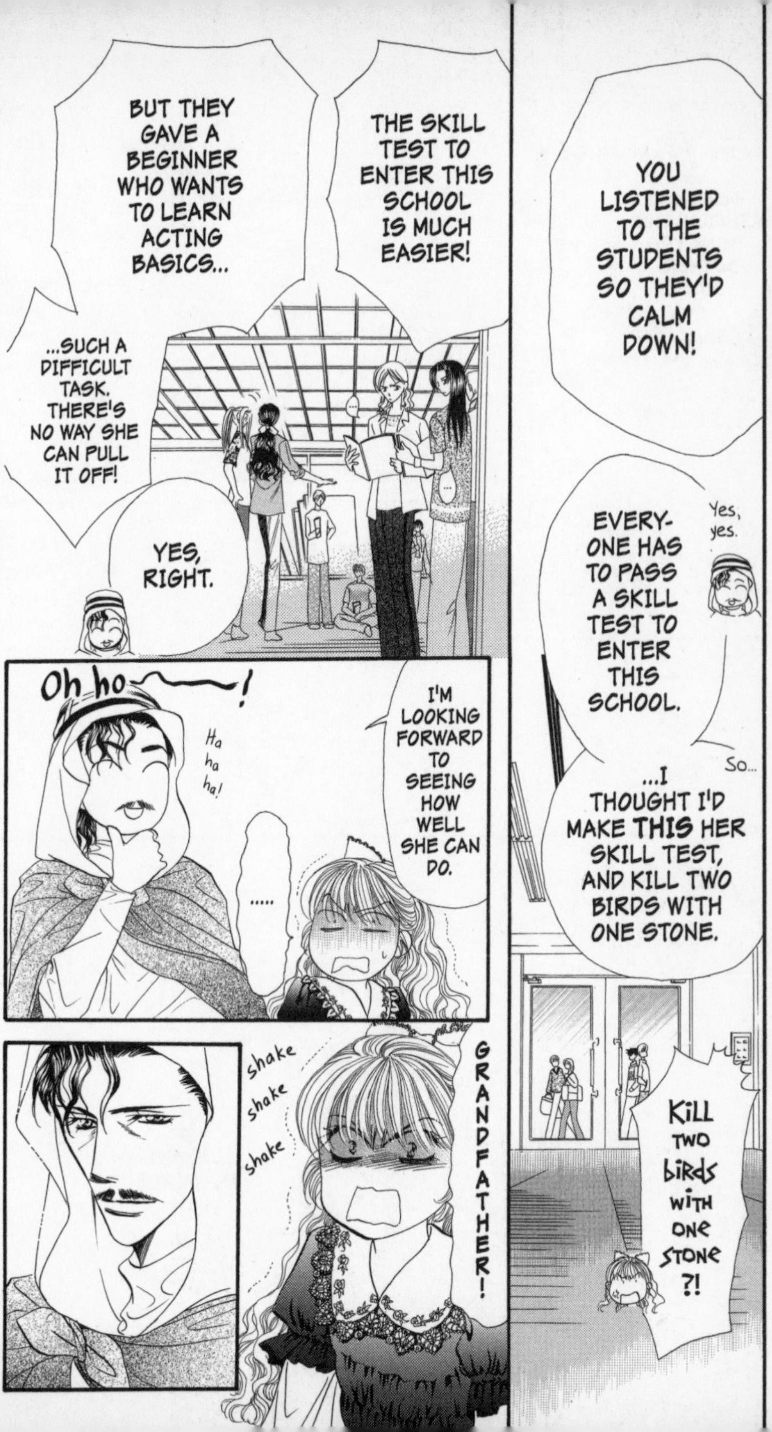
YOU LISTENED TO THE STUDENTS SO THEY'D CALM DOWN!
EVERYONE HAS TO PASS A SKILL TEST TO ENTER THIS SCHOOL.
Yes, yes.
So...
...I THOUGHT I'D MAKE THIS HER SKILL TEST, AND KILL TWO BIRDS WITH ONE STONE.
Kill two birds with one stone?!
THE SKILL TEST TO ENTER THIS SCHOOL IS MUCH EASIER!
BUT THEY GAVE A BEGINNER WHO WANTS TO LEARN ACTING BASICS...
...SUCH A DIFFICULT TASK. THERE'S NO WAY SHE CAN PULL IT OFF!
YES, RIGHT.
Oh ho~!
I'M LOOKING FORWARD TO SEEING HOW WELL SHE CAN DO.
Ha ha ha!
.....
GRANDFATHER!
shake shake shake

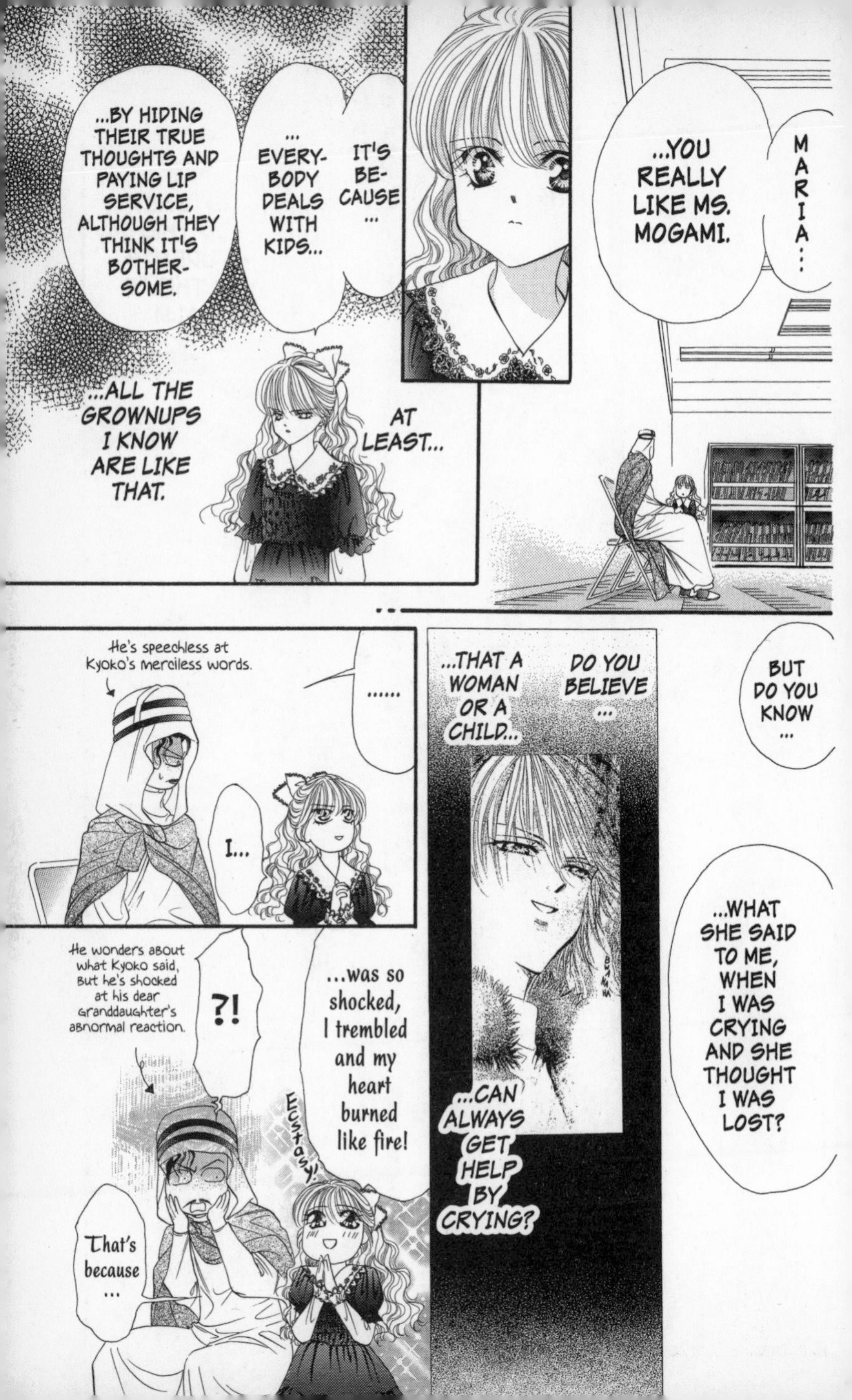
MARIA...
...YOU REALLY LIKE MS. MOGAMI.
IT'S BECAUSE...
...EVERYBODY DEALS WITH KIDS...
...BY HIDING THEIR TRUE THOUGHTS AND PAYING LIP SERVICE, ALTHOUGH THEY THINK IT'S BOTHERSOME.
AT LEAST...
...ALL THE GROWNUPS I KNOW ARE LIKE THAT.
BUT DO YOU KNOW...
...WHAT SHE SAID TO ME, WHEN I WAS CRYING AND SHE THOUGHT I WAS LOST?
DO YOU BELIEVE...
...THAT A WOMAN OR A CHILD...
...CAN ALWAYS GET HELP BY CRYING?
......
He's speechless at Kyoko's merciless words.
I...
...was so shocked, I trembled and my heart burned like fire!
?!
He wonders about what Kyoko said, but he's shocked at his dear granddaughter's abnormal reaction.
Ecstasy!
That's because ...

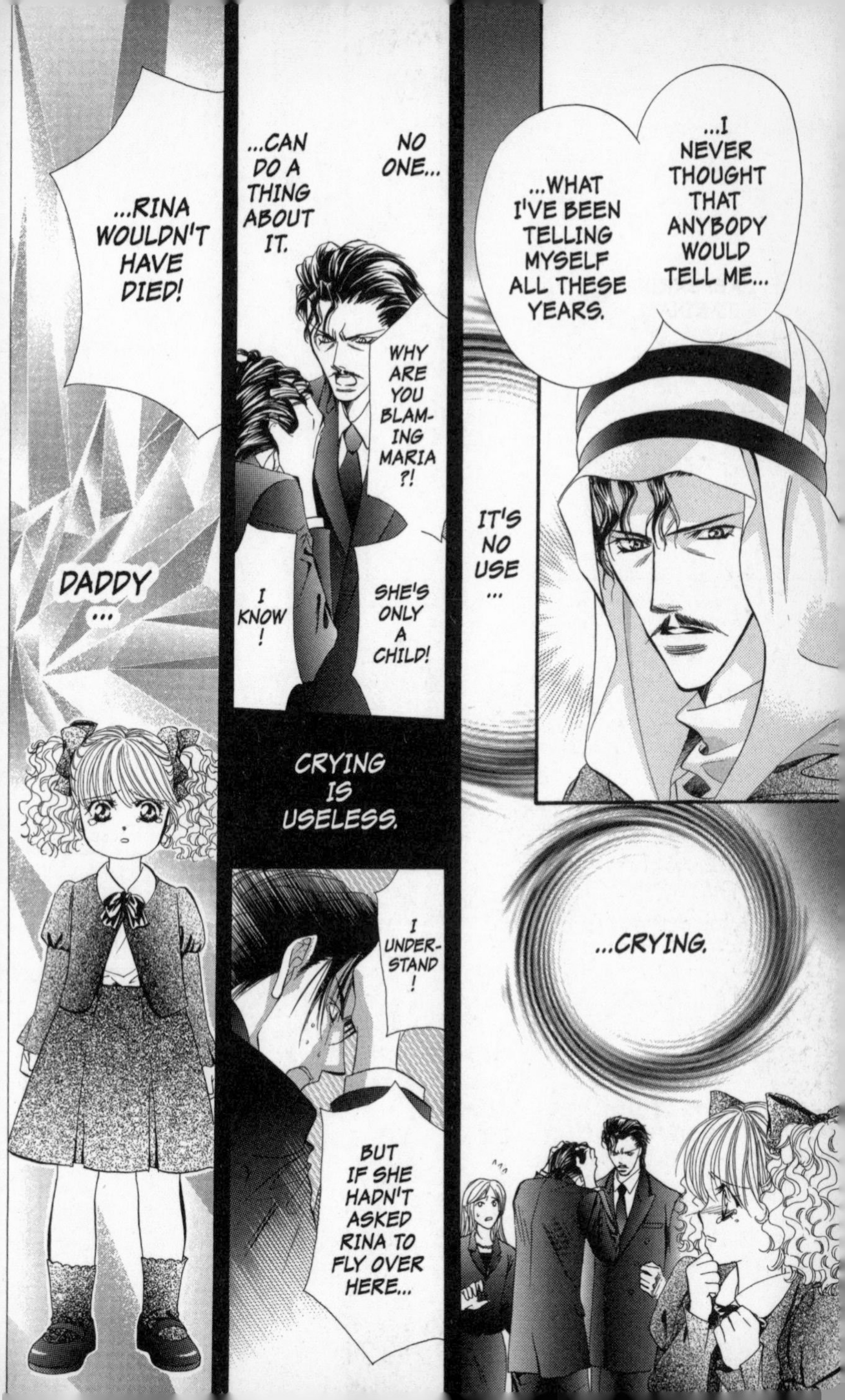
...I NEVER THOUGHT THAT ANYBODY WOULD TELL ME...
...WHAT I'VE BEEN TELLING MYSELF ALL THESE YEARS.
IT'S NO USE...
...CRYING.
NO ONE...
...CAN DO A THING ABOUT IT.
WHY ARE YOU BLAMING MARIA?!
SHE'S ONLY A CHILD!
I KNOW!
CRYING IS USELESS.
I UNDERSTAND!
BUT IF SHE HADN'T ASKED RINA TO FLY OVER HERE...
...RINA WOULDN'T HAVE DIED!
DADDY...

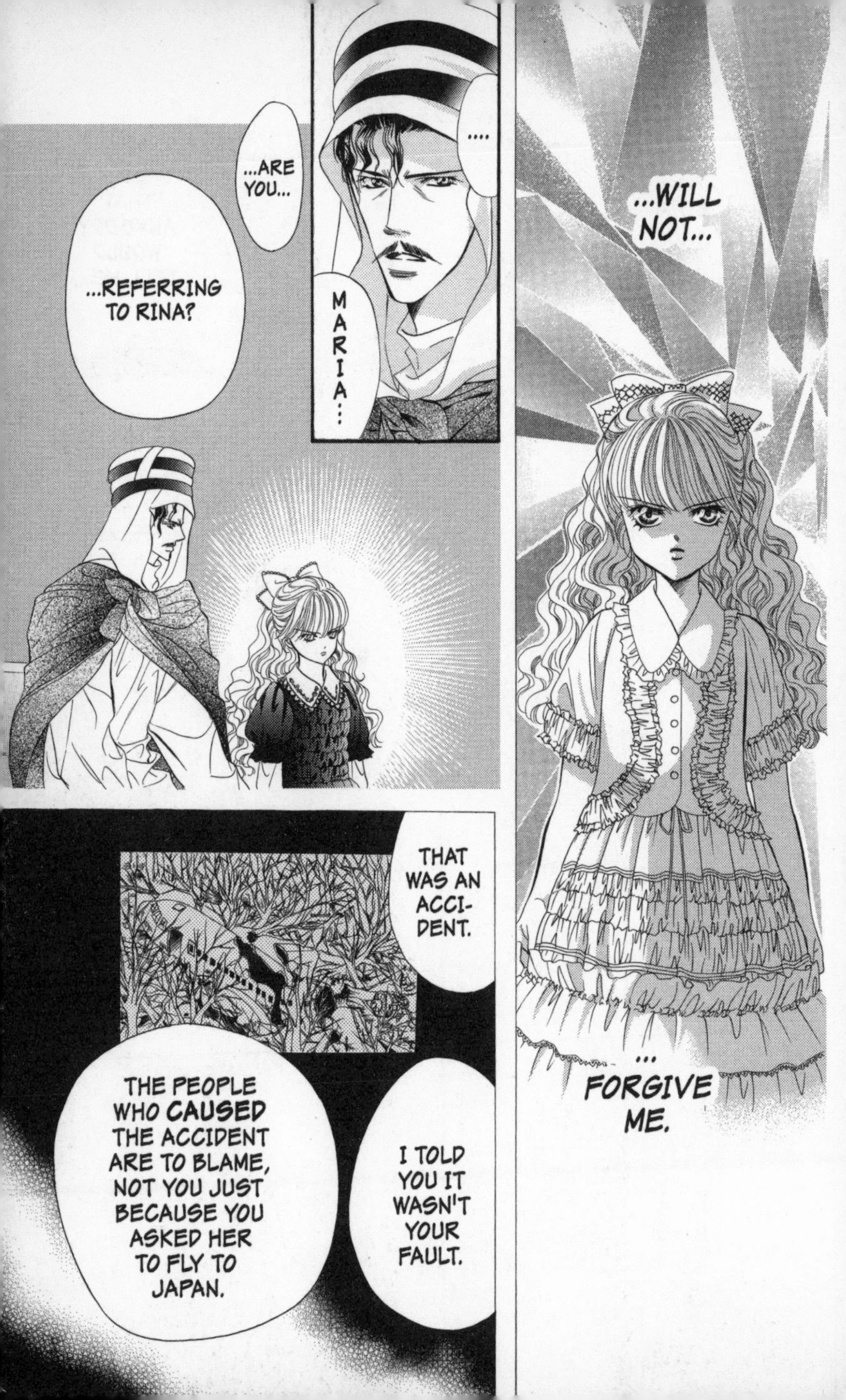

...WILL NOT...
...FORGIVE ME.
....
MARIA...
...ARE YOU...
...REFERRING TO RINA?
THAT WAS AN ACCIDENT.
I TOLD YOU IT WASN'T YOUR FAULT.
THE PEOPLE WHO CAUSED THE ACCIDENT ARE TO BLAME, NOT YOU JUST BECAUSE YOU ASKED HER TO FLY TO JAPAN.

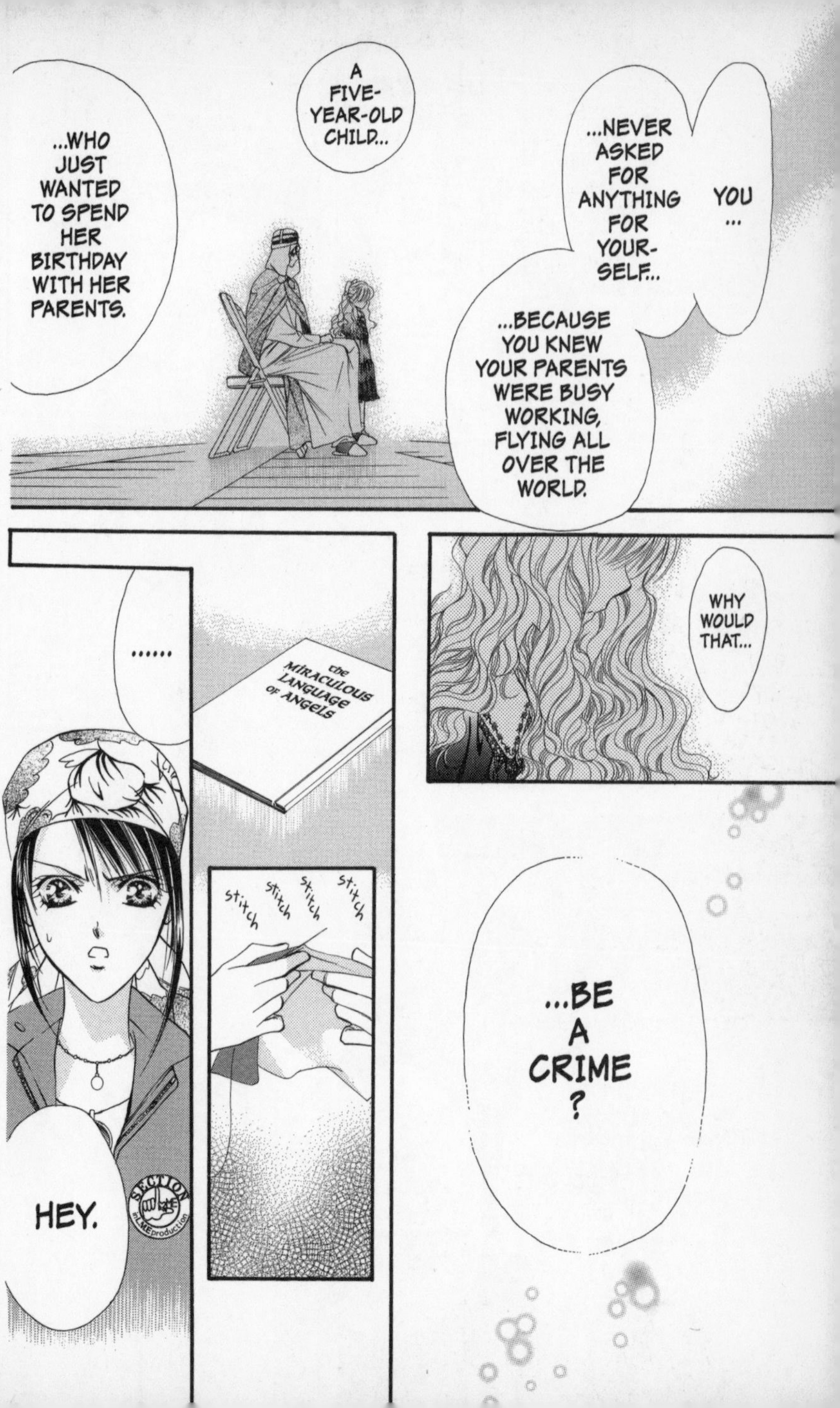
YOU...
...NEVER ASKED FOR ANYTHING FOR YOURSELF...
...BECAUSE YOU KNEW YOUR PARENTS WERE BUSY WORKING, FLYING ALL OVER THE WORLD.
A FIVE-YEAR-OLD CHILD...
...WHO JUST WANTED TO SPEND HER BIRTHDAY WITH HER PARENTS.
WHY WOULD THAT...
...BE A CRIME?
the MIRACULOUS LANGUAGE of ANGELS
stitch stitch stitch stitch
......
HEY.
SECTION inLMEproduction

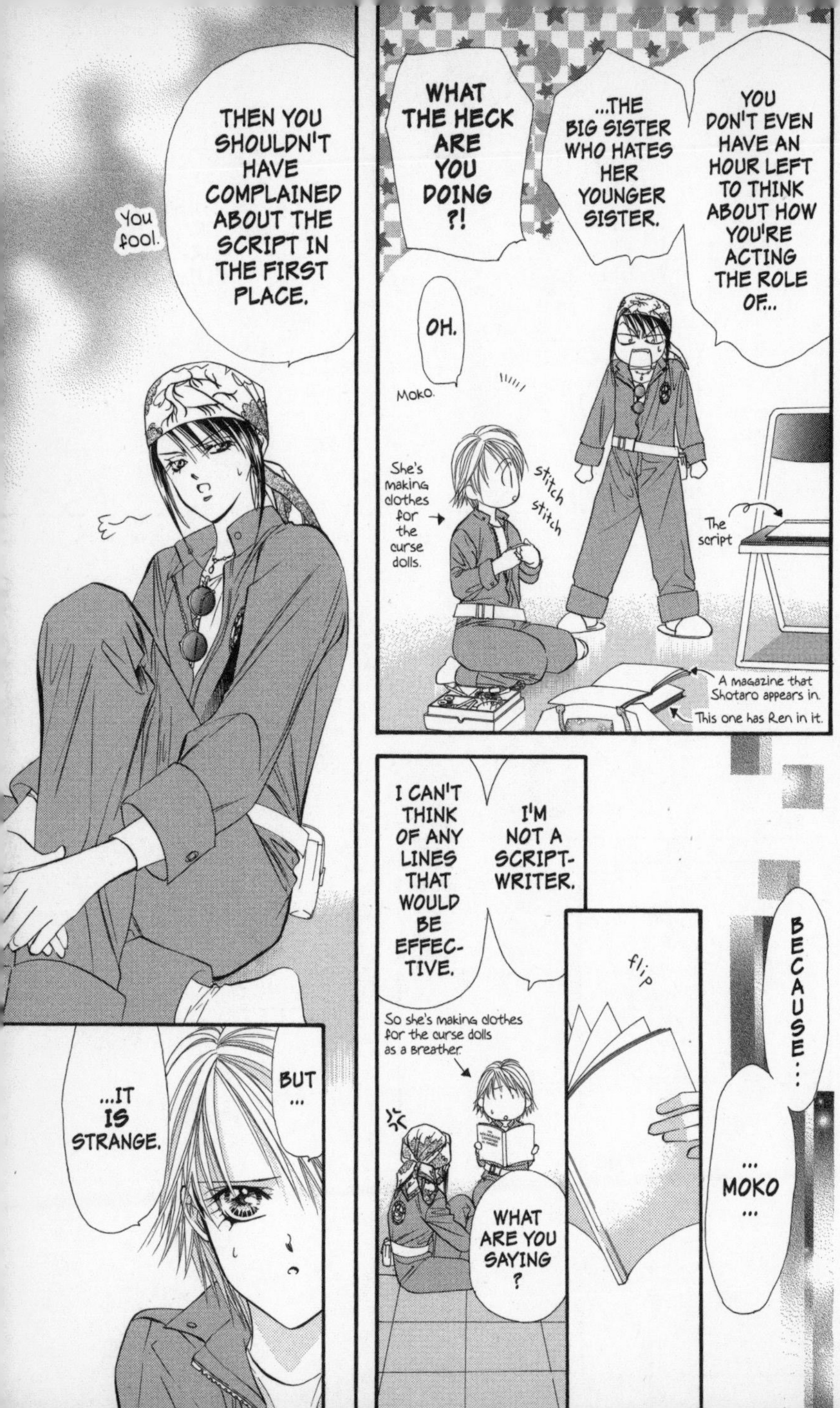

YOU DON'T EVEN HAVE AN HOUR LEFT TO THINK ABOUT HOW YOU'RE ACTING THE ROLE OF...
...THE BIG SISTER WHO HATES HER YOUNGER SISTER.
WHAT THE HECK ARE YOU DOING?!
OH.
Moko.
stitch stitch
She's making clothes for the curse dolls.
The script
A magazine that Shotaro appears in.
This one has Ren in it.
THEN YOU SHOULDN'T HAVE COMPLAINED ABOUT THE SCRIPT IN THE FIRST PLACE.
You fool.
I'M NOT A SCRIPT-WRITER.
I CAN'T THINK OF ANY LINES THAT WOULD BE EFFEC-TIVE.
So she's making clothes for the curse dolls as a breather.
WHAT ARE YOU SAYING?
BECAUSE...
...MOKO...
flip
BUT...
...IT IS STRANGE.

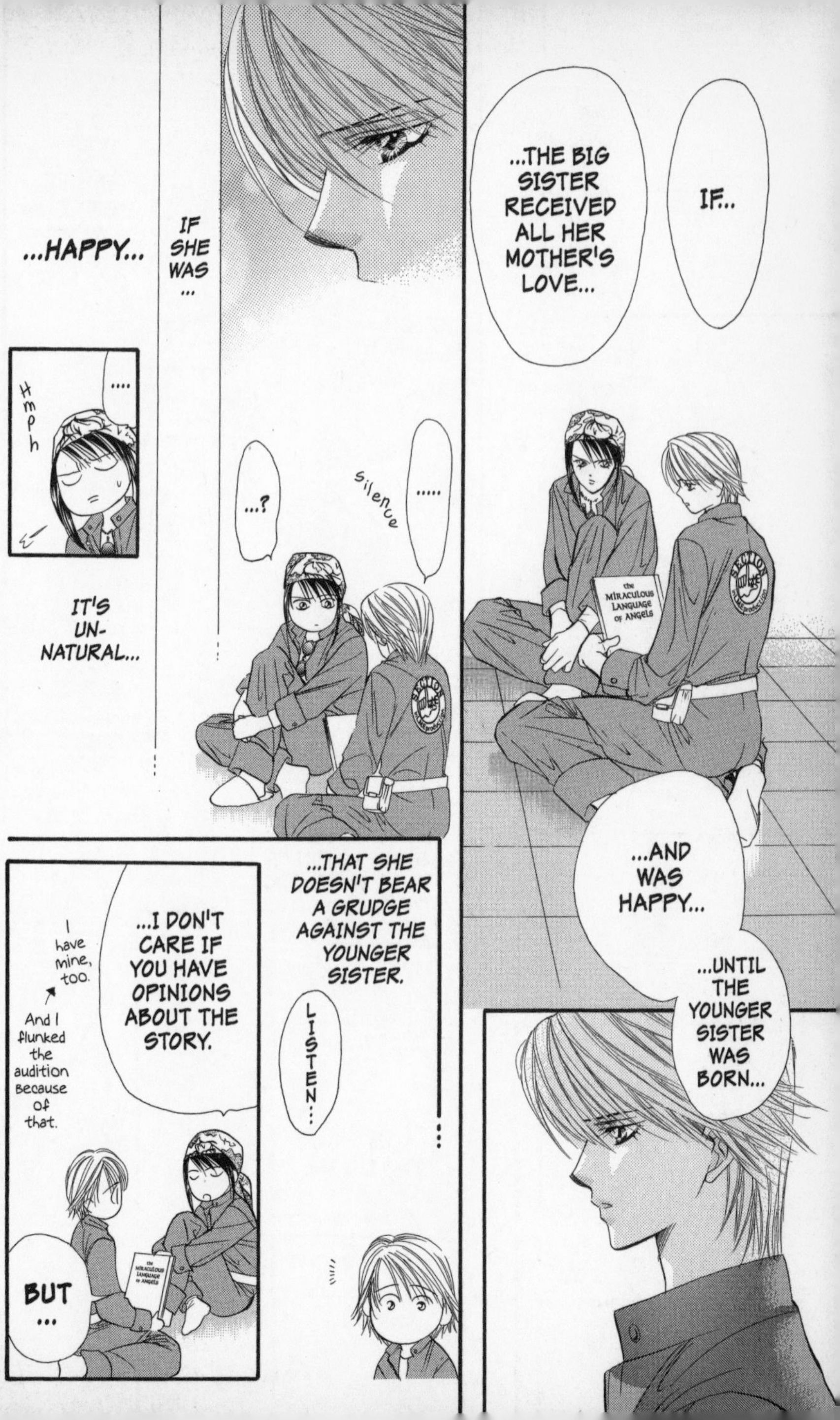
IF...
...THE BIG SISTER RECEIVED ALL HER MOTHER'S LOVE...
...AND WAS HAPPY...
...UNTIL THE YOUNGER SISTER WAS BORN...
IF SHE WAS...
...HAPPY...
IT'S UN-NATURAL...
.....
...?
Silence
....
Hmph
...THAT SHE DOESN'T BEAR A GRUDGE AGAINST THE YOUNGER SISTER.
LISTEN...
...I DON'T CARE IF YOU HAVE OPINIONS ABOUT THE STORY.
I have mine, too.
And I flunked the audition because of that.
BUT...

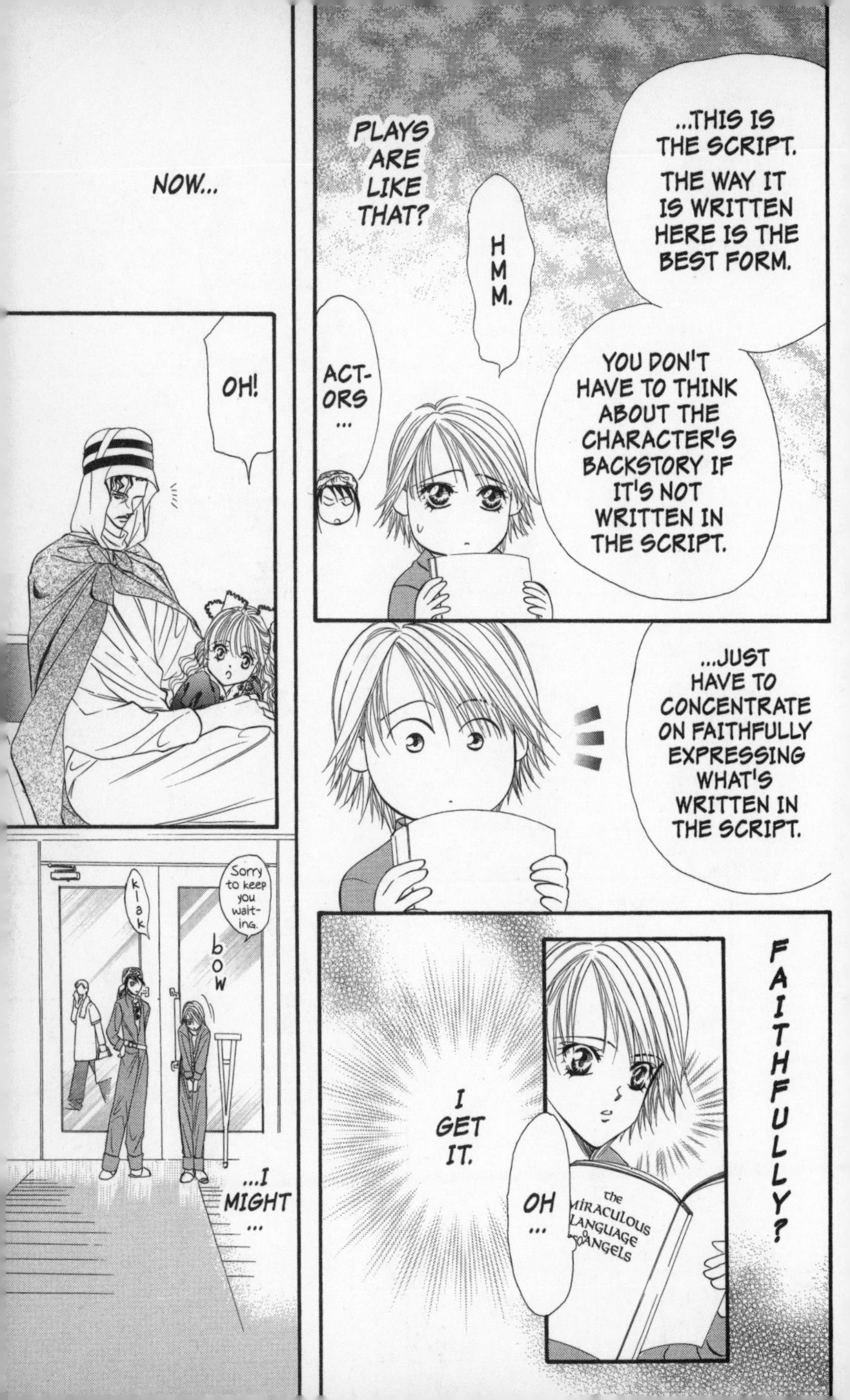
...THIS IS THE SCRIPT.
THE WAY IT IS WRITTEN HERE IS THE BEST FORM.
YOU DON'T HAVE TO THINK ABOUT THE CHARACTER'S BACKSTORY IF IT'S NOT WRITTEN IN THE SCRIPT.
HMM.
PLAYS ARE LIKE THAT?
ACT-ORS...
...JUST HAVE TO CONCENTRATE ON FAITHFULLY EXPRESSING WHAT'S WRITTEN IN THE SCRIPT.
FAITHFULLY?
I GET IT.
OH...
The MIRACULOUS LANGUAGE of ANGELS
NOW...
OH!
Sorry to keep you wait-ing.
klak
bow
...I MIGHT...

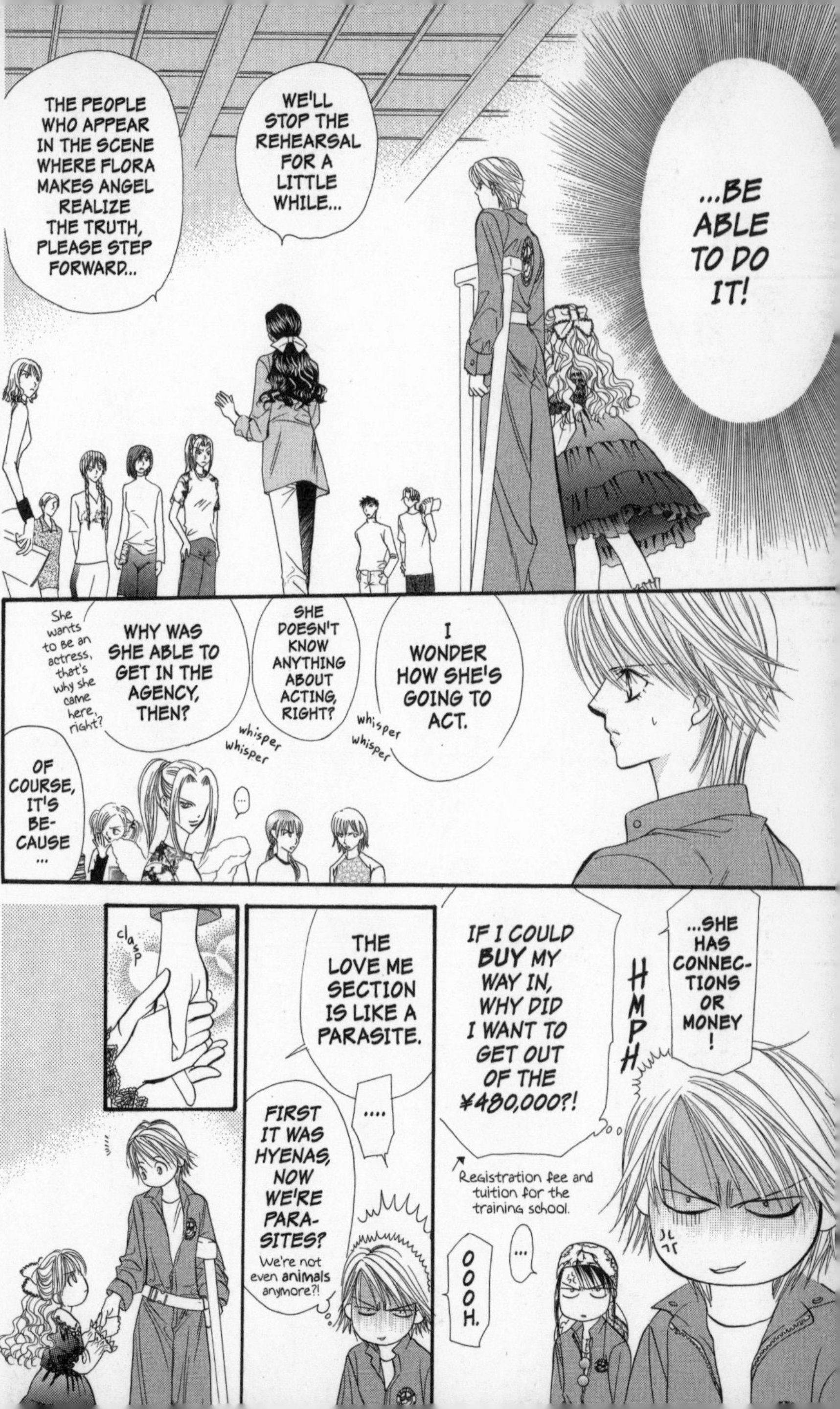
...BE ABLE TO DO IT!
WE'LL STOP THE REHEARSAL FOR A LITTLE WHILE...
THE PEOPLE WHO APPEAR IN THE SCENE WHERE FLORA MAKES ANGEL REALIZE THE TRUTH, PLEASE STEP FORWARD...
I WONDER HOW SHE'S GOING TO ACT.
whisper whisper
SHE DOESN'T KNOW ANYTHING ABOUT ACTING, RIGHT?
WHY WAS SHE ABLE TO GET IN THE AGENCY, THEN?
She wants to be an actress, that's why she came here, right?
whisper whisper
...
OF COURSE, IT'S BE-CAUSE...
...SHE HAS CONNEC-TIONS OR MONEY!
HMPH
IF I COULD BUY MY WAY IN, WHY DID I WANT TO GET OUT OF THE ¥480,000?!
Registration fee and tuition for the training school.
...
OOOH.
THE LOVE ME SECTION IS LIKE A PARASITE.
....
FIRST IT WAS HYENAS, NOW WE'RE PARA-SITES?
We're not even animals anymore?!
clasp

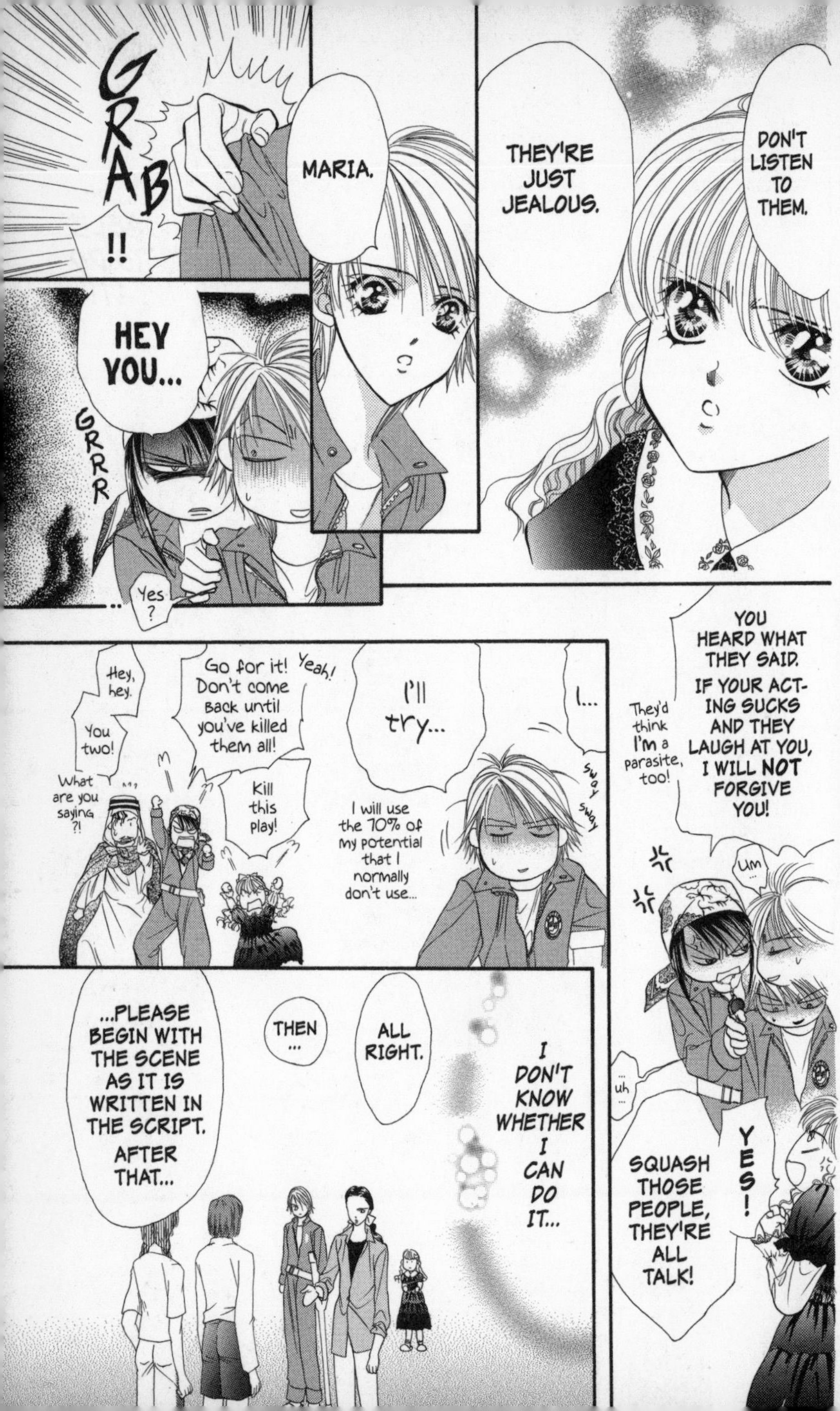
DON'T LISTEN TO THEM.
THEY'RE JUST JEALOUS.
MARIA.
GRAB!!
HEY YOU...
GRRR
...Yes?
YOU HEARD WHAT THEY SAID.
IF YOUR ACTING SUCKS AND THEY LAUGH AT YOU, I WILL NOT FORGIVE YOU!
They'd think I'm a parasite, too!
Um...
...uh...
YES!
SQUASH THOSE PEOPLE, THEY'RE ALL TALK!
I...
sway sway
I'll try...
I will use the 70% of my potential that I normally don't use...
Yeah!
Go for it! Don't come back until you've killed them all!
Kill this play!
Hey, hey.
You two!
What are you saying?!
I DON'T KNOW WHETHER I CAN DO IT...
ALL RIGHT.
THEN...
...PLEASE BEGIN WITH THE SCENE AS IT IS WRITTEN IN THE SCRIPT.
AFTER THAT...

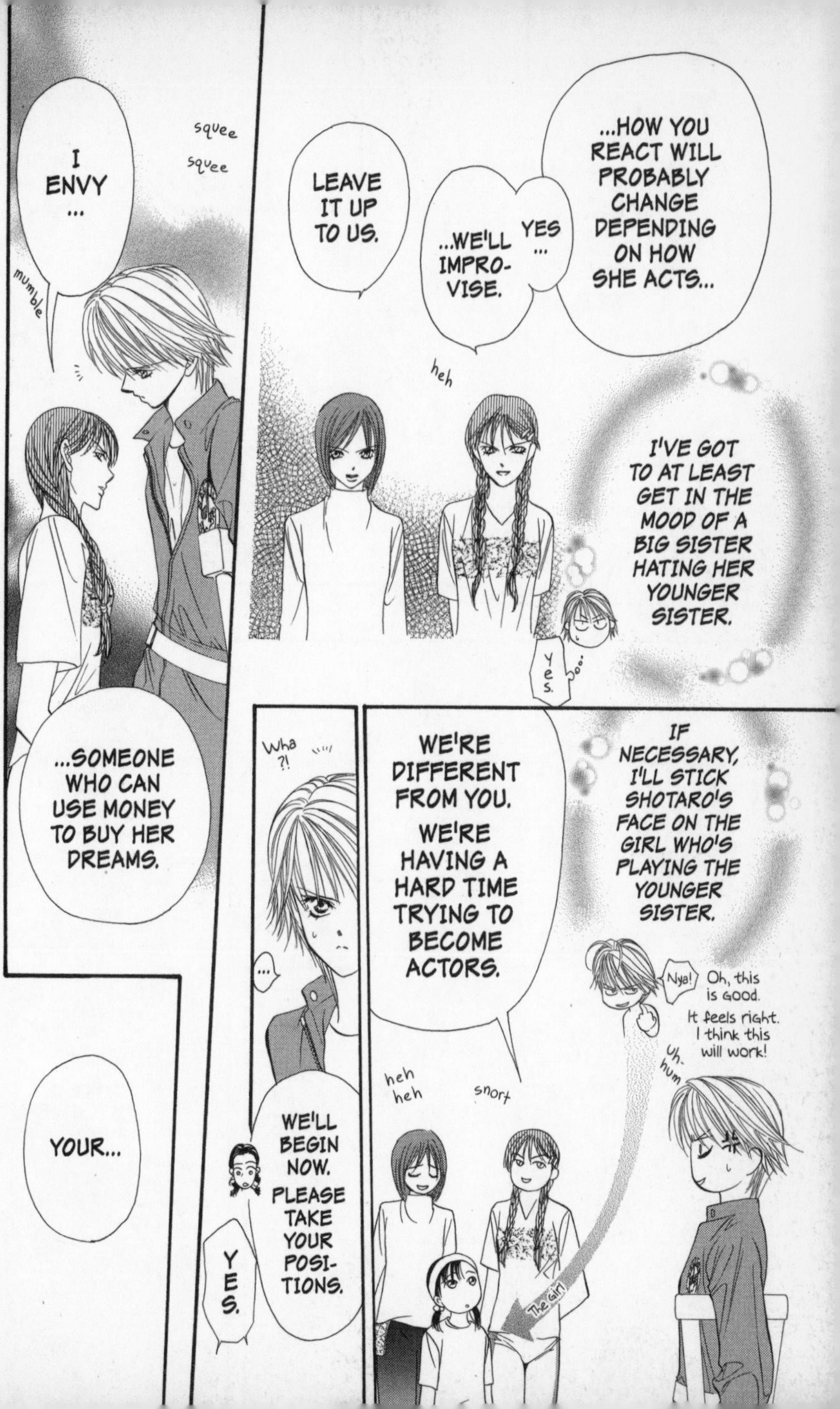
...HOW YOU REACT WILL PROBABLY CHANGE DEPENDING ON HOW SHE ACTS...
YES...
...WE'LL IMPROVISE.
LEAVE IT UP TO US.
heh
I'VE GOT TO AT LEAST GET IN THE MOOD OF A BIG SISTER HATING HER YOUNGER SISTER.
Yes.
IF NECESSARY, I'LL STICK SHOTARO'S FACE ON THE GIRL WHO'S PLAYING THE YOUNGER SISTER.
WE'RE DIFFERENT FROM YOU. WE'RE HAVING A HARD TIME TRYING TO BECOME ACTORS.
Nya!
Oh, this is good. It feels right. I think this will work!
Uh-hum
snort
heh heh
The Girl
Wha ?!
...
WE'LL BEGIN NOW. PLEASE TAKE YOUR POSITIONS.
YES.
squee
squee
I ENVY...
mumble
...SOMEONE WHO CAN USE MONEY TO BUY HER DREAMS.
YOUR...

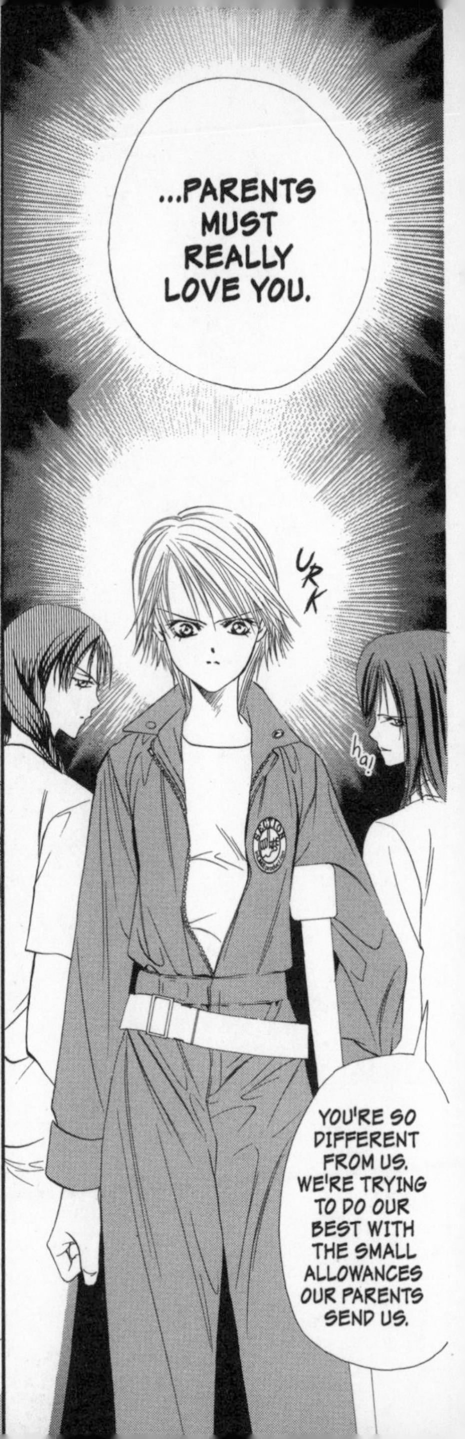
...PARENTS MUST REALLY LOVE YOU.
URK
ha!
YOU'RE SO DIFFERENT FROM US. WE'RE TRYING TO DO OUR BEST WITH THE SMALL ALLOWANCES OUR PARENTS SEND US.
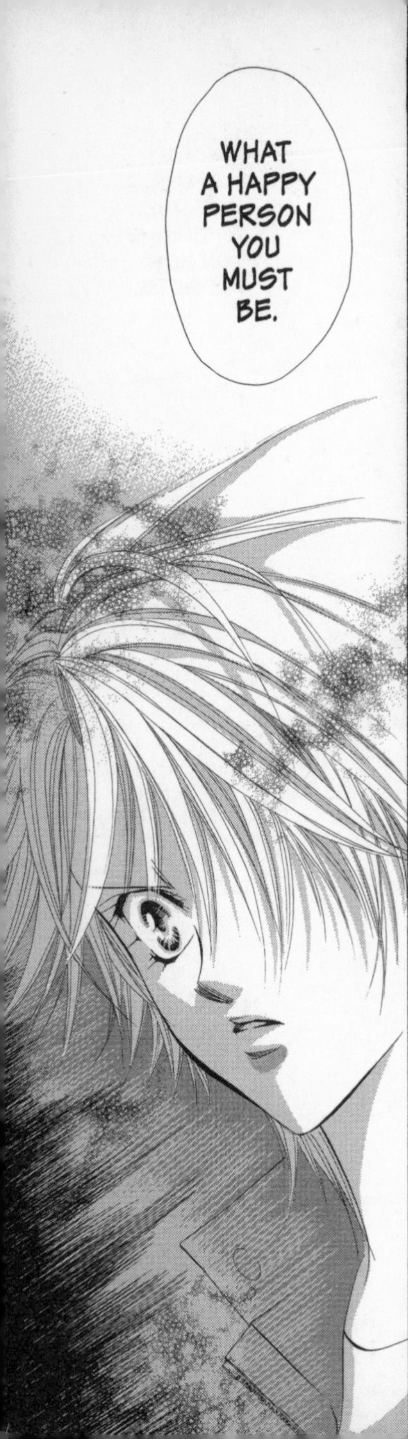
WHAT A HAPPY PERSON YOU MUST BE.

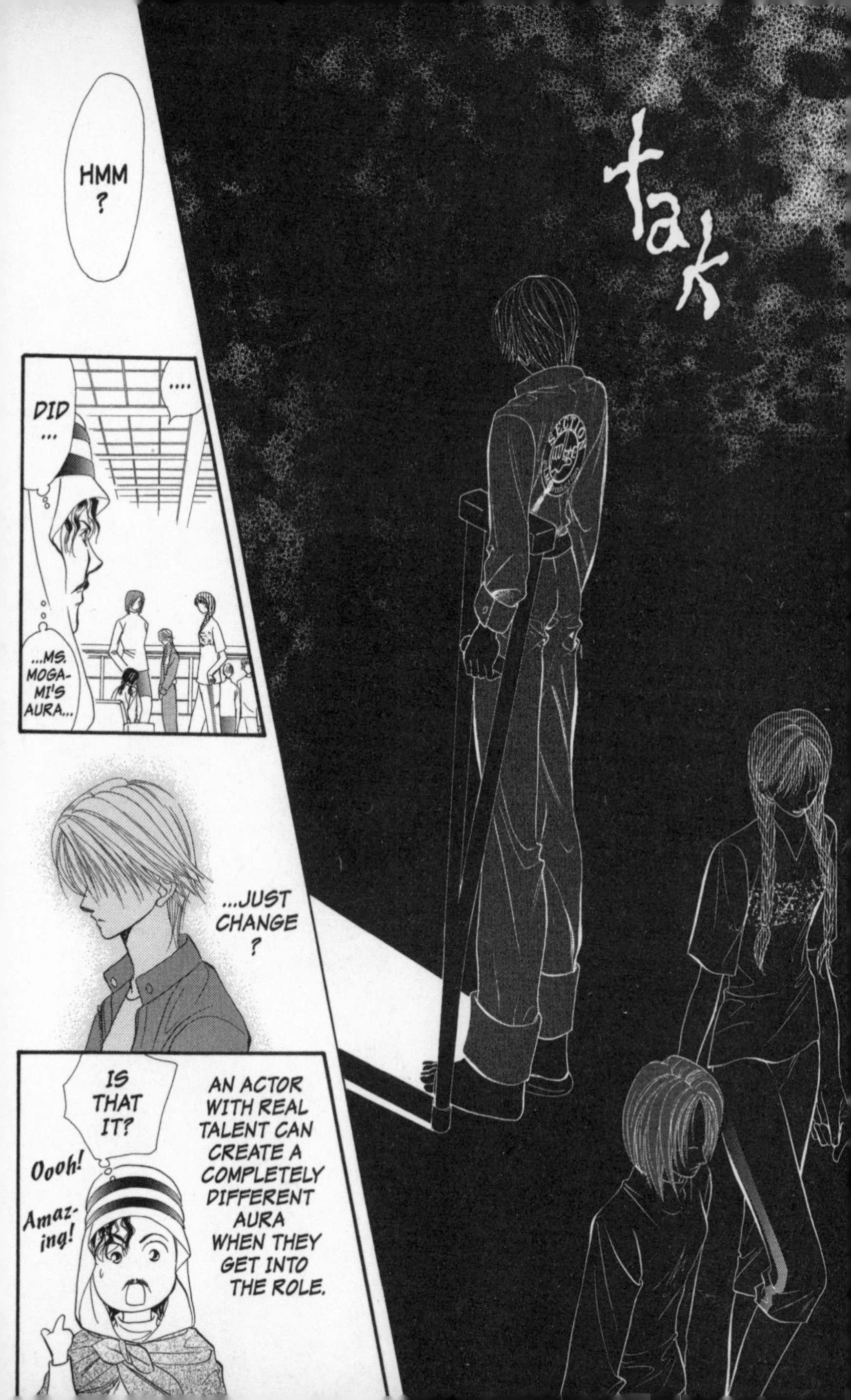
tak
HMM?
....
DID...
...MS. MOGAMI'S AURA...
...JUST CHANGE?
IS THAT IT?
AN ACTOR WITH REAL TALENT CAN CREATE A COMPLETELY DIFFERENT AURA WHEN THEY GET INTO THE ROLE.
Oooh! Amazing!

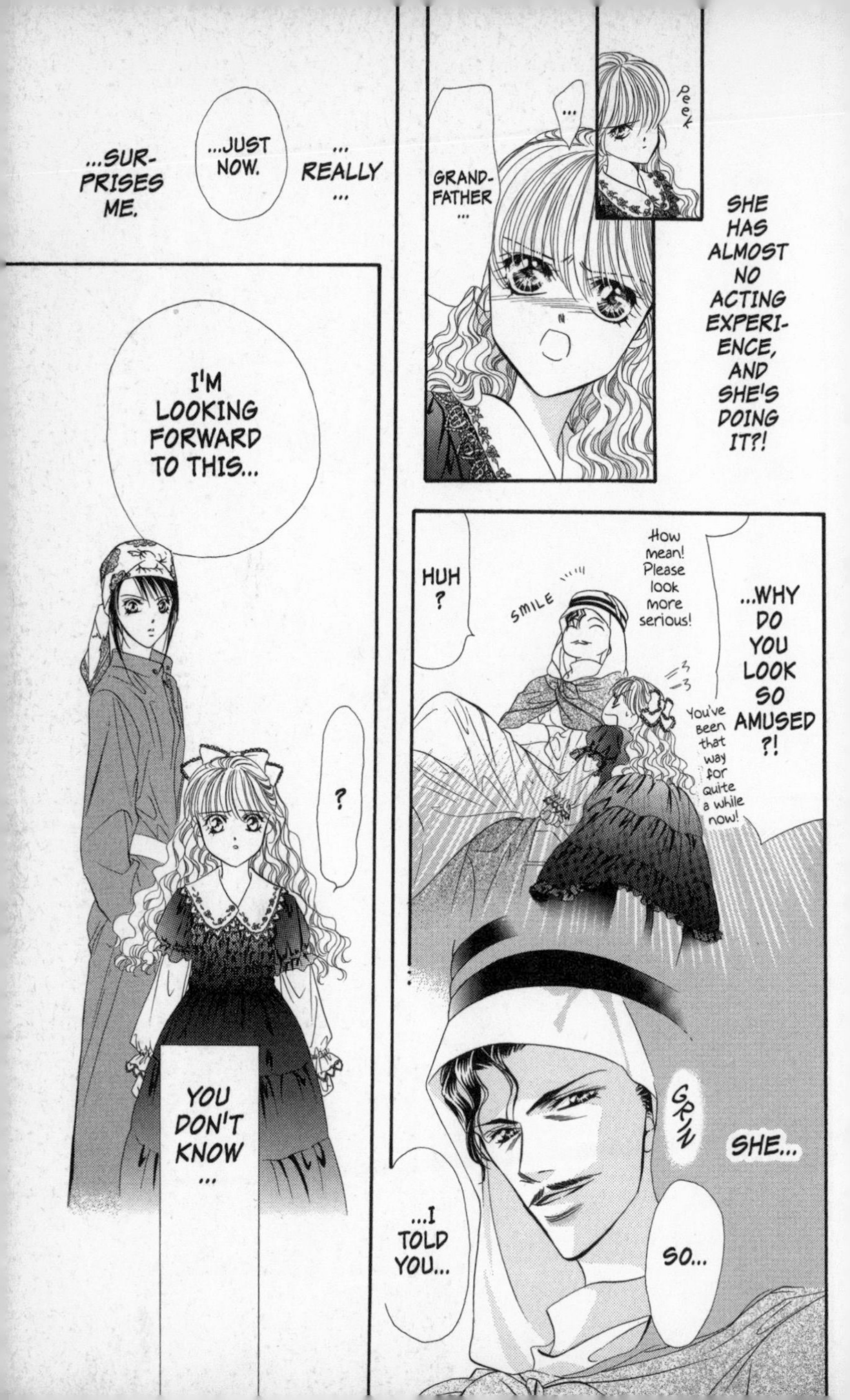
Peek
...
GRAND-FATHER ...
SHE HAS ALMOST NO ACTING EXPERIENCE, AND SHE'S DOING IT?!
... REALLY ...
...JUST NOW.
...SUR-PRISES ME.
HUH ?
SMILE
How mean! Please look more serious!
...WHY DO YOU LOOK SO AMUSED ?!
You've Been that way for quite a while now!
GRIN
SHE...
SO...
...I TOLD YOU...
I'M LOOKING FORWARD TO THIS...
?
YOU DON'T KNOW ...

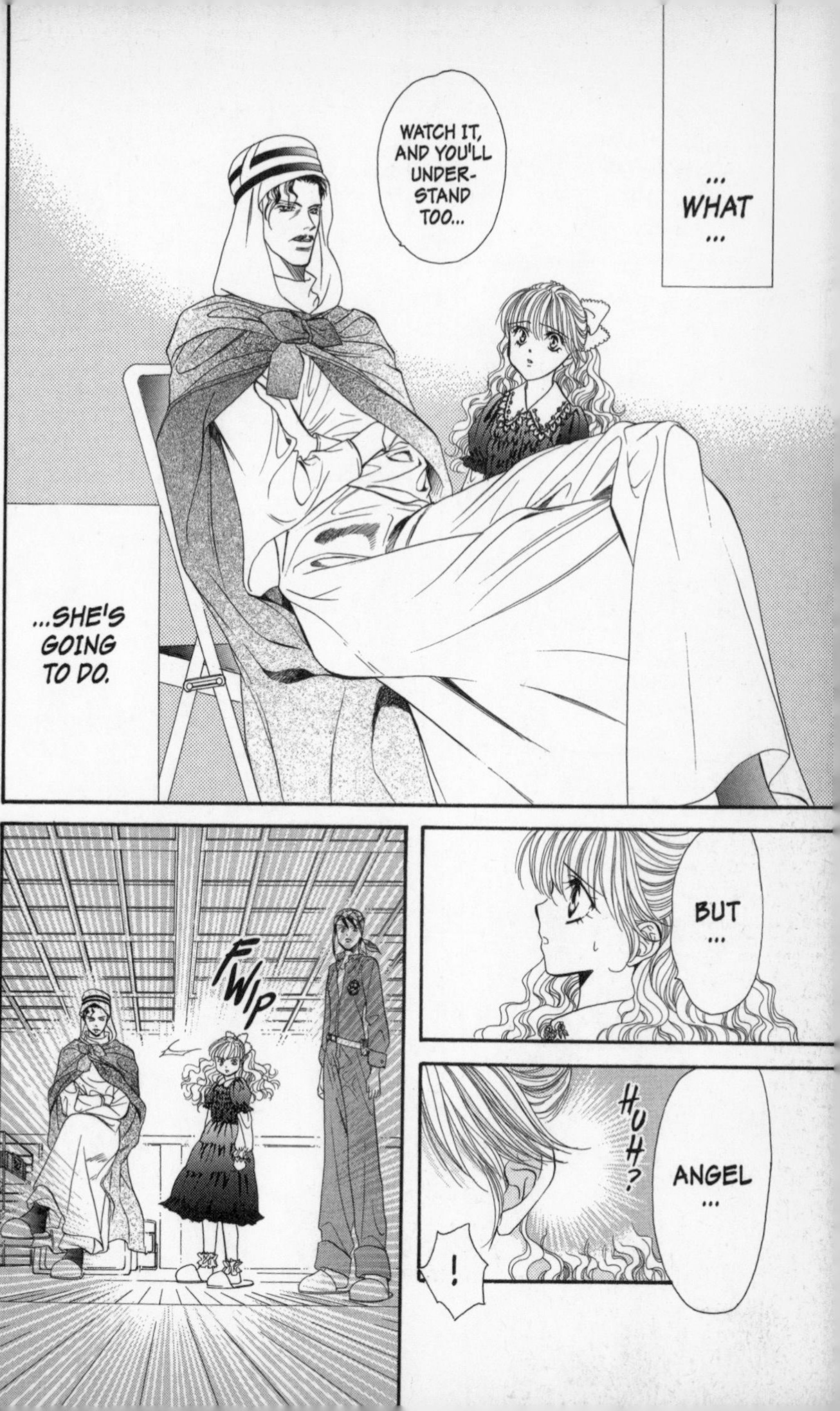

... WHAT ...
WATCH IT, AND YOU'LL UNDER-STAND TOO...
...SHE'S GOING TO DO.
BUT ...
ANGEL ...
HUH?
!
FWIP

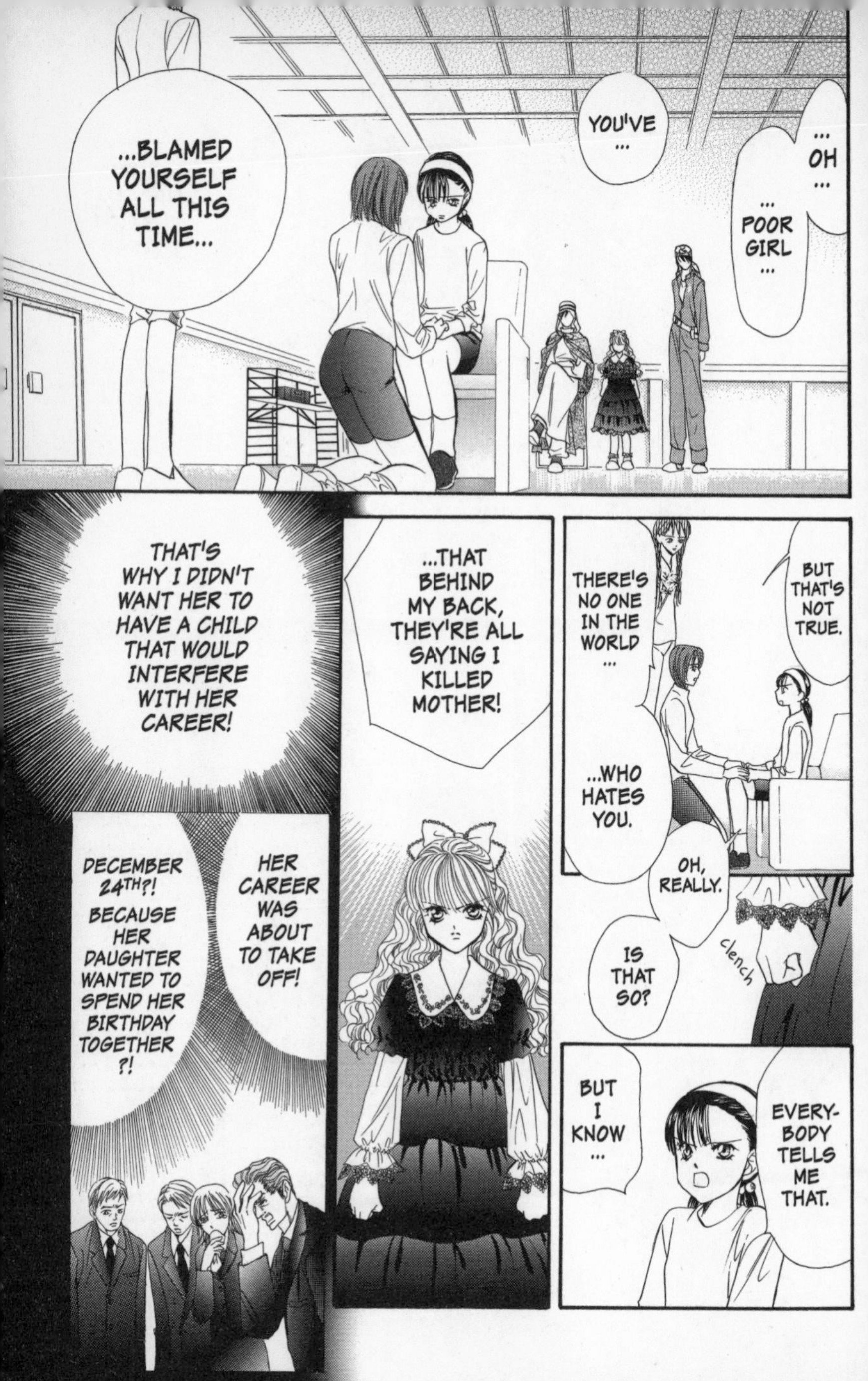
...OH... ...POOR GIRL...
YOU'VE...
...BLAMED YOURSELF ALL THIS TIME...
BUT THAT'S NOT TRUE.
THERE'S NO ONE IN THE WORLD...
...WHO HATES YOU.
OH, REALLY.
IS THAT SO?
clench
EVERY-BODY TELLS ME THAT.
BUT I KNOW...
...THAT BEHIND MY BACK, THEY'RE ALL SAYING I KILLED MOTHER!
THAT'S WHY I DIDN'T WANT HER TO HAVE A CHILD THAT WOULD INTERFERE WITH HER CAREER!
HER CAREER WAS ABOUT TO TAKE OFF!
DECEMBER 24TH?! BECAUSE HER DAUGHTER WANTED TO SPEND HER BIRTHDAY TOGETHER?!

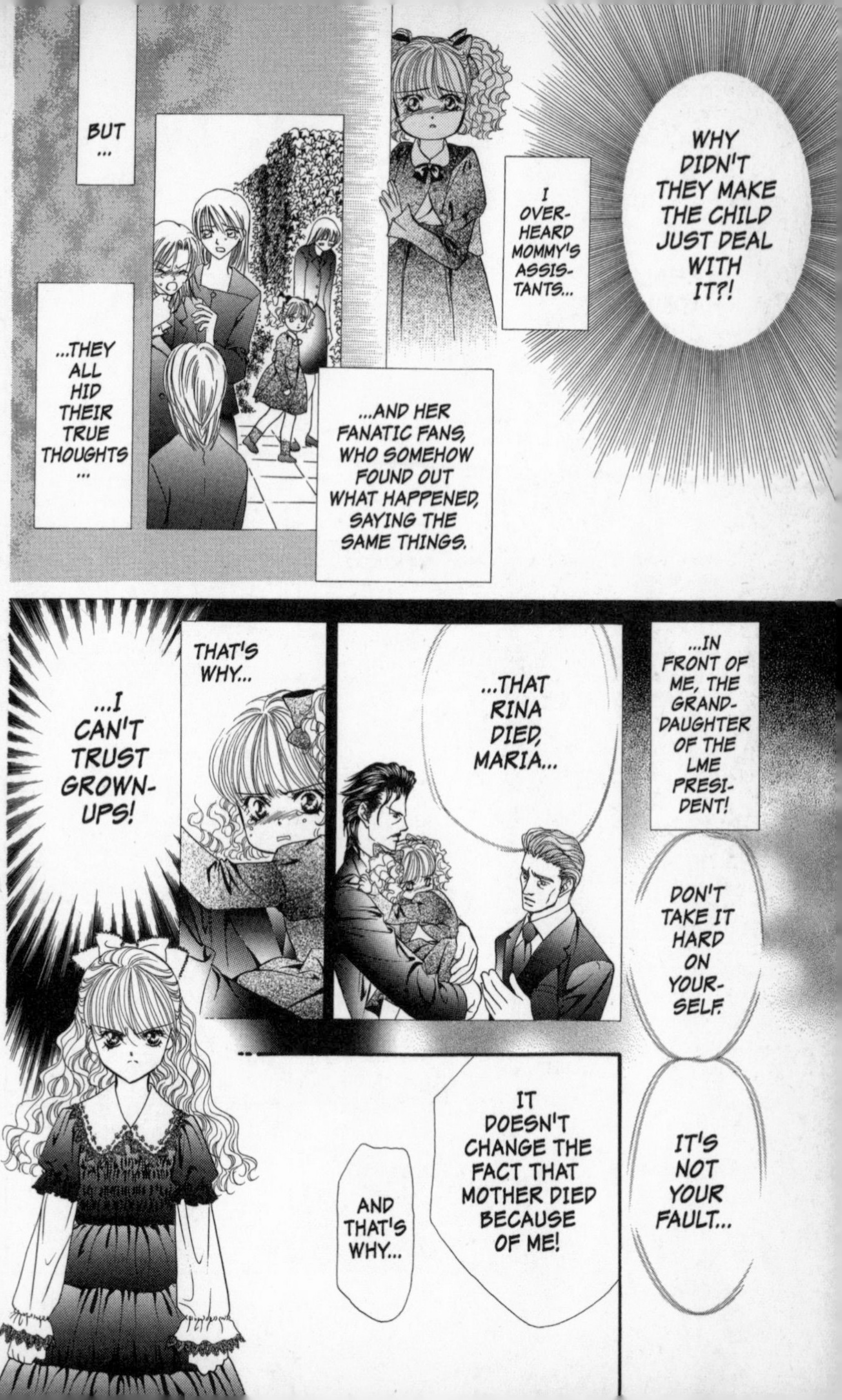
WHY DIDN'T THEY MAKE THE CHILD JUST DEAL WITH IT?!
I OVERHEARD MOMMY'S ASSISTANTS...
...AND HER FANATIC FANS, WHO SOMEHOW FOUND OUT WHAT HAPPENED, SAYING THE SAME THINGS.
BUT ...
...THEY ALL HID THEIR TRUE THOUGHTS ...
...IN FRONT OF ME, THE GRANDDAUGHTER OF THE LME PRESIDENT!
DON'T TAKE IT HARD ON YOURSELF.
IT'S NOT YOUR FAULT...
...THAT RINA DIED, MARIA...
IT DOESN'T CHANGE THE FACT THAT MOTHER DIED BECAUSE OF ME!
THAT'S WHY...
AND THAT'S WHY...
...I CAN'T TRUST GROWN-UPS!

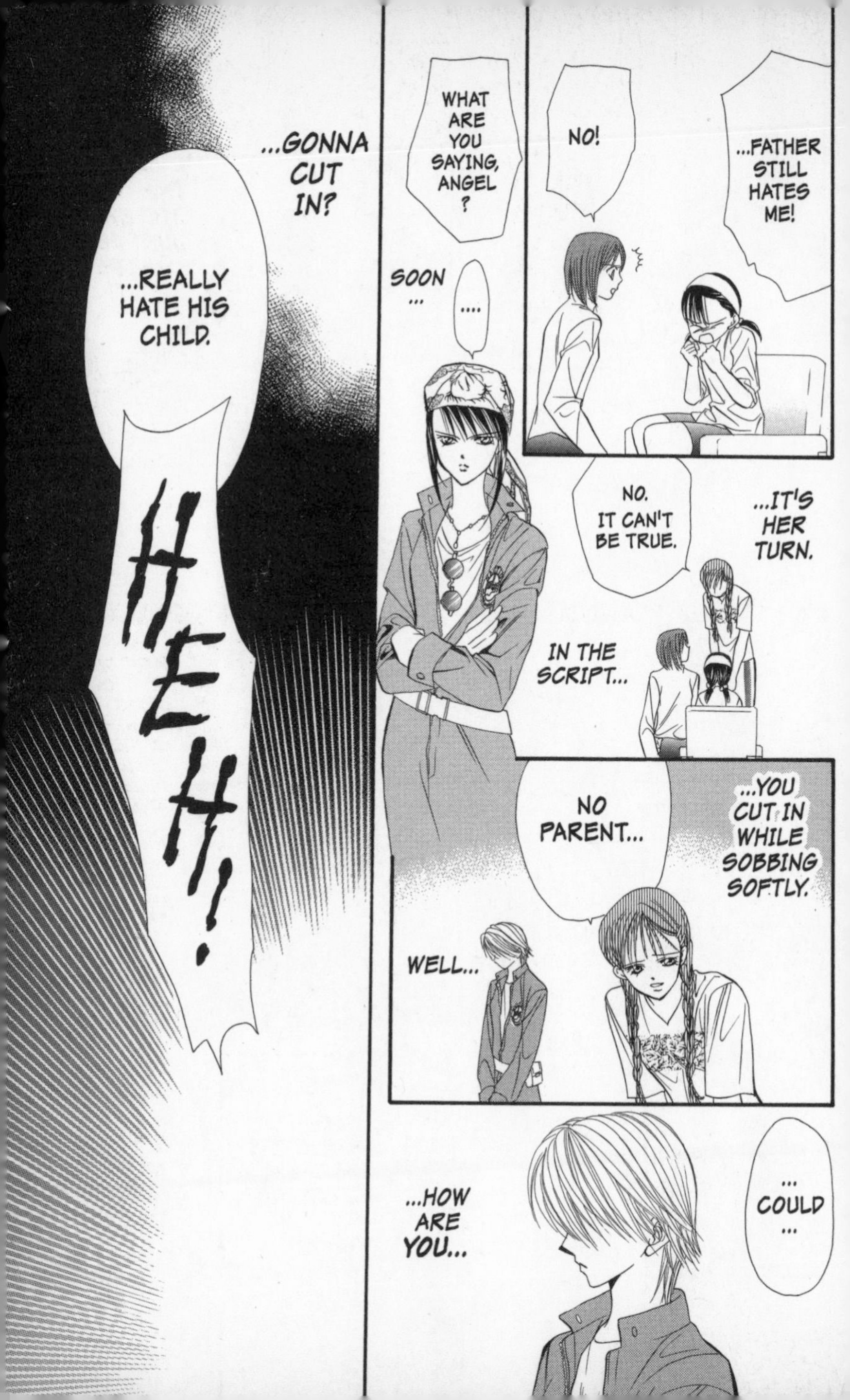
...FATHER STILL HATES ME!
NO!
WHAT ARE YOU SAYING, ANGEL?
....
SOON...
...IT'S HER TURN.
NO. IT CAN'T BE TRUE.
IN THE SCRIPT...
...YOU CUT IN WHILE SOBBING SOFTLY.
NO PARENT...
WELL...
...COULD...
...HOW ARE YOU...
...GONNA CUT IN?
...REALLY HATE HIS CHILD.
HEH!

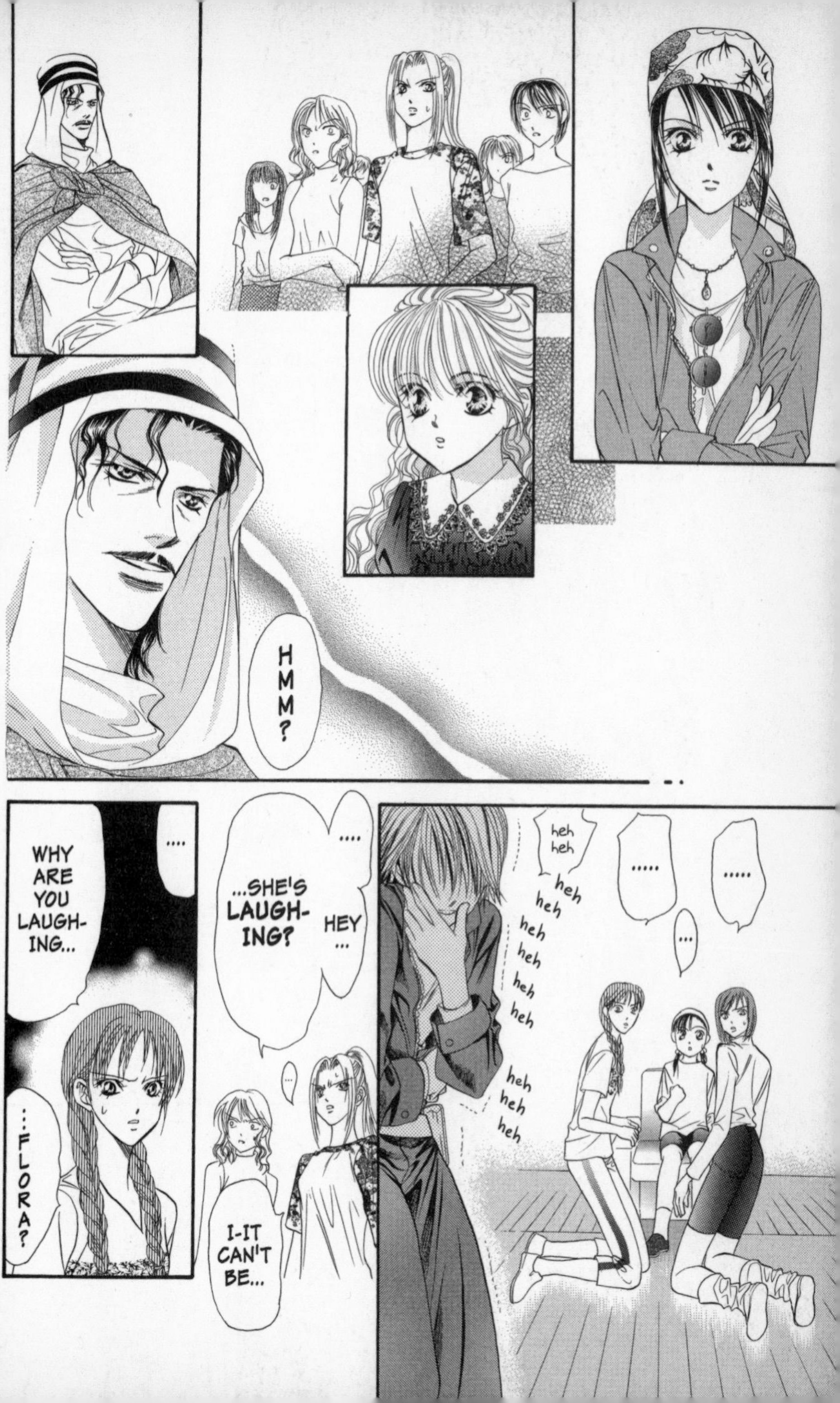
HMM?
......
......
heh heh
...
heh heh heh heh heh heh
heh heh heh
....
...SHE'S LAUGHING?
HEY ...
...
I-IT CAN'T BE...
....
WHY ARE YOU LAUGHING...
...FLORA?

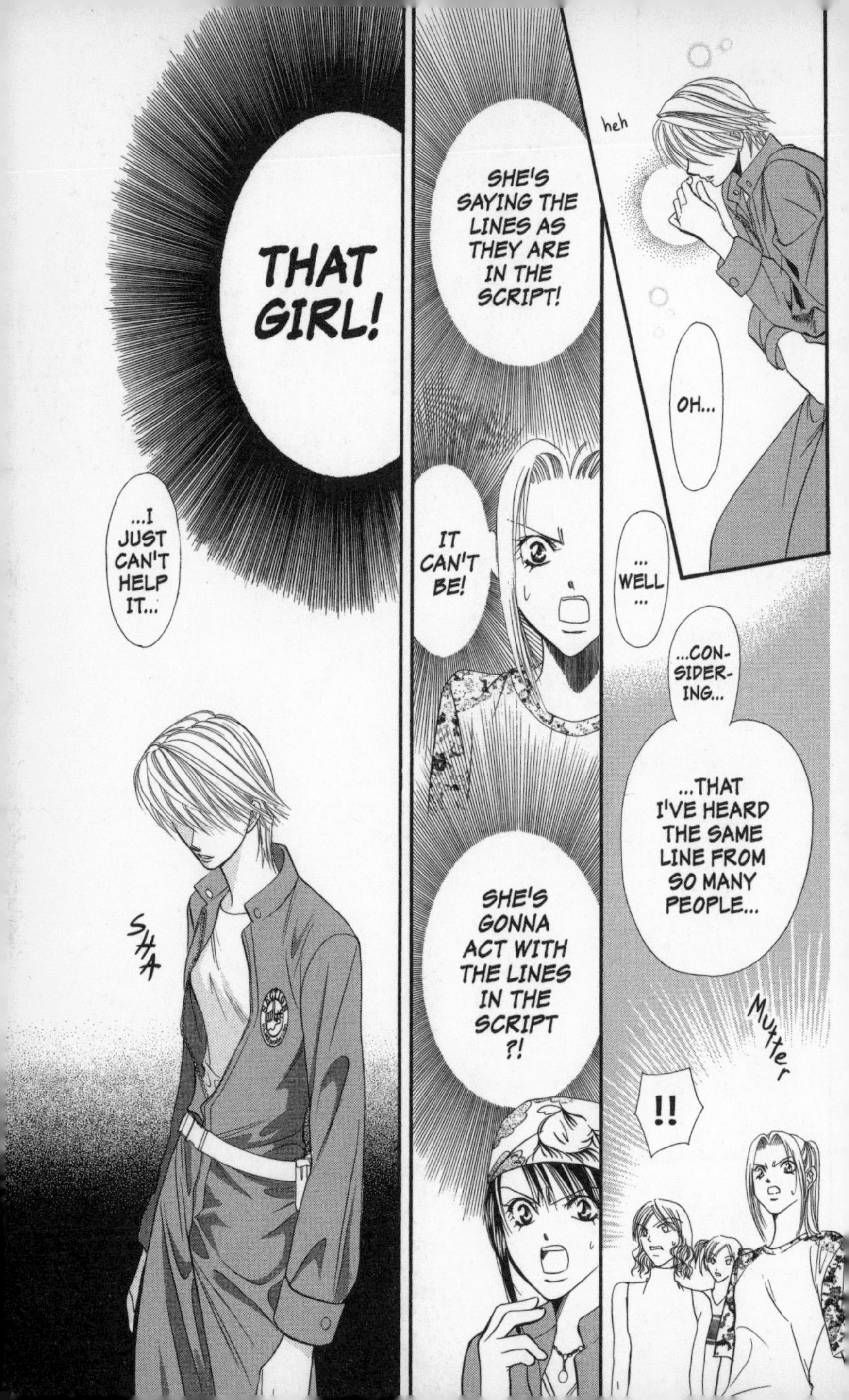
heh
OH...
...WELL...
...CON-SIDER-ING...
...THAT I'VE HEARD THE SAME LINE FROM SO MANY PEOPLE...
Mutter
!!
SHE'S SAYING THE LINES AS THEY ARE IN THE SCRIPT!
IT CAN'T BE!
SHE'S GONNA ACT WITH THE LINES IN THE SCRIPT?!
THAT GIRL!
...I JUST CAN'T HELP IT...
SHA

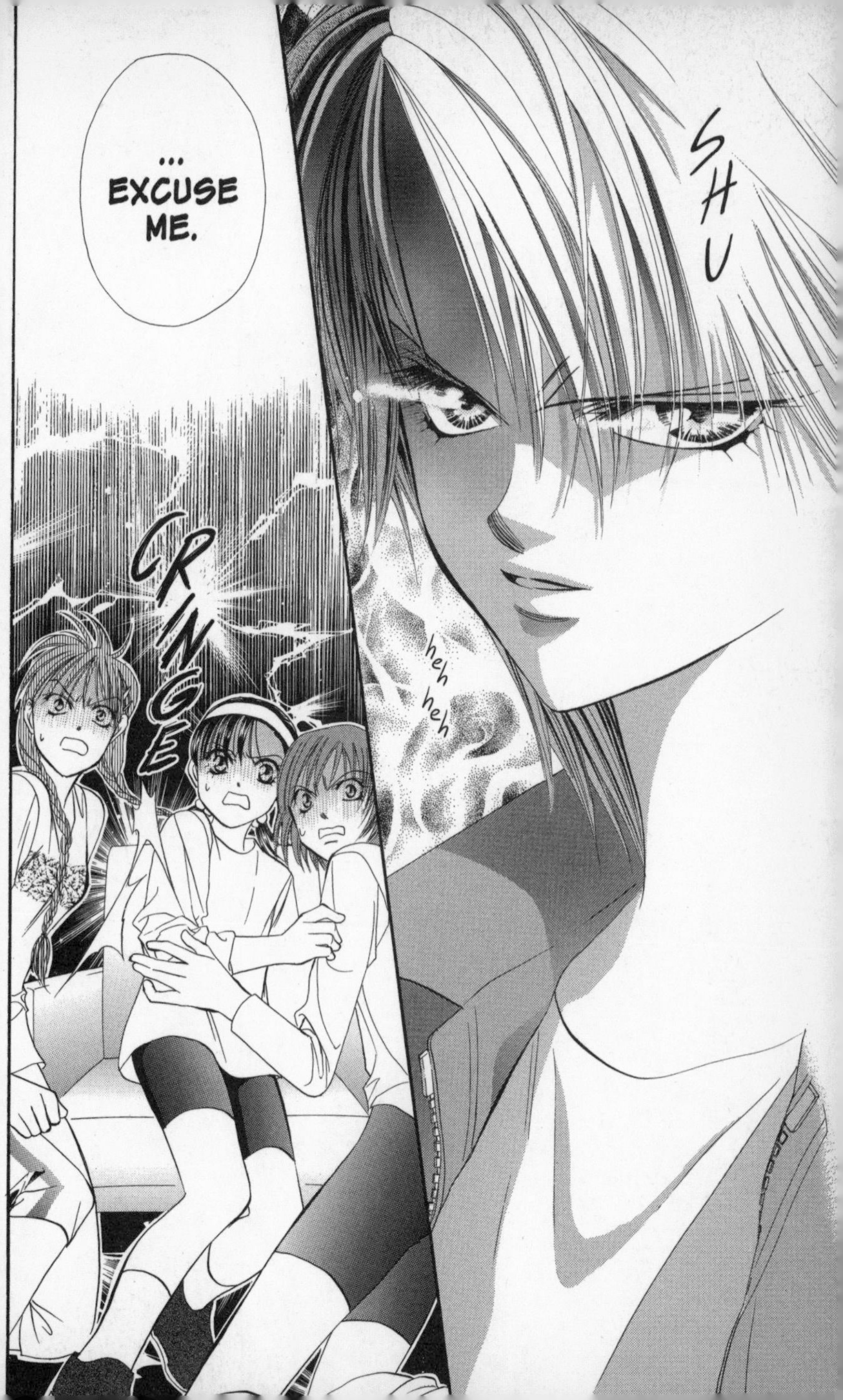
SHU
heh heh
... EXCUSE ME.
CRINGE

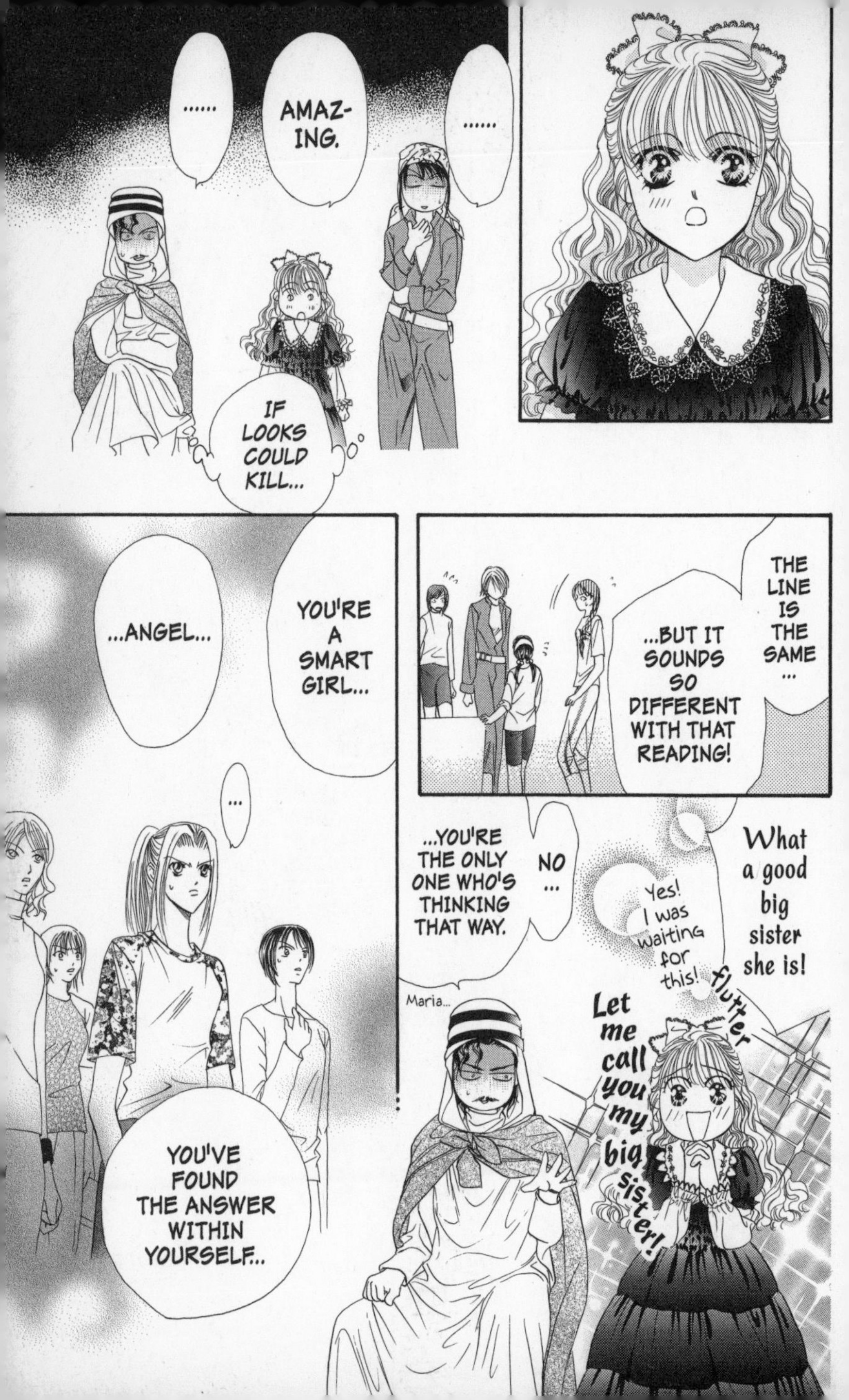
......
AMAZ-ING.
......
IF LOOKS COULD KILL...
THE LINE IS THE SAME ...
...BUT IT SOUNDS SO DIFFERENT WITH THAT READING!
What a good big sister she is!
Yes! I was waiting for this!
flutter
Let me call you my big sister!
NO ...
...YOU'RE THE ONLY ONE WHO'S THINKING THAT WAY.
Maria...
YOU'RE A SMART GIRL...
...ANGEL...
...
YOU'VE FOUND THE ANSWER WITHIN YOURSELF..

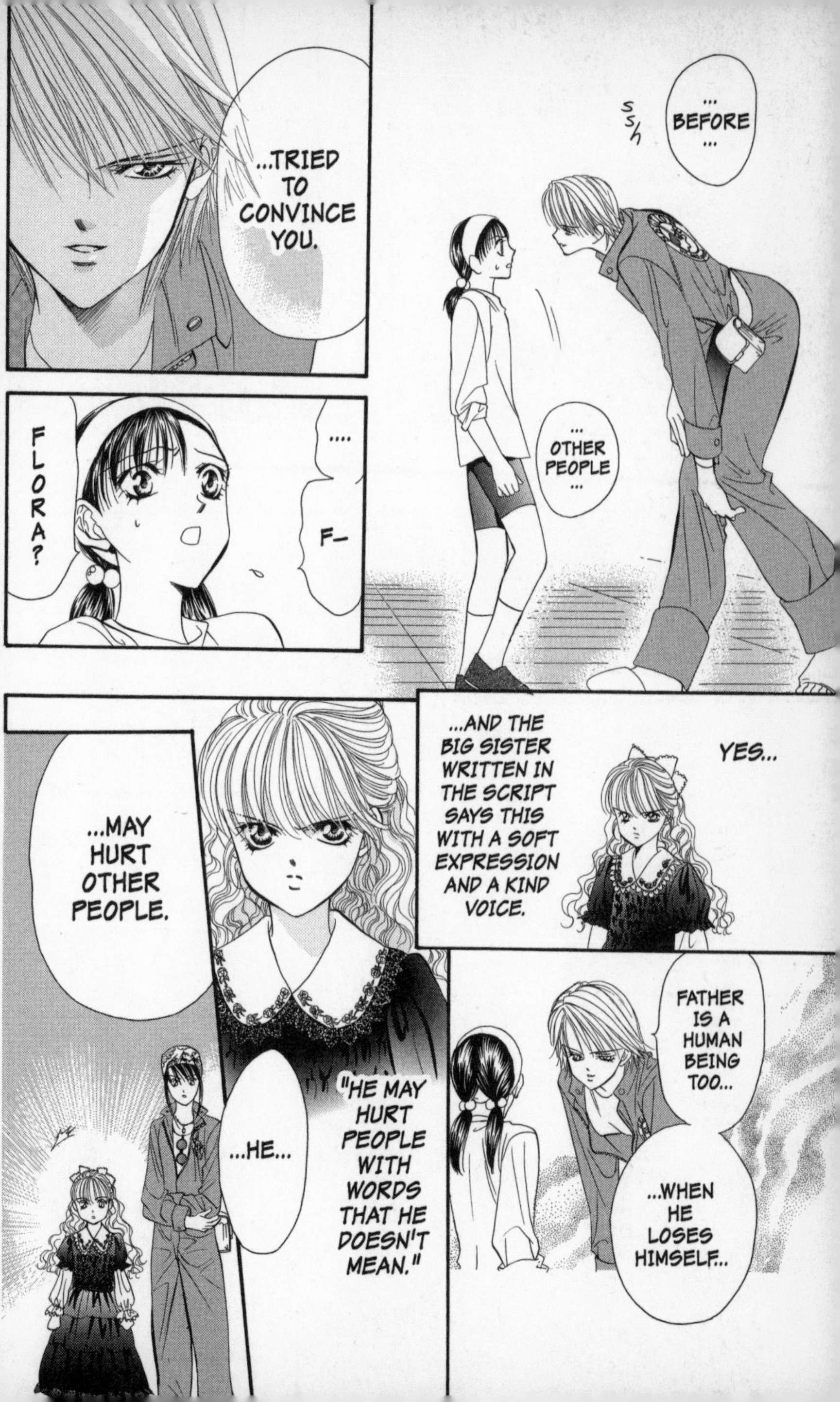
... BEFORE ...
SSH
... OTHER PEOPLE ...
...TRIED TO CONVINCE YOU.
.....
F—
FLORA?
YES...
...AND THE BIG SISTER WRITTEN IN THE SCRIPT SAYS THIS WITH A SOFT EXPRESSION AND A KIND VOICE.
FATHER IS A HUMAN BEING TOO...
...WHEN HE LOSES HIMSELF...
...MAY HURT OTHER PEOPLE.
"HE MAY HURT PEOPLE WITH WORDS THAT HE DOESN'T MEAN."
...HE...

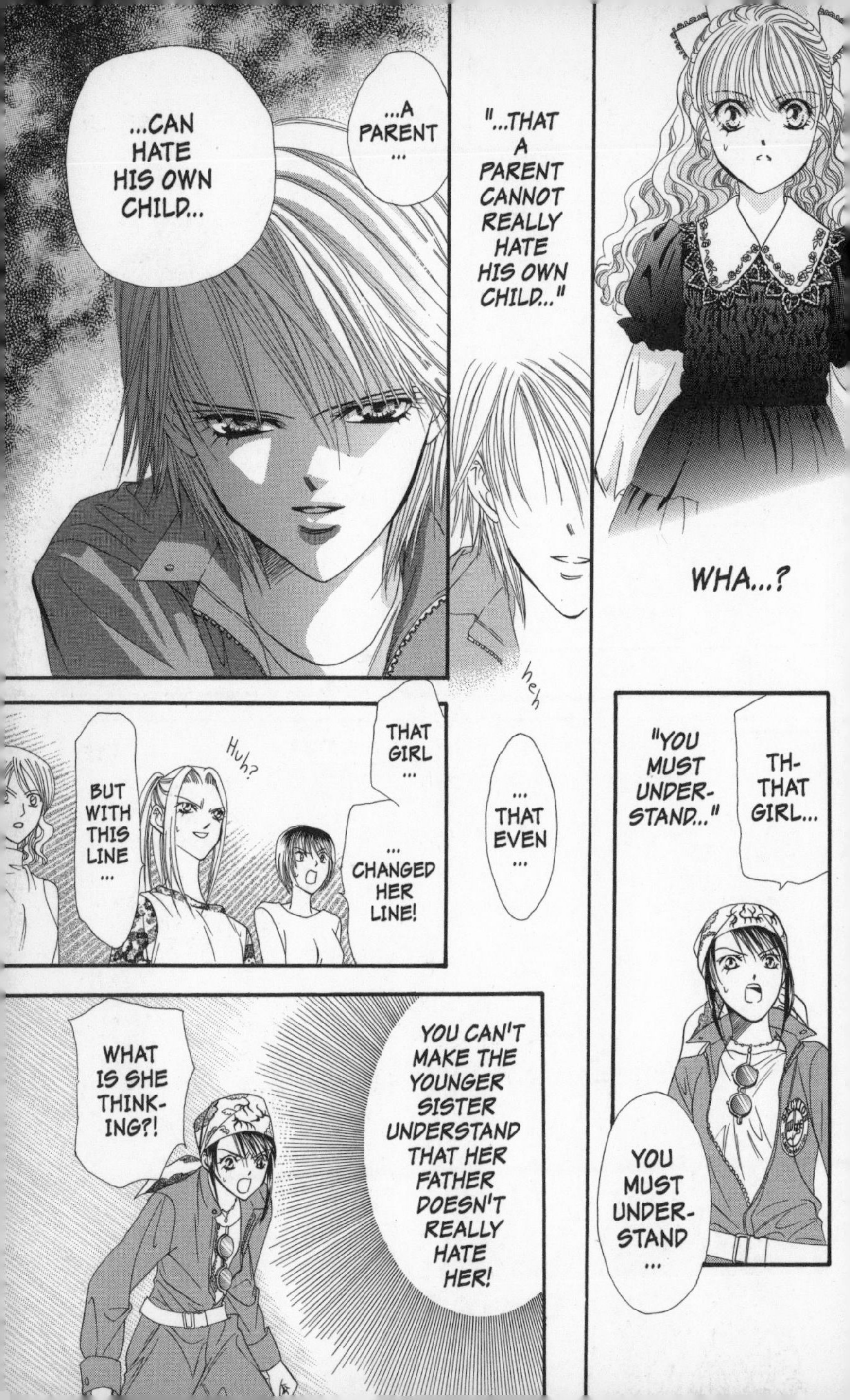
WHA...?
"...THAT A PARENT CANNOT REALLY HATE HIS OWN CHILD..."
...A PARENT ...
...CAN HATE HIS OWN CHILD...
heh
"YOU MUST UNDER-STAND..."
TH- THAT GIRL...
YOU MUST UNDER-STAND ...
... THAT EVEN ...
THAT GIRL ...
... CHANGED HER LINE!
Huh?
BUT WITH THIS LINE ...
YOU CAN'T MAKE THE YOUNGER SISTER UNDERSTAND THAT HER FATHER DOESN'T REALLY HATE HER!
WHAT IS SHE THINK-ING?!

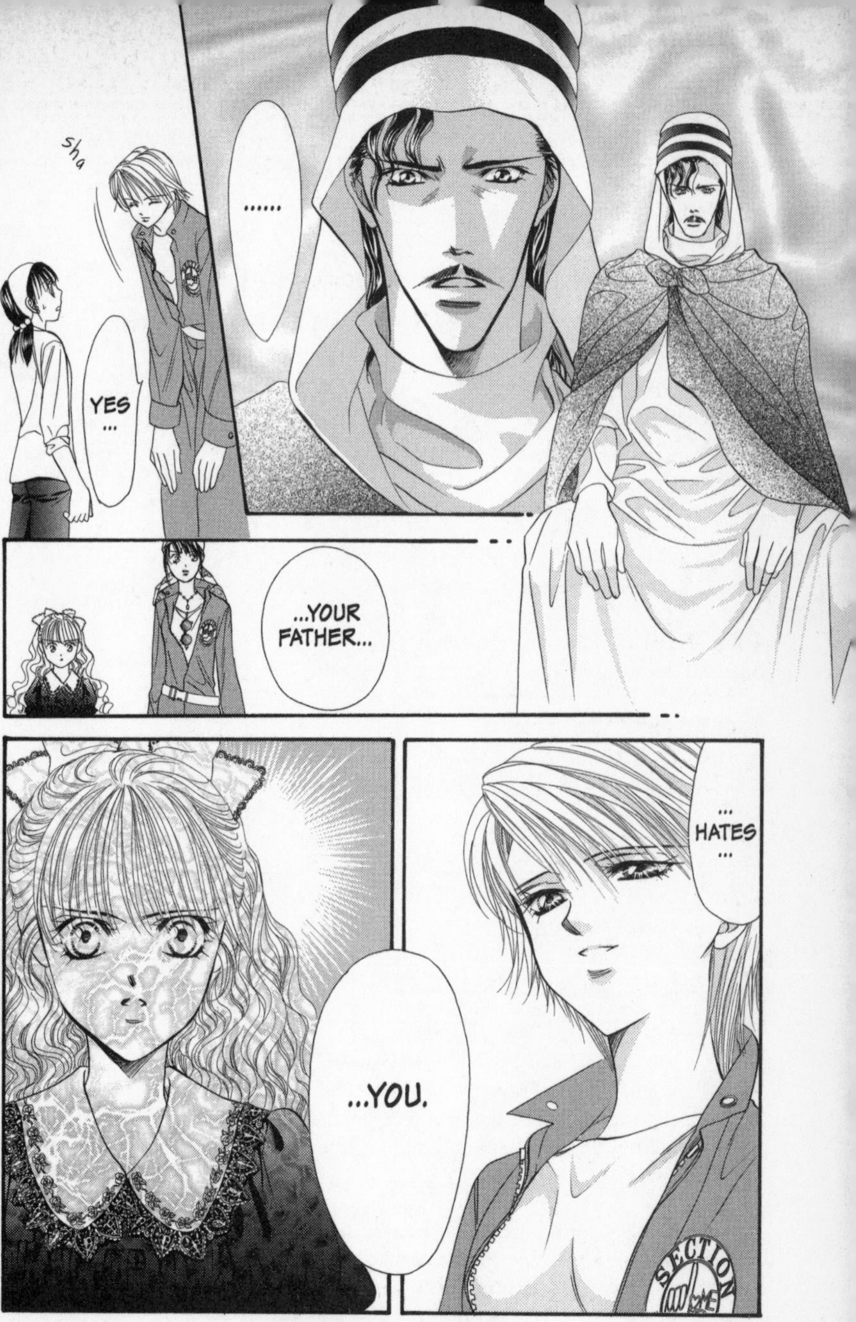
......
Sha
YES ...
...YOUR FATHER...
... HATES ...
...YOU.

End of Act 17

Skip-Beat! End Notes
Everyone knows how to be a fan, but sometimes cool things
from other cultures need a little help crossing the language barrier.

Page 9: Tea ceremony
The Japanese tea ceremony is a ritual stemming from Zen Buddhism, where
the powdered green tea, called *matcha*, is prepared and served in a serene
setting. *Cha no yu* refers to the ritual itself, while *chado* or *sado* refer to the
study of the tea ceremony. Practitioners of the tea ceremony must know
about calligraphy, flower arrangement, ceramics, incense, kimono, and other
traditional arts, along with the tenets of the particular teachings of her or his
school. It takes many years to become masterful at the tea ceremony.

Page 32, panel 1: Suzunari coast
Suzunari means "where the bell tolls."

Page 53, panel 1: Gel pad
In Japanese, these are called *hiepita*. They are disposable pads filled with a
cooling gel that you stick on your forehead when you have a fever.

Page 117, panel 6: Kanashibari
The Japanese term for a form of paralysis that occurs due to the presence of
a ghost or evil spirit. Most often occurs just after waking.

Page 124, panel 4: Manzai
This is a form of Japanese stand-up comedy involving a straight man and a
funny man. The jokes usually revolve around misunderstandings, puns, and
other verbal gags. The term was first used in 1933, in Osaka.

Page 127, panel 8: Purikura
This is a contraction of the Japanese pronunciation of "print club," and refers
to the photo booths found in arcades and game centers, and the photos they
dispense.

Page 149, panel 1: Katsura-muki rose
This was Kyoko's skill in the preliminary auditions in volume 1. She carved a
rose from a daikon radish using a unique Japanese chef technique.

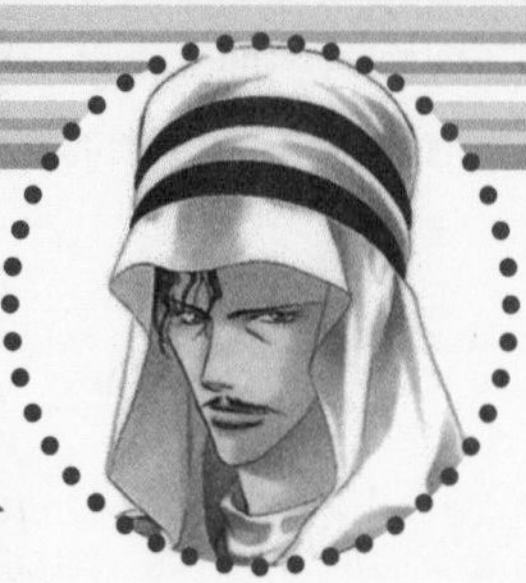

Yoshiki Nakamura is originally from Tokushima prefecture. She started drawing manga in elementary school, which eventually led to her 1993 debut of *Yume de Au yori Suteki* (Better than Seeing in a Dream) in *Hana to Yume* magazine. Her other works include the basketball series *Saint Love*, *MVP wa Yuzurenai* (Can't Give Up MVP), *Blue Wars*, and *Tokyo Crazy Paradise*, a series about a female bodyguard in 2020 Tokyo.

SKIP·BEAT!
Vol. 3
Shojo Beat Edition

STORY AND ART BY YOSHIKI NAKAMURA

English Translation & Adaptation/Tomo Kimura
Touch-up Art & Lettering/Sabrina Heep
Design/Yukiko Whitley
Editor/Pancha Diaz

VP, Production/Alvin Lu
VP, Sales & Product Marketing/Gonzalo Ferreyra
VP, Creative/Linda Espinosa
Publisher/Hyoe Narita

Skip·Beat! by Yoshiki Nakamura © Yoshiki Nakamura 2002. All rights reserved. First published in Japan in 2003 by HAKUSENSHA, Inc., Tokyo. English language translation rights arranged with HAKUSENSHA, Inc., Tokyo.

Some art has been modified from the original Japanese edition.

Printed in Canada

Published by VIZ Media, LLC
P.O. Box 77010
San Francisco, CA 94107

10 9 8 7 6 5 4 3
First printing, November 2006
Third printing, November 2009

www.viz.com

www.shojobeat.com

High Seas Hostage!

WANTED

BY MATSURI HINO, CREATOR OF *MERUPURI* AND *VAMPIRE KNIGHT*

In search of her kidnapped first love, Armeria disguises herself as a boy to join the crew of the pirate ship that abducted him. What will happen when the former songstress' cross-dressing cover is blown?

FIND OUT IN *WANTED*—MANGA ON SALE NOW!

On sale at **www.shojobeat.com**
Also available at your local bookstore and comic store

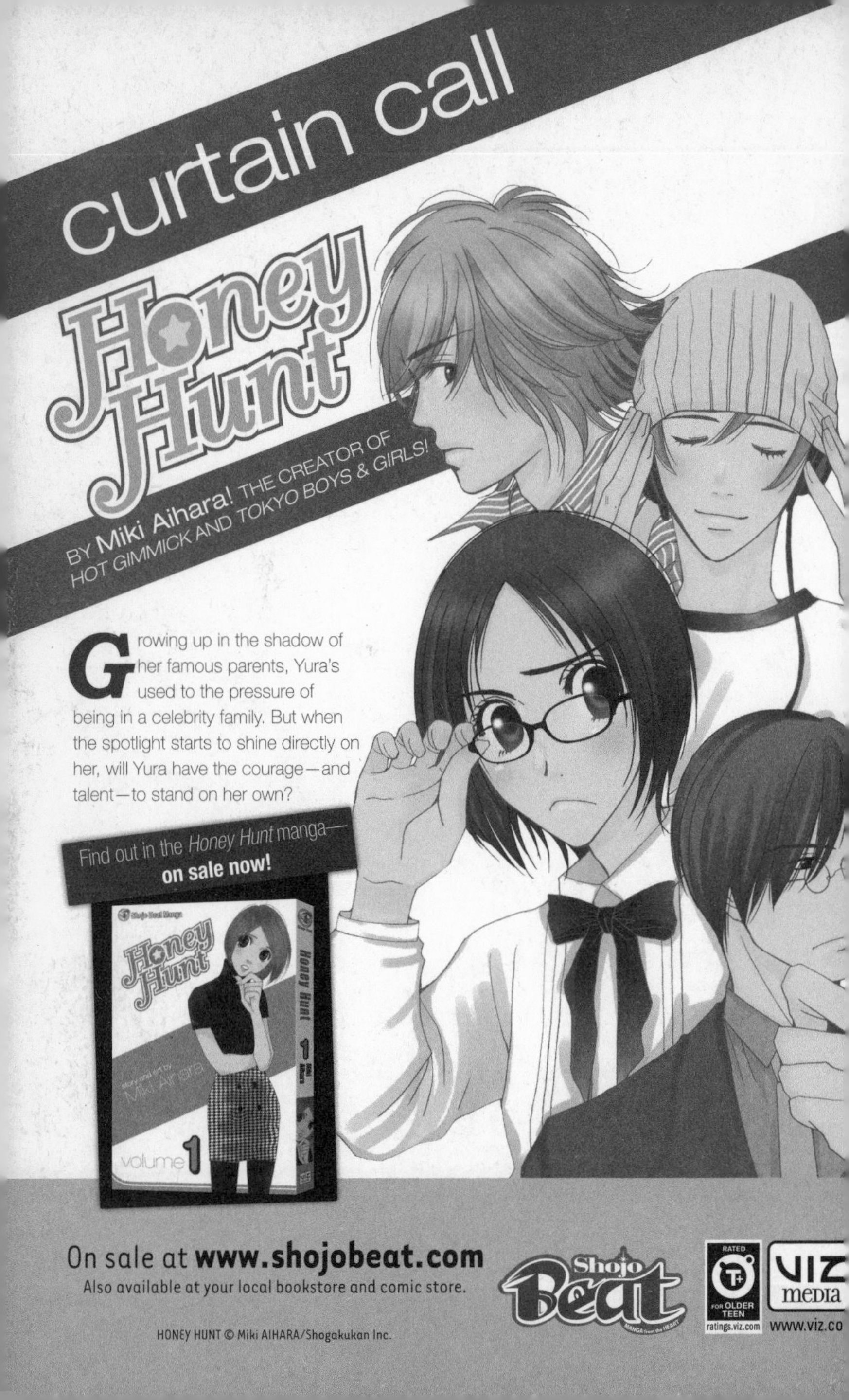

curtain call
Honey Hunt
BY Miki Aihara! THE CREATOR OF
HOT GIMMICK AND TOKYO BOYS & GIRLS!
Growing up in the shadow of her famous parents, Yura's used to the pressure of being in a celebrity family. But when the spotlight starts to shine directly on her, will Yura have the courage—and talent—to stand on her own?
Find out in the Honey Hunt manga—
on sale now!
Shojo Beat Manga
Honey Hunt
story and art by
Miki Aihara
volume 1
On sale at www.shojobeat.com
Also available at your local bookstore and comic store.
HONEY HUNT © Miki AIHARA/Shogakukan Inc.
Shojo Beat
MANGA from the HEART
RATED
T+
FOR OLDER TEEN
ratings.viz.com
VIZ media
www.viz.co

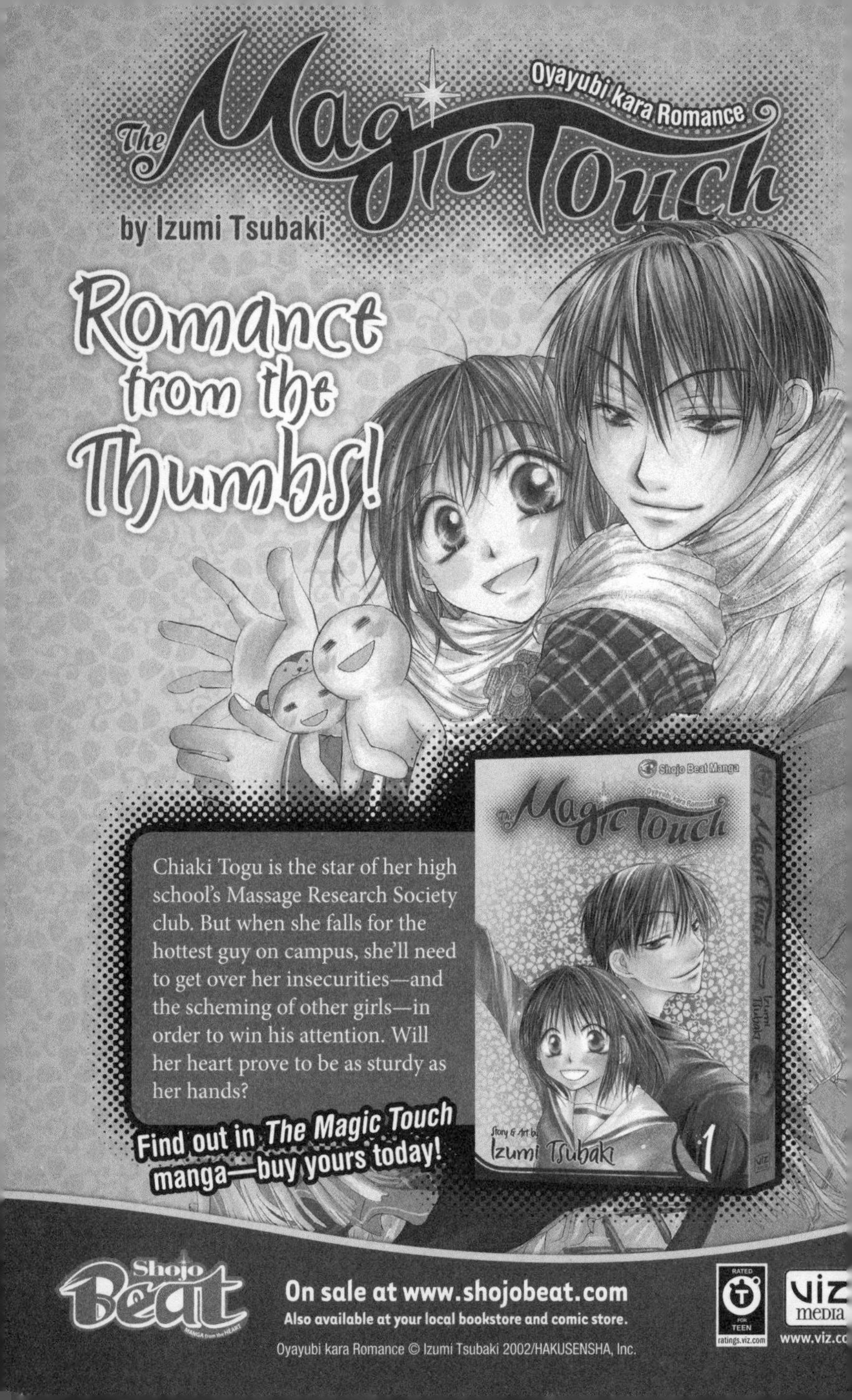

The Magic Touch
Oyayubi kara Romance
by Izumi Tsubaki
Romance from the Thumbs!
Shojo Beat Manga
Oyayubi kara Romance
The Magic Touch
Story & Art by Izumi Tsubaki
1
Chiaki Togu is the star of her high school's Massage Research Society club. But when she falls for the hottest guy on campus, she'll need to get over her insecurities—and the scheming of other girls—in order to win his attention. Will her heart prove to be as sturdy as her hands?
Find out in The Magic Touch manga—buy yours today!
Shojo Beat
MANGA from the HEART
On sale at www.shojobeat.com
Also available at your local bookstore and comic store.
Oyayubi kara Romance © Izumi Tsubaki 2002/HAKUSENSHA, Inc.
RATED T FOR TEEN
ratings.viz.com
VIZ media
www.viz.co

Hot Gimmick

If you think being a teenager is hard, be glad your name isn't Hatsumi Narita

With scandals that woul
make any gossip girl blus
and more triangles than yo
can throw a geometry boo
at, this girl may never figur
out the game of love!

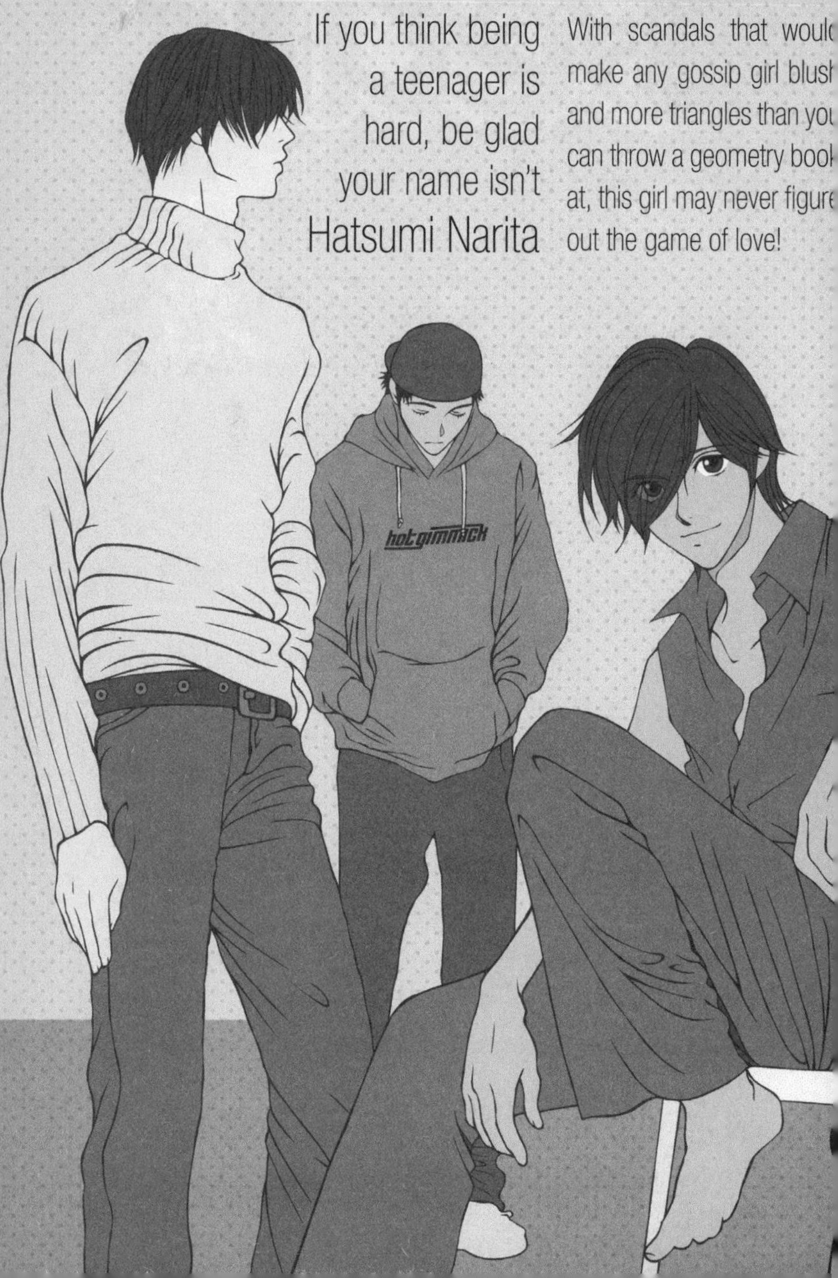

hotgimmick

OTOMEN

**STORY AND ART BY
AYA KANNO**

VAMPIRE KNIGHT

**STORY AND ART BY
MATSURI HINO**

Natsume's
BOOK of FRIENDS

**STORY AND ART BY
YUKI MIDORIKAWA**

Want to see more of what you're looking for?

Let your voice be heard!

shojobeat.com/mangasurvey

Help us give you more manga from the heart!

VIZ MEDIA
www.viz.com